To my dad
Francis "Poppop" Tkacik
For believing in me long before anyone else did.

When love is not madness, it is not love.
—Pedro Calderón de la Barca

CHAPTER 1

NOVEMBER 1988

It was the same conversation, week after week. Kate didn't know why she even bothered anymore. She forced a smile at the two girls passing in the hall, then leaned into the pay phone on the wall outside her room.

"You said I could come home after homecoming." She spoke in a hurried whisper. "That was two weeks ago."

"You can't still be homesick," her mother said, irritation creeping into her voice. "Isn't there a club or something you could join?"

She slumped against the wall. "Don't you miss me?"

"Don't be ridiculous. You'll be home for Thanksgiving. That's only two weeks away."

"I'm not being ridiculous. I just want to come home for the weekend."

"I'm sorry, no. And since you're determined to make this into such an issue, perhaps it's best to limit your calls. We'll call you Sunday evenings like always. There's no point in calling home every day just to whine."

"Mo-omm!"

"That's enough," her mother said. "It's Friday night. Go do something. It wouldn't kill you to make some new friends. Your life didn't end when Joey moved to New York."

Kate twisted the phone cord around her finger until it turned purple. *Actually, it kinda did.*

Joey had been her best friend since third grade. They'd been practically inseparable. At least until he and his father had a falling out. Afterward, Joey took off for the big city in search of fame and fortune, something he was convinced he'd reap in spades.

As for Kate, she'd lost her North Star.

Her mother droned on for a couple more minutes, lecturing her about something she must be doing wrong, but she'd stopped listening. When she was finally dismissed, with a warning not to call unless it was an emergency, she returned to her room, unlaced her Docs and stretched out on her bed, staring up at the stained acoustic tile overhead.

The pale yellow walls of her dorm had seemed cheery in the waning days of summer when she'd first arrived at Rutgers. But in the dreary cold of November, it was like being imprisoned inside a sickly stick of butter. Even though her room at home was childish and way too pink, she missed it. It was safe. Familiar.

College life wasn't at all what she'd expected. Coming from a long line of alumni, she had always known that she'd go to Rutgers. It had been a relief at first, to be away from home, out from under the shadow of her mother's critical eye. She thought she'd finally be able to breathe, spread her wings. But it turned out that even though her parents weren't there telling her what to do and how to do it, she had fallen into the same routine she'd grown up with. And without Joey to stir things up and pull her out of her little bubble, surviving college was beginning to seem hopeless. As sad as it sometimes made her, her old routine seemed the much safer option when faced with so many unknowns.

Perhaps it wasn't the walls of her room that made her feel like a prisoner after all.

She picked up her *Anthology of British Literature* and was trying to wrap her head around *Beowulf,* when the door burst open and her roommate rushed in, dumping her backpack on the floor with a loud thud.

"What in God's name are you doing?"

Kate peered over the top of her book. "Um . . . reading?"

"Not tonight, you're not." Toni grabbed the book and pitched it over her shoulder, hitting the wall with a satisfying thud. She tossed two fake IDs in its place. "We're going out, and I'm not taking no for an answer."

Toni could be a bit overwhelming, although she was a lot like Joey. They were both loud and gregarious, everything Kate wasn't.

Toni gave her a threatening look. "Seriously. Get up and get gorgeous, or I'll throw a bag over your head and drag you all the way to Kildare's."

"I have a test Monday." Kate pointed around her roommate at the anthology splayed open in the corner, its spine twisted.

"It's Friday," Toni reminded her. "You have plenty of time. C'mon. Chop-chop."

Kate opened her mouth to argue, but the prospect of another evening reading names she couldn't begin to pronounce was too depressing.

And besides, hadn't her mother insisted she get out and make new friends?

Stepping off the elevator a few hours later, Kate frowned at her reflection in the lobby window. She was wearing too much makeup, and her crimped hair looked huge. Reason enough to cut and run.

"So what's going on at Kildare's?" She tried to adopt a casual attitude as she and Toni headed down George Street.

"There's a rock duo there tonight. They're supposed to be really good. Plus, I hear they're both gorgeous." Toni winked. "So if we're lucky . . ."

Kate slowed to a halt. Maybe she should turn around, head back to *Beowulf.*

"What's wrong?"

"I don't know if I'm looking to 'get lucky.'"

Toni crossed her arms and jabbed a finger into Kate's chest. "Listen,

Mousy Brown. You've had your nose stuck in a book since you got here. You haven't been to one football game or one party. It's almost Thanksgiving. If you don't get out tonight, you won't have anything to talk about when you get back to East Bumblefuck, so let's get moving!" She linked her arm through Kate's and tugged.

Stumbling along beside her, Kate regretted her choice of footwear. How could she be expected to take a leap out of her comfort zone, when her boots were already pinching her toes?

Kildare's was crowded and smoky and loud. Any other time, Kate would have turned and walked out. Instead, she braced herself and followed as Toni pushed her way to the bar and commandeered the bartender's attention, flashing her fake ID and a little cleavage and ordering two Fuzzy Navels.

She had only had alcohol one other time. The summer after freshman year, Joey swiped a mason jar full of vodka from his dad. They hiked into the woods behind the high school and mixed it with iced tea. They got so drunk that on a dare, they each stripped out of their shorts, T-shirts, and underclothes. A lot more than curiosity had been stirred up when Joey stood naked before her. On the other hand, he took one look at her, exposed and vulnerable, and shook his head. "Nope, nothing—sorry." It was as if she'd tried to tempt him with a piece of dry toast.

They didn't see each other for several days after that. Humiliated and hung over, she spent the next day with her arms wrapped around the toilet. When she hadn't returned his calls, Joey waited until her parents went out, then threw pebbles at her window. At first she ignored him, but as the stones grew larger, she became afraid he'd eventually break the glass.

"What?" She stuck her head out the window, glaring down at him.

"Just in time." He dropped the small boulder he'd been about to lob at her window and brushed the dirt from his hands. "I want you to know you're the most beautiful girl I've ever seen. If I could, I'd whisk you away from your ivory tower and make mad, passionate love to you right here on this very spot, you dark-haired Rapunzel, you." He pointed to the grass beneath his feet, then looked up at her with a sweet smile. She crossed her arms and tried to look angry, but it didn't matter, she couldn't stay mad.

"C'mon down and let me give you a big, wet kiss right on the lips."

"Not necessary. I get it. I'm not your type."

He lowered his voice. "Well, not exactly—but I do love you." He folded his hands over his chest, just like he'd done playing Romeo in the eighth-grade play.

Their relationship had been like that since grade school. She was the yin to his yang.

"Here." Snapping her back to the present, Toni handed her a glass of something orange and sweet-smelling. "Follow me." She pushed her way through a wall of people to lay claim to a recently vacated table near the stage.

Bon Jovi shook the speakers on the walls as Kate took a seat and wondered how long it would be before her head cracked open like a ripe melon. Between the noise and the smoke, the chances of making it through the evening looked pretty slim.

There were few faces Kate recognized in the crowded bar, and no one she knew well enough to engage in conversation, unlike Toni, who had turned away to speak with someone at the next table. Kate crossed her ankles and tapped one foot rapidly against the other. She twisted a strand of hair around her finger. Invisible—that's how she felt. Not that she wanted to be the center of attention. God no! But she could be invisible back at her dorm just as easily, and a lot more comfortable. She tried to wiggle her toes, and when she couldn't she cursed Joey. She should've never let him talk her into buying these high-heeled boots.

Her discomfort, like the crowd, was growing rapidly.

One drink and I'm outta here.

She poked a finger in the orange concoction, gave it a stir, and then popped it in her mouth. *Not bad.* She took a cautious sip and then another. *OK. Maybe two drinks.*

Downing the contents of her glass, she watched as one of the musicians climbed onto the stage. He set a bottle of Budweiser on an amp and picked up a guitar.

"I saw him first," Toni shouted over the music. "You can have the other one."

Yeah, right. She snickered. "I didn't realize they were ours for the choosing."

"Why not?" Toni gave her a nudge, followed by a wicked smile.

"So is the other one the one with the nice personality?"

"Beats me," Toni answered, just before someone else snagged her attention.

Kate laughed until she saw "the other one" making his way through the wall of people to leap onto the stage. His dark blond hair brushed the tops of his shoulders as he slipped his guitar strap over his head, buttoned it, and turned toward his amp.

An ear-splitting squeal shot through the speakers behind her.

Squinting into the light, he shielded his eyes and flashed a sheepish grin in her direction. "Sorry," he called out. "Forgot to turn my volume off."

Her heart beat loudly in her ears. It could have been from the sudden assault to her hearing, but it also could have been because the most beautiful man she'd ever seen had just smiled at her. She continued to stare as he turned away to adjust his amp.

A sharp jab caught her in the ribs.

"I think I spoke too soon," Toni yelled over the steady thump of the jukebox.

Buoyed by false courage from the drink she'd polished off too quickly, Kate shook her head and grinned. "No backsies!"

Toni sat back, looking impressed. "Oh, really? Be my guest!"

Kate chewed on the stirrer from her empty glass and watched the second guitar player tune his instrument. *I wonder what it would be like to be kissed by someone who looked like that.* He was definitely not her type—not that she had a type. Her experience was limited to that embarrassing naked romp with Joey and getting felt up in the front seat of a Buick by her prom date. Her crushes had always been the clean-cut, studious types, the kind of boys her parents might approve of. Not men with long hair, earrings, and ripped jeans. Not, God forbid, a man with tattoos peeking out from beneath his rolled-up sleeves.

But still, he was certainly something to look at.

CHAPTER 2

Billy Donaldson buttoned the strap on his Fender Stratocaster. He gazed out at the crowd of twenty-somethings, at least six deep at the bar. If Viper kept packing them in like this, especially on the college circuit, it was only a matter of time before they would hook up with a concert tour.

As he tightened his strings, he tried to pick out the students from the townies. College girls looked the part, especially at a school like Rutgers. It might not be Ivy League, but the girls were a lot like the ones at Princeton. They came off smug, and although they were easy enough to hit on, they were usually looking for something more intellectual. Not that he wasn't up for that. But after playing a four-hour gig, that wasn't usually what he had in mind.

Townies were easy to pick out. Big hair, too much makeup. Only problem was, sometimes teenagers would sneak in with fake IDs. Last thing he needed was to get arrested for banging a fifteen-year-old.

He caught another glimpse of the dark-haired girl near the speakers, the one who had nearly jumped out of her skin when his amp screeched. He couldn't quite peg her. She looked like a townie, but the chick she was with was definitely a student. The two didn't usually mix. He caught her watching, but every time he smiled at her, she looked away. It was kind of cute, actually. Usually when he zeroed in on a girl at a gig, she'd not only smile back, she'd let him know that whatever he was thinking, she was willing. This was not one of those girls. But damn, she was pretty.

When the set ended, he sauntered over to the bar and ordered a Jack Daniels. He let the whiskey roll over his tongue, savoring the taste while he watched the table in the corner.

"What's the girl over there drinking?" he shouted over the jukebox. "The one with the dark, kinky hair."

The bartender followed his gaze across the room. He shook his head and motioned for a waitress.

"Fuzzy Navel, but I prefer something with a little bite myself." In case he missed her meaning, the waitress sank her teeth into her lower lip.

"Thank you, darling," he drawled, slipping into his "aw, shucks" Midwestern accent. If things didn't work out with the brunette, the waitress was a definite possibility.

"Another Jack and a Fuzzy Navel," he told the bartender. The waitress shrugged and collected her tray of drinks, then pushed her way back into the crowd.

While he waited, the brunette's friend stood and left with a jock in a varsity jacket. *Perfect timing.* He picked up the drinks and squeezed through the crowd.

"Hey." He flashed one of his trademark smiles and held out the drink. "I think this is yours."

Wide eyes, the color of a stormy sea, looked up at him, and for the briefest moment, he felt like a man falling overboard. There was a vague sense of familiarity. *Had they met before?*

"I hope your friend didn't abandon you," he said, taking a seat, trying to regain his swagger.

Her eyes followed him. "No. They just went out to the parking lot. She'll be right back."

He extended his hand. "Billy McDonald," he said, introducing himself with his stage name.

"Kate Daniels," she answered, taking his hand.

"Katherine, or Kathleen?"

She shook her head. "Just plain Kate."

"Oh, Katie." He leaned in closer. "There's nothing plain about you."

Deep pink stained her cheeks.

"Your hand is freezing," he said. Reaching for its twin, he rubbed them between his own. "Better?"

"Yes, thank you." She pulled her hands back as soon as he let go and tucked them under her legs. With an appraising look, she rocked forward in her seat. "Are you a model or something?"

Caught off guard, he laughed. "Nope. Just a musician." He rested his forearms on the table and leaned closer. "You're pretty cute, Katie. Did you know that?" Her smile was slow and a bit off-center.

Guns N' Roses was playing on the jukebox. He glanced at his watch. There was time before the next set.

"C'mon." He pulled her to her feet. "Dance with me."

Kate pointed to the small space in front of the stage and shook her head. "I don't think they allow dancing."

"I don't care." He leaned so close, his nose almost touched hers. "I wanna dance with you."

"Sweet Child O' Mine" wasn't exactly suited to slow dancing, but he'd make it work. He'd never done anything like this at a gig before, and he wasn't sure why he was doing it now. Well, that wasn't completely true. He wanted an excuse to touch her. He felt her body tense as he slipped his arm around her waist. She tried to step back, but he tightened his hold until he felt her relax. In spite of the pace of the music, she followed him easily.

After a while, she giggled.

"That tickles."

It took a moment to realize he'd been mindlessly playing the notes to the lead break against her spine. "Sorry," he whispered, catching a soft, citrusy scent as he lowered his head.

"It's OK." She sighed and rested her forehead against his chest.

He slipped his hand beneath the hem of her shirt, then played the bare skin along her vertebrae like he was fingering the frets of his guitar. He felt her tremble. Sometimes it was almost too easy.

When the song ended, he twirled her to her chair, whispered a quick thank-you, and hopped back onto the stage.

Throughout the next set, Kate couldn't focus on much more than the memory of his calloused fingertips against her spine. He didn't ask her to dance again, but he bought her drinks and sat with her during every break, ignoring the crush of girls that mobbed him at the bar. She'd gone from being invisible, to feeling as if she was the most important person in the room.

It was pretty awesome, and other than a tricky trip to the ladies room, steadying herself along the crush of bodies, she was having fun.

Toni frowned as Kate staggered back to her seat. "I think you've had enough." She moved a drink that had appeared soon after Kate had finished the last one.

Kate shook her head, almost losing her balance, and plopped into her chair.

"I'm fine." She leaned forward, bumping the table and knocking over a half-empty bottle of beer. "I don't think I've ever been finer!"

"You're officially flagged." Toni chuckled as she reached for a handful of napkins to sop up the mess. Kate tried to help, but was unable to pluck the napkins from the holder.

"Ready to head out?"

She shook her head, sending the room into a spin. Bad idea. "No," she said, keeping her head perfectly still. "I wanna hear the band."

"I think they're about done. It's almost two. Besides, I have plans. I want to make sure you get back safely." Toni scanned the crowded barroom. "Anyone here you know?"

"Just him." She pointed at Billy.

Toni cocked an eyebrow. "I don't think so. I think that one might be trouble."

When Kate looked up to disagree, Billy caught her eye and grinned. A thousand butterflies took flight inside her chest.

Toni moved closer. "Look, I have someone waiting for me. Either you go with me now or find another way home."

She didn't want to go, but Toni wasn't giving her much choice. She was fighting with the twisted sleeve of her jacket when Billy leaned away from the microphone, calling out to her.

"Where're you going? We're not done yet."

Dragging the offending garment behind her, she took a few steps toward the stage. "I have to go. My walk is leaving."

"Don't go. I'll take you home." He glanced at Toni, mouthing the words, "I promise."

Toni hesitated, then stalked across the dance floor and motioned for Billy to lean forward. She ignored the dirty look from his partner, who was belting out a lyric from Sonic Youth's "Teen Age Riot."

"Don't fuck with her," she yelled up at him. "I swear to God. Don't fuck with her."

"Cross my heart," he said. Then turning to Kate, he winked.

She stared up at him, doe-eyed, a dreamy smile plastered across her face. This girl was freaking adorable—and hot, in an innocent sort of way. She had a dancer's body, but softer. No hard edges. At least, none he'd detected on the dance floor.

Bouncers herded the last of the stragglers out the door. Up on the stage, Pete unplugged instruments and wound cords as a tipsy blonde sat nearby, jabbering away. Definitely Pete's type; he'd likely score a quick blow job in the parking lot or head to her place for a couple hours.

Billy could've easily found someone like her if he'd wanted. He wasn't sure what to expect from Kate, but he was willing to find out. And she was certainly pretty. In a couple years, she might even be what he would call beautiful. Too bad he wouldn't be around to see that.

"Do you want another drink?" he asked. "Maybe some coffee?"

Coffee? What the hell? He wasn't typically one to sober a girl up, unless she had to drive, and that was usually later.

"No." Kate sighed, her eyes half-closed, her chin resting on her open palm. "I'm good."

He almost laughed. She wasn't good; she was smashed. "Okay. You sit tight. Then I'll get you home."

After everything had been loaded into his van, Billy drove around front. The temperature had dropped, and he blew on his hands to keep warm while he waited for someone to unlock the door. Kate sat on a wooden bench inside the entrance. She jumped when he knocked, then gave him a loopy smile.

He felt guilty. In spite of the way she looked, this was not the kind of girl he should be messing with. He should just take her home, call it a night.

After the bartender let him in, he helped her to her feet.

"Wanna dance?" Leaning against him, she looped her arms around his neck.

"There's no music," he answered, breathing in the scent of her hair. *Oranges?* No. Sweeter. Whatever it was, she smelled amazing.

She pouted, and he found he couldn't resist. Singing softly, he waltzed her toward the exit. When he opened the door, she stumbled.

"You OK?" He tightened his grip around her waist.

She looked startled, then nodded. "I'll be fine once the air hits me."

Only she wasn't. As soon as they stepped into the frosty night, her head rolled back and her knees buckled.

"Shit!" He caught her before she hit the sidewalk. Lifting her up, he carried her to the van and propped her against the door.

A pair of jocks in Rutgers jackets passed as he fumbled for the keys.

"Need any help?" one called. "We'll take her off your hands."

"I got it," he snarled. They snickered and strolled on, boasting about what they'd do with a drunk girl, given the opportunity. If his hands hadn't been full, he'd have banged their heads against the sidewalk a few times, although the subtlety would've probably been lost on them. "Dickheads," he muttered as he lifted Kate into the van and buckled her seatbelt. He rushed around to the other side and climbed in beside her, then he lowered her seat and adjusted her head. He opened her window a few inches. Maybe the cool air would bring her around.

He shifted the van into gear, then slammed on the brakes. Where the hell was he taking her?

"Katie," he called, tapping his fingers gently on her cheek. Nothing.

"Damn it." He dug through the pockets of her jacket, finding a wallet, some keys, a wad of dollar bills, and her ID.

"Nice try, sweetheart," he said, scanning the ID. "No way in hell are you twenty-three."

He dipped into her wallet and pulled out her driver's license: July 19, 1970. *Eighteen*. He sighed in relief, then checked the address. *Where the hell is Belleville?* She probably lived on campus. At least he hoped so. He didn't want to worry about her father calling the cops when she didn't come home—but she was left in his care. His only option was to take her with him.

She was still out cold when he pulled into the motel parking lot. He maneuvered her out of the van, then lifted her into his arms, holding her tighter when she shivered against his chest.

"Good thing you don't weigh much," he muttered, slowly climbing the metal steps. He was making his way along the balcony when a door opened. A thickset man in a sleeveless undershirt stepped out, a foul-smelling cigar clenched between his teeth.

"Everything all right?" the man asked, angling his head for a better look at Kate.

"Yeah," Billy grumbled. "We're newlyweds."

"She don't look so good."

The jerk was taking up half the walkway.

"Yeah? Well, she's fine."

He unlocked the door to his room, kicking it closed behind him as he carried Kate to the bed.

"This is not how I pictured this evening ending." He grunted as he pulled off his jacket and tossed it onto the floor. He raised Kate into a sitting position and slipped off her jacket. As he knelt to unzip her boots, she moaned.

It was an all too familiar sound.

"Hang in there, sweetheart." He scooped her up and raced toward the bathroom, but before he reached the toilet, she vomited over them both. Foul orange bile soaked their shirts and wet her hair.

"Shit." He placed her on the floor, squatting behind her to keep her upright and pulling her hair out of the way as she continued to retch.

When she was finally done and had slipped back into semiconsciousness, he tugged his shirt off over his head. He ran a towel under warm water and wiped around her mouth, then began dabbing at the black smears pooled beneath her eyes. She was beginning to look a bit like Alice Cooper. In spite of the mess, he chuckled.

"See," he said, cleaning her face, "I knew you'd be a beautiful girl." When he'd finished, he peeled off her shirt and pants, explaining as he went along, even though she probably couldn't hear him. "Sorry, honey, but I'm gonna bet you don't wanna stay in these wet clothes. Besides, you kinda stink."

He grabbed a paper coffee cup from the vanity, rinsed it out, then leaned her against the edge of the tub and washed her hair, careful not to move her too much so she wouldn't get sick again. He wrapped her clean hair in a towel and moved her into the corner, propping her between the tub and the sink so she wouldn't fall over.

After stripping out of his soiled pants, he rooted through his suitcase until he found a long-sleeved T-shirt. Behaving himself—although at this point, he didn't know why—he turned her away from him, unsnapped her bra with one hand, then dropped the shirt over her head.

She moaned.

"Are you gonna be sick again?"

"Unh-uh."

"That's a good girl."

He carried her into the bedroom, pulled back the covers, and guided her between the sheets.

"Here you go, sweetheart. Time for bed."

She looked younger with her hair wet and with less of that black crap around her eyes, but she was still pretty, even like this. He ran a finger across her face, removing a damp strand of hair that clung to her cheek. Then he sat beside her, waiting until her breathing was soft and regular. When he was certain she was okay, he finished cleaning up, and took a quick shower.

It was after four when he finally slipped into bed beside her. He lay awake for a long time, staring at the ceiling, just listening to her breathe.

CHAPTER 3

Pain stabbed behind her eyes and through her temples. If she lifted her head even a fraction of an inch, she was afraid it might explode. As her eyes adjusted to the dim light, Kate realized not only didn't she know where she was, but she wasn't alone. Someone much bigger pressed up against her. An arm draped over her waist, pinning her in place.

She wanted to scream, but no sound came from her dust-dry throat. She blinked frantically. Slowly, she lifted the blanket. In the light coming from a partially opened door, she could make out a braided leather bracelet and the bold, black strokes of a tattoo. She jerked, then froze as Billy shifted against her.

Oh my God! I'm a groupie!

Incoherent thoughts skittered through her marinated brain.

Kildare's. And those peach-flavored drinks. At the thought, her stomach lurched so violently, she was surprised Billy didn't feel it. She gulped for air, then tried to slow her breathing, afraid she would hyperventilate. *Never again.* She would never have another drink as long as she lived.

First things first. She needed to pee, but as she tried to slip out from under Billy's arm, he tightened his hold around her waist.

"Not yet," he mumbled into the back of her head.

She tried to remain still, but couldn't.

"I have to use the bathroom," she whispered.

"Hmm. Hurry back." He raised his arm.

She staggered to the bathroom, groaning when she found her bra and jeans hanging on the rod over the shower. Her tank top was soaking in the sink, along with Billy's blue chambray shirt. The shirt she was currently wearing, which grazed the middle of her thighs, must be his as well.

Bracing herself on the edge of the tub, she leaned into the shower to wash her hands and face. A tube of toothpaste sat on the counter. She grabbed a clean washcloth, wet it, and used it to scrub her teeth and tongue. No matter how hard she rubbed, she couldn't eliminate the bitter taste.

She stared at herself in the mirror. Her skin looked pasty and there were dark smudges beneath her eyes. A shaving kit sat on the sink. On the floor next to the tub was an overnight bag. The counter was cluttered with minuscule bottles of shampoo and conditioner. A tiny bar of soap rested on the sink.

Where the hell am I? A motel?

Swallowing the nausea that burned her throat, she grabbed another washcloth, and as she scrubbed at the remaining black around her eyes, she tried to figure out what to do. She couldn't sneak out. Even if she knew where she was, her clothes were wet. Besides, she was dizzy and her head hurt, and unfortunately, she needed to lie down or she was going to be sick— again. Fragments of memory assaulted her. Bad idea. Maybe forgetting was the way to go.

Billy didn't open his eyes as she approached; he just lifted the covers. Against her better judgment, if she even possessed such a thing, she yanked the back of the shirt between her legs, then slid in beside him.

"Morning," he whispered, curling himself against her back.

"Morning," she answered, her throat scratchy. "But it might be afternoon."

"I'm not surprised. We were up pretty late."

"We were? What were we doing?"

He chuckled. "Wouldn't you like to know?"

Probably not. What she did know was that she should have been freaking out over waking in the arms of a stranger. Instead, she'd willingly climbed back into bed beside him.

And she was also pretty sure this wasn't what her mother meant when she said Kate needed to make new friends. At this moment? She didn't really care.

~

Kate opened her eyes awhile later, surprised that she'd somehow fallen back to sleep. This behavior was so unlike her, she wondered if maybe he'd slipped something into her drink last night. She didn't have much time to think about it as Billy stirred, yawned loudly, and rolled onto his back.

"I'm starving. You?" He addressed her as casually as if he woke up beside her every morning.

The throbbing in her head had receded, and she no longer felt seasick. "I might be able to eat."

"Sounds good." He slapped her on the ass, climbed out of bed, and shuffled toward the bathroom.

She was about to comment on his irksome sense of familiarity when he walked past her—naked. She clamped her eyes shut, but the image was already imprinted in her brain. Long, lean, and muscular, he looked like a Greek statue she'd seen at the Metropolitan Museum of Art. Scratch that. He actually looked better than any statue she'd ever seen. She opened her eyes for another quick peek just as bathroom door snapped shut.

What is wrong with you, Kate, and what the hell was in those drinks?

She rolled toward the wall. In addition to drinking too much, maybe she'd fallen and hit her head.

The door opened a few minutes later.

"Going back to sleep?"

She stretched but didn't turn around. "I'm awake."

Billy chuckled. "Katie?"

Here goes nothing. She peeked over her shoulder. Still shirtless, he'd slipped into a pair of torn, faded jeans. She forced her eyes up from the hard stomach muscles and perfect pecs.

"There's a restaurant on the corner," he said, dragging a T-shirt over his head. "Tell me what you want, and I'll bring it back. Your clothes are still wet."

She sat up, rubbing her eyes. "Something light. Maybe a bagel and some tea. I'm feeling a little better, but I don't want to take any chances."

He grimaced. "Good idea."

She groaned and pulled the covers over her head, which is where she stayed while he finished dressing.

"So tea and toast. Anything else?"

"No, thanks." She peeked out from behind the sheet. He'd pulled his hair back into a low ponytail and was zipping up a black leather jacket.

"Holy shit!" He stood back from the open door.

She slipped out of bed to find that everything outside was white. Several inches of snow were already on the ground, and it was coming down hard. In the parking lot below, Pete was clearing off a station wagon.

"Hey, Rip Van Winkle!" he shouted when he saw Billy. "You're on your own tonight. I called the bar in Tewksbury. They're canceling because of the weather." When he saw Kate, he laughed. "Guess you got it covered, though."

She ducked behind Billy.

"That's OK," Billy answered. "I can use a night off. Where're you headed?"

"Well, unless you feel like sharing, I'm in search of a little entertainment of my own. Then I'm heading home." He paused as if he seriously expected Billy to invite him up. When no invitation was forthcoming, he shrugged and climbed into his car. Kate watched him slide sideways out of the parking lot, glad he was gone.

When Billy turned toward her, his grin made her forget all about Pete's sleazy proposition and the cold air swirling around her bare legs. "So, snow. What shall we do?"

She made like she was giving this serious consideration. "Since I have a shirt and no pants, snow angels are out of the question. But if you can find a carrot, I might be persuaded to make a snowman."

"Good point. Although snow angels could be a lot of fun." He winked, and her face grew warm.

"Let me see if this rat trap has a laundry room. That may solve a few of our problems. Not that I find you having no pants a problem, just so you know."

Her cheeks were on fire.

He returned a few minutes later, on a mission to take their clothes to a Laundromat around the corner. "I'll be right back, and I'll come bearing gifts."

"Just come bearing food. And maybe some aspirin."

"There's aspirin in my travel bag." He nodded toward the bathroom. "Help yourself."

She tapped two into the palm of her hand, then followed them with some metallic-tasting water. After trying to clean her mouth again, she climbed back under the covers to consider her predicament.

They were definitely in a cheap motel—dirty, off-white walls, a generic oil painting, jewel-tone curtains and bedspread. In the corner were two guitar cases. She wondered if the rest of Billy's equipment was with Pete. She didn't know what to make of him, although she could guess what his kind of entertainment entailed. Then again, she was all but naked in a stranger's motel room. That didn't say much about her, either.

To be honest, once she'd gotten past the fear of not knowing where she was or who she was with, waking up in Billy's arms had been nice. She might even go so far as to say she liked it—a lot.

Careful, Kate. You don't know this guy. He could be a crazy rapist. Of course, if that were true, he would have raped her by now. Then again, throwing up all over him might have diminished his ardor for college virgins.

She picked up the phone and dialed the number for her dorm. It rang three times before Toni picked up.

"Hi, it's me."

"Where the fuck are you?" Toni screeched so loud she had to pull the phone away from her ear.

"I'm okay," she sputtered. "I kinda passed out last night when we left

Kildare's. Billy brought me back to his motel."

Two, maybe three beats of silence. "Where?"

Good question.

"I'm not really sure . . ." She searched through the drawer in the nightstand. Beneath the standard-issue Bible, she found the television channel guide with the name of the motel stamped at the bottom.

"Murray's Motorlodge."

"Where the hell is that?"

Beat's me. She flipped the guide over. The address was printed at the bottom. "Lincoln Boulevard in Bound Brook."

"Jeez, Kate. Do you want me to find someone to come get you?"

Did she?

"Um . . . Look—he's being really nice. He just went to get us something to eat." She shot a quick glance at the door. "I'm okay, really. I'll call you if I need a ride."

"Give me the number there," Toni demanded. "If I don't hear from you in an hour, I'm hunting him down—and I'm bringing reinforcements."

After assuring Toni repeatedly that she was fine and promising to call later, she hung up and burrowed deeper under the covers. Using the remote, she turned on the television, flipping through the channels until she found one of her favorite old movies.

Billy stomped through the door a few minutes later. The way his eyes lit up when he saw her made her feel like Santa had left her under his tree. All she was missing was a big, red bow.

"I was cold," she pointed out. "And pantsless."

"Not for long. As soon as we eat, I'll go throw your clothes in the dryer, then I'll take you home. Which I would've done last night, if I knew where you lived."

"Oh." She flushed. *Idiot.* She was only there because he hadn't known what to do with her. "Sorry about that."

He set two cups on the nightstand, tossed the bag of food on the bed, then flopped down beside her. Her stomach clenched as she caught a whiff of greasy French fries.

"Nothing to be sorry about," he said, opening the bag and pulling out a fried egg sandwich and a bagel. "I needed to wash those clothes anyway. It'll save me the trouble when I get home."

He seemed sincere, but he was probably just being polite—a nice guy stuck with a drunk girl. After they'd eaten and her clothes were dry, he'd take her back to her dorm. The end.

She tore off a tiny piece of bagel and chewed slowly. It didn't threaten to return, so she tried a second bite.

"What're you watching?"

Her heart stuttered as he licked a dab of egg yolk off his bottom lip.

"Just a silly old movie. I love Cary Grant, but I think I like the house even more. I watch lots of movies because I like the houses. I picture how my life would be if I lived there. I guess it's my way of getting away from—" She had started off rambling. Now she hesitated, not exactly sure what she wanted to say.

"Go on. Getting away from what?"

"I don't really know." She tore another piece from her bagel. "Maybe it's not really the houses after all." He was listening so intently that she felt even more exposed. "Um . . . Maybe it's more about trying on someone else's life. See if it might be a better fit, you know?"

He nodded. "So where do you see yourself fitting in? What do you want to do with your life?"

"Honestly? I think I'd like to write. Be a novelist, or maybe children's books. My parents want me to teach—they're both teachers." She twisted a long strand of hair around her finger. "Of course I also want to fall in love and get married one day to a man who adores me." She couldn't help but smile. "And I want lots of kids. I want a big, crazy, noisy life."

He laughed. "Is that what you're used to? Lots of noise?"

"Oh God, no. No siblings. No pets. Just me. I was raised in a museum under a microscope so that all my flaws were enlarged and exaggerated." She couldn't believe she'd just spilled her guts to a stranger, but her frankness didn't seem to bother him.

When she glanced up, he was no longer smiling.

"Flaws? I don't see any flaws."

A soft laugh escaped, although there was no humor in it. "I'm pretty sure they're there."

Uncomfortable when he didn't respond right away, she reached for her tea. It had grown cold but she drank it anyway. She tried to focus on Mr. Blandings and his dream house, but she'd begun to feel as if she were back under the microscope.

"How many?"

She looked up, horrified. "Flaws?"

He chuckled. "No. Kids. How many kids?"

"Oh." She smiled. "Five—three boys and two girls." Wrinkling her nose, she lowered her voice, as if her future children might be listening. "Girls can be kinda bitchy, so two, even one would be fine with me."

"Based on my experience, I would agree." He shoveled the last of his fries into his perfect mouth. "I can't say for sure about all that other stuff, but the adoring you part should be easy. You're pretty adorable."

If he kept smiling at her like that, she was going to melt into a big pile of goo.

"So what do you want?"

He wiped his hands on his thighs, then leaned back against the pillows, folding his arms behind his head. "That's easy. I want it all. I wanna play my music. I wanna hear my songs on the radio and see my picture on the cover of *Rolling Stone*. I want the screaming fans and everything that goes with it."

"Don't you want someone to adore you, too?"

"I don't know. Fans love you. That's not what you mean, though, is it?"

She shook her head.

"I'm not really sure I believe in all that, but if I can find the right girl someday, one who understands my needs and what's important to me and what I do, one who can stand behind me no matter what . . ." He shrugged. "Maybe."

"How about a girl who stands *beside* you?"

The corner of his mouth quirked up. "Oh, I get it—women's studies minor, right?"

She laughed. "Not exactly."

"Okay. Guess you're right. That might be better."

CHAPTER 4

After the movie, Billy left to finish their laundry while Kate took a shower. Since he'd already told her she could check his bag for aspirin, she didn't think he'd mind if she looked for a hair dryer. Rooting through the bag, she came up with a copy of *Ulysses*.

"No way!" She turned the large volume over in her hands. She wouldn't have guessed he was a reader, let alone James Joyce. She'd read this book in high school and hated it. It was torture. She couldn't imagine anyone tackling Joyce without a gun to his head. "Guess you can't judge a book by its cover."

And oh, what a cover. It was easy to get swept up in Billy's looks, his smile. Last night he'd had the bad boy thing going on, but today he was different. More sensitive. Of course, she was probably wrong. She'd known him just a few hours. Still, if he'd made a move on her that morning, she would've let him. It would be nothing more than a one-night stand; she knew that. But the way he looked, the way he moved, and the few times he'd touched her, she had all but turned to jelly. Impressive.

She put away the dryer and was running his brush through her hair when Billy came in, stomping snow from his feet.

"It's brutal out there. When I passed the diner, they were getting ready to close, so I bought us some dinner. It was that, or we don't eat again until spring."

He grinned when he saw her. "I like your hair like that."

She thanked him, cheeks burning, and pulled back the drapes to look out the window, feeling the cold radiating from the glass. Maybe there was a pill she could take so she wouldn't blush whenever someone paid her a compliment.

The snow was deeper now and showed no sign of stopping.

"I guess you're stuck with me."

He tossed the clean clothes onto the bed. "I could think of far worse things."

Her cheeks remained pink as she disentangled her bra from a pair of his briefs, trying hard not to giggle at the intimate relationship their undergarments had formed while being tossed around inside a hot dryer. She ducked into the bathroom to finish dressing, slipping Billy's shirt back on top, since it was much warmer than the tank top Toni had loaned her.

Crap. Toni!

"Do you mind?" she asked, picking up the phone. "I need to check in with my roommate before she calls out the National Guard."

"Be my guest. Definitely don't wanna tangle with any guys with guns."

It took a few tries to convince Toni that she was fine, but in the end, she gained her roomie's blessing.

"Don't do anything I wouldn't do," Toni teased.

"And what might that be?"

"With a hot guy like that? Beats the hell out of me."

In spite of the annoying warmth creeping up her cheeks—again—Kate was laughing when she hung up.

Billy had set their dinner on a little table in the corner, but she had a better idea. While he folded his clothes, she pulled the bedspread onto the floor. He gave her a curious look.

"Picnic," she explained.

His grin went through her like an electrical charge. She busied herself with the food, setting it in the center of the blanket, then grabbed two clean washcloths from the bathroom.

"Cloth napkins?"

"Only the best," she answered, arranging them neatly on the bedspread next to the paper plates and plastic utensils the diner had provided.

"Only thing missing is ants," he said, dropping down beside her. He moved his place setting so that they were knee to knee, while she ladled out the food. They dined on room-temperature turkey with mashed potatoes, a stuffing of unknown origin, congealed yellow gravy, and mushy green beans. For dessert, there were huge slices of devil's food cake.

"Isn't it amazing how these desserts look so yummy spinning around in those carousels, but when you eat them, they're as dry as stale bread?" she asked.

"Just goes to show you can't judge a book by its cover."

She nodded, thinking of the copy of *Ulysses* stashed in his duffle bag.

Reaching across their unfinished picnic, Billy ran his hand through a strand of her hair. Shiny and straight, it hung nearly to her waist. "I really do like your hair this way."

"Without the vomit?"

He laughed. "Yeah. That's exactly what I meant."

When they finished, she cleared away the containers while he unfastened the latches on his guitar case.

"I was ten when my grandfather gave me this." He lifted out an acoustic guitar. C.F. Martin was written in script on the head near the tuning keys. "I don't play it at every gig, but I always have it with me." He ran his hand over the dark wood body before drawing the strap over his shoulder and fastening it. It was a deliberate gesture; one that told her he cared very much for his grandfather.

She lay across the bed and listened as he turned rock tunes into complex acoustic ballads. Then he surprised her with a classical piece by Bach. What she loved most, though, was one of his own songs, hard and edgy, filled with pain and longing. He practically growled the lyrics.

"You're incredibly talented," she said when the song ended. "Someday, I'll tell everyone that I knew you when." He looked at her a long while, as if weighing his response. In the end, all he did was mumble something about it getting late.

He returned the guitar to its case and took out a small cloth bag. From that, he pulled out a smaller plastic bag, and although she'd never been anywhere near it, she knew exactly what it was.

"You don't mind, do you?" he asked, taking out a small wooden oval. When he flipped it open, it became a pipe.

She did mind, but she wasn't about to complain.

She picked at the nubby texture of the bedspread and tried to sound casual, like she was used to people smoking pot around her all the time. "So, where're you from? You have a bit of an accent."

"Kansas, but we moved a lot when I was younger." He filled the pipe as he spoke, then sat down beside her on the bed. "My old man was in the army. After he took off, I lived with my grandparents. When my grandfather died, it was just me and my grandmother for a while. I've pretty much been on my own since I was seventeen."

He sucked hard on the pipe, drawing in the acrid smoke. She tried not to make a face. "What about your mother?"

"Gone," he answered in a tight voice, holding his breath. He offered her the pipe, but she shook her head.

"Really?" He seemed surprised. "Helps me relax, loosen up, you know?" He took another hit and held it in.

"I don't smoke," she said, trying to sound casual. "I wouldn't even know what to do."

Still holding the smoke in his lungs, he leaned toward her. She thought at first he was going to kiss her. He pressed his lips gently against hers and then, parting them slightly, exhaled into her mouth.

"Breathe in," he instructed. "Hold it for a few seconds."

She did as he said. When her throat started to burn, she blew it out quickly, then started to cough. *What a dork.*

"Not so fast next time." He took another hit and moved closer. She leaned forward, more for the feel of his mouth on hers than anything else. She closed her eyes and held the smoke in until he told her to let it out, then exhaled slowly. This time she didn't cough. After a few more times, she realized he was right. She felt relaxed. Better than relaxed.

"How're you feeling?" he asked as she lay back on the bed. "Zoning out?"

"Pretty good."

He ran a finger along her jaw. The side of his mouth curled up. "Can I kiss you, Katie?"

Her heart was doing double-time inside her chest. She swallowed, then nodded.

His kisses were soft at first, sweet and smoky. He cradled her face, his thumb stroking her cheek. He flicked his tongue over the corner of her mouth. A sound escaped from her throat. Was she actually purring? She felt him smile against her mouth.

"I've been wanting to do that all day," he said, drawing her arm up over her head and threading his fingers between hers. He leaned forward and kissed her again.

She didn't know if it was the pot or Billy, but her body responded in ways she'd never experienced before. Rising up to meet him, it was like bodysurfing, and she was ready to ride this wave wherever it took her. She swallowed a giggle. She felt like Sleeping Beauty, and he was kissing her back to life.

Deepening his kisses, Billy gently parted her lips. His tongue slipped into her mouth, seeking hers. His hand slid under her shirt and along her ribs. Raising it higher, he leaned back. When she didn't protest, he slipped the two shirts over her head, his intense blue-gray eyes fixed on hers.

Some tiny part of her nagged that this was wrong, she shouldn't be here, shouldn't be doing this, but in that moment, it didn't matter. Her hands reached around his neck and tugged the elastic from his hair, allowing it to fall, thick and silky, around his face. She stroked the soft skin at the nape of his neck and pulled him toward her. She was hungry, starving in a way she'd never known existed.

His kisses grew more urgent. He nipped at her lip, then pressed his mouth against her throat. She made a gurgling sound. Yep, she was purring all right.

Rolling her toward him, with a quick flick he unfastened her bra. She almost stopped breathing and fought the instinct to cover her breasts. Instead, she let Billy slide the straps from her shoulders. Her skin pebbled under his touch. Closing her eyes, she embraced the rush of excitement and adrenaline that washed over her. Her breath came in short, rapid bursts as he ran his tongue lightly along the outside of her ear, then down the side of her neck. He planted tiny kisses from her shoulder along her collarbone until he reached the hollow of her throat.

Her fingers tangled in his hair, traced the curve of his ear, and caressed the ridges of muscle beneath his shirt. She wasn't sure what she was doing, but it felt right.

Billy ran a finger under the waistband of her jeans. When he got to the button, he wrapped his fist around it, practically lifting her off the bed. Their eyes locked. *Yes.* She wasn't sure if she'd said it aloud or only thought it, but he understood. He unfastened her jeans and slid them off slowly, along with her panties, his long fingers trailing her skin. Unwilling to look at her nakedness, she stared at the ceiling, focused on the soft circle of light from the bedside lamp.

"You're beautiful," he whispered, brushing her hair off her shoulders, leaving her totally exposed. The words were soft, reverent. "You are really beautiful."

She lowered her eyes to meet his. The way he spoke, she almost believed him.

Lightly, he traced her shoulders, her breasts. Every place he touched came alive. Lowering his head, he swirled his tongue around her nipple, then captured it into his mouth, sucking gently. When his eyes met hers, they burned with such intensity, she wanted to fall into them. She was waking up, coming to life. For the first time ever, she was truly in the moment. A certain numbness she hadn't even realized she'd possessed fell away. She felt raw and vulnerable, but she wasn't afraid. She was alive. The scratch of scruff against her breasts and the silkiness of his hair in her hands. The taste of his mouth and the saltiness of his skin. The scrape of his teeth. The spicy, intoxicating hint of lemongrass curled around her. She heard her heart beat, felt her blood move through her veins. She felt it all.

Billy's mouth burned its way from her breasts to her belly, each kiss searing her. He ran his tongue along the sharp wings of her hip bones.

Trembling beneath him, she dug her fingers into his arms, afraid she couldn't pull enough air into her lungs to keep from fainting—and when he nipped the soft skin at her waist, she almost did.

He stood and slipped off his clothes. Then he wrapped his arms around her, pulling her against him. She melted into him, no longer knowing where she ended and he began. He wound a handful of her hair around his fist, and tilting her head back, not quite rough, he buried his face against her throat, alternating between soft bites and long, slow kisses.

"I want you, Katie." His voice was low and thick, and with that simple sentence, her life changed.

She lowered her eyes, then looking up, met his. "Yes."

Poised above her, Billy gently pushed her legs apart with his knees. He teased at first, coming close, yet holding back. Some primal part of her knew what to do, and her body took over. She pressed her thighs against his.

Still he held back.

"Are you a virgin?" he asked, dragging his nose against hers.

She bit her bottom lip, then nodded.

He searched her eyes. "You sure about this?" It sounded almost as if he were in pain.

"I am," she whispered. She was past the point of no return.

Long past.

He responded by pressing his mouth against hers, his tongue probing deeply. A tiny growl escaped from deep in his throat. She moaned. As if that was a signal, he lifted his face.

"Look at me," he whispered. "Stay with me."

She was drowning in honey-flecked pools of blue, but she felt anchored, safe. She moved beneath him, wanting more, wanting him. And with one quick thrust, he was inside her. The pain was sharp and stabbing, and although she had expected some measure of it, it still surprised her. Crying out, she pushed against him, but he held her tightly. He bent his head over hers, whispering her name, promising it wouldn't hurt for long. He kissed her neck and her face.

When the pain faded, she began to move. He pulled her knees up, one at a time, and wrapped them around his hips. Then he moved inside her, rocking, slowly at first. As the momentum built, her head rolled back and he buried his face against her throat.

"Open your eyes," he said after a while, his breathing ragged. "I wanna see you."

Eyes locked, she held onto him, digging her fingers into his back. She was afraid to blink; afraid to break the connection. What was left of her inhibitions cracked, the delicate fragments floating away, until nothing remained but the two of them. Finally, he shuddered several times. His mouth found hers once more before he collapsed beside her, cradling her in his arms.

Not a single word existed that could describe all that she was feeling. And she felt everything all at once: happiness, contentment, completion, adoration, even sadness. But the thing that resonated most within her? She felt wanted.

She trembled from the scope of emotion. Silent tears trailed her cheeks.

"Does it still hurt?"

"No. I don't know why I'm crying."

He kissed away her tears, then reached over and turned out the light. Holding her close, he tucked the covers around them.

In the dark, he cradled her face in one hand and kissed her again, deeply.

Sleep beckoned. But before she gave in, she tried to commit every detail of what had just happened to memory, praying she would never forget one single moment.

CHAPTER 5

Snow fell over New Brunswick. Kate and Billy slept tangled in each other's arms. Every few hours, he stirred. His mouth found hers. His hands claimed her body. Each time, she unfolded into him, and barely awake, he made love to her again.

In the morning, as thin strips of daylight crept out from behind the curtains, Kate felt a touch of sadness. Not for what she'd done—she would never regret that—but because whatever this had been, it would soon come to an end.

Nestled into the crook of Billy's arm, her bare leg draped over his, she studied his face as he slept. He looked younger but just as beautiful. His hair, splayed across the pillow, reflected a thousand shades of gold. Judging by the quiet breaths coming from his slightly parted lips, he was in a deep sleep. With the tip of her finger, she traced defined stomach muscles to the thin line beneath his navel, then over the coiled black serpent inked along the sharp V of his lower abdomen. Unable to resist, she reached down further. His eyes shot open, followed by a sleepy smile.

That was one way to wake him. He rewarded her until she lay there panting, the sheets gripped tightly in her fists.

"I guess you liked that?" he said, smiling up at her, his chin propped on her belly.

She nodded, still unable to catch her breath. If she'd read every romance novel ever written, she still wouldn't have been prepared for the last twelve hours.

"What have you done to me?" she asked when she could finally speak.

With a devilish gleam in his eyes, he nipped the inside of her thigh. "Did I hurt you?"

"No," she answered, her chest still heaving. "That's not what I meant. I'm not the same girl who walked into Kildare's Friday night."

He gave her a disarming smile, then ran his tongue in a straight line up her stomach, between her breasts, and over her throat. When he reached her mouth, he asked if she was sorry.

"No." She sighed as she cupped his face in her hands. "Not at all."

～

Most of the day was spent in bed. They alternated between watching TV, having sex, and eating day-old cake washed down with instant coffee. It was late afternoon before Billy dragged her into the bathroom for a shower—a very long shower.

"Hungry?" he asked, slipping his arms around her waist as she finished drying her hair.

"Starving."

"Get dressed. We'll go get some real food."

After stepping into her jeans and tank top, she reached for her jacket, but he stopped her. "You'll freeze in that." He slipped one of his sweaters over her head, following it with a kiss in the center of her forehead. A small flame of hope ignited deep within her.

Nearly a foot of snow had fallen. The parking lot had been plowed, and now two feet of snow blocked Billy's van. He borrowed a snow shovel from the office, and while he dug them out, Kate brushed snow from the windows with her hands. It wasn't long before they were stinging from the cold, so she stood nearby, watching and feeling useless.

"If you're not going to sit in the car, then at least stick your hands in your pockets," he scolded. "You're going to get frostbite."

Stick her hands in her pockets, when there was all this snow? She ducked in front of the van. A few seconds later, a snowball whizzed past his head. He whipped around as the second found its target. He dropped the shovel and raced toward her. Letting out a loud screech, she tried to escape, but her boots wouldn't cooperate and she landed face down in a snowbank. Scooping up a handful of snow, he flipped her over and pressed himself on top of her.

"No!" she screamed with laughter. "You'll get your sweater wet!"

"I'm not wearing it." His hand got dangerously close. "Why should I care?"

She tried to wriggle free, but it was no use. "Go ahead." She squeezed her eyes shut and grit her teeth. But instead of dousing her with snow, he kissed her. Long and hard. She was breathless by the time he pulled away, and only after the front desk manager started yelling for them to take it inside.

"Cool your jets, buddy," Billy yelled as he helped her to her feet. She brushed the snow from her jeans and climbed into the van, feeling warm in spite of the temperature. He returned the shovel, then climbed in beside her. He blew on his hands to warm them, then did the same with hers.

"Where to?"

"I would kill for a pub burger and a wedge salad. Do you mind going back to Kildare's?"

"Works for me."

Although the place was empty compared to Friday, Billy still commanded quite a bit of attention. Kate steered him to a booth in the back. As the waitress headed toward them with menus, she asked him to order her a cup of tea while she ducked into the ladies room to wash her hands. When she returned, she was surprised to see the waitress still talking with him, even more so when she slid a piece of paper across the table. Billy winked, then picked it up and slipped it into his pocket. As Kate approached, the girl gave her a cool once-over before heading to the bar to get his beer.

"I guess she recognized you from the other night," Kate said, swallowing her disappointment as she slipped into the booth across from him.

He shrugged and smiled.

"Did you decide what you're going to have?" she asked, suppressing an irritating pang of jealousy.

"Pub burger, wedge salad, Thousand Island dressing."

"Excellent choice."

"You come here often?"

She peeked at him over her menu. "You're a little late with that line, aren't you?"

His chuckle was low and throaty.

"Actually, my dad used to bring me here when I was little. We'd come for football and basketball games. He's an alumnus. That's why I'm here—family tradition." She began plucking sugar packets from their holder, one by one, aligning them on top of one another. "But in recent years, only twice before the other night. Once when they brought me and Joey before I applied to Rutgers. The other time was when they dropped me off in August." She made sure the pile was perfectly square, then one by one, returned them to their rightful place.

"Who's Joey?"

"My best friend."

"She go to Rutgers, too?"

"He. And no. He graduated a year ahead of me. There was some trouble at home, so he moved to New York. We keep in touch, but I haven't seen him in months. I should just get on the train and go, but my parents would be furious."

"What kind of trouble?"

She hesitated for a second, then shrugged. "Joey's gay. When he told his father, he threw him out."

"That sucks. Did you know he was gay?"

"Not until high school. I never really thought about it until I found myself with the biggest crush on him."

He grimaced as he reached for his beer. "Ouch."

"I was hurt and embarrassed, but it's all good. I love him with all my heart." Billy raised an eyebrow. "You know. Like a brother. Maybe more than a brother. He'd do anything for me, and vice versa."

"New York's not that far. Your parents wouldn't even know. Seriously, you've probably done worse things than go to New York without permission." He waggled his eyebrows, making her laugh and blush at the same time.

"I love New York," he added. "All that energy. We have a gig in Manhattan in a couple weeks."

"Ooh, where? Madison Square Garden?"

"Someday, maybe."

She rested her head on the heel of her hand. *God, he has a beautiful smile.*

The food came, and she was pleased to notice that other than a polite thank you, Billy didn't give the waitress a second glance. While they ate they talked about everything, from their favorite cereals—Cheerios for him, farina for her—to books.

"Let me guess," he said, sizing her up. "*Pride and Prejudice?*"

She nodded. "And you? *Ulysses?*"

"Definitely not my favorite, but I'm trying to read all the great novels."

"Ugh!" She stuck out her tongue. "I wouldn't call it great. For the first forty or fifty pages, I thought it was a story about a couple priests who lived in a tree house near the beach."

He choked on his beer. "What the hell?" Laughing, he wiped his mouth with a napkin.

"I think my mind wandered so much, I didn't know what the heck Joyce was talking about. That stream of consciousness stuff? Seems like he was a drug-addled pervert, if you ask me."

"Some of my best friends are drug-addled perverts."

He'd said it so seriously, she hesitated until she saw the corner of his mouth twitch. "My apologies for your friends, but as far as *Ulysses* is concerned, I think it's like *The Emperor's New Clothes.*"

Now he just looked confused. She dabbed her mouth with a napkin and continued.

"The emperor's told he's wearing fine new garments, and he struts around believing it. Everybody thinks it's just them who don't see the clothing, so they act like they do. It's the same with *Ulysses*. Scholars act like it's a masterpiece, so wannabe scholars go along so they won't look stupid."

He picked up his burger, but hesitated, as if trying to digest what she'd said. "I'll take your comments under advisement and come to my own conclusion when I finish."

"As long as it's your conclusion and not that of the rest of the kingdom," she said, waving a French fry.

"It will be. I'm not easily swayed."

Back at the motel, Billy sat on the bed as she slipped off his sweater and began gathering her things. When she walked past, he grabbed her hand.

"Stay," he said, embarrassed by the pleading tone of his voice.

She bit her bottom lip, and he felt it all the way into his groin. "I can't. I have a paper to write and a test to study for, not to mention a nine o'clock class."

He stood. Tucking a strand of hair behind her ear, he drew his fingers along her neck and down her chest to the space between her breasts. Her eyes were wide and dark. If he pushed a little harder, he knew she'd stay.

Instead, he did the sensible thing and helped her into her jacket.

The crisp air outside cleared his head. It was like he'd been in a trance or something. What the hell had he been thinking? This had been fun, but she was just a kid. He had a lot of plans, none of which included a girlfriend—at least, not now. This is what he'd wanted since his grandfather handed him that Martin. He was going places, and small-town New Jersey wasn't one of them.

He stole a glance at Kate, clinging to his arm as she dodged patches of ice. This was a girl who could get under his skin. If he was smart, he'd take her back to her dorm and kiss her good-bye. Remembering the taste of her skin nearly derailed him. He bent and scooped up a handful of snow, rubbing it on the back of his neck.

"What're you doing?" she cried, struggling to remain upright while still hanging onto his arm.

"Are you planning to fall down again?"

"I don't know," she said with a laugh. "It was so nice last time, I just might. Of course, you could always carry me."

In one swift movement, he scooped her up. "Now that I have you where I want you, I'll just carry you back upstairs."

She managed a sad smile, then looped her arm around his neck and rested her head on his shoulder. Fighting the insane urge to again beg her to stay, he turned and carried her to the van.

The ride to her dorm seemed to last only a few minutes. "Walking or riding?" he asked, helping her out of the van.

"I'm pretty sure I can make it the rest of the way." She rolled her lips and looked up at him expectantly.

"Well, Katie my love," he said, channeling his stage persona. "It's been a real pleasure."

Her body stiffened, and she gave him a tight smile. He knew she sensed the difference—he was a real shit.

She stood on her toes and gave him a chaste kiss on the cheek.

"Goodnight, Billy. It was nice meeting you." She hesitated for a moment. "Good luck with everything." Then she turned and tottered off on those ridiculous heels. She didn't look back. Not once.

He stood there long after she was gone, waiting. For what, he wasn't quite sure.

Sex.

For a musician, it was everywhere. You could be fat and bald. It didn't matter. If you played well enough, there were always girls waiting in the wings—a blow job backstage, a quick fuck in the parking lot. Then it was on to the next gig, the next town, the next girl. Older women, younger women. Teachers, secretaries, lawyers, doctors.

Billy had done them all. It was no secret; women were always looking to fuck someone in the band. Even for a guy like him who never had trouble getting a date or any woman he wanted, it had been a bit overwhelming at first.

Over the past few years, he had played out several times a week. Most nights, someone was there to take care of his basic needs—sometimes more than one girl a night, depending how he was feeling, and sometimes more than one girl at a time. Usually all they asked for was a guitar pick to remember him by. There had been hundreds of women, and the future promised more of the same. He had no interest in settling down. Not now, maybe not ever. It was easier this way. No strings. No attachments. Besides, he was having fun.

So then why, knowing he had a long way to go before he was ready to settle down—if he ever did—why couldn't he stop thinking about her?

Did he owe her something because he'd taken her virginity? Some misguided sense of decency? He'd been with plenty of virgins, although probably not since high school.

He'd been careless, too. He'd never encountered a college girl who wasn't on the pill, but he'd never gone without a condom. Too risky. But this had been Kate's first time, and he was afraid if he stopped to wrap up, she'd have changed her mind. He wouldn't have forced her, but he wanted her, and not just because she was willing and available. He'd just . . . wanted her. She was all soft curves and wide-eyed innocence. And her smile. It started in her eyes. Then the corners of her mouth quirked up. By the time it spread over her face, he was smiling, too. It was contagious. And dangerous.

He'd tried to keep it casual when he dropped her off. Maybe too casual. Maybe he'd hurt her feelings.

Although he turned on the lights and turned up the heat when he got back to the motel, the room felt as if the life had been sucked from it. The sheets lay jumbled at the foot of the bed. He saw a flash of arms and legs, felt silky chestnut hair fall like rain across his chest.

"You're losing it," he said aloud, determined to lay this particular ghost to rest.

He picked up his guitar and played mindlessly, until he realized he was playing the same silly tune he'd shown Katie that afternoon. He put the guitar away and picked up his dog-eared copy of *Ulysses*, but all he could think of was her wacky analysis of the book.

He reached into his pocket for the number the waitress had given him. It was almost ten. She said she would be getting off about now. He wouldn't even have to pick her up.

"Fuck this." He crumpled the paper and threw it into the trash.

If he was smart, he'd pack his shit up and check out. He should've left this morning, taken Katie back to her dorm and said good-bye. There was no reason for him to be there, and if he wasn't so damned tired, he'd leave now. But since he'd already had to pay for three nights—which more than ate up what he made Friday—he might as well stay.

He smoked a bowl and finally felt himself beginning to relax. But as soon as he turned out the light, she was back. The sheets had the faintest scent of sweet citrus. Clementines. That was it—she smelled like clementines. He imagined her lying there just beyond his reach. He rolled to the far side of the bed, punching his pillow in frustration. Before long, he was back, cradling her pillow in his arms, losing himself.

First thing tomorrow, he was getting the fuck out of there.

CHAPTER 6

Kate expected an earful from Toni, so she was glad her roommate wasn't around when she returned. She changed into her pajamas, brushed her teeth, then stretched out on her bed with *Beowulf* to reread it for the hundredth time—and wonder for the hundredth time why she'd taken British Literature. She'd thought she'd be reading Jane Austen and the Brontë sisters, not work from the Middle Ages. It was her own fault for not reading the syllabus. She wouldn't make that mistake again.

Tribes, wars, and mythic heroes were not her cup of tea, to be British about it. Her favorite hero of literature was Mr. Darcy. But the lord of Pemberley that came to mind now was not the Mr. Darcy of her teenage dreams but one with golden hair and blue-gray eyes. She closed her eyes and imagined herself back in Billy's arms—the softness of his lips, the scent of his hair, the warm tingle of his touch on her skin.

She jerked awake as her stuffed tiger landed on her head. Opening her eyes, she squinted up into her roommate's irritated face.

"Spill," Toni demanded.

She wiped her eyes, trying to clear the cobwebs.

"What time is it?"

"Ten thirty. Start talking." Toni dropped heavily onto the foot of Kate's bed.

"I'm not sure what you want me to say." She shrugged. "I already said I was sorry."

"Not that. What happened? Did he, ya know?" The corner of her mouth quirked up. "Did you?"

Kate hoped her face didn't give her away.

"Oh my God! You did." Toni slapped her arm. "You little hussy."

She shook her head. "No. It wasn't like that."

"So you didn't have hot sex with the hottest guy on the planet?"

"Um . . ."

"Exactly. Hussy." Toni threw her head back and laughed. "I can't believe it. Good for you. Damn, girl." She leaned forward, lowering her voice. "How was he?"

Kate's cheeks were burning. "Toni!"

"Hey, appropriate went out the window when he had to carry you out of the pub Friday night."

Kate shrugged.

"How many times?"

"Stop!"

"That many, huh?"

There was a good chance her cheeks might melt right off her face.

"You gonna see him again?"

Fingering the faded and frayed collar around the neck of her childhood toy, she shook her head. Growltiger had seen her through a lot. Of course, a banged-up heart might be more than a stuffed tiger could manage.

Toni looked at her like she'd lost her mind. "Why not?"

"Because. We both know what that was. It wasn't a date. He's a musician, remember? I bet he has plenty of girlfriends. Besides, I don't even know where he lives, and he didn't ask for my number or anything." She shrugged, trying to sound casual. "It was just a . . . a one-night stand."

"Well, that kinda sucks."

"Not really. It was very . . . memorable." She forced a smile. "I'm okay."

She wasn't. Not really. But she would be.

Toni was asleep when Kate woke the next morning. She rose quietly and dressed in the shared bathroom down the hall, then headed for the common area. Finding a sunny spot near the window, she finished *Beowulf* with a quick Hail Mary, praying she'd retain enough of it to pass her test. If she hurried, she'd have just enough time to grab a cup of coffee.

Sunlight glinted off deep piles of snow lining the sidewalks. She trudged along, head down, wishing she'd remembered her sunglasses while she tried to mentally sort out Grendel, Hrothgar, and the various Danes, Swedes, and Geats. She'd gone about a half-block when she heard someone call her name. Shielding her eyes, she peered across the snowy quad.

A light breeze lifted Billy's hair. Dressed in black and framed against the snow, he looked like a movie star.

"Morning," he said when he caught up to her.

She stared up at her distorted reflection in his mirrored sunglasses, clueless as to why he was there or what to say.

"Hey." *Well, that was clever.*

"Need a lift?"

"Not really. My class isn't that far."

"Can I walk with you?"

"Yeah. Sure." She jammed her sweaty hands into the pockets of her jacket.

The temperature had risen since Sunday, melting any snow remaining on the sidewalk. She picked her way over the puddles.

"Nice kicks," Billy said of her red Converse. "No stiletto boots today?"

She laughed and shook her head. "What class are we going to this morning?"

We? She pointed across the street. "There. The Murray building."

He rested his hand against the small of her back as they crossed.

"So," she said, feeling completely unnerved, even though less than twenty-four hours ago she'd been tangled up naked with this man. "What's up?"

"Not much." He looked down as a smile tugged at his lips. "You?"

"Oh, you know. Same old, same old." *Talk about the cat having your tongue.*

Kate couldn't help but notice the looks other girls gave Billy as they passed. In the three months she'd been on campus, she'd never seen anyone command such attention, not even the football players. Billy moved through the crowd like he was already a rock star.

By the time they got to the steps outside Murray Hall, she decided she had no idea what he wanted, and she was beginning to think he didn't either.

"So."

"Wanna have lunch?" The question popped out so fast, it seemed as if the idea had just occurred to him.

"It's not even nine o'clock," she said, laughing. "But lunch would be good. Around lunchtime." Billy had an unnerving effect on her, and it seemed as if she might be having a similar effect on him. He acted almost tongue-tied.

"Where can I find you?"

"Right here, around twelve fifteenish? I have another class after this. It should be over by then, depending how much my professor loves hearing his own voice."

"Noonish it is." As he leaned down, she lifted her face, but all he gave her was an innocent brush on the cheek. Still, it made her melt inside. He gave her hand a quick squeeze, then strolled back down the sidewalk to George Street.

"Well, I'll be damned," she said softly.

Billy had no idea what he was doing or why—at least none he was willing to admit, even to himself. He should be home by now. Instead, here he was, planning to spend another night in New Brunswick.

There was something about Katie he couldn't shake. It had been a long time since he felt a connection with anyone. What harm could there be in spending some time with her? Get to know her outside the bedroom. Maybe the attraction would fade. While he appreciated a good time in the sack, he had little patience with women who couldn't hold a conversation. Pete wasn't much for deep thoughts, and the people he met on the road were either all business or all pleasure. Besides, he was leaving tomorrow and wouldn't have another gig near here until the end of December. It wouldn't hurt to spend a little time with a nice girl for a change.

Back at the motel he practiced for a bit. He changed his strings, even though they didn't need changing, and when it still wasn't time to leave, he collapsed on the bed and watched sitcom reruns until after twelve so he wouldn't seem overanxious. He was already behaving out of character, and he didn't like not having the upper hand. What he hadn't counted on was lunch-hour traffic. It was nearly twelve thirty when he pulled up. Kate was nowhere in sight. He was hurrying up the sidewalk as she burst through the double doors.

"Oh my God," she cried. "I'm so sorry. My professor just wouldn't shut up. I hope you weren't waiting long."

He felt foolish for plotting a late arrival. Kate didn't possess one ounce of pretense. When she smiled at him, he felt the same weird, exposed feeling he'd had in the club when they first met. And when she reached up onto her toes and pressed her lips against his, he began to think it might just be game over.

~

The pizza joint Kate suggested was bright and loud. Students filled the tables and booths. After laying claim to a rickety table in the back, Billy ordered a pitcher of beer.

The waitress took one look at Kate and frowned. "And for you?"

"Diet Pepsi."

He looked away to hide his smile. What the hell was he doing with a girl who wasn't even old enough to drink? When the waitress had taken their order and left them alone again, he asked how she'd done on her test.

"*Beowulf?*" She rolled her eyes. "Who knows?"

"Really? I liked it. I read it in college."

Her eyes widened. "Where'd you go to college?"

"Don't sound so surprised," he scolded, grinning as color crept into her cheeks. "University of Kansas. I was a music major, but I minored in English. I went for a couple years. I even had a scholarship, but I couldn't afford it after—" He caught himself in time. "I just couldn't afford it. I made enough to support myself playing, and since music was what I wanted, I quit."

"That explains your love for *Beowulf* and Joyce," Kate said. "I mean, I'm an English major, sort of, but I'm no fan."

"If you want to be a writer, you better get on board with the classics." He lifted his eyebrows as he brought his glass up to his lips.

"Yeah, yeah," she said. Then keeping a lookout for the waitress, she reached forward and hijacked a sip of his beer.

They split a thin-crust pizza, half pepperoni for him, half veggie for her, although she barely finished her second slice. She did manage to sneak enough beer to get a little buzz and was feeling pretty brave when they stepped outside, so when Billy asked if she had any other classes that afternoon, she lied and said she didn't.

"So you're all mine?"

"All afternoon and into the evening," she said, hoping he'd take the hint. He didn't answer. He just smiled as they walked along Bartlett Street, his hands jammed into the pockets of his leather jacket.

They walked in silence for a while. Kate leaned hard to the right, bumping his arm. They took a few more steps. She did it again, this time much harder.

"You're gonna find yourself in a snowbank in about two seconds," he said.

She swung her hip into his thigh, taunting him. "I dare you."

Before he could react, she spun toward him and grabbed the collar of his jacket, stretched up onto her toes, and kissed him. His fingers snaking through her hair, he deepened the kiss until she felt boneless.

"Don't start anything you're not about to finish, little girl," he whispered before letting go.

She staggered backward, trying to catch her breath. "Who said I won't finish?" It would have sounded much sexier had she not squeaked the words out.

He reached for her hand, threading his long fingers between hers. He planted a gentle kiss on the inside of her wrist, then he asked for a tour of the campus. She wasn't expecting that, not after that kiss, but being with him again was more than she could've hoped for when she woke that morning.

They walked up to Kirkpatrick Chapel, then to the Old Queens building. On their way back to College Avenue, she led him over to Still Bill.

"William the Silent." Billy read the name engraved on the statue's base. He cocked his head. "What's his deal?"

"Legend is you can hear him whistle if a virgin walks past."

"Damn." He burst out laughing. "You mean we just missed out on a whistling statue?"

Her cheeks burned. "No. It has to be a woman in her senior year. That's supposedly why he's remained silent all these years." She couldn't help but wonder if she hadn't met Billy whether she might have been the first to make Willie whistle.

Still laughing, Billy settled his hands along her hips. "Doesn't matter. I wouldn't trade the last couple days with you, even if old Bill would climb off that pedestal and tap dance while singing the 'Hallelujah Chorus.'"

"Really?" she asked, skeptical. "That's quite an image."

"Really." His eyes dropped to her mouth. She thought he would kiss her again, but he didn't. He just cleared his throat and asked where they were headed next.

Back to his motel was where she wanted to go, but instead she led him toward the Alexander Library, where she pulled him into a dark corner of the graduate reading room. There he didn't hesitate. He kissed her up against the stacks until they were interrupted by some uncomfortable throat-clearing. After that, she declared the tour complete.

"What do you want to do now?" he asked as they walked along College Avenue. The sun hung low in the sky behind them, reflecting off the taller buildings downtown.

She wasn't sure how to suggest what she wanted to do without sounding exactly like the hussy Toni had accused her of being. They walked in silence for a bit.

"Well?"

She looked up at him with a shy smile. "Maybe we can . . . um . . . go watch TV or something."

"I think we can do that . . . or something."

They went at each other as if they'd been apart for months, stopping only long enough for Billy to untie her sneakers and yank them off so he could get her jeans out of the way. Afterward, while she finished undressing, he pulled out his stash and filled his pipe. Then they made love again, more slowly this time. She reveled in how alive each kiss, each touch made her feel.

"Oh, Katie," he groaned as he collapsed beside her. "What have you done to me?"

She didn't have a clue, but that didn't stop her from feeling pleased with herself.

"Will you stay with me tonight?" he asked, brushing his lips across her temple. Tired and content, she'd been trying not to think about her eight o'clock sociology class or her unfinished paper. She nodded, closing her eyes and losing herself in the peppery scent of lemongrass.

He looped an arm across her chest and curled into her. "I'm leaving tomorrow. I have to get home and repack, then I'm heading to Pittsburgh in the afternoon. We're there for a few nights, then on the way back we're booked in State College, Scranton, then up to Vermont for a few days. I'll be in New York the day after Thanksgiving."

All her wonderful feelings came to a grinding halt.

"I won't be back this way for a while."

No words came to her. She'd known him for three days. Last night, she'd been convinced she would never see or hear from him again. Now, it felt as if a large hole had opened up inside her.

"Katie?" He lifted up onto one elbow and looked down at her.

She tried to look away, feeling stupid and emotional. Of course this would happen. This was still a one-night stand, more or less. She'd be crazy to think—

"Well?"

She'd been so focused on maintaining control of her emotions, she hadn't heard what he said.

"What?"

"I said come with me."

Her heart was beating so fast he had to feel it.

"I know it's crazy, but I don't want to say good-bye. I've never met anyone like you." His lips grazed her shoulder. "I'm not sure what I'm doing. I'm just not ready for this to end. I think we could have a lot of fun together. I want you to come with me."

Leave school? Drive around the country in a van—with another guy? She blinked rapidly, convinced she was losing her mind, because she was actually considering it. Had he suggested robbing Franklin National Bank, she might have given that equal consideration as well. There were a couple brain cells still functioning in her drug-addled mind, however.

"I can't," she heard herself say. The remaining brain cells and a chorus of her heart and other parts of her anatomy screamed: *Don't listen to her!*

"Please, Katie." He planted tiny kisses around her face, then dragged his nose along hers. God, she loved when he did that. "Come with me."

"I don't want this to be over either, but I can't. What about school? What about Thanksgiving and my parents?"

"You'll catch up," he said, trying to convince her. "I'll buy you a turkey for Thanksgiving. Hell, I'll buy you a live one if you want."

She laughed. "Where would I keep a turkey?"

"I'll build you a pen with wheels so we can take him with us."

A marijuana-fueled vision of a van pulling a turkey in a cage sent her into a fit of giggles. Billy wasn't laughing; he just stared down at her, his face nothing but serious. She struggled to compose herself.

"If I leave now, I'm throwing away an entire semester. My parents would kill me."

"Are you here for your parents or for you? You said you wanna be a writer. So write. I don't think that's something anyone can teach you. If you wanna be a teacher, I guess you don't have a choice, but if your dream is to be a writer, go for it."

What he said made sense, but she was pretty sure that was only because she wanted to go with him.

"I'm following my dream, Katie. You can come with me and follow yours." The incongruity of his statement wasn't lost on her, but she dismissed it and slipped her arms around his neck.

"Is that a yes?"

When she shook her head, he pulled away until he was sitting on the edge of the bed. She scrambled after him. She definitely did not want this, whatever it was, to end.

"How about I meet you in New York? I won't go home for Thanksgiving. I'll tell my parents I'm staying here, and I'll take the train to New York." She pressed her naked flesh against his back. "Please. That's the best I can do."

He pulled her forward until she was kneeling in front of him.

"Please?"

Looking disappointed, he ran his thumb over her mouth, then shrugged. "Guess it's better than nothing."

CHAPTER 7

Kate spent an anxious few days trying to figure out a suitable lie to convince her parents to let her stay in New Brunswick over Thanksgiving break. Considering that she'd been begging to come home every weekend since they dropped her off, it needed to be a doozy. She had enlisted Toni's help, but so far they hadn't come up with anything she thought her parents would believe.

"I'm tapped out," Toni told her Saturday afternoon as they walked back to campus. "You've nixed every one of my ideas."

Kate transferred the bag of detergent and shampoo from one arm to the other. It banged heavily against her thigh. "I know. I just can't see them buying any of this. I'm screwed."

They walked along in silence. About a block up Albany Street, she spied a woman in a dirty, worn-out coat at least two sizes too big sitting on a wall outside the Reformed Church. Her stringy gray hair sprang out from beneath a knit cap that looked as if it would unravel at any moment.

Kate shoved her shopping bag at Toni. "Here, hold this. I'll be right back."

"Where're you going?"

"Give me a sec."

She darted into the corner sandwich shop and returned with a Styrofoam cup of soup and some crackers.

"Here you go," she said, holding the cup out. The woman flinched as if she'd expected Kate to toss the hot liquid at her.

"It's vegetable beef." Kate smiled. "It's my favorite." She continued to offer the cup until the woman extended her arm. When she'd taken it, Kate held out the crackers. "I don't like crackers with my soup, but that's just me." The woman snatched the sleeve of crackers and slipped them into her pocket.

Kate reached into her own pocket and pulled out two singles and a handful of change. "It's not much, but if you like the soup, it's enough to buy more later."

The woman looked at the money in Kate's hand, then back at her. The hard lines etched into her face softened. She unfolded her hand, and Kate pressed the bills into them, then the change on top of that. The woman snapped her hand closed and shoved the money into the same pocket that had moments earlier swallowed up the crackers.

Toni handed Kate her bags, then pulled out a five of her own to offer the woman. When she turned back, a wide grin split her face.

"What?" Kate asked as they resumed walking.

"You're gonna wanna kiss me."

"Why is that?"

"Because I just had a brilliant idea."

⌒⌒

Sunday evening, Kate paced the hall in front of the payphone. When it rang, she about jumped out of her skin.

"Hello, Kate," her mother said. "How is school?"

Nerves got the better of her, and she began to ramble. "Great. I got a B on my British Lit test, and an A-minus on my research paper. My philosophy class is going well, although sometimes the concept seems so abstract—"

"An A-minus? I would have thought after all that research, you would have aced that paper. I'm really quite surprised." Kate could see her mother's frown as clearly as if she were standing in front of her.

"To be honest," her father chimed in from the extension in his study, "I would've expected a much better grade in British Literature. You said you loved British Lit when you registered for that class."

"Yes, I do, but I meant Jane Austen. I didn't realize it was a class on the Middle Ages—"

"Like *Beowulf?*" her mother asked.

"Exactly. *Beowulf.*"

"It's a folktale, Kate, filled with interesting characters. I don't understand your inability to follow such a—"

"You're right." She could interrupt, too. "I'll reread it. Even if it doesn't help my grade, just so I have a better understanding of a classic work of literature." She almost gagged.

"I would hope so," her mother said with a long-suffering sigh.

"Umm, listen. I'm not coming home this week." Telling them, rather than asking them, wasn't the smartest approach, but that's what came out of her mouth.

"What?" they said in perfect unison.

"Umm, Toni—my roommate?—she and I joined this organization, and they need students to help at a shelter for Thanksgiving. I kinda got caught up in the whole idea of helping the less fortunate. Ya know, it's the Christian thing to do . . ." She was going to hell. "And you've always taught me to put others first. I guess I wasn't thinking. I signed up, and then I thought about you guys. But the organizers were so grateful, because, ya know, they really need the help, because most of the other students are heading home for the holiday. So I was like, yeah sure." She snatched a quick breath. "Please don't be mad. I'm just trying to do the right thing. I thought you'd be proud."

Billy was right. She didn't need a diploma to spin a creative tale. This lie was turning into a real masterpiece.

Her mother spoke first. "Please don't say 'ya know.'"

Kate chewed on the pad of her thumb to keep from answering.

"What about the rest of the weekend?" her mother asked.

"I'll be staying with Toni. Her parents live in Somerset. Actually, they're divorced. We'll be staying with her dad and stepmom. Having a late dinner Thanksgiving night. Then since we're already giving up our holiday vacation . . ." She couldn't stop now. Her ticket to hell was bought and paid for. "We'll be working at the mission store the rest of the weekend. They sell things that are donated. Like the Salvation Army."

At the rate she was going, she might not even get to see Billy. The floor might just open up and swallow her—straight to hell.

"It sounds very admirable," said her father.

"To be honest, the thought of not having to spend all that time in the kitchen—I won't miss it," said her mother.

"What do you mean? You're not gonna make Thanksgiving dinner?"

"Not if you're not coming home."

"But what about Daddy?"

"I don't even like turkey," he said.

"So you won't have any holiday dinner?"

"It's fine with me," said her mother. "I have several books I'm looking forward to, plus I'll have papers to grade. A four-day weekend with no cooking sounds like heaven to me."

At least someone will be enjoying heaven.

"I hope you won't miss me too much," Kate said, feeling a little put out, even though she was getting exactly what she wanted.

"Don't be ridiculous," said her mother. "You have a wonderful time!"

"I'll be working with the homeless—people who have no place to live? They can't bathe, so they'll probably smell pretty bad. You know. Those people. I don't know how wonderful it'll be."

Worried that she'd been a bit too snarky, she dialed up the sweetness. "Do you want me to call you over the weekend?"

"That's not necessary. Make sure to bring a hostess gift to your friend's parents. Pick out something suitable. We'll call you Sunday."

"Okay, but I'm not sure what time I'll get back. It'll depend on when her dad can drive us."

"We'll call you Monday evening then," said her mother.

"Well, happy Thanksgiving," Kate said sullenly.

"Same to you," said her mother.

"You too, sweetheart," added her father.

The line went dead.

She stared at the phone before hanging up.

"Well, okay then."

CHAPTER 8

Because Kate couldn't bear telling a lie, especially one that traded on the less fortunate, she spent Thanksgiving Day volunteering at a downtown church, serving meals to the homeless. For several hours, she lugged heavy trays of mashed potatoes and large canisters of gravy, then ladled it all onto hundreds of plates. Her face hurt from smiling, and her feet ached from standing. She was still excited about seeing Joey, who would be waiting for her at Penn Station since Billy wouldn't arrive in New York until the next afternoon, but by the time she boarded the train, all she wanted was sleep. Which is exactly what she did. She didn't open her eyes again until the train lurched to a noisy halt.

Blinking several times, she squinted into the bright light, her eyes scanning the platform. It took a few moments to pick him out from the squirming sea of humanity moving outside the window. But if she hadn't, the loud squeal that erupted as soon as she stepped off the train would have alerted her as to his whereabouts. He rushed forward and twirled her around while she giggled like a little girl.

"C'mon," he said, finally letting go and grabbing her suitcase. "Let's get out of here before we get mugged."

"Oh, stop." She rolled her eyes. "It's not that bad."

"No?" He eyed her, straight-faced. "You're lucky someone isn't already wearing your underwear."

Shaking her head, she followed at a quick pace as Joey led her out onto Forty-Second Street. When they reached the subway, he searched until he found the car with the most passengers and the ones he said least looked like murderers.

"How long?" she asked as they settled into a seat, hoping he'd say "Five minutes and the train stops next to the bed."

"About forty minutes."

She squeezed his hand. "That'll give us time to catch up."

"Then we have to walk about eight blocks." She squeezed harder. "Ouch!" He pulled his hand away. "I can't help it if I'm poor!"

"It's fine," she said as the train inched forward. "After all this sitting, a walk will do me good."

"Well, in my neighborhood it might be more of a brisk jog, but we'll see how it goes."

She rested her head on his shoulder and yawned, tracing a finger over the crease he'd ironed into his jeans.

"So tell me about the rock star."

"He's not a rock star. Not yet, but he will be."

"I see we're a smitten kitten," he said, gently bumping her shoulder. "What's he look like?"

"He's the most beautiful man I've ever seen—other than you, of course." Joey's hair had grown out into a halo of dark, unruly curls, although she knew there was nothing haphazard about them. She studied him intently. "On second thought, he's even more beautiful than you."

"I'm crushed."

"You'll get over it. He has dark, maybe medium blond hair, but it's streaked, like he spent a lot of time in the sun."

"Highlights." He nodded.

"No, it's natural."

"Bullshit. No one in the northeast has natural highlights in November. Trust me. We have plenty of men who come into school for highlights—plenty of straight men. Of course, if he's this handsome, could there be the slightest chance, that maybe—"

"No way." She shook her head.

Gasping dramatically, he clutched his chest. "Katy-did?"

Slipping her hand into the crook of his arm, she leaned in. "Katy-most-certainly-did." Lowering her voice, she added, "Katy-did until she almost couldn't walk."

"You didn't!"

She grinned and nodded.

"How was it?"

If she closed her eyes, she could almost feel Billy's arms around her. "More than I dreamed it could be. But it scares me, too. It was wonderful—everything you see in the movies, you know? Bells, whistles, and you think 'Yep, that's exactly how I wanted it to be.' I'm afraid no one else will ever live up to this? He's set the bar pretty high. I mean, my experience is pretty limited. Other than the prom."

"Ugh, Digger." He groaned. "I told you I'd have taken you."

"I know, but I knew how hard it would be for you to come back. I didn't want to put you through that."

"So you went with that Neanderthal." Disgust lined his face. "I still can't get over that."

"Well, he liked me, that's for sure."

She remembered prom night too well. As soon as they'd left the dance and gotten into his father's Buick, Digger was all over her. She practically had to knee him in the groin. They were supposed to go to Seaside Heights the next day, but she feigned a headache and spent the day reading while her friends went to the shore. Having to fight Digger off all day wasn't worth it.

He'd called several times over the summer and even stopped by the house, but she refused to speak to him. After a while, he got the hint.

"Go on," Joey prodded. "He's blond, and angels come at night and paint highlights in his hair. What else?"

"He has blue eyes."

"Of course he does. What hunk doesn't?"

"You want me to tell you or not?"

"Sorry." He waved her on. "Continue."

"He has blue-gray eyes with little flecks of gold. He's growing a goatee. And he's really tall, like six four or something, and slim but not skinny. He looks like a Greek statute, you know." She lowered her voice. "Naked."

"I'm shocked! Three months at college doing nothing but studying, and the first time you venture out, you meet and fall in love with Adonis."

"Pretty much."

He laughed, but she was serious. That was exactly what had happened.

~

The streets of the city were teeming with Black Friday shoppers and crowds trying to catch a glimpse of the decorations at the major department stores. Normally, Kate would have loved ogling the windows at the stores along Fifth Avenue, but all she wanted this time was to see Billy. He'd told her he would be at the club by five thirty, six at the latest, but it had taken her so long to get ready, it was well after six.

She had packed a couple different outfits, not really sure what one wears to a New York club. Joey had nixed both her ideas. Instead, he pulled different pieces from her suitcase until he came up with something he considered almost suitable. After some heated debate, they agreed on a rose-printed black velvet dress with a V-neck, black tights, her leather jacket, and high-heeled boots.

When it was time to finish her look, she'd dug in her heels.

"I don't want big hair or heavy makeup, and I don't wanna look like Madonna," she'd insisted as she sat on a stool in his tiny living room.

"If you don't suck the life out of a party, I don't know what," he responded tersely, eyeing her up as if he knew he had his work cut out for him. "Okay," he said resolutely. "We'll just have to give him Kate with a little—pizzazz!"

"Put the jazz hands away. Just give him Kate, with a little—I don't know . . ."

"Pizzazz?" he asked dryly.

"Whatever."

Although she had fought against him doing anything to her hair— he wanted to cut it, while she liked it long, straight, and parted down the middle—she allowed him to give her some deep bangs. Then he played up the green in her eyes and gave her a dramatic cat-eye sweep of black eyeliner. When he was done, he tied a thin black ribbon around her neck.

"Nice," he said, twirling her around to get the full effect. "Kind of *Little House on the Prairie* meets Stevie Nicks."

He ducked just in time.

When they'd left his apartment in the Bronx, she had been feeling excited and confident. Now, as they made their way up Second Avenue, her stomach was doing somersaults. She struggled to keep up with Joey's long-legged stride, cursing her unfortunate choice of footwear—again.

"Slow down," she begged, tugging on the sleeve of his navy pea coat. "I can't keep up, and these boots pinch my toes."

"You're the one who's in a hurry," he reminded her.

She screwed up her face.

"What's wrong?"

"I dunno. Nervous, I guess."

"Oh, honey. You look beautiful." He gave her a squeeze. "He should fall on his knees and beg you to have his babies."

She attempted a laugh, but the sound that came out of her mouth was more like a strangled noise.

"Oh God," she murmured, her fingers digging into Joey's arm as they waited to cross Fifty-First Street. "There he is."

Billy was easy to spot. Wearing a black leather jacket, ripped jeans, and boots, he stood beneath a marquee that announced Viper would be playing Friday and Saturday nights. Although they'd spoken on the phone almost every night since she'd last seen him, she was inconveniently reminded that she hardly knew him.

"I think I'm gonna throw up."

"No, you're not." Joey linked his arm through hers. "Just breathe. Where is he?"

Billy hadn't seen her yet, so she pointed. "There. Blond ponytail, leaning against the building."

Joey's mouth dropped. "Good lord. He looks like he stepped right off a Times Square billboard."

She looked up, grinning. "Told you!"

They were separated by a sea of yellow taxis and hordes of holiday shoppers, but Billy couldn't miss her. Kate stood on the corner, beneath the blinking do not walk sign. She lifted her hand and waved, and he was blindsided by two unexpected emotions. The first shocked the hell out of him. Her smile, even from across the street, seemed to light up the entire block. His chest tightened as an unfamiliar tingle spread through him. He wiped his sweaty palms hastily on his thighs before curling them into fists as the second emotion took hold—pure jealousy. They stood arm in arm, waiting for the light to change, and the sight was unsettling. This Joey was a good-looking guy. Kate said he was gay, but seeing him so familiar with her made Billy want to set him straight, just in case he wasn't as gay as she thought.

He took a few steps as she darted into the street, surprised by how excited he was to see her. Words bubbled in his throat, but he swallowed them. It was too early, too crazy to say them. Let alone feel them.

"Katie!" His voice sounded strange and husky. He wrapped his arms around her, and to keep from saying anything, he kissed her so long and so hard that her friend pointed out that they were causing a disturbance in the middle of Second Avenue. Kate looked embarrassed when she pulled away. She made the introductions, but not before reaching up and wiping her lip gloss from his mouth.

He shook hands with her friend, then reached for her suitcase, swinging a possessive arm around her neck. "I missed you," he whispered in her ear, hesitating long enough to take a whiff of her citrus-scented hair.

They stood in front of the club. Waiting. The silence had become awkward.

"Thanks for dropping her off," he said finally. "I've got it from here."

Joey's eyes widened.

"I hope it's okay." Kate rushed to explain. "I asked Joey to stay, at least for a little while. Actually, I wanted him to take pictures, if that's all right. He's a great photographer."

"Pictures?" He'd rather this dude would just leave, but there wasn't much he could do about it. "Sure, why not?" He led Kate toward the door, his arm still around her neck. "C'mon," he called over his shoulder. "I'll introduce you around, buy you a drink."

"Super," Joey muttered.

Billy smiled. He'd gotten the message—Katie was his now.

The club was huge compared to Kildare's and twice as dark. She and Joey settled at a table near the stage while Billy went to the bar. The moment he was out of earshot, Kate scooted closer to Joey.

"Well?" she asked, practically bouncing out of her seat.

He gave her a tight-lipped, wide-eyed smile.

She felt her own smile slide from her face. "What?"

Clearly stalling, he picked at a nonexistent spot on the cuff of his jacket.

"What?" she repeated, annoyed. "You've known him for less than a minute. You already have an opinion?"

"No-oo. Not really."

"Then what? He's not good-looking enough for you?"

"No. He's gorgeous. Just like you said."

"And?"

"And . . ." He folded his arms across his chest and stuck out his chin. "I bet he knows it."

She snorted. "Really, Vanity Smurf? You can't walk past a mirror without stopping to say hello."

Judging by the look on his face, he was about to answer with something cutting, but instead he shushed her as Billy approached the table.

He handed her a club soda and Joey a Diet Pepsi, then went back to the bar and returned with a mug of tea.

"It's good for my vocal cords," he explained, patting his throat. "Especially when it's cold. Plus, there's a shot of whiskey in it."

She caught Billy watching Joey over the rim of his cup. A glance in Joey's direction showed him narrowing his eyes, trying to look equally threatening.

This wasn't going well at all.

"Show him the pictures you took last summer," she chirped, trying to disrupt the Mexican standoff that seemed to be brewing. "Joey's a great photographer."

"Yeah. You said that." Billy cast a quick glance her way.

Joey glued on a phony smile and pulled a plastic sleeve of photos from his wallet. Still irritated, she snatched it from him and handed it to Billy. Most of the photos were of her, but there were several of them together.

"You guys are pretty close," Billy said, looking through the photos.

"Yes," Joey stated, rather emphatically. "We are."

"These are good," Billy said of the first few.

She took the sleeve from him. "Those are older. Look at the ones in the back—the black-and-white ones."

Billy flipped through the photos, pausing to study each one. "The quality is exceptional. Katie's pretty, that's for sure, but these—she's stunning."

Her cheeks grew warmer.

"I really like this one." Billy held up one of her sitting on the steps in a turtleneck and cardigan, the wind blowing her hair. He bookmarked that photo with his thumb as he flipped through the rest.

"That's my favorite too," Joey said.

"It's okay," Kate said, "but this is my favorite." She pulled out a shot that showed her looking more provocative than preppy.

Billy nodded in a distracted way. "That's beautiful. But this? This is you." He looked at Joey. "You captured her soul here."

"My soul? I think I look sexy in this one."

Joey laughed. "Honey, you can't look sexy when you barely even know what it means, so don't even!"

If he weren't sitting right next to her, she would have kicked him. Hard, too.

Billy laughed, then raked his eyes over her in a way that made her forget the pain she had been about to inflict on her best friend.

"So if you were to take her picture now, she'd look even sexier and more beautiful?"

There was a good chance her face was now exactly the shade of the roses in her dress.

"Oh yeah," Joey assured him.

Billy drummed his fingers against the nicked surface of the table. "Then that's what you should do. I'll pay for the film, developing. I'd like to see more pictures. Maybe something I can take with me when I'm on the road."

She smiled. At least she hoped she was smiling. This was all so new. She already hated the idea of him going away.

"In the meantime, can I keep this?" Billy held up the photo of Kate on the steps.

When Joey hesitated, she gave him a tiny nod, silently begging him to say yes.

"Sure. I might still have the negatives somewhere." Joey's eyes swept her face. She knew exactly where those negatives were—or where they'd been—in a box under Joey's bed back home. By now, his father would have thrown all his things away. She reached under the table for his hand. When she found it, she gave it two squeezes.

Thank you.

⁓

The night had gone well. The crowd was receptive, and the club remained packed right up until closing. The manager had booked them for a return weekend in April and again in May, with the understanding that Billy would be expanding from a duo to four or five pieces.

As exciting as all that was, none of it was responsible for the steady drumbeat of his heart against his ribs. He set his guitars down near the door of their hotel room as Kate slipped out of her jacket and draped it over a chair. Her hair fell in gentle waves down her back. The dress she wore, although innocent enough, emphasized her narrow waist and the swell of her hips. And those boots. He couldn't remember how many times he'd pictured her wearing them and nothing else over the past two weeks. His body thudded against the door.

He hadn't touched another woman since they'd met. That kind of celibacy had never happened before. *Never.* Two weeks. It was the longest he'd gone without sex since his first time.

And she hadn't asked him to be faithful. Probably hadn't even expected it. Neither had he, to be honest. But no one else interested him. It was the longest two weeks of his life. And now it felt as if his blood had begun to boil. If he didn't have her soon . . .

Kate turned to find him staring. "Is anything wrong?"

Wrong? Yeah. She had somehow managed to turn him inside out. He nodded. "You."

She looked as if he'd just told her that her puppy had died. *Shit.*

"No," he added quickly. He searched for the right words. "It's me, actually." He ran his hand through his hair. "I don't want to scare you, but I'm about two seconds away from slamming you down on that bed. I can't decide between acting like a caveman or taking my time and making love to you all night long."

God, he sounded like an idiot.

A corner of her mouth quirked up.

"What do you want?" he asked, trying to ignore the growing discomfort in his already tight jeans.

She moved toward him until she was close enough for him to smell clementines. Lifting her chin, she looked up at him with those stormy sea-green eyes.

"You." She pressed her hands into his chest, gripping the fabric of his shirt. "Just you."

He ran his hand along the side of her face. Then weaving his fingers in that glorious hair, he kissed her. When she moaned into his mouth, he deepened the kiss and his heart cracked open, just wide enough to allow her to slip in the rest of the way.

CHAPTER 9

The next afternoon, while Billy returned to the club to audition drummers and bass players, Joey met Kate at the hotel for her photo shoot. Some of the pictures he took were definitely more risqué than she would normally have been comfortable with, but she wanted to give Billy something that would make it hard for him to forget her. She was pretty sure they'd done exactly that. She couldn't wait to see the finished photos.

Lunch, on the other hand, had been a disaster. Billy had given her money to treat Joey, but he had insisted on paying for himself. She realized why as soon as he started trying to convince her that she was making a mistake falling for Billy. She listened politely, then told him to stuff it. When she'd gotten up to walk out of the restaurant, he had followed and apologized until she had no choice but to forgive him. Still, it hurt that he didn't have enough faith in her to know her own mind, let alone her heart.

The hotel room was empty when she returned. She drew a warm bath to shake the late November chill, then spent the rest of the afternoon getting ready. She was applying an extra layer of lip gloss when she heard the door open.

"Katie?"

"Just a sec." She gave herself one last hit of hair spray. It might take a week to get a brush through her hair after this.

"Sorry I was gone all afternoon," Billy called. "I didn't think it would take so long. I picked up a pizza—" He froze when he saw her standing in the doorway. "Wow. Look at you."

On her way back to the hotel, she'd stopped at a little boutique and bought a pair of black spandex pants, a satiny off-the-shoulder top, and a pair of gold hoop earrings. None of it was anything she would have considered wearing less than a month ago. Given his reaction, perhaps she'd made the wrong choice.

She turned so he could get the full effect. "Well?"

"Wow."

She hooked her hands on her hips. "Good wow, or wow, what the hell did you do?"

"You look amazing." He seemed rooted in place. "Wow."

"You said that." She took another look in the mirror. "Maybe it's a little much. I just wanna fit in. I noticed the other girls last night, and I thought maybe that's what you like. Besides, Pete said I should 'dress the part.' I'm not sure what he meant, but—"

"Pete's a dick," he said, breaking the spell. "Don't worry about what he says. You looked beautiful last night, you look beautiful now, and you look beautiful first thing in the morning with no makeup and sleep in your eyes. I don't want you to be anyone but who you are—but I gotta tell you, you look pretty hot."

She met his grin with a confident smile of her own. "How'd the auditions go?"

"Good. I'm definitely going with the drummer, and I think I found our bass player, too. I'll tell you more later. Right now, I have to eat and jump in the shower." He gave her a look she could feel all the way down to her toes. "But to be honest, I'd rather jump you."

"That sounds better than pizza."

He took her into his arms and nuzzled her neck. "It's pretty good pizza."

"It better be." She twisted away and grabbed a slice, feeling playful and even a bit powerful. Was this what it was like to have someone wrapped around your little finger? She almost laughed out loud. She couldn't imagine anyone, especially her, having Billy McDonald at their beck and call.

After his shower, she watched as he stood over his suitcase in nothing but a towel, sorting through his clothes. He was so gorgeous, she should be black and blue from pinching herself. *Here goes nothing*. She tossed the book she'd been reading aside, stood, and looped her arms around his waist. "I want you."

He looked at his watch, which she'd noticed was always the first thing he put on and the last thing he took off. "You've got five minutes," he said, tossing her onto the bed. "You better make 'em count."

They missed his five-minute deadline, but Billy wasn't complaining. Pete, however, was pacing by the time they got there, even though their equipment was still set up from the night before.

"I don't think he likes me," Kate whispered to Billy after Pete grunted in response to her greeting.

"Fuck him. He's just jealous."

She wasn't sure what that meant. Pete wasn't interested in her. She'd only been around him a couple times, but was definitely not his type. Over the course of the night, she'd seen him with several girls. He'd disappear with one on a break, then later he'd slip out with another. When she asked Billy where they were going, he had just smiled and told her not to worry about it. She had a pretty good idea, though. Some of the girls, like the ones she saw him leave with at the end of the night, looked pretty wild, but they didn't all fit the groupie image.

Did Billy see her that way? A groupie? That powerful feeling she'd had earlier began to ebb. With all the women vying for his attention, he could tire of her and walk out on the next break with someone else. She had no claim on him. Wondering how he behaved when she wasn't around made her stomach clench.

With anxiety gnawing at her nerves, she headed for the restroom shortly before the end of the second set, then waited in line to find only two of the three toilets were working. The place was so filthy she couldn't bring herself to use it no matter how badly she needed to pee. The jukebox was already playing over the speakers, which meant Billy was on break. She headed backstage, hoping to find him, but the dressing room was empty. Cursing herself for waiting so long, she practically danced across the room to the private toilet and yanked open the door.

Pete was leaning against the wall, his eyes closed, his hands tangled in the hair of the blonde kneeling in front of him.

"Oh my God! Sorry!" Kate exclaimed, backing up and tripping over her own feet. She scrambled for the door.

Pete called after her.

"Hey, Katie, don't go. You can be next." His laughter followed her into the hall even after she pulled the door closed behind her.

By the time she'd used the disgusting rest room and scrubbed her hands until they were raw, Billy's break was nearly over. She found him standing at the bar, surrounded by women—women who might jump at the opportunity to do for Billy what Pete's friend had been doing for him. A cold nugget of apprehension lodged itself into her chest.

"Where were you?" he asked, breaking away when he saw her.

"Bathroom."

He grimaced. "Gross, huh? You should've just used the one in the dressing room. It's not much better, but at least you don't have to fight to get a seat."

She nodded, too embarrassed to say anything. At least she knew now what Pete did between sets.

He ran his hand up her arm. "You okay?"

"Uh-huh. Fine."

Pete didn't reappear until it was time to go back on. She did her best to avoid looking at him, but whenever he caught her eye, he'd smile and wink. Billy had been right; Pete was a dick.

"So what was your favorite part?" Billy asked as they waited for a table at the deli across from the Winter Garden Sunday evening. That morning he'd surprised Kate with tickets to *Cats*. The entire weekend was costing him a small fortune, but when the lights went down and the overture began, the look on her face convinced him it was worth every cent.

"I loved it all," she gushed. "But if I had to pick my favorite, it would be 'Growltiger's Last Stand.'"

"Not 'Memories'?"

"I love that, too, but when they started singing opera, I felt it." She placed her hand on her heart. "I have no idea what they said, but it touched me. It's how I feel sometimes when you play, especially the acoustic. It's so beautiful, I could cry. Don't you ever feel that way?"

"I don't know that I've ever heard a piece that made me cry." He thought for a moment, then laughed. "Although, to be honest, bagpipes make me want to bawl my eyes out. Guess it's my Scottish blood."

Smiling coyly at Billy, the hostess motioned for them to follow her to a two-top in the back.

"So, you like opera?" he asked after they were seated.

Kate picked up her menu and shrugged. "After hearing that, I'd be willing to give it a shot. It would have to be something romantic, though, and Italian." She crinkled her nose. "I don't know that I could get all teary about a German opera like *Die Fledermaus*, especially if it's about a real mouse."

He tried not to laugh. "Pretty sure that's a comedy. And *die fledermaus* is a bat."

She shuddered. "Even worse. So what was your favorite part?"

Watching you, he wanted to say. He'd found himself spending more time glancing down at Kate's face than he had watching the show, and finding her way more captivating. Could he possibly get any cheesier?

"Oh, I think it was all pretty good."

She flipped her hair over her shoulder, and he imagined the weight of it dragging across his chest. He wanted to lean forward and kiss every freckle from one cheek to the other, then get lost in her gray-green eyes. He wanted to skip dinner and go back to the hotel. Instead, he fumbled with his menu and asked what she was going to have.

"Chopped liver with onion and a giant pickle."

69

"Jeez, I hope that comes with a side of Listerine," he muttered.

Her face fell. "Do you want me to get something else?"

"No, that's OK. I'll just eat onions, too, and hope for the best."

Later, as they walked back to the hotel, holding hands and taking in the lights and the sounds of the city, he asked if she'd ever want to live there.

"As much as New York has to offer, I'd rather just visit. I like the peace and quiet of the country. I like to see the stars. What about you?"

"The big city's pretty exciting. It might be fun for a while. I guess it would be difficult with kids, though."

"So now you're having kids?" She poked him gently in the ribs. "You weren't even sure you wanted to fall in love."

He guided her over to a store window, out of the path of the other pedestrians. "A guy can change his mind, can't he?" Then he leaned down and kissed her.

"Hmm. Liver."

⌒

Billy hadn't even left yet, and Kate was already missing him. They'd returned to New Brunswick around midnight. He carried her suitcase up to her room. She then insisted on walking him back down to the lobby where they kissed for so long her lips were swollen and her face burned from the scruff of his beard.

"I don't want you to go," she said finally.

"I don't want to go without you."

"It's such a long time." She studied his face. "You're gonna meet someone else and forget about me. Probably some snow bunny."

"I won't. No one could make me forget you."

A heavy weight settled on her chest.

"I'll call you every night, I promise. Every night before the gig."

"I'd rather you call me every night after the gig, from your lonely hotel room."

"I'll do that then, if you don't think it will bother your roommates. I'll call whenever you want. Just tell me when." He twirled a long strand of her hair through his fingers. "I'll see you in two weeks. You take the train into the city Friday, and I'll pick you up at the station. Then we'll drive out to Long Island."

"What about Christmas?"

"I'm booked up in Stowe, but I'll be back the Tuesday after Christmas, and then Tewksbury on Friday and Asbury Park for New Year's Eve." He cradled the back of her head in his hand, then kissed her so hard her knees turned to rubber. "I want you with me for New Year's." The words brushed softly against her ear.

It hadn't been too difficult to fool her parents this time, but they thought she was doing charity work. They would never let her go away with Billy overnight. "I hate lying again, but I'll think of something. In the meantime, come see me when you get back. That Thursday, come meet my parents."

"I don't know, Katie." He rested his forehead against the top of her head. "Maybe that's not a good idea."

Her heart sank. "Don't you want to see me?"

"Of course I do, but your parents seem pretty strict. I'm not your average boyfriend material."

"Am I your girlfriend?"

He gave her the half-smile that made her tingle. "Oh baby, you are most definitely my girlfriend."

"Then please. It'll be fine."

He didn't look convinced, but he agreed. She had no idea if her parents would like him, or even accept him. But as long as she did, wasn't that all that mattered?

CHAPTER 10

Christmas vacation dragged, especially since it would be another week before she would see Billy again. To pass the time, Kate had baked dozens of cookies. She made trays for the volunteer firefighters and the rescue squad. She made a bûche de Noël from scratch, with chocolate fudge icing that looked like bark and meringue mushrooms dusted with cocoa powder. When she got sick of baking, she took long walks. She even helped decorate the Presbyterian church in the town square after she saw the minister and his wife struggling to unload boxes from their Jeep.

She couldn't remember ever having this much energy, but whenever she stopped moving, she physically ached for Billy.

On Christmas Eve, she and her parents went to midnight Mass, after which they'd gathered in the family room, where she was permitted to open one present. It was the same each year, a Christmas nightgown or pajamas. This year it was a flannel nightgown that looked like every other flannel nightgown she'd ever received: a half-circle of lace around the yoke, buttons on the cuffs, and buttons in the back. It would cover her from the tips of her ears to the tips of her toes.

She wondered what Billy would say if he saw it. No matter. That wouldn't happen.

To try and stir things up, make it a little more fun this year, she surprised her parents with pajamas of their own. For her mother, bright pink flannel covered with dancing lobsters wearing Santa hats—a tribute to their summers in Maine. And for her father, a pair of forest green flannels printed with red Christmas balls.

"Oh my," her mother said as she opened the box. Her father said nothing.

Kate giggled. "Aren't they great? I saw them at the mall, and since you always get me PJs for Christmas, this year I thought we'd all wear them." She scrambled to her feet. "Go put them on. I'll set up the camera so we can get a picture in front of the tree."

"Oh, I don't know," her mother said. "I'm not sure they'll fit." She looked at the tag under the collar. "These are a six. I'm only a four."

"Can't you at least try them?"

"If your mother says they're too big, then they're too big."

She tried not to let the hurt feelings show. "What about you, Daddy? Can you put yours on?"

He made a face. "These really aren't my style. It's a lovely gesture, though. Thank you."

She looked from her father to her mother. "I'm not asking you to wear them to a faculty meeting. I just thought it would be fun."

"Your father's right. It's a lovely sentiment. Thank you." Her mother put the lid on the box and the conversation, then picked up a plate of neatly arranged cookies.

"Cookie?"

Swallowing her disappointment, Kate shook her head and stood. "No, thank you. I think I'll just go to bed."

After kissing her parents goodnight and hanging up her stocking on the highly polished marble fireplace in the front parlor, she headed upstairs, feeling lonelier than ever. She slipped out of her plaid jumper and tights and pulled her new nightgown from the box. But instead of putting it on, she tossed it on the bed and then locked her bedroom door.

Standing in front of the full-length mirror, she stared at her reflection. She reached back and unhooked her bra, then she slipped out of her panties. She'd never really looked at herself like this before, although she'd always been critical of her perceived misfortunes: her legs were too thin, her breasts too small, her neck too long.

But when she looked at the girl in the mirror, she didn't see any of those things. A woman looked back at her. She saw what Billy saw, and she wasn't disappointed. Pulling her hair up on top of her head, she turned to one side, then the other. She was proud of her body. And if someone like Billy, who had girls throwing themselves at him nightly, saw something special in her, then maybe it was true.

She climbed into bed, thinking of Billy, unable to sleep. She rolled onto her side. It was a little past one. Picking up the phone, she dialed the long distance number he'd given her. A tiny thrill went through her when she heard his voice.

"You're still awake?"

"Hey, babe. We finished up a couple hours ago. I was just about to go to bed."

"I'm already in bed. I miss you."

"I miss you, too. I wish you were here, right now, in my bed." His voice dropped an octave. "Do you know what I'd do if you were here?"

She twisted the cord around her finger. "No. Tell me."

He chuckled. It was low and throaty. "I think you know exactly what I'd do to you."

"Tell me."

It was quiet for a few seconds. "You promise to do exactly what I tell you?"

"Uh-huh."

"What're you wearing?"

"Nothing."

"Then we're off to a good start."

—⁓

Christmas at home was quiet. After the wrapping paper had been carefully folded and put away, and the opened gifts arranged neatly under the tree, Kate and her parents gathered in the front parlor. They sat in their respective places, each reading one of their Christmas gifts. Kate stared at the pages of *Beloved*. Her father was reading *The Closing of the American Mind*, a book her mother had given him—a perfect choice, she thought with a small grunt. When he glanced up over the top of his book, she cleared her throat and went back to staring at the same page, flipping it for effect.

Her mother was reading a leather-bound volume of *The Wings of the Dove* Kate had picked up in New York.

"This is a beautiful book, Kate." She ran her hand over the gold embossing. "Where did you say you found it?"

"I didn't." Kate hesitated. "Actually, there's a little bookstore in New Brunswick. Lots of oddities, some rare books. I saw it, and I knew you'd love it."

"Yes, I do." Her mother gave her a bland smile. "Funny thing is, there's a bookmark inside from Argosy's Old and Rare Books in New York."

Kate tried not to fidget under the sudden scrutiny. She drew her legs up under her. "Maybe that's where it was before I got it. It's an old book, Mom. It's been around."

"Perhaps."

"That's probably what happened." She buried her face back in her book. She was a terrible liar. If they pushed her, she'd probably cave and admit to getting it in New York. But then she would need an excuse for having gone there. She would just say that she took the train into the city to see Joey and—

"Kate?"

"Huh?"

"Please don't say 'huh.'" Her mother closed the book and set it on the table next to her chair.

"Sorry. I didn't hear you."

"I asked you to set the table."

"Yes, ma'am."

She scrambled to her feet, grateful for an excuse to escape. She removed her grandmother's china and the family silver from the butler's pantry and took down three crystal goblets and two wine glasses. Then she arranged the place settings the way she had been taught. The candles in the silver candelabra would be lit just before they sat down to their traditional goose. She hated goose. Even the smell of it roasting in the oven was nauseating. Her dinner would consist of salad, green beans almandine, and a scoop of duchess potatoes. That was her tradition. It made no sense to her why, if one-third of the family refused to eat the meal, it remained a tradition. But it was also a tradition, it seemed, not to discuss changing traditions.

As they ate, nondescript Christmas music played in the background, accented by the tinkle of heavy silver on fine bone china.

Kate steered a green bean through her potatoes. She cleared her throat. "I have a friend coming to visit Thursday. I hope that's okay."

"Oh?" Her mother looked up. "Who might that be?"

"His name is Billy." Just saying his name made her smile.

"Is this the young man who's been calling every day?" her father asked.

"Yes. I want him to meet you, and I'd love for you to get to know him."

Her mother placed a forkful of potatoes in her mouth and chewed.

Kate waited. *How long does it take to chew fancy mashed potatoes?*

"How do you know this boy?" her father asked.

"He's not exactly a boy."

"Oh?" Her mother's brows shot up. Kate winced. Wrong answer. "How old is this young man then? He is a *young* man, isn't he?"

"Yes, of course. He's in his early twenties."

"How early?" asked her father.

"Um, twenty-one." Billy was almost twenty-four.

Her parents exchanged glances. Raising the heavy linen napkin from her lap, her mother dabbed at the corner of her mouth. "Is this a boy—sorry—a young man you met at school?"

"Kind of. Toni and I went to this, um, restaurant one night, and I met him there. He's very nice. I think you'll like him." She looked from her mother to her father. They were unreadable. "He's very talented. He's a musician."

Her father coughed. "A musician? What kind of musician?"

"The kind who plays music. What do you mean, what kind of musician?"

"No, dear," her mother said as if speaking to a five-year-old. "What type of instrument does he play?"

"Oh. Pretty much everything—piano, mandolin, guitar, anything with strings."

Her mother took a sip of her wine. Her father sliced through a piece of dark meat. Kate waited, impatient.

"Well? Can he come for dinner?"

"Of course, that should be fine," said her mother.

"Thank you," she answered, with just a little too much attitude.

"Excuse me?" Her father seemed somewhat taken back.

"I'm sorry." She gave them both her sweetest smile. "I'm just nervous. I want you to like him."

"I'm sure we will," her mother said, already sounding bored. "If you like him, what's not to like?"

CHAPTER 11

After trying on just about every outfit in her closet, Kate settled on a long-sleeved Laura Ashley dress sprinkled with tiny flowers, paired with dark tights, and flats. She needed to look as demure as possible. If her parents caught a glimpse of what she'd been wearing lately, they'd lock her in her room. She stared at her reflection in the mirror. Other than having her two front teeth, she didn't look much different than she had in kindergarten.

To kill time until Billy arrived, she went downstairs and began setting the table, pulling out the linens and the good china.

Her mother stopped her.

"I don't think that's necessary. We don't want your friend to feel uncomfortable."

"Why would he feel uncomfortable?"

"I don't know. Perhaps he's not used to the finer things."

"Why would you say that?" She didn't have a clue if Billy was used to finer things or not, but for her mother to assume he wasn't was just wrong. Her mother smiled her typical smile, the one that said "I'm not discussing this, so don't waste your breath."

"Fine. What would you like me to use?"

She handed Kate the everyday dishes.

"Paper napkins, too?"

"Don't be ridiculous. We don't have paper napkins."

Kate had wanted to make dinner, but her mother insisted on handling it. That was probably a good thing, as the less time she spent around her mother, the less likely she would say something to get herself in trouble. Her father was less of a problem, since he spent the day in his study.

As dinnertime neared, Kate waited anxiously at the window, spotting Billy's van just a few minutes past four. He climbed out and looked up at the house—a three-story, Italianate Victorian with a mansard roof. For a second, she feared he might get back in and drive away. She rushed to the front door and yanked it open, barely able to contain herself as he came up the walk.

Billy grinned when he saw her, and she wondered how he could possibly be even more beautiful than the last time she'd seen him. He'd shaved his beard and mustache, and his hair was pulled back into a neat ponytail. Of course, that exposed the two small gold hoops in his left ear. He was wearing his leather jacket and a gray sweater, jeans, and cowboy boots that made him even taller. He carried a large bouquet of red roses and a box wrapped in Christmas paper.

"Hello, beautiful." He leaned down as if to kiss her, but whispered in her ear instead. "I'm here to see your older sister. Is she home?"

Kate rolled her eyes. "Funny." She heard her mother coming from the kitchen, so she whispered quickly. "You're twenty-one."

"What?"

"You're twenty-one, if anyone asks." He nodded, then seeing her mother, he smiled.

Kate turned to gauge her mother's reaction. Upon seeing Billy, her hand flew up to her neck and she began to fidget with the string of pearls peeking out over the shell of her red sweater set.

Damn. He even has that effect on her. She ducked her head to hide her smile.

Her father came down from his study, and Kate made the introductions. Billy shook their hands, calling her mother "ma'am" and her father "sir." So far, so good, she thought, taking his jacket and hanging it in the hall closet. He handed her mother the roses. The wrapped box, he gave to her father.

"They're beautiful," her mother said. "Let me get these in some water."

Her father invited Billy to join him in the parlor. As he followed, Billy pushed up his sleeves, revealing the tattoos on his forearms. Kate gave the sleeve a quick tug, along with a pleading look. He winked as he smoothed the sleeves back in place, then took a seat on the horsehair loveseat. To her dismay, her father perched next to him and began unwrapping his gift. Kate sat in the wing chair opposite them, just itching to get her hands on Billy.

"What have we here?" Her father asked as he pulled out a round brass box.

Billy reached out. "May I? Kate says you collect stamps. This is an antique magnifying glass. You just slide this here, and it opens up." A circle of glass popped out from the center.

"My goodness, would you look at that?" Her father peered through the glass and smiled. "Thank you, young man. I'm sure I'll get a lot of use out of this." He flipped the glass back and forth, then lifted it to his eye to study it closer.

When her mother called for him to help, he slipped the magnifier into his shirt pocket and patted it with his hand. "It's perfect."

Kate waited until she heard voices coming from the kitchen, then rushed to the sofa. She kissed Billy so hard, she almost knocked him over.

"I've missed you," she said between kisses. "I'm miserable."

"Me, too," he whispered, holding her close, burying his face in her hair. He kissed her again, gently this time. "Can we go out later? Just to be alone for a bit. A movie? Anything?"

She nodded. "I'll think of something."

Billy pulled a small box from his pocket. "Merry Christmas."

She carefully slipped her finger under the tape so as not to tear the paper.

"What're you doing?" He looked amused.

She shook her head and grinned, then tore at the paper. Inside the box was a thin gold bracelet with a heart in the center.

"It's beautiful." She held out her wrist for him to fasten the clasp.

"You're not gonna believe what I got you." Laughing, she jumped up and ran to a table between the floor-to-ceiling windows. From the drawer, she pulled out a box a little bigger than the one he had given her. It was wrapped in gold brocade paper and tied with a green velvet ribbon.

"Fancy," Billy said, shaking the box. "Do I need to open this carefully?"

"Unh-uh. Go for it."

In the box was a bracelet, but this one was made out of steel guitar strings. A silver tube slid onto the wire, covering the clasp. It was engraved with the letters B and K.

"Wow. This is something."

"It's yours," she explained, fastening it just below the leather and metal strap he wore. "I mean, of course it's yours—but it's your guitar strings. I saved them after you changed them and brought them to this head shop in New Brunswick where some guy makes these. Do you like it?"

"I love it." He tilted her chin and kissed her.

When dinner was ready, he followed her into the dining room. Kate's mother carried in a bowl of mashed potatoes.

"Everything smells wonderful, Mrs. Daniels. Can I help you with something?"

"No, Billy, thank you. Mr. Daniels has the meat loaf."

"Meat loaf?" Kate exclaimed. Her mother never made meat loaf for company.

"I love meat loaf," Billy said. "It's one of my favorites."

"Well, you're in for a real treat then," said her father, who hated meat loaf.

Kate surveyed the meal her mother had prepared: meat loaf, topped with a can of tomato soup, mashed potatoes, canned green beans, and a salad made with iceberg lettuce, hothouse tomatoes, and bottled salad dressing. This was not the type of dinner her mother served to company. This wasn't even the type of dinner she would serve to her family.

The men waited for her mother to sit, then settled in.

"Would you say grace, darling?" her mother asked.

Kate shot her mother a look. Usually her father led the blessing. This was for Billy's benefit. She made the sign of the cross and caught her mother watching to see if Billy did the same. He didn't, although he bowed his head. When Kate finished, her mother picked up the potatoes, helped herself, and then passed the bowl to Billy.

"I see you're not Catholic. Do you mind if I ask what religion you practice?"

"No, ma'am." He took a scoop of potatoes and passed them to Kate's father. "I grew up Methodist, but I haven't practiced in a long time."

"Ah," said her mother, arching an eyebrow in Kate's direction.

Dinner went as well as could be expected, although Kate was fuming. She knew her parents well enough to recognize their questions for what they were. They were trying to make Billy look foolish and uneducated, but they were failing.

"Billy's a fan of James Joyce, aren't you?" she said abruptly, interrupting a series of increasingly personal questions.

He looked up, surprised, then wiped his mouth with his napkin. "I don't know that I'd call myself a fan exactly, but I appreciate his writing."

"Do you? That's surprising," her father said. "So many young people don't appreciate the classics."

"I do," Billy continued. "Although I prefer Faulkner to Joyce."

Kate's father seemed impressed, but her mother was unmoved.

She plowed on.

"He's also quite the expert on *Beowulf*. Really helped me on that one. Good old Grendel." Judging by the look her mother gave her, Grendel was the dragon. *Takes one to know one.*

"Did you go to college, Billy?" her mother asked, zeroing in.

"Yes, ma'am, but I dropped out during my junior year. I was raised by my grandparents. My grandfather died when I was eleven, and my grandmother when I was seventeen. I went to school for a couple years, but it was too hard to support myself and go full time. Music is what I planned to do anyway, and I can make a living at it, so that's what I do."

"You can never undervalue the benefits of an education, Billy," said her mother. "I hope Kate appreciates the sacrifices we've made so that she can have the very best."

Her mother looked at her, as if waiting for her to agree. She was too annoyed to express any gratitude. Instead, she swirled the remaining meat into her potatoes until her mother reached across the table and stilled her arm.

"What kind of music do you play?" her father asked. "Kate hasn't told us very much."

Because you wouldn't listen if I did.

"Hard rock, mostly. Some indie stuff, punk, alternative. I have an audition next month. If that comes through, I'll be putting my band on hold for a bit and heading out on tour."

His eyes met Kate's. This was the first she heard about any audition.

"I suppose if it works out, you'll be on the road most of the time?"

"Yes, sir. For a few months, at least."

Kate smiled, but it felt fake. She could only imagine how it looked.

When dinner was over, her father ushered Billy into the parlor while she helped her mother clear the table.

"Meat loaf?" she whispered viciously as soon as they were in the kitchen. "That's what you make the first time I bring someone home for you to meet?" She took her anger out on the dishes as she scraped them over the garbage disposal.

"I don't see a problem. He said he loved meat loaf."

"I know what you're doing. You've made up your mind you don't like him."

"Nonsense."

"Whatever. We're going out for a while."

"I don't think so. You can visit right here."

Kate bit her tongue. It was a battle she would lose, so why bother? She set the coffee to brew, then carried the tray of mugs into the dining room before joining her father and Billy in the parlor. Her father was adding another log to the fire while Billy just looked uncomfortable.

"Dad, Mom wants your help in the kitchen."

"Certainly." He gave Billy a wink. "You two behave."

As soon as she heard the kitchen door swing shut, she raced to the hall closet for their jackets.

"Let's go," she whispered, pushing him toward the door and closing it softly behind them.

It was bitter cold outside. Kate could see her breath as they dashed toward Billy's van. As usual, she'd forgotten her gloves.

"Are you okay?" he asked as he pulled away from the curb.

"Meat loaf?" she cried, expecting him to be as offended as she was. "What kind of meal was that?"

"I don't know. I like meat loaf. Besides, any home-cooked meal is better than bar and diner food."

Her outrage was too great, and she continued as if he hadn't spoken. "I'm so embarrassed. You tried. You even shaved. They had their minds made up before you even got here—at least, my mother did."

They drove aimlessly before she directed Billy to the high school parking lot. He parked behind the dumpsters and climbed between the bucket seats into the back, then helped her climb in back beside him. They squeezed into the small space left between the front seats and the amps, monitors, and speakers.

She shimmied onto his lap and settled in against his chest as he rubbed his hands up and down her arms. "Listen, Katie. I honestly didn't expect your parents to like me. It would've been nice, but I'm not the kinda guy most parents cozy up to. In fact, they're more likely to hide their daughters."

"How many parents have you met?"

"Not as many as you might think." He kissed the top of her head. "I'm not the guy girls usually look to bring home to meet Mom and Dad."

"It doesn't matter. They're wrong."

"If a long-haired musician with a couple earrings, some tattoos, and a questionable background showed up to date your daughter, what would you do?"

"I don't judge people on how they look or what they do."

"That's admirable, but there aren't too many people like you. Maybe by the time you have a daughter and she brings home a musician or a guy with a blue Mohawk or a biker, you won't be so generous."

"I hope I never change. I don't ever want to be like my mother."

He captured her hand, rubbing his thumb over her cold fingers.

"Being home these past few days, my life seems so empty. It wasn't so bad when Joey was around, but now . . ." Her voice drifted off. It was like peeling back a scab. It was one thing to examine her life on her own, but here she was, sharing the darkest parts, the parts she'd even tried to hide from herself. It wasn't as hard as she thought it would be, at least not with Billy.

"They have their routines, you know? Every night my mother makes dinner. Afterward, she and my father do the dishes. I'm excused. My help isn't wanted. Then my mother sits in the parlor and reads while my dad heads to his study. Every night. It's like I don't even belong there. I feel like an outsider who's overstayed her welcome. I was always quiet and obedient. Always on my best behavior. Being away at school just made it more obvious when I got home that I'm still not good enough. The weekend we met, I'd begged my mother to let me come home, but she said not until Thanksgiving. I hadn't seen them since August. No family weekends, no visits, no care packages. Just a phone call once a week to criticize me. They actually gave me grief about an A-minus for a paper on Shakespeare and for a B for my test on *Beowulf*."

"You got a B on your *Beowulf* test? Seriously? You didn't even know that Grendel was the dragon."

"Are you kidding me?" She tried to pull away, but he held her tighter.

"I'm sorry. I just don't understand how you got a B." He chuckled softly before kissing her tearstained cheek. "Don't get mad, but do you think you might be reading too much into your parents' being threatened by a new boyfriend?"

"Not just a new boyfriend. You're the first boy I've ever brought home, other than Joey. Don't you think they'd be like 'Hey, at least she's not a homosexual'?" She wiped her eyes. "I'm sorry. I don't want to spend our time together talking about my parents."

"It's okay. I'm happy just being with you." He tilted her face toward his. "I missed you." His hand slid along the inside of her thigh.

"What if they say I can't see you anymore?" she asked in a sudden panic.

His hand stilled. "That's up to you, but I'd hate that."

"I couldn't do it. If I can't see you, I'll leave. I'll go back to school."

She settled in, comforted by his touch and the familiar scent of lemongrass.

A thin shaft of light from a street lamp illuminated his face. Reaching up to touch his cheek, she searched his eyes. She hesitated at first, but she couldn't hold it back anymore.

"Billy," she whispered, "I love you."

He wiped away a stray tear, his eyes locked on hers. He didn't speak right away, as if weighing his options. Just as a tiny seed of fear began to sprout, he answered.

"I love you, too. So much."

When his mouth found hers, nothing else mattered. It had been over two weeks since they'd been together, and she wasn't about to be denied.

She kicked off her shoes and slipped off her tights. He turned up the heat, then loosened his jeans and lowered them. She straddled him as he guided her into place. His hand snaked its way underneath her dress. He slipped his finger under the edge of her bra to push it up, freeing her breasts. One hand cupped a breast while the other held her around her waist.

"If I wasn't worried about you freezing to death and having to take you home naked, I'd tear this dress right off you," he growled into her shoulder.

A beam of light flashed across the fogged-up window.

"Out of the van! Now!"

"Shit," Billy mumbled.

She buried her face in Billy's shoulder while he reached into the front and rolled the window down an inch. "Look, buddy. Could you get that light out of my eyes?"

"You heard me. Out!"

Kate raised her head and squinted into the light. "Digger?"

"Kate?"

That idiot. "Yes!" she yelled, as the beam of light dropped. "Go away!"

"Get out of the van, Kate. You and your friend."

This was all too much. If he thought she was getting out of that van, he was out of his mind.

"Beat it!" she growled.

"Jesus, Katie. What're you doing?" Billy muttered.

"Seriously, Digger! I'm not in the mood."

"What're you doing in there?"

"What the fuck does it look like? Get the hell out of here." She'd never used that word before. It felt good.

"Is he a cop?" Billy asked.

"He's no cop. He's just a boy from high school."

"I'm not a cop. Yet. But I work security," Digger answered, as if that should impress them. "You're trespassing. If you don't get out of the van, I will call the cops."

"And if you don't get out of here, I'll call your mother and tell her what you did to me on prom night," she yelled back.

"Kate . . ." The authority in his voice faded.

"I'm gonna count to ten, Digger, and you better be pulling out of this parking lot before I hit nine."

"Katie," Billy whispered. "What're you doing?"

"One!" she yelled, feeling pretty brave for a girl with her panties stuffed into her coat pocket. "Two!"

"Kate," Digger whined.

"Three!"

Billy pulled back. "You're yelling in my ear."

"Four!" She lowered her voice.

"Sonofabitch." Digger turned off the flashlight and headed for his rent-a-cop car. "You'll be sorry, Kate!" he yelled over his shoulder.

"Five!"

Billy stuck a finger in his ear.

When Digger finally pulled away, Billy erupted with laughter. She remained straddling him, her knees tucked into his armpits.

"What the fuck, Katie! You kiss your boyfriend with that mouth?"

She wrapped her fingers around the lapel of his jacket. "Every chance I get."

⁓

It was after two when Kate slipped in the front door. The house was dark. She'd almost expected her parents to be waiting, but that would've meant staying up past their bedtime.

She was tired, but she didn't want to go to sleep, not when she could still feel Billy touching her, inside her, still had his scent on her skin. She tiptoed into the kitchen and put the kettle on, then pulled out her favorite Christmas mug and scooped cocoa mix into the top of Santa's head. Before the kettle could whistle, she snatched it from the stove, filled her mug, and carried it upstairs.

After changing into a pair of sweats and a T-shirt, she sat on her bed, fingering the bracelet Billy had given her. Already missing him, she slipped on her headphones and drank her cocoa while listening to a cassette he'd made for her.

When the first side finished, she got up to brush her teeth. Taped to the mirror in her bathroom was a note written in her mother's neat parochial school script.

Don't make plans for tomorrow. We need to talk.

She tore the note off the mirror, crumpled it, and tossed it into the trash, where it unfurled, refusing to be ignored. She slipped into bed, then rolled onto her side and gave her pillow a hard thump.

"I'm an adult now. What can they possibly do?"

CHAPTER 12

It seemed Kate had barely closed her eyes before she woke to the sound of gentle tapping on her door. She stuck her head under the pillow. When the knocks grew louder, she forced herself to climb out of bed.

She yanked the door open. "What?"

Her father's eyes widened, but he ignored her surliness. "Your mother and I would like to see you in the kitchen in five minutes."

"What time is it?"

"Seven o'clock."

"Seven?" she croaked. "Can't it wait?"

"Five minutes."

Grumbling, she washed her face and brushed her teeth. She pulled on a fuzzy chenille robe and a pair of thick socks, then headed to the kitchen where her parents waited. The radio, usually tuned to NPR first thing in the morning, was silent. The quiet was unsettling. Kate walked to the cupboard, as her mother instructed her to sit.

"Can I get some coffee? Jeez."

"You don't drink coffee," her mother pointed out.

"I do now," she snapped.

"Kate," her father warned, "I don't care for your tone."

Taking her time and struggling to remain calm, she poured her coffee, then dropped heavily into a chair.

Her mother took the lead. "As you can imagine, we're very disappointed in your behavior last night."

"Really? Can I tell you how disappointed I am?"

"You may not. We allowed your friend to come to our home, and we treated him politely—" Kate began to speak, but her mother held up a finger. "I'm not finished. It's come to our attention that you've been having relations with this boy. To say we're deeply disappointed doesn't begin to express how we feel."

"Oh my God. Why would you even—"

Her mother raised her hand again. Kate slumped lower into her chair. She picked up her coffee and glared at her mother. Her father sat quietly, twiddling with his spoon, looking like he'd rather be anywhere but there.

"When I was looking through your things—"

Kate bolted upright. "You went through my room?"

Her mother continued as if she hadn't spoken. "When I was looking through your things, I came across these." She placed the envelope with the pictures that Joey had taken in New York on the table.

Kate reached for it, but her mother was quicker.

"Those are mine. Joey took them. You know he's a photographer. He asked me to pose, and I did. Big deal!"

"We all know the purpose of these photographs. No good girl does something like this."

Picturing her mother going through the photos that had been meant for Billy, Kate's stomach turned. Still, she fought to remain in control. She lifted her chin. "Now I'm not a good girl?"

Her mother slipped her hand into the envelope and pulled out the disk holding Kate's birth control pills. Although it was a new prescription, the tray was empty. All of the pills had been removed. She lowered her eyes and stared at the mug in her shaky hands.

"I would say no, not based on what's going on here."

Even though she should be used to disappointing her mother—she'd been a disappointment for as long as she could remember—Kate felt as if she'd been punched in the stomach. She should be indignant, stand up for herself. She was an adult, dammit—

"You will not see that boy again nor have any communication with him other than to tell him you can no longer see him. That you will do over the telephone."

"No!" Kate sprang from her chair.

Her mother continued as if she hadn't reacted. "Your father will drive you to Rutgers next week to collect your things. You'll enroll in community college for the coming semester. If you do well and obey our rules, we'll discuss the possibility of returning to Rutgers in the fall—or better yet, the following spring."

Kate spun toward her father. "You're okay with this?"

He glanced nervously at her mother, then nodded.

Bursting into tears, she kicked back her chair and raced up the back stairs to her room, where she collapsed on her bed, sobbing. She cried even harder when she realized that her phone was gone. They had to have taken it last night, while she was out. She'd been too tired and too distracted to notice.

When she ran out of tears, she tried to think. She wouldn't be able to call Billy, at least not while her mother was home. But her mother had a hair appointment that afternoon, and in the evening, her parents would be going to a Christmas party. In the meantime, she'd just stay in her room and hope Billy didn't call.

⌒⌒

When Kate heard the front door close, she stood by the window and waited until the car pulled away, then she snuck down the back stairs and through the kitchen. Her father was asleep in front of the TV, so she hurried back upstairs to her parents' room. She had to find those photos. She searched through her mother's chest of drawers, careful not to disturb the neatly folded lingerie and sweater sets. The scent of Chanel No. 5 wafting from the drawers was so strong, she turned to be sure her mother wasn't standing behind her. Finding nothing, she made sure everything was back the way she'd found it, then entered the large walk-in closet.

There was no sign of the envelope on the shelf that ran the length of the closet, but she did find a box tucked in the back corner. Inside were dozens of leatherbound notebooks. Curious, she reached for one and opened it, but when she realized it was a journal, she put it back. Then again, privacy amounted to nothing as far as her mother was concerned. She snatched it up.

The book was filled with diary notations, poems, and story ideas, snippets of her mother's life. Any other time, Kate might have been fascinated by a side of her mother she'd never been privy to, but right now, she needed to find her pictures. She returned the journal to the box, but when she tried to slide it back into place, it wouldn't go. She shimmied the box out again. A book had fallen and was wedged in the way. She pulled it out and, wondering if it was also a journal, flipped it open. The inside cover was dated September 1, 1969. She thumbed through the pages. The last entry—July 23, 1970—had been written four days after she was born.

My heart is truly broken, and I have not been able to stop crying. Arthur has tried to console me, but in my heart I will never forgive him for this. He promised I would feel differently after the child was born, but I don't. I feel nothing—nothing but anger and resentment. All of my hopes and dreams have been crushed under the heel of a foot that is barely bigger than my thumb.

The blood thrummed so loudly in her ears, it was almost as if someone were knocking at the closet door. Kate slid from her knees onto the floor and stared at the words until they swirled on the page like a black and white kaleidoscope. Maybe it was the beginning of a story her mother once wanted to write—a story about someone who had a baby, a baby she didn't want.

She read the entry a second time, then a third. The more she read, the sicker she felt.

It was the beginning of a story all right; it was the beginning of her story.

Numb, Kate sat on her bed, the journal open beside her. When her eyes could focus again, they zeroed in on the framed photograph on her dresser, the one Joey had taken a few summers earlier. She was grinning, her arms around each of her parents. Her father had looked away just before the photo was snapped, and her mother wore a thin, tight smile. The Portland Head Light rose up behind them, majestic, surrounded by deep blue water that reflected a cloudless sky.

Balancing on shaking legs, she crossed the room, picked up the frame, and slammed it into the trash.

Neither of them wanted her. It was right there, neatly penned in black and white, every ugly word. She'd read them all. The entire journal. Her father had yielded because he didn't believe in abortion and wouldn't condone an illegal one. Her mother had been willing—determined, even—to take her chances.

Painful as it was, her entire life began to make sense. She felt like an outsider because she was one. She was a mistake that couldn't be fixed.

"Not anymore."

After tucking the journal between her mattress and box spring, she grabbed a jacket and headed down the back stairs—straight into her father.

The tips of his ears grew pink when he saw her, and she remembered how uncomfortable he'd looked that morning when her mother held up her empty pack of birth control pills. He held up a jar of mayonnaise.

"Are you hungry? I can make you a sandwich."

"No, thank you," she answered, curtly.

She was starving, actually, in spite of her distress. She peeled a couple slices of ham from the packet of lunch meat open on the counter.

"Kate, don't—"

The words dried up with the look she gave him.

"I'm going to Debby's."

"Debby? I didn't think you two were that friendly."

She shrugged. "I haven't had a chance to see her since I got home. Unless I'm not allowed to have any friends at all."

He looked at her sadly. "Of course not. Tell her parents I said hello, although we'll probably see them tonight."

She forced a smile. "That's right. The Romanos' Christmas party."

Shivering in her light jacket, Kate raced across the yard. She knocked on the neighbors' back door harder than necessary, but she had to be quick. Her mother wouldn't be so easily duped. A dog barked, and soon a tall, pretty blonde came to the door.

"Hey, Kate. What's up?"

"Can I use your phone?"

"Your phone not working?"

"Um, it is. I need to call my boyfriend, and I don't want my dad to know." She shifted her feet nervously. "Parents, right?" She waved her finger around her ear to indicate they were crazy.

"Yeah, I hear you!" Debby pointed to a green wall unit with an extra-long cord. "You can use this one. It'll even reach into the pantry." She motioned toward a door under the stairs.

A few moments later, sitting on the floor of the pantry next to an extra-large bag of dog food, Kate dialed Billy's number. It rang several times. *Please, please, please.* When he finally answered, she knew she'd woken him.

"Billy?"

"Hey, babe. What's up?"

Cradling the phone against her neck, she pressed the heels of her hand against her eyes. "Can you come get me tonight? I have to get out of here."

"What's wrong?"

"Everything. Please." She was trying not to cry. "I can't see you anymore, and they're pulling me out of Rutgers and making me go to community college."

"Holy shit," he mumbled. "What're you gonna do?"

She hesitated. What was she going to do? "I don't know. Maybe I'll stay with Joey."

"Oh man, Katie. Let me think. I guess I can be there in a couple hours."

"No. Not now. They're going to a party tonight. They'll probably leave by six thirty or seven. Can you come around seven thirty?"

"You sure you want to do this?"

"Positive."

Billy waited down the block until her parents left, then pulled into the alley behind the house. Kate had left the back door unlocked. When she heard it open, she darted down the stairs with a load of her things, kissed him, then turned and ran back up.

"Katie, c'mon!" he yelled after her. "I have a gig tonight, remember?"

"Go!" she called over her shoulder. "I'll be right there."

She took one last look around her room and tried to imagine what she might take if the house were on fire—her pillow, a photo album, the cassette Billy had made her, and a jar of sea glass she had collected in Maine. Her mother's journal had already been packed in her suitcase. Before she turned out the light, she opened her diary. If her mother's journal had been meant to destroy her, then she would make sure her mother would know that she hadn't succeeded.

In bold black marker she penned one last entry: *And she lived happily ever after.* She bookmarked it with the pen and set it in the middle of her bed. Then she raced downstairs and out the back door, straight into the arms of the unknown.

CHAPTER 13

Billy pushed the metal door open and held it. "Welcome home." He attempted a smile but didn't quite pull it off.

Kate squeezed past him into a long narrow hallway, careful not to scrape the wall with her suitcase, although the plaster was already in pretty rough shape. The kitchen was immediately to her left. The light was off, but she could see the room was large enough to hold a small table and not much more.

The living room at the end of the hall held a battered-looking orange sofa, a television and elaborate stereo system, several guitars and amps, and a weight bench and weights. Other than a poster of Jimi Hendrix thumbtacked over the sofa, the walls were empty. Her heart sank. She didn't know what she'd been expecting, but it wasn't this.

She set down her purse and suitcase.

"I'll get the rest." Billy pointed toward the bedroom at the end of the hall. "There's a set of clean sheets on the dresser. I haven't emptied any drawers for you yet, so there's no point in unpacking." He spoke as if he'd rented a room to a stranger.

Nodding, she blinked back tears. It was almost three thirty. She assumed he was tired. He'd done a lot of driving, from Bayonne to Belleville, then back to Tewksbury, and then Bayonne again, not to mention playing for four hours and lugging all their stuff. The new guys were great, and the band sounded phenomenal, but there seemed to be a lot of tension between him and Pete. Or maybe she was reading too much into it.

Tossing her coat on the sofa, she headed for the bedroom, where she found a king-sized bed taking up most of the room. While she stripped the bed and put on clean sheets, Billy noisily dropped off another load and headed back through the large cement courtyard to the van. She hadn't been able to see much of the neighborhood, but the building was old and rundown, and the hallway had smelled rancid, like something had gone bad. It didn't matter. She wasn't going back.

After she'd located her overnight bag and gotten ready for bed, she found Billy in the dark kitchen with a bottle of Molson's, staring out the window at the city lights in the distance. She slipped her hands around his waist.

"Is that New York?"

He stirred as if he'd just realized she was there. "Yeah. The shitty side of Staten Island."

"Oh." She waited a moment. "Are you okay?"

"Yeah, why?"

"You don't seem like yourself. You don't seem very happy."

He snorted. "Happy? What am I supposed to be happy about?"

Her hands fell to her sides, and she took a step back.

"I'm sorry." He turned and leaned against the windowsill. "That didn't come out right."

"Not really, no."

"Look, Katie. I love you, I really do, but this is a big step. I don't wanna stop seeing you, so I get this is the only way, but I'm kinda freaking out here. I'm just not sure I'm ready—that either of us is ready for this. Hell, this apartment isn't even big enough for me, but it's the best I can do."

Tears burned her eyes. "I'm sorry. I'll call Joey in the morning."

Even in the dark, she noticed the tightening of his jaw. "No," he insisted. "I don't want you to live with Joey. We'll just make the best of it."

We'll make the best of it? She blinked several times and bit the inside of her cheek to keep from crying.

Billy set the empty bottle on the counter and took her hand.

"C'mon. I'm tired. We've got a long day tomorrow."

He led her to the bedroom, leaving her on her own while he used the bathroom. She dropped her robe and climbed into the enormous bed, not sure which side to lie on. After moving back and forth several times, she split the difference. When he slipped in beside her a few minutes later, she leaned over to kiss him, but all he did was brush her lips.

"I'm sorry, babe. I'm beat. I just can't." He rolled away from her onto his side.

She moved to the far side of the bed, afraid to speak. Afraid of what sound might escape if she tried. Everything that had happened over the past twenty-four hours replayed in her head, taunting her in the dark.

It was too soon to live together, but she wouldn't go home. If he didn't want her, she'd stay with Joey. Her head throbbed. She was so tired the room seemed to be moving. The sheets were clean, but cheap and scratchy, and cold against her bare skin. She curled into a ball and shivered. She hadn't bothered to pack pajamas, but right now, she'd settle for that hideous Christmas nightgown.

"You cold?"

"Uh-huh."

"C'mere." He rolled toward her and draped his arm and leg over hers. "I love you," he murmured, kissing the back of her head.

The tears came anyway, but her heart didn't hurt quite as much.

~

There was no point in going to Rutgers to pick up her things, since they had no way to get into the building. There was only one person Kate could think of who might be able to help.

"What's up, Buttercup?" Toni said when she heard Kate's voice.

"I hate to bother you, but I have a huge favor to ask." She told Toni everything except the part about the journals.

"Holy shit! Let me think. I might know a guy. Let me make some calls and see what I can do."

The phone rang a short time later. "Any luck?" Kate blurted.

"Er . . . Hello?" It wasn't Toni.

"Sorry," she apologized. "I was expecting someone else."

"I guess." The woman's voice sounded disinterested. "Is Billy there?"

"Just a minute."

Billy sat in front of the TV with the sound off, changing strings and tuning his guitars.

"It's for you."

He looked up from his Stratocaster. "Who is it?"

"I don't know. Do you want me to ask her?"

His expression darkened. She'd tried to keep the jealousy out of her voice, but clearly hadn't succeeded.

Although she wasn't eavesdropping, it was such a small apartment, it was difficult not to overhear their conversation, including Billy's laughter and "my girlfriend probably wouldn't like that." It felt good to know he referred to her as his girlfriend, but she couldn't help wondering what the woman had proposed.

He wasn't about to tell, either. When he returned, he sat down, picked up his acoustic, and began snipping the strings.

The phone rang again a few minutes later.

"Would you rather I not answer that?" she asked.

"Why wouldn't I want you to answer the phone?" he asked pointedly. "You live here now, don't you?" He went back to his strings, while Kate headed for the kitchen.

It turned out that Toni had been able to track down someone who knew someone who knew a janitor with a key. He would let Toni into the building on Monday to pack Kate's things. Then she would stash them in a friend's room until Kate could pick them up.

When Billy finished changing his strings, she gave him an update.

"So the only problem right now is I don't have anything to wear tonight. How dressy is this place?"

"Not dressy. I don't think you have anything to worry about. Besides, you'd look good in anything."

It was the nicest thing he'd said since she'd gotten there.

He set the acoustic in its case and snapped it shut. "It's going to be a long night. If I were you, I'd just worry about being comfortable."

He had to be kidding. "We've been together six weeks. I'm not ready to dress for comfort yet."

"You know what I mean." He stood. "Since we don't have to leave for a couple hours, I think I'm gonna take a nap."

Kate nodded and settled in on the couch. MTV was counting down the top music videos of the year, although without the sound, it seemed rather pointless.

Billy gave her a strange look, then snapped off the TV, took her hand, and helped her to her feet. "I said I was gonna take a nap." Slipping his hands under her sweater, he kissed her just below the ear. "Don't you want to take a nap?"

"Oh. That kind of nap."

"Yeah, that kind of nap. You're pretty smart for a college dropout."

She winced.

"Too soon?"

"A bit, yeah."

Walking backwards, he pulled her toward the bedroom. "Sorry. Let's see if I can make it up to you."

CHAPTER 14

They checked into the motel, then headed to the club for setup and sound checks.

There was just one not-so-minor problem.

"Are you kidding me?" Kate wrung her hands and paced in short circles, stopping in front of Billy. "No way!"

"You can do this," he assured her.

"I get nervous singing in the shower. I sure as hell can't sing in front of all those people!"

"It's either this, or you wait in the van all night—and it's gonna be a long night, because we play until three."

She resumed pacing the dressing room, stopping when she caught Pete mid-snicker. "I bet he had something to do with this."

"He better hope he had nothing to do with it." Billy gave him a murderous look, and Pete raised his hands to proclaim his innocence. She wasn't buying it.

"Please don't make me do this." She wove her fingers between the buttons of Billy's shirt and tugged. The greasy cheeseburger she'd downed in the car turned to lead in her stomach, and she wouldn't have been at all surprised if it decided to suddenly reappear.

"It'll be okay." He coiled a strand of her hair between his fingers. "I promise."

Denny, the new drummer, entered the dressing room and handed her a tambourine. "Here you go."

"I don't know what to do with this!" The tambourine rattled as she thrust it out in front of her.

"Perfect," Billy said, lowering her arm. "Just like that."

"Please." She was practically whimpering. "I can't do this. I'll be so nervous I'll pee my pants."

"Look." He leaned closer. "I'll give you a little something to take the edge off so you won't be so scared, okay?"

She shook her head.

"That's the only way. Since you're under twenty-one, you can't be in the club unless you're in the band. They think you're in the band, so you have to get on that stage and make like you're in the band, or you'll ring in the New Year with the seagulls on the boardwalk."

She folded her arms and frowned. "What're you gonna give me?"

"Nothing strong. Just a little downer. It'll relax you."

She didn't want to take any kind of drug, but she didn't want to wait in the van, either. The only other option was to go back to the motel and spend New Year's Eve alone.

"Okay, but if I wet myself . . ." She was only half-kidding.

"I'll clean it up. I've done worse." He set down his beer and reached into the bag where he kept his microphone and guitar cords.

"Wait!" She grabbed Billy's arm. "I'm not really dressed appropriately, am I? Someone told me to be comfortable."

Judging by the look on his face, he didn't think her sweater and jeans would work, either.

"I'll trade outfits with you," Pete's date volunteered. Kate and Delilah were about the same size, although Delilah was a little taller and had a set of breasts on her that could stop traffic. So essentially, they weren't the same size at all. Billy had also said she was a stripper, and she sure as hell wasn't wearing anything Kate would've chosen for herself.

If she was panicking before, she was about to go into full-blown apoplexy.

"I can't ask you to do that."

"I don't mind. Besides, I'm freezing. C'mon."

Delilah grabbed her hand and pulled her toward the bathroom. Kate shot Billy a desperate look.

"What the fuck?" Pete yelled. "Don't do that! I like the way you look."

"You'll like me just as much in a turtleneck."

"I doubt it," Pete muttered as the bathroom door closed.

Kate wasn't sure which was worse: having to strip down to nothing but her underwear in front of a perfect stranger, or having to step out of the bathroom wearing Delilah's dress. Since spending the night in the bathroom wasn't an option, she took a deep breath and pulled open the door.

Billy whistled when he saw her.

Delilah, who was currently stretching the front of Kate's sweater out so much she'd never be able to wear it again, gave her the thumbs up. "Knock 'em dead!" she called before heading out the door.

The band was already warming up onstage.

"Please don't make me do this." Kate was shivering uncontrollably, either from the skimpy outfit or fear, although it was probably a combination of both. Delilah's dress had no back or sides. The front, which was little more than a strip of fabric draped around the neck, was attached to the waist with a large rhinestone sunburst. If she moved too far to one side or the other, she was certain one of her breasts would pop out. "How am I supposed to bang on a tambourine without exposing myself?"

"First of all, I don't want you to bang on it. Just tap it lightly. Denny set up a microphone right behind me." He winked. "I've always wanted a backup singer."

She gave him a hard look, which he chose to ignore.

"Now, take this." He handed her half of a small white tablet.

"You expect me to get up in front of hundreds of people with my boobs hanging out on aspirin?"

"It's not aspirin." He handed her his beer. "Just take it. Hurry up."

"You sure half is enough?"

"For you?" He snorted. "Plenty." He swallowed the other half.

"What is it?"

"It's like a tranquilizer, but more fun."

"Why'd you take it? You nervous?"

He laughed and took her hand. "No, I just don't like to be left out. Ready?"

"No."

"Good. Let's go."

Kate was beginning to relax. When she started rocking back and forth like Stevie Wonder, Billy commandeered a stool for her to sit on. He also rearranged the set list with several songs in a row where her tambourine and vocal skills, such as they were, weren't needed, then handed her off to Delilah, who ushered her to the band's table.

"You're doing great!" Delilah crowed. "You're a natural."

"What a rush! I'm still scared, but I don't really care."

Delilah gave her a squeeze. "I couldn't do it—although I gotta tell ya, if Billy told me to crawl on my hands and knees through broken glass and bark like a dog, I'd do it in a heartbeat."

What? "Why would he do that?"

"Oh my God," Delilah glanced at the girls who'd come with Denny and Steve. "This girl's a hoot." She leaned in closer. "So what's he like?"

Kate shrugged. "Like?"

"In bed, silly. What's he like in bed?"

Although not much was bothering her at the moment, Kate could feel the familiar warmth creeping up her neck. Not so much from Delilah's question, which was really none of her business, but from the long, slow look she gave Billy as he fingered Jimmy Page's iconic riff. "I bet he likes it rough,"

Delilah shouted.

Billy was lost in "Whole Lotta Love." The hair on her skin stood up as she watched him. Eyes closed, head thrown back, he coaxed the notes from his guitar, and they fell over her like a shower of sparks. Her body vibrated along with the strings of the Strat. Billy played guitar with the same intensity he played her.

As the last strains of the repetitive rhythm faded with whatever was left of her inhibitions, she climbed clumsily onto the stage and threw her arms around his neck. He swung the guitar to his side and pulled her closer. His hands burning against her bare skin, he kissed her as if they were alone.

"I need you to fuck me," she whispered, catching his earlobe with her teeth, before stumbling to her place on the stool behind him.

A few minutes before midnight, Billy jumped off the stage. "You get this," he called to Pete. "You owe me." He reached up and grabbed Kate around the waist, stole a bottle of champagne from a passing waitress, and led her backstage.

Slamming the door to the dressing room, he pushed her up against the wall, hiked up her skirt, and tore off her panties with one hard yank. She fumbled with his belt and while she tugged at his pants, his fingers found their way inside her. Her head rolled back as he planted open-mouthed kisses along the curve of her neck.

With the edges of her vision growing dim, he lifted her up so she could wrap her legs around his waist. Cold cinderblocks scraped her bare flesh. In the distance, she heard fireworks amid shouts and cheers. They were coming from inside her head, or the New Year had arrived. Either way was fine with her. The revelry continued as Billy carried her to the couch, where they collapsed onto the stained, dingy cushions. Not quite finished with him, she slid to the floor between his legs, but when he realized what she was about to do, he lifted her back onto the couch.

"Stop, Katie, stop," he said, trying to catch his breath. "I don't ever wanna see you kneeling on the floor backstage, ever." He closed his eyes and leaned back. After a few seconds, he looked at her again. "Promise."

"You love that." She reached for him again.

"Not here," he insisted. "Not that. You understand?"

She nodded, although it made no sense, especially after what they'd just done.

"I love you," he said. "You're not a groupie. Don't act like one." He laced his fingers in her hair. Cradling the back of her head, he circled his arms around her. The kiss was gentle this time, very much unlike the rough, demanding way he'd kissed her minutes earlier. Then he raised the bottle of champagne to his lips.

"Happy New Year, baby."

CHAPTER 15

The kitchen was a disaster. Salad greens soaked in the sink. Ribbons of bright orange lay next to a handful of half-peeled carrots. Steam escaped from beneath a rattling lid on the narrow stove. Dirty dishes were piled on every available surface.

Judging from the look of things, the mouthwatering aroma was coming from his own kitchen.

"You can cook?"

"I'm trying," Kate said, sliding her hands into a pair of oven mitts. "I got the recipe from Mrs. Adelman. Smells good, doesn't it?"

"Who the hell is Mrs. Adelman?"

"Your neighbor." She looked up, surprised. "Across the hall? Don't you know your neighbors?"

"Nope. Not interested in any neighbors. I don't like people knowing my business." He grabbed a chocolate chip cookie from a wire rack where Kate had set them to cool.

"Saying hello and learning people's names isn't the same as someone knowing your business." She slid the roasting pan out of the oven. Drops of juice sizzled as she basted the fat, brown bird.

Wait a minute. I don't own a roasting pan.

She returned the chicken to the oven. "What do you have to hide anyway?"

"Nothing." He pushed aside her hair and planted several kisses along her shoulder, pausing to nip her ear. "So you're beautiful, a great fuck, and you can cook?"

"You're a real sweet-talker, you know?"

"I try. Speaking of which." He reached under her sweater and unhooked her bra. "When are your friends getting here?"

"About half an hour. Hook me back up. I'm not finished."

"Sorry." He snapped off the heat under the potatoes and led her toward the bedroom. "I haven't seen you since this morning. You don't want me to carry you off in the middle of dinner, do you?" He cocked an eyebrow, as if that was a real possibility. "Now take everything off except those oven mitts. You're sexy when you cook."

She laughed. "You're insatiable. What did you do before I moved in?"

"I took lots of cold showers. Because of you, I leave drought conditions wherever I go."

She beamed. "Good answer."

He kicked his jeans across the room. "For you, maybe. For the environment, not so much."

⌒

"Honestly, how're you doing?" Toni asked after dinner. Eric, her new boyfriend, drove a Suburban, so Toni had offered to deliver Kate's things from the dorm. As a thank-you, Kate had invited them to stay for dinner.

"It's kind of like becoming a grownup overnight." Kate felt a wave of sadness but pushed past it. "But it's okay. Besides, I'm in love."

Toni looked skeptical. "Love or lust?"

Color rose in Kate's cheeks as she recalled what happened minutes before they arrived. "Definitely both."

"What about school?"

Kate pulled four mismatched dishes from the cabinet and arranged them on an aluminum tray she'd found at a secondhand shop. "Maybe I'll take a class during the summer. But if I do, I wouldn't be able to travel with the band, so probably not right away."

Toni's face turned sour. "So you're a groupie now?"

"No. I'm just saying, given the choice, I'd rather be with Billy on the road than alone here."

She watched as her former roommate surveyed the small kitchen: a refrigerator that was shorter and older than they were, a tiny stove, white metal cabinets, padded chairs and a Formica table that was so old she wasn't sure if it was campy or simply a relic. The only bright spots of color came from a few yards of discount fabric she'd used to cover the open pantry and to make a curtain for the window that looked out onto the dismal courtyard.

"I guess." Toni rolled her eyes. "But I love what you've done with the place." She snatched a cookie off the counter and headed into the other room to join the guys while Kate finished assembling dessert: ice cream sandwiches made with homemade chocolate chip cookies.

As she pressed the last cookie into place, Kate could hear Billy laughing and talking. He'd hardly said a word during dinner, but now he seemed animated and friendly.

Other than that disastrous dinner with her parents, the only time she'd seen him interact with other people was with his band. He couldn't be socially awkward. He had no problem climbing onto a stage and charming an audience. Then again, there'd been that time with Joey—although to be fair, they disliked each other equally.

She wondered if the scent of marijuana mixing with the leftover aroma of roast chicken was responsible for his sudden gregariousness, but as she stepped into the living room, she could see there was more to it—much more.

His head bent over a mirror on the weight bench, Billy finished a line of coke. She'd never seen anyone snort cocaine. It was like walking in on someone with his hand down his pants, a copy of Hustler in his lap. She wanted to go back to the kitchen with her stupid ice cream sandwiches, but she was rooted to the cheap carpet.

Billy smiled when he saw her. "Hey babe." He held out a rolled up dollar bill. "C'mon. Your turn."

She stared at the mirror—three neat white lines and a razor blade—while she tried to work out what to say.

"Um . . . I don't think so." Ice cream was dripping over the edge of a cookie. They really should eat them now.

"C'mon, Kate," Toni said. "It's no biggie. Just do a line."

The longer she stood, the heavier the tray became. She set it down at the end of the bench and knelt beside Billy. "I've never done this before."

He laughed, and she shot him a pained look. No wonder his mood had changed; he was stoned.

"I'd never let you do anything that might hurt you," he said, running his nose around the edge of her ear. In spite of the little nugget of anxiety growing inside her, the skin along her arm pebbled under his touch.

Swallowing half a pill was one thing. So was pot. Everyone smoked pot. But snorting cocaine? She hadn't even known Toni did it.

"Don't you trust me?" Billy asked.

She gave him a little shrug and nodded.

"Watch. Like this." Leaning forward, he covered his nostril with his index finger, touched the bill to a line, then sniffed in hard.

The three of them looked at her expectantly, their eyes shining, noses running. Not the most attractive look. Not the look you'd expect from someone who'd been preparing to serve a tray of homemade ice cream sandwiches.

Billy slid closer and put his arm around her waist. She pinched the bill between her fingers and grimaced. The thought of putting something in her nose that had just been in three other noses was disgusting. Should she ask for her own dollar? Probably not. Leaning forward, she was startled by the face in the mirror staring up at her. *What are you doing?* it asked. Ignoring her reflection, she did as she was told while Billy held her hair. The inside of her nose burned and her eyes watered. She coughed. He laughed, then leaned over and kissed her as if she'd done something wonderful.

One line and the melting desserts remained.

"Who's in?" Billy asked.

"I'll drive," Toni told Eric. "Knock yourself out. I'm gonna have one of these." She picked up an ice cream sandwich and ran her tongue between the cookies, catching the drips.

"Keep that up and we're leaving now," Eric said with a lascivious wink.

"Looks good," Billy said. When Kate looked up she realized his attention was focused on her, not on her dessert.

It was late when Toni and Eric left. Once the door closed, Billy had her up against the wall with such urgency she banged her head. His mouth found hers before she could utter a sound, while his hand yanked at the button on her jeans. He grasped her thighs, then lifted her so she could wrap her legs around his waist. She took in a great gulp of air when he pulled his lips from hers.

"I want these clothes off, now," he grumbled, carrying her into the living room and dropping her onto the couch. He stripped out of his clothes while she watched, a bit stunned. Impatient, he reached down and gave her jeans a sharp tug.

"Off," he demanded, pointing at the sweater. She tugged it over her head, but before she could remove her bra, he pushed her down and climbed between her open thighs, sinking deep inside with a low, throaty growl. He reached behind her, and unfastening her last remaining item of clothing, pulled it down and tossed it across the room. "That's better," he mumbled against her breast.

As hastily as he'd begun, he slowed now, teasing and playing until she found herself falling over the brink with him. As she did, he quickened his pace until, with one final thrust, he grunted and sank his teeth into the softness of her shoulder. She cried out, a combination of pain and pleasure.

His body turned to dead weight. She pushed against him. When he didn't budge, she pushed harder. He mumbled incoherently into her ear.

"Billy, I can't breathe," she whispered, pushing her palm against his chest. He shifted his weight just enough for her to expand her lungs. His eyes were closed, his face turned to hers. She wondered if he'd fallen asleep.

When he finally peered out at her, she was watching him.

"What?"

"Are you okay?"

The corner of his mouth tugged upward. "I'm very okay. Are you okay?"

She shook her head.

"You're not okay?"

"No. I mean, yes. I'm fine. That's not what I meant."

He sighed. "What is it, Katie?" His pupils were so dilated that his eyes were almost black.

"Sometimes when you take me like that, it seems like there's barely a hair's breadth between passion and anger. I feel like you're on the precipice of destroying me or consuming me. It can be a little scary."

He chuckled. "Precipice, huh?"

"Don't tease me." She fought a sudden urge to cry.

"Do you want me to stop?"

"No. Not really. I just wonder why you're so angry."

He raised himself off her. "If I frighten you so much, why don't you fight back? Tell me to stop?"

She struggled to find the right words.

"Because you never really hurt me—it just seems like you might. Maybe I sound crazy, but in some ways, it's exciting and dangerous."

What she couldn't explain was that standing on a precipice was familiar. Getting hurt was familiar. But how could she explain when she didn't understand it herself?

She shrugged. "Besides—I trust you." She gently tucked a strand of hair behind his ear and touched his temple. "I just wish I knew what was going on up here."

Hours later, still wired from the cocaine and Kate's words, Billy stood over the bed and watched her sleep. The sheets were tangled between her legs, and the light from the hall washed over her bare skin. In the dim light, he could see the circle his teeth had left on the fleshy part of her shoulder. A bluish-purple bruise bloomed near her hip bone.

Guilt flowed through him like ice water.

Yes, he was angry. He'd been angry for years, but it had nothing to do with her. If anything, she'd softened his harder edges. The world was no longer just black and white.

He loved her, and he didn't want to hurt her. So then what the fuck was he doing? Fate had somehow dropped her in his lap. Now what? Was he trying to possess her? He couldn't keep his hands off her. Even now, knowing she was sound asleep, he wanted to climb into bed and kiss her until she woke.

Maybe that was part of it, the feeling of not being in control, always wanting. He'd never felt like this about any girl before. He'd barely allowed himself to feel before.

When he thought he could trust himself, he climbed into bed, gently slipping his arm beneath her head and wrapping himself around her.

"What's wrong?" she murmured.

"Nothing." He kissed the top of her head. "I'm sorry."

She peered up at him. "For what?"

"I don't want to hurt you."

He felt her warm breath on his chest. "You didn't," she answered sleepily. "We're good."

Her eyes fluttered. "Just remember, you can let me in. I won't hurt you, either."

He didn't answer for a long time, and not until he was certain she was asleep.

"Don't," he whispered to the darkness.

CHAPTER 16

Kate pressed her way through the grocery store aisles along with everyone else who was trying to stock up before the winter storm hit. She filled her cart with enough food to tide her over until Billy got home. Toilet paper was on sale, so she tossed in a few extra rolls and wondered how long it would be before she spent Sunday afternoons clipping coupons.

When she moved in with Billy, she had assumed she'd be going on the road with him, but in reality that would have been way too expensive. So while Viper toured the southern states, she found herself alone in Bayonne at the end of January, thumbing through the latest issue of *People* and contemplating Drew Barrymore's hairstyle. She tossed the magazine into the cart. She needed a pick-me-up. And if she were being honest about her new lifestyle, it probably wouldn't hurt to read about the thirteen-year-old's drug and alcohol issues, either.

The first snowflakes fell as she finished chopping carrots for her vegetable beef soup. She set the pot on a low simmer, pulled on one of Billy's old sweatshirts, and settled on the couch with her magazine. Just before five, there was a loud knock at the door.

She peeked through the peephole, recoiling when a huge eye stared back.

"Who is it?" she asked, deepening her voice.

"Let me in before I get mugged!"

Joey burst in as soon as she opened the door, stomping his feet and kicking snow all over the doormat and floor.

"Why didn't you tell me you lived in the projects?" he demanded. "This place makes my apartment look like The Plaza!"

She threw her arms around his neck. "Don't start."

After exchanging hugs and kisses, she took his coat and hung it on the rack she'd had Billy install near the front door. "You should've told me you were coming. What would you've done if I wasn't here?"

"I'd have waited five minutes until you got back," he replied, straight-faced. "Where would you possibly go, with Romeo on the road?" He peeked into the kitchen and tsked. "Look at you," he said sadly. "You're like a bird in an ungilded cage."

"Be nice."

"Oh, I am. You should hear what I really think." He shook droplets of snow from his curls.

Best to change the subject. "How did you get here?"

"I took the Lexington Avenue local to City Hall, walked to the E, took that to Port Authority, then took the PATH to Newark, the Hudson-Bergen Light Rail to 34th Street, then a bus the rest of the way." He looked at his watch. "And it only took twelve hours."

"Funny."

He lifted his chin and gave the air a sniff. "What's that wonderful smell?"

"Vegetable beef soup. It should be ready soon. Meanwhile, let me give you the grand tour."

She started in the kitchen, pointing out her handiwork to make it sound more impressive. At the living room window, she pointed out that the lights flickering in the distance were New York.

"If that's New York, I'll swim across the Hudson next time. It'll be quicker."

"Actually, it's Staten Island."

He crinkled his nose. "Never mind."

In the bedroom, Joey waved his arm at the king-sized bed. "I assume this is where the women's gymnastics team practiced for the Olympics before you moved in."

She wordlessly guided him toward the kitchen.

"Are you staying over?" she asked as she ladled soup into bowls.

"I was planning to, but I have a class Monday afternoon, so I should probably leave now."

"Funny."

"Of course I'm staying. I haven't seen you since Thanksgiving. I'm worried about you."

"I'm fine. But I'm glad you're here." She set a bowl of soup down in front of him, then fixed one for herself. "I've been going crazy. There's nothing to do. I've cleaned everything that could be cleaned. I've read every book Billy owns. I even bought some knitting needles and yarn, but I can't figure out what I'm doing. All I've made so far is a mess."

"Knitting? What has this clown turned you into?"

"Joey, please. He's not making me knit. I was just looking for something to do while he's away."

"Let me get this straight."

"Can you?"

He flashed her an evil look. "You leave home to run off with this wannabe rock star. Leave your family, friends, and drop out of college so you can follow him all over the globe, or at least the Mid-Atlantic States. Yet here you sit in this godforsaken little city, all alone on a Saturday night, while Romeo is performing in front of adoring women a thousand miles away, supposedly alone."

"I'm not alone. You're here."

He put down his spoon. "Talk to me. Something's wrong. I hear it in your voice over the phone, and now that I'm here, I see it in your eyes."

Uncomfortable under the scrutiny, she stood and reached into the refrigerator and pulled out a bottle of white zinfandel. "Wine?"

"No, thanks." He smiled brightly. "I'm not old enough to drink, remember?"

If Joey had a clue what she'd been doing in addition to drinking, he'd knock her over the head and drag her back to the Bronx. She filled her glass, and after they resettled on the couch, she reprised the story of what happened with her parents.

"Sweetie, I know they're wrong, but maybe after a few days, things would've calmed down and you could have reasoned with them. At least you could've stayed in school, even if you had to sneak around for a while. They'd have gotten over it. Now this," he waved his hand to encompass the tiny apartment, "this is your world—three small rooms and a ginormous bed. That's a metaphor for your life and what's important. It's not right. What about your plans?"

A lone tear trickled down her cheek.

"Kate, honey." He patted her leg. "You can go home. It's not too late to go back to school, even. You'd catch up."

She shook her head. "I can't."

He sat back with a huff. "Now you sound like me, and you're being ridiculous."

She'd been holding them back for so long, once started, the tears wouldn't stop. Joey wrapped his arms around her.

"They don't want me. They never wanted me." Although it was a relief to finally say it, it felt as if she'd just ripped off a bandage, exposing a wound that hadn't had time to heal.

When the tears slowed to a trickle, Joey lifted her face, taking in the red eyes and runny nose.

"You are not a pretty crier. You better never let Romeo see you like this. Yuck! Good thing I love you." He kissed her on the head, starting her tears anew. "Stop! No more crying. Start talking!" He picked up her glass and shoved it at her. "Here, drink this, you alcoholic!"

In spite of the tears, she laughed. When she had calmed somewhat, she excused herself and came back with her mother's journal, which she'd kept hidden in a shoebox in the bottom of the closet. She turned it to the last page and handed it to him.

His face turned stony as he read. "What is this?"

"Look at the date."

He read it again, then he thumbed back a few pages. His brow furrowed as he read some of the earlier entries. He folded the journal and set it in his lap. "Could it be that you're reading this out of context? Maybe it was just postpartum depression or something. It's hurtful, but—"

"That's the last entry. There were no more journals after that."

"That doesn't mean—"

Now that the lid was off, it all came pouring out in a rush. "She'd been offered a grant to some big writers retreat and was planning to take a sabbatical, but then she found out she was pregnant. She wanted an abortion—she begged my father to support her—but he refused. Not because he wanted a baby, no, but because it was illegal. That was his main concern. And since she'd had such bad morning sickness, she couldn't follow through with her writing. She missed the retreat and lost the grant, and the publisher pulled his offer. So instead of following her dream, she gave birth to her worst nightmare: me."

As she spoke, the color drained from Joey's face. For once, he seemed speechless.

"So at least my father was against killing me. That's a good thing, right?" She forced a smile. "Over the course of the pregnancy, not only did she document her feelings, she saved them. She wanted me to know I ruined her life."

Joey seemed to be having a hard time digesting what she'd just told him.

"Don't you think she got over it? I mean, you're the sweetest person I've ever known. There's nothing about you that could keep someone from loving you once they know you. Look at Romeo. He's probably had every girl on the East Coast. He spends one night with you, and he's over the moon."

The ice that formed around her heart whenever she thought of her mother began to melt. "Do you really think so?"

"For as much as he swept you off your feet, I'm pretty sure the same goes for him. That doesn't mean I like him any better—but yeah, he's hooked."

The pain of revisiting her mother's journal began to ease. "As for my mother 'getting over' it—she didn't." She held up the journal. "I think this explains why when I said I wanted to be a writer, she insisted I become a teacher. My father agreed, but if it wasn't for her, I don't think it would've mattered, as long as I went to Rutgers. My mother wasn't gonna let me pursue my dream because she blames me for crushing hers. And meeting Billy? It was more than she could handle."

Joey looked at her like she was crazy. "What does he have to do with this?"

"You should've seen her when she met him. It's the same with every woman. He has this effect on them. They stumble over their words and giggle. When he shook her hand, she actually clutched her pearls. I was stunned then, but I see it everywhere. The women at the A&P practically jump out of their smocks when he pushes his cart into their aisle. Girls at concerts and clubs hang out by the stage, trying to get his attention. I can't even think about what it's like when I'm not there." Her eyes met his. "She accused me of having sex with him."

He raised his eyebrows. "Um, sweetie . . ."

"I know—but she didn't have the tone you'd expect from a parent who's worried that her daughter was too young or might get hurt. This was different. She was jealous. She wasn't disappointed, which I would understand. She was angry. And she knew if she said I couldn't see him, I'd leave. Instead of having to deal with me for the next four years, she found an early out. Not early enough, but better late than never."

She could tell he was struggling to find something positive to say. Before he had a chance, she asked him about school.

He jumped up from the sofa. "That reminds me!" he cried, yanking off one of her socks. She retracted her foot, afraid he was about to tickle her, but he was more intent on insulting her. "Just as I thought. Look at you. You're a mess. Look at those feet. These hands. Are you working construction?" He headed for his overnight bag. "I need to practice my mani-pedis and you're my guinea pig. Go put hot water in the tub and soak those nasty things."

Once her feet had been soaked, scrubbed, and exfoliated, Joey worked his magic. "French manicures are big right now, but you're a rocker chick. Look what I brought." He pulled out a bottle of strawberry pink nail enamel. "This will look gorgeous on you!"

"Nice," she said, as he started to paint her toes. "Speaking of which, hand me that magazine." She pointed to the copy of *People* she'd dropped earlier.

His face fell. "Seriously? You're gonna ignore me and read a magazine like I'm your manicurist?"

"No. I want you to see Drew Barrymore's hair. What do you think?" She held the magazine in front of her face.

"She's thirteen," he said dryly.

"She doesn't act it. Besides, she still looks older than me."

"True." He studied the picture. "I'll have to cut a good ten, twelve inches."

"I know, but I need a change."

"Pizzazz?"

"Don't start."

"Actually, this would be kinda cute on you. I'd wanna add some highlights to bring out the layers and give it more . . . more oomph."

"I can deal with oomph. Pizzazz scares me."

"How about Tuesday?" he asked, his volume rising. "You can be my model. You won't even have to pay for supplies."

She perked up. "That would be great. I could surprise Billy when he gets back."

"So now that you brought Romeo up again, what did he say about your mother?"

"I didn't tell him."

"Why?" He looked up, the brush poised midair over her big toe.

"Why tell him I was unwanted? What would he think?"

"What difference would it make? You're hurt and it shows. Don't you think he should know what you're hurting about? I could tell over the phone something was wrong. I'm sure he can see it in your eyes."

"No, I don't want him to know I'm damaged goods."

"What the hell is that supposed to mean? You're not damaged. You're perfect."

She pulled her foot away from him. "My entire life was built on a foundation of sand that's been washed away. I can't fix that. It's who I am. Who'd want to be with someone who's broken?"

"I know that's how you feel, but look at me. I was wanted—but when it became clear who I was, my father chose to throw me away."

It still made her sad, remembering the night he'd run away, how she'd hidden him in her room until first light, then said good-bye, not knowing when she'd ever see him again. His pain was still very real for her, almost as real as her own.

He reached for her foot. "I won't let my father define me. I'm a good person. I'm smart and talented, and I'm gonna make something of my life. You just wait. Success is the best revenge, and then my father and brothers can kiss my ass." He all but spat the last few words.

"You will be a success. But me? I'm just broken. I don't know how to put it all back together. Billy may love me now, but someday he may see I haven't much to offer."

"He's lucky to have you, and I bet he knows that!" He bent over her foot again with the polish. "Have you thought about talking to someone?"

"What? Like a shrink?"

His eyes drilled into hers. "Yes, a shrink."

"Where would I get money for a shrink? I'll be fine. I'll deal with it."

"Tell Billy."

She yanked her foot back again. "No—and don't you, either. I don't want to talk about it anymore."

With a great flourish, he pulled an imaginary zipper across his lips. He may have agreed to drop the subject for now, but judging from the look in his eyes, it was far from over.

～

From the kitchen window, Kate could see Billy climbing out of his van. She darted into the bedroom to light some candles, threw her robe into the closet, and hopped into bed.

The front door burst open. "Honey, I'm home," he called in his best sitcom dad voice.

"In here," she answered sweetly.

"Where?" As if the apartment was so big it would take him a while to find her.

"I'll give you one guess."

"Sounds good to me." Guitar cases thumped against the living room floor. "But I need a shower." He stopped in the doorway when he saw her. "Well, hellooo. I was looking for my girlfriend, but you'll do."

She tossed her head so that the curls bounced and fell against her shoulders. "You like?"

"I do." He pulled off his jacket. "But I really need a shower first."

She sat up. "Billy, it's been two weeks. I don't care what you smell like."

He grinned as he yanked off the rest of his things. "Okay. But don't say I didn't warn you."

Later, as they lay tangled up in each other, she asked if he liked her hair.

"I do. You look beautiful, but you always look beautiful."

"Which do you like better?"

He laughed. "I'm not stupid, Katie, but I'll say this. I love your long hair. It's still long, just not as long. That said, I love it."

"Pass."

He positioned himself over her, preparing for round two. "Good. I'd hate to piss you off right away. I'd rather take my time. Make it worthwhile."

CHAPTER 17

Kate would've enjoyed another day with Billy to herself, but she also looked forward to getting out and doing something fun, even if it was just a party at Pete's. Billy had been by her side most of the evening, but had been coaxed up to the make-shift stage by a tall, willowy blonde. Kate watched from the back of the large finished basement, while he jammed with Denny, Steve and Fat Bernie, relieved that once he'd picked up his Strat, he seemed to have forgotten about the blonde. She was about to search for something to drink when Pete beat her to it.

"You look thirsty," Pete said, cutting her off and handing her a plastic cup.

"What's this?" She sniffed it suspiciously.

"Not a Fuzzy Navel." He gave her a mischievous smile.

Her stomach lurched. "God, I hope not."

"Kamikaze. Not too sweet, but effective."

She took a sip. "Not bad, actually. Thanks."

His response was drowned out as Billy launched into "Eruption."

"He's fucking amazing, isn't he?" Pete yelled over the wail of Billy's guitar.

And he was. She had nothing to do with Billy's talent, but she couldn't help feeling proud when she watched him play. She was also feeling the effects of the overcrowded, overheated room and a lack of food. She'd mistakenly assumed a party meant more than chips and pretzels—although there was an impressive amount of alcohol and drugs to be had.

Feeling light-headed, she moved to an open window and rested against the sill. She couldn't help but notice as Pete kept busy playing host, surprised that he possessed some rudimentary social skills.

As the final vibrato of Billy's Strat died away, Pete cupped his hands. "'Free Bird'!"

Billy scanned the room, saw it was Pete, and shook his head. Pete yelled again, and others began chiming in. When it turned into a full-on chant, and Steve fingered the first few notes, Billy had no choice. The opening strains of "Free Bird" filled the basement. Billy glanced at the guys backing him up and frowned. Before beginning the lead work, he flipped Pete the finger, then leaned into the microphone and made a dedication. "This is for Pete. Fuck you," he said, laughing.

Kate finished her drink, and before she could set the cup down, Pete appeared with another. Again he surprised her. Usually, he barely spoke to her, but tonight he was the charming host. She took a few sips. It was good, but combined with the two or three beers she'd had earlier, it was hitting her hard. The room tilted on its axis.

"What's wrong?"

"I feel kinda dizzy." She tried to focus. "Is there a bathroom down here?"

Pete took her drink and led her down a narrow hall to a back bedroom. "In here. Are you OK?"

"I don't know. They really sneak up on you, don't they?" When she stumbled, he tightened his grip on her arm.

"You want me to get Billy?"

She nodded. "When he's done."

Inside the small bathroom, she rested her head against the cold porcelain sink and waited for the room to stop spinning. She could still hear the muffled strains of "Free Bird" through the walls, and hoped Billy wouldn't launch right into another song," like he usually did.

She was surprised to find Pete waiting when she emerged from the bathroom. He'd shoved the pile of coats to one side and was motioning toward the bed.

"Billy said to lie down. He'll be in soon."

He was being nice, but she still felt uncomfortable with him there. She wished he would just go, take care of his guests, and was about to say something along that line when the floor rolled up to meet her. Pete caught her and guided her to the bed. He slipped a pillow behind her head. A chill ran through her as he brushed a strand of hair from her face. He trailed his fingers along her neck and over her shoulder.

"You really are kinda pretty. I can almost see why Billy's so taken with you."

She tried to scoot away but was blocked by the pile of coats. Was he smirking at her?

"Personally, I think you're kind of annoying, but there must be something pretty special about you to hold his attention for so long."

Before she could react, he'd pinned her down and slid his hand under her sweater, grasping at her breast. He crushed his mouth against hers. The strong odor of garlic and alcohol on his breath was nauseating. Bile rose in her throat. She pushed against him, but it was no use. He wasn't as big or strong as Billy, but he was much bigger than she was.

She tore her mouth free. "What the hell? Stop it!" She raised her hand to hit him, but he caught her wrist, then slapped her, hard, with his other hand.

The world went gray and fuzzy, and somewhere beneath the buzzing in her head, she could taste something bitter. Blood? A hand clamped over her mouth, and as her vision cleared, she saw him yanking at the top button of his jeans.

~

Watching Lynyrd Skynyrd perform in person was one thing. Playing this damn song was another. Billy was pissed at Pete for calling it out, especially since nearly everyone was wasted. Pete knew they'd rise to the bait, and he knew Billy found it boring—the same riff played over and over. Any kid with a few months of guitar lessons could play that song, and it was usually the first song they wanted to learn.

He scanned the room for Kate. She'd been talking to Pete earlier, which surprised him. Pete didn't like Kate, but he'd learned to keep his mouth shut, especially after Billy had warned him the next time he said something out of line, he was finished. He didn't see either of them now, and when they didn't reappear as the song wound down, it began to bug him.

He motioned for Bernie, who'd been playing rhythm, and handed off the Strat without missing a note. He caught up with a few people outside, passing around a joint, but none of them had seen Kate.

She would have had to have passed him to go upstairs, so the only other place she could be was the bedroom at the end of the hall.

He rattled the doorknob, then knocked. It was hard to hear, especially with the amps turned up high. Pressing his ear against the door, he called her name. Something wasn't right. He backed up, lifted his foot, and kicked the door open.

Pete was standing beside the bed, holding his hand, while Kate was struggling to stand. Her sweater was pushed up, and he could see her bra as well as an angry red welt on her cheek.

Tugging on his zipper, Pete tried to push past him. "Look, man, she came on to me."

A loud roar filled his ears. Whether it was out loud or in his head, he wasn't sure. He lunged. Pete stumbled into the door jamb, then turned and dashed down the hall. Billy caught him by his shirt and hauled him around. His punch glanced off the side of Pete's face. Pete swung blindly. Billy lowered his shoulder, and drove himself into Pete's midsection, sending him crashing into a table. Liquor bottles smashed onto the floor as Pete's stunned guests scrambled out of the way.

Someone grabbed him from behind and pinned his arms, allowing Pete one clear shot. Fueled by adrenaline and anger, he wrested himself free and lunged again, catching Pete around the middle and crashing to the ground. As they wrestled on the floor amid spilled whiskey and shards of broken glass, something inside Billy snapped. Self-control vanished. He drove his fist into Pete's face as the other hand wrapped around his throat, choking him.

It took three large men to pull him off. Then Denny was driving his shoulder into Billy's chest, shoving him backward.

"Jesus!" Denny shouted. "Billy! You're gonna kill him!"

"Good," he said, still trying to yank free.

Pete lay at his feet, panting and bleeding, his face barely recognizable. Billy was breathing hard, but he was finished. He knew he had it in him to kill Pete right then if he didn't stop.

Twisting away, he glimpsed Kate, pale and wide-eyed, across the room.

"Get your coat," he barked. She disappeared down the hall.

"You're fired, you lousy piece of shit," he said turning back to Pete. It took every ounce of self-control he had to keep from kicking him.

When he went to get his guitar, Denny stopped him.

"I'll get it. You better get to the hospital. You need stitches."

He hadn't noticed the blood running down the side of his face. Swiping at it now, he could feel an inch-long gash in his cheek. His eye was starting to swell, and the knuckles of his right hand were throbbing beneath the scrape he'd gotten from Pete's teeth.

"Son of a bitch," he muttered. He glowered at Denny. "Bring it by tomorrow. And you and Steve leave now, or you're both fired too."

Since he was having a hard time seeing, Kate insisted on driving. They weren't more than a mile from Pete's when she veered onto the shoulder, threw the van into park, and jumped out. She ran toward the woods, then stopped and bent over. Cursing, he climbed out after her.

"What the hell are you doing?" he yelled, swiping at the blood still oozing from his cheek. She was shaking when he reached her. "What's wrong?"

She raised her hand just as she began to vomit.

"Ah, jeez." He grabbed her hair and held it until she was done. "Are you finished?" he asked, trying to sound supportive, although he wasn't exactly feeling it at the moment.

She nodded, then stood and wiped her mouth with the back of her hand.

He put his arms around her and held her until the shaking stopped.

"You okay?"

She was pale in the streetlight, her face inscrutable as she looked up at him and nodded.

"Okay, let's go before this—ow!"

Son of a bitch. She had punched him in the stomach—hard.

"What the fuck was that for?"

She let out a strangled noise that sounded like a laugh, although the look on her face was something more like horror.

"I don't know. You scared me."

He threw his hands up in the air and stalked off, then whirled back around, stopping when his face was just inches from hers.

"So you hit me? Didn't you see I just got the shit kicked out of me? Over you, I might add."

She glared right back. "You almost killed him. He landed one punch."

"Well." He wasn't quite sure how to respond. "It was a good punch."

She continued to glare at him, wide-eyed, her chest heaving.

"Get in the van," he ordered, running the sleeve of his jacket over his face to wipe away the blood. He reached for her elbow and led her to the passenger door. "I'm driving."

~

Billy ended up with eight stitches and a tetanus shot, and his eye was black and blue and swollen shut. The only good thing was he had no gigs scheduled for the weekend. Not only was he not presentable, he no longer had a rhythm guitar player.

They'd sat in the emergency room for hours before a plastic surgeon finally arrived to stitch him up. The doctor did the best he could but said Billy would probably have a scar.

By the time they got home, it was almost five.

Kate still wasn't feeling well. She got up around seven, made herself a piece of toast, and climbed back into bed after her stomach had settled. When she woke a few hours later, Billy lay on his back, staring at the ceiling with his good eye.

She rolled onto her side and threw her leg over his. "I'm sorry about last night."

"Why? You didn't split my face open."

"No, but it's kinda my fault."

"How do you figure?"

How did she figure? She hadn't led Pete on; hadn't even thought he liked her, let alone in *that* way. She dragged a toe along the inside of Billy's calf.

"Pete's a jerk," he said, not waiting for a response. "I've wanted to cut him loose for a long time." He slipped his arm beneath her head. "Last night just gave me a good excuse."

"I guess."

"You guess? I find you with your shirt up around your neck and that dickwad on top of you, and you don't think I had every right to beat the shit out of him?"

"He wasn't on me. He'd already jumped up."

Billy pulled himself up on one elbow. "That's better?"

"I bit him. He had his hand over my mouth, and I bit him."

He huffed loudly. "Then maybe you should've gotten a tetanus shot."

"Perhaps, but you could've gotten yourself killed—or killed him."

"That was his choice." He lay back down. "He only got what he deserved."

"Maybe, but it was scary."

"Is that why you hit me?"

She thought about it for a long minute. "I don't know what came over me."

"You never saw a fight before?"

She shook her head. "I could hardly sleep after we got home. I kept hearing the sound of your fists, the furniture crashing, the glass breaking." The memory still gave her the willies.

His face was stony. "I'm sorry defending your honor was so scary. You want me to ignore the next guy who makes a pass at you?"

She shrugged. She couldn't tell if his eye was open or closed.

"You have a bad temper," she said after a while.

His expression softened. "I know."

She rested her chin on his chest and absentmindedly traced circles around his nipples and down to his belly button, then back again.

"Should I be afraid?"

"Of what?" He lifted his head so he could see her.

"Of you. What if I make you mad?"

He lay down with a grunt. "I'll punch you in the nose."

"I'm serious. I've never seen anything like that before. My parents never raised their voices. I could only tell when they were angry because every sentence ended with 'Yes, dear' or 'dearest.' Emotion wasn't acceptable in my house—good or bad."

Billy cupped her chin and looked at her with his good eye. "I'll never hurt you. I promise."

She felt the words as much as heard them. They took root inside her and became something tangible; something she could believe in, hold on to.

She nodded, unable to speak at first. But there was something that still bothered her.

"It's just . . . it's something Pete said."

"Pete's a dick."

"Still."

"Okay. I'll bite. What did he say?"

"He said there must be something special about me to keep your interest for so long. What does that mean?"

"How do I know what he means?"

"Haven't you had other girlfriends?"

"Yes."

"Then why would he think there's something special about me?"

"Because you are special." He ran his finger down her forehead, stopping to tap her on the nose.

"I'm serious."

He rolled onto his side with a grunt. "I can see I'm not gonna get anymore sleep, so let's knock this out. Then we can get something to eat, because I'm not only tired, I'm hungry."

She sat up and hugged her legs against her body, waiting.

"I've had two girlfriends. One for a couple years in high school, and one for about a year in college. We broke up when I quit school and moved east."

"So you've only been with two girls?"

He laughed, then quickly looked contrite. "I didn't say that. I said I had two girlfriends. I never said anything about being with just two girls."

"Oh."

"What about you? Tell me about your boyfriends."

"One."

"One? Just one before me?"

"No. Just one including you."

He slapped his palms against the mattress in mock frustration. "C'mon, Katie. You never dated anyone before me?"

"Not really, just Digger. And that was a huge mistake."

"Oh yeah, prom boy." He chuckled.

She wasn't going to let him off so easily. "So? How many women?"

He shifted uncomfortably. "You don't want to ask me that."

"Yes, I do. I wanna know what he meant. He made it sound like being with me was some Olympic feat or something."

"What he probably meant was that given the way I've behaved with women in the past, or at least since he's known me, the fact that I'm faithful to you must make you pretty damn special." He kissed her neck and along her chin, giving her goose bumps, but she still wanted an answer. "He was right. You are pretty damn special."

"In what way have you behaved with women in the past?"

He stopped nibbling and looked her in the eye. "We're gonna have this conversation once, okay?"

She nodded.

"You're not gonna like the answer."

"Just be honest."

"You want honesty?"

She nodded again.

He propped his head up on his elbow, his face blank. "What do you want to know?"

"How many women have you dated?"

"I don't know."

"That's not fair. You said you'd be honest."

"I am. I don't remember how many women I've *dated*."

"I'll make it easier, then. How many women have you slept with?"

"Exact number?"

Now he was deliberately being a jerk. "No. Just round up or down."

He studied her face until she began to grow uncomfortable.

"If you want me to be honest, Katie, I can't. Not because I don't want to, but because I really don't know. I'm embarrassed to admit this, but you seem determined to know the answer, so my best guess is between four and five hundred."

She blinked several times and opened her mouth slowly, although there were no words.

"You okay?"

She nodded.

"I told you, you wouldn't like it, but let me add something. Since I've been on the road and playing music full time, I haven't had any type of relationship except with you, and not for over four years. You're very special to me, and I have no desire to be with anyone else. I don't even look at other women."

It took a few seconds for it all to sink in, but his last comment brought her around pretty quickly.

"You're full of shit."

He laughed guiltily. "Okay—I look. But I'm not interested, and that's the truth. The flirting onstage, that's part of the act. When I'm on the road and you're not with me, I pack up and I'm back to the hotel before the rest of the band finishes their last beer. I promise." He put his arms around her. "I mean it. I wouldn't do anything to jeopardize what we have. You hear me?"

"Yeah, but—"

"But what?"

She lay one palm flat against his chest. "Why me?"

"Why you, what?"

"I don't understand why you want me when you've been with so many women. It doesn't make sense."

"Maybe to you it doesn't make sense."

She shoved him gently. "Seriously. I have no experience in the bedroom, other than what I've learned from you."

He smiled wickedly. "Well, I'm a very good teacher."

She plowed onward. "And I have no life experience. I grew up in a small town, and the only time I ever left was for summer vacations in Maine. Other than that, I've had one semester of college. I have nothing to offer. That's 'why me.'"

"Do you want me to say I'm no longer interested?"

"No." She hoped he wasn't serious. "I guess I'm afraid someday you will say that."

"Katie. For the last time today, as I'm sure you aren't gonna let this go, you have a lot to offer. In addition to being beautiful on the outside, you're beautiful on the inside. You're kind, generous, and gentle. You're supportive and nurturing. You're smart, funny, and clever, even though you never give yourself credit for any of it. You've carved a spot for yourself right here." He moved her hand over his heart. "If you were to go away and leave that spot empty, it's so big, I don't know if I'd ever be able to fill it."

She closed her eyes and felt his heart thump steadily beneath her fingers.

"Now." He nipped her bottom lip. "Can we please go get something to eat?"

CHAPTER 18

The break Billy had been waiting for came in the form of a phone call Monday afternoon.

"This is Christa Dunphy with Bennett-Friedman. Davy Steinman gave me your number. He said you're in need of an agent, and I'm the best in the business."

Humble, too. He made a polite noise of agreement.

"Davy tells me you're something to see and hear. Can we get together sometime this week?"

His fingers leapt to the thin black thread holding his cheek together. "This week isn't good for me. How about next Monday?"

"I'm flying to LA Sunday. It's important that we meet. Davy and I have been discussing something you might be perfect for. You sure you can't squeeze me in?"

"I guess."

"Don't sound too excited!"

"Sorry. It's just that I had a little accident over the weekend, and I still have a few stitches in my face."

"I don't care if you don't."

They met the following afternoon at Sardi's on Forty-Fourth Street. When Billy told the maître d' he was meeting Ms. Dunphy, he was directed to "her table." He had no idea who or what to expect, and he was pleased when an attractive blonde, probably in her early thirties, made her way toward him. She was small in stature, but her spiked heels and the way she carried herself let everyone know she was important. She shrugged her long black overcoat into the waiting arms of the maître d, unveiling a dark red suit so tight he was surprised she could move. He rose as she approached, taking her outstretched hand.

"Oh my," she said, holding on to his hand. "You are a tall drink of water. And you're even more handsome than I expected, in spite of your little boo-boo." She settled into her chair, her eyes never leaving his face. "So, Billy, have you ordered a drink?"

"No, ma'am."

"'Ma'am'? You must be from the south. Call me Christa."

"Midwest."

She shrugged. "Same thing. Unless of course you want to play country music."

"No, ma'am—sorry. Christa. I don't play country."

"So I hear." She pulled a cigarette from a quilted case and held it to her lips. "I must say, I've been dying to see for myself the man Asher Drake turned down because he was too good-looking." She snickered.

"I beg your pardon?"

Her eyes remained fixed on his as he lit her cigarette.

"Asher Drake?" She blew a cloud of smoke over his head. "Didn't you just audition for Asher's band?"

"Yeah, but Davy said they went with someone else."

"He didn't tell you why?" A sly smile tugged at the edge of her crimson lips.

He shook his head.

"This is precious!" She leaned forward, as if everyone in Sardi's was waiting to hear why he hadn't landed the lead guitarist spot with Asher Drake. "Asher nixed you himself. I think the boy was worried you might steal some of his thunder. Now I can see why. You look like a young Robert Redford, only with all that gorgeous blond hair."

"I'm an excellent guitar player," he said evenly.

"So I've been told. Of course, I'll have to hear for myself, but Davy is singing your praises."

"I brought a couple cassettes." He slid a manila envelope across the table.

"Wonderful." Christa took a sip of the martini that appeared, even though she hadn't ordered. "Billy? What are you drinking?"

"Just a beer," he told the waiter. "Whatever you have on tap."

"Beer?" With a cursory glance at the waiter, Christa leaned back and studied Billy carefully. "I take you for a Jack Daniels man. Single malt?"

"Yes, ma'am." He grinned. "That'll do fine."

"So." Christa snuggled into her chair. "Tell me about yourself."

"Well, I'm a damn good lead guitarist. I have my own style, but I might lean a bit toward Eddie Van Halen or Slash. "

"Mason Edwards!"

"Not really. Although I admire him."

She didn't hear him as she'd already bounced from her seat and into the arms of a dark-haired, bearded man. Billy listened, awed, as the two exchanged small talk.

"Mason, sweetheart, I have to introduce you to someone who just might give you a run for your money."

Billy wiped a sweaty palm on his jeans and stood. He was several inches taller than Edwards, but he still felt like he was standing next to a giant.

"I'm a huge fan," Billy said, extending his hand.

Edwards smiled as he touched his finger to his cheek. "Woman or money?"

His hand rose to his sutures, and he shrugged. "Woman."

"Only thing worth fighting for," Edwards said with a wink. He gave Christa another peck on the cheek, wished Billy luck, and left.

The waiter brought their lunch, a hamburger that cost more than Billy had ever paid for steak along with a Cobb salad for Christa.

"So, woman trouble?" Christa asked, spearing a sliver of chicken.

"Excuse me?"

"You told Mason you were fighting over a woman."

"Oh, yeah. Someone got out of line with my girlfriend."

She grimaced. "I don't like to hear that."

"It won't happen again. I fired him."

She waved her fork dismissively. "I don't mean that. I have no problem with the bad boy image. I don't like to hear that you have a girlfriend."

Looking up from his drink, he gave her a sly smile. "Sorry. I'm spoken for."

She reached across the table and patted his hand. "Not for me, silly. For all the other women. They'll want to believe you're available. They want to imagine going home with you and doing all sorts of nasty things. I'm just saying it would be a lot easier to sell you if women jump on board from the get-go. You've got the makings of a real heartthrob."

This wasn't going the way he'd expected. He wasn't looking for tail. The quicker they got that out of the way, the better.

"Listen, Christa. I want to play my music and be judged for that, not for my looks."

"Aren't you precious?" She slapped his hand playfully before diving back into her salad. "I'm not telling you to dump the girlfriend. I'm just saying don't broadcast that you have one." She arched an eyebrow. "Who needs to know?"

He didn't like his personal life being open for discussion. What he did and with whom was nobody's business. It was especially not the business of someone he'd known less than an hour.

"Where does she live?"

"Katie? With me."

She studied him closely. "How old are you?"

"I'll be twenty-four in March."

"You're a baby! Let's keep this between us."

When the waiter asked if they wanted dessert, she ordered them each another drink. Billy declined, but ordered a slice of cheesecake to go.

Christa arched an eyebrow. "Too full to eat that now?"

"It's not for me."

"That's what I thought. I don't think you're listening to me."

"I'm listening. I'm not sure I agree."

A flicker of irritation crossed her face. "I guess that's all I can ask." She decided to skip her drink as well, then instructed the waiter to put the cheesecake on a separate check. "You're on your own with that one, sweetheart."

"Understood."

As she stood, the maître d' materialized with her coat. "I'm going to give these a listen, and I'll be in touch." She swept up the manila envelope, leaving him in a cloud of blue smoke and expensive perfume.

~

When Christa didn't call right away, Billy became unbearable to be around. If he hadn't scheduled auditions to replace Pete and band practice for Friday afternoon, Kate didn't think he would have moved more than a few feet from the phone, let alone left the apartment. And just like a watched pot, Christa called almost as soon as he drove away.

Kate tracked him down at his rehearsal space to pass along the numbers Christa had left. That had been shortly after four o'clock. It was almost one when she woke to the familiar thump of guitar cases on the living room floor. She squinted up at him in the flickering blue light of the television.

"Well?" she croaked, her voice heavy with sleep.

He picked up her legs, plopped down on the couch alongside her, and dropped them into his lap, then leaned back and pretended to snore.

She shoved him with her foot. "Nuh-uh. Start talking."

He opened his eyes and grinned. "Christa loved my demos, and we discussed some possibilities. There are a couple things she wants to flesh out with her agency, but what she wanted to talk to me about tonight was a job for Davy Steinman."

"Who?"

"Remember the producer I auditioned for last month?"

"But I thought he said no."

"No, he didn't say no. He liked me. Asher Drake said no."

"Right." She yawned. "Because you're too good-looking. Sorry, I have to agree. You're much better looking than Asher Drake—although he's not bad."

Billy snorted. "Sounds like a jerk." He lifted her foot and started kneading the sole with his knuckles. She sighed contentedly. If someone could figure out how to bottle a guitarist's hands and fingers, they'd make millions.

"Probably. You wouldn't want to work with someone that insecure anyway." She nudged him. "Keep talking."

"Davy's filming a music video in a few weeks, and that's why he suggested Christa contact me. He thinks I need an agent, and he wants me to back Bailey Swift on a song called 'Phoenix Rising.' Christa wants to represent me. She's gonna negotiate a deal with Steinman for me to play lead guitar in the video."

Kate threw her arms around his neck, then wrinkled her nose as she sniffed his hair.

"Why do you smell like cigarettes?"

"Christa smokes."

"I thought you talked to her on the phone."

"I did. Then she wanted me to meet her at her hotel, so I went straight to the city after practice."

Her eyebrows shot up. "Her hotel?"

"Yes, her hotel. In the bar. Okay? Although her agency has an office in New York, her base is in LA. So when she's on the East Coast, she often works from her hotel."

"How convenient."

He ignored the snarky comment. "She's also gonna start setting up some gigs for the band, try to hook us up on some tours."

"Are the other guys are on board?"

"Dunno. I didn't discuss it with them. They've only been with me a couple months. I'm not sure if they're willing to go on long cross-country tours."

Her stomach turned over. "Is that what's gonna happen?"

"Probably. No one's gonna sign me if they never heard of me. I have to build a fan base."

Fear and uncertainty settled in around her.

"You knew this was my dream, babe." Billy cupped her cheek, angling her face toward him.

She nodded.

"It won't change anything. If you can come, then you'll come. If not, you stay here until I come back. I'll still take care of you."

Although he probably didn't mean it the way it sounded, she'd gone from girlfriend to burden; like a plant that would need to be watered while he was away. Memories of being less, of not belonging, buried just below the surface, reawakened.

"Oh—and hey!" His excitement surged. "Do you think you can get Joey here? Maybe next weekend?"

"I can ask. Why?"

"Christa thinks I should bleach my hair. She thinks it will give me more of the bad boy vibe she wants to promote."

The stitches had been removed, but the remnants of last weekend's fight were still clearly visible.

"You already have a bad boy vibe. Does she want you to actually kill somebody?"

"I play hard rock, Katie. She likes my look. She just wants me to have more of an edge. If I wasn't okay with it, I wouldn't do it."

"So she doesn't think you're too good-looking?" she asked, turning up the sweetness.

"No," he said with a perfectly straight face. "She thinks I'm just good-looking enough."

That made her laugh and helped lighten the dark feelings she'd had moments earlier. She reached for his throat, but he caught her hands and held them.

Teasing, he moved in, running his nose along her jaw line. "What about you, Katie? You think I'm pretty?"

The sarcastic remark on her tongue dissolved. All she could focus on was his warm breath on her face. He was as beautiful as ever, in spite of the purplish bruises around his eye and the angry red scar. "I do."

"You're in for a real treat, then." He swept her up from the couch and carried her off to bed.

CHAPTER 19

The following week, his hair bleached a yellow-blond, Billy dropped Kate off at The Met before heading uptown for his meeting with Christa. He was relieved they were meeting at the agency this time. He'd been picking up some pretty strong signals, and he just wasn't interested. A few months ago, perhaps, but not now.

He thought she'd gotten the hint, but almost as soon as he signed the contract, she started in on him again.

"I'm sure she's adorable, but you have to look at the bigger picture." She perched on the edge of the enormous mahogany desk, leaning forward to give him a clear shot of the black lace bra hugging the curve of her breasts.

"You're incredibly handsome and extremely talented. You think women want you now? Baby, you have no idea. A girlfriend is just going to hold you back. You've got the goods, and I can make you a star either way. But I can also lay the world at your feet if you want it." She moved closer, lowering her voice until it was just a whisper. Her lips brushed his ear. "That's how good I am—and that's just one of my many talents."

He remained focused on the skyline outside the window.

"Let's just say when I'm done with you, you can have your pick of any woman you want."

He swept her with a sidelong glance. "I already do."

"Fine." She threw her hands up and pulled away. "Don't complain later."

"That'll be my problem, not yours."

Barely hiding her irritation, she went on to tell him about the video. It would pay much less than he expected, and she'd get fifteen percent of that. But it was a start, she promised, and if Steinman was happy, it was just the beginning. As an unknown, Billy wouldn't take away from Davy's new star, but he would gain some serious music cred.

Filming was slated for a soundstage in Brooklyn. Three models dressed in black leather would be hoisted over the set, which would include a funeral pyre.

"What about the models? Did you hire them yet?"

Christa gave him a wicked smile. "I thought you weren't interested, Mr. McDonald."

"I'm not, but if they haven't been cast, I'd like you to suggest Kate."

She tugged a cigarette from her fancy case and dropped it on the desk. "You're killing me, you know that?" She glared at him as she lit it. "Is she tall and leggy?"

He shrugged. "Tall enough, I guess. Definitely leggy."

"Picture?"

He reached for his wallet and pulled out his favorite, the one of Kate sitting on the steps.

Christa cooed as if he'd shown her a cute, cuddly kitten. "Adorable!" Then she frowned and tossed the picture on the desk. "She looks like jailbait."

He pulled out two Joey had taken over Thanksgiving, one of Kate in bed wearing nothing but a sheet and another with a strand of pearls between her teeth, her hands over her breasts.

"Let me see the others," she said, wiggling her fingers, impatiently. She sat back and flipped through them, pursing her lips as if reluctant to speak. "Okay. She's beautiful. Whoever took these is a genius—and the stylist, very talented. I'm impressed."

"Does she have the job?"

"How tall is she?"

Billy held his hand to his chest. "About here. Taller than you."

"Fine." She tossed the photos onto the desk and leaned back in her chair. "Have her call the office and we'll set it up. She'll need to go for a fitting. The bikinis are being made specifically for the girls."

His mouth dropped open. "A leather bikini?" *Shit.*

She smirked. "Problem?"

"No, ma'am," he lied.

~

It was after four by the time he got to the museum. The meeting had taken a lot longer than he anticipated, and he'd spent another forty minutes searching for Kate. As soon as he saw her standing in front of a room from an old English castle, he felt guilty. Christa had finally berated him into keeping their relationship quiet. It had seemed like an acceptable compromise at the time. Now he wasn't so sure.

"What do you think?" he asked, sneaking up behind her as she studied the ornate ceiling and the walls draped with heavy tapestries. "Should we do this in the dining room or the front parlor?"

She smiled up at him, looking tired and pale.

"You OK?"

Nodding, she slipped her hand in his. "I think I'm a bit done in."

"You sure you're all right?"

"Uh-huh. I'm hungry, too."

"That I can fix. There's a little restaurant on the corner where I parked. About two blocks away."

"Good. I'm starving, and my feet are killing me."

He bent down as if he intended to lift her up, but she jumped aside.

A passing docent, leading a troop of green-clad Girl Scouts, shot them a disapproving look. "Don't!" Kate laughed. "They'll take my membership card away!"

A half-hour later, as she pushed chunks of fatty pot roast around her plate, she wasn't laughing. "If I didn't want to get up on stage fully clothed and sing, what made you think I'd want to hang half-naked from a trapeze?"

"If I remember correctly, you were half-naked the first time, too." Judging by the look on her face, his attempt at humor wasn't working. "Eat." He pointed with his fork. "You said you were hungry."

"I didn't realize I should've just ordered a lettuce leaf."

"You'll look amazing."

"Will I? You've never seen me in a bikini, especially a leather one."

The rise in her voice prompted a man at a nearby table to lean forward, his eyes raking over her. Billy gave him a menacing look, then ordered her to lower her voice.

"Look, I don't blame you for being pissed. I wouldn't want to be swinging around in a leather thong either. It's just that we could use the money. I don't have as many gigs booked as I'd like. Plus I have to give Christa fifteen percent of my earnings now."

"I have money in the bank."

"You're not touching that. It's there in case you really need it."

He'd been adamant that she open another savings account after she closed her old one. And other than a couple hundred dollars for some clothes and a few personal things, he hadn't let her touch it. He'd nearly shit a brick when he learned she had almost $8,000 saved up. While it would come in handy right now, she might need that money someday if things didn't work out between them.

He watched as she mashed her carrots into pulp, then mixed them into her potatoes. It was nothing really, but the mess she made on her plate when something was bothering her, drove him crazy—that and her complete disregard for the concept of time.

"Don't we really need it?" she asked, stirring the rest of her pot roast into the slop.

"Katie, listen." He reached across the table, covering her hand with his own to get her to stop playing with her food. "If you could make a few hundred dollars for showing off your beautiful body for a few hours, isn't that better?"

She gave him a dark look. "Things a pimp says," she muttered, pulling away and mashing her food into a mushy, brown blob.

Sensing she was wavering, he hurried to close the deal. "Plus, we'll be together. I'll be there the whole time. If not, think of all the hours I'll be in New York without you. There's rehearsals and dress rehearsals." He put on his best pleading expression.

"You can be a real pain in the ass sometimes."

"Excuse me?"

"You heard me. And one other thing." She eyed him mischievously. "I'm getting you a leopard-print thong, and you're wearing it around the apartment."

"Deal." There wasn't such a thing, was there?

CHAPTER 20

Billy pulled up to the corner of Seventh Avenue and Thirty-Seventh Street. Kate had an appointment to get measured for her costume, and he was heading to Brooklyn for his first rehearsal with Bailey Swift.

"Listen," he said, as she gathered her things. "I should have told you this before, so you have every right to get mad."

She eyed him warily. "You mean madder than I already am for making me do this?"

"Yeah." He rubbed his finger under his nose. "Probably."

"Oh, shit."

If he wasn't already in the dog house, he'd have laughed at the face she made. Instead, he cleared his throat.

"Christa isn't happy I have a girlfriend. She thinks it'll negatively impact my career."

Her jaw dropped. "So you're dumping me? In the middle of Manhattan?"

He started to laugh, then realized she wasn't joking. "No, I have no intention of dumping you. I told her that." He stopped to clear his throat. "But I did kind of agree to keep you under wraps."

The hurt on her face tore at him.

"So you want me to act like we don't know each other?"

A horn blasted behind them. He flipped off the driver, then turned back to Kate.

"I know it sounds bad. It sounds even worse coming from your mouth."

"Oh, I don't know. Sounded pretty bad coming from yours."

"Forget it. I'm sorry I said any—"

"No." She grabbed her bag and opened the door. "I get it."

"Katie." He unbuckled his seatbelt and tried to grab her arm. "Just forget it."

"It's okay, Billy. I get it!" She slammed the door and started walking.

He jumped out and called after her, but she wouldn't stop. The other driver laid on his horn. If he hadn't been blocking a lane of traffic and she hadn't been walking the opposite direction up a one-way street, he would've gone after her. Instead, he pounded his fist into the hood of the jackass with the horn, then climbed into his van and headed to Brooklyn, feeling like a first-class piece of shit.

✦

Kate had a hard time reading the paper gripped between her shaking fingers. She blamed the cold wind howling down Thirty-Seventh Street, but her tears had nothing to do with the temperature. When she finally figured out where she was going, she was surprised to see Joey waiting when she stepped off the elevator.

One look at her and his smile faded. "You look awful."

"Thanks. I love you, too."

"Seriously. Your eyes are all red, and you look like you haven't slept."

"I'm fine. Just tired. I thought you weren't meeting me until later."

"My morning class was cancelled, and I was dying to see a bona fide costume studio, so . . . Voila!" He threw his arms open.

After she checked in with the receptionist, Joey dragged her off into a corner near the water cooler.

"Compose yourself," he warned. "Your competition is here."

"What? What competition?"

He motioned with his head toward two women sitting on a long, low sofa. They were all boobs and legs. One was blond and the other a brunette. "Those are the other models," he whispered. "For the video."

She covered her mouth with her hand. "What are they, like six feet tall?"

"I know," he said, leaning in close.

"Do you mind?" Irritated, she wiped his moist breath from her ear.

He snapped back and dropped a hand onto his hip. "Don't be bitchy with me. I didn't do anything."

"Sorry."

"You sure you're okay?"

"Fine. Did you tell them you were waiting for me?"

"Why? They would know who you are?" he asked sarcastically.

She looked around to make sure no one was listening. "Apparently, no one is supposed to know Billy is attached. So I'm not supposed to say I'm his girlfriend."

"What?"

Everyone in the waiting room looked up. She smiled benignly.

"It's his new agent. She thinks it could hurt his career."

"No! Why didn't you tell me?"

"I just did."

"I mean before."

"I just found out. As I was getting out of the van."

His mouth dropped open. "Coward!"

She resettled her bag over her shoulder and leaned against the wall. "I understand, kind of, but that doesn't mean I like it. It also doesn't mean he should've told me like this."

"What're you gonna do?"

She shrugged.

"Are you gonna act like you don't know him?"

"I guess."

"You're an idiot."

She pinched him, and he yelped. Rubbing his arm, he dragged her over to the two girls sitting on the sofa.

"Tiffany, Crystal, this is my friend Kate. She's gonna be working with you."

The blonde lowered her magazine, looked down her nose at Kate and then up to the top of her head. She snapped her gum. "How tall are you?"

"Me? About five six."

She glanced significantly at her fellow Amazon, then went back to her magazine. Apparently, the conversation was over.

"Nice meeting you," Kate said as Joey pulled her back across the room. "Oh, yeah," she grumbled once they were out of earshot. "This is gonna be loads of fun."

Joey followed Kate in for her fitting a few minutes later, even though she had to strip down to her bra and panties. When the seamstress was done taking Kate's measurements, she reminded her to make sure she waxed before the next fitting.

"I'm sorry, what?" Kate's eyebrows inched toward her hairline. Images of boiling wax and blistering skin flashed in her head.

Standing quickly, Joey dropped the magazine he'd been reading. "Of course." He rolled his eyes as if to say, *You have to ask?*

Kate shot him a questioning look, and he touched his fingers to his lips. As soon as the seamstress left the room, she wheeled on him.

He held up his hands. "You need to get waxed on your lady parts."

"What?"

"Shhh. You want someone to hear you?"

"I don't care. My lady parts? What does that mean?"

"You don't know what your lady parts are?"

She drew a circle around her bikini area with her finger. "Here?" *Hot wax? There? What sicko came up with that idea?*

He nodded.

"Waxed?"

"Yeah."

"Sounds painful."

"Pretty sure it is, but I know someone who can do it. I bet she can even do it today. That way, the redness and irritation will be gone before your next fitting."

"Redness and irritation?"

"Why are you parroting everything I say?" He ducked out of her way when she reached for him, pointing an accusatory finger in her direction. "Don't you dare! Save those sharp little pinchers for when you get home."

It was close to midnight by the time Kate climbed the stairs to her apartment. She was fumbling with the key when the door flew open.

"Where've you been?" Billy demanded. "I've been worried sick."

She gaped up at him. "Where do you think I've been? I was where you left me."

"That was twelve hours ago," he bellowed. His voice echoed through the empty hall. "It didn't take that long to get fitted for a bathing suit."

She pushed him into the apartment, closing the door behind her.

"Not a bathing suit. Two pieces of leather dental floss."

He blanched. "That bad?"

"Oh yeah. You're not gonna have to worry about me telling anyone I'm your girlfriend, because if I know you, the first guy who looks at me wearing that thing will be looking for his nose somewhere behind his ears."

"Shit. I'm sorry." He reached for her, but she waved him off.

"You don't get off that easy. That was only half of it."

He looked worried.

"I've never worn anything so revealing. Which meant I needed to pay a visit to a lovely Brazilian woman with a masochistic streak."

It didn't take long for him to figure out what she was talking about. He tried to hide his smile.

She nodded. "I figured a man of your vast experience would be familiar with the term. Sad thing is, I had no idea what it was. Good thing I had Joey."

"Joey did it?" The little muscle in his jaw began to pulse.

"No! I said a Brazilian woman, didn't I?"

"I thought it was a euphemism."

She threw her hands up in the air. "You're ridiculous, you know that?"

He shrugged.

"Let's just say this wasn't my finest day. I was hurt, humiliated, had to borrow money from my best friend to have this little, albeit expensive, procedure done—in Harlem, no less—and then, I got to bounce around on a hard bus seat for a half-hour before I could drag myself into a smelly taxi for the last leg of my trip home. And you're upset it took twelve hours."

"If I'd known you'd be so late, I would've picked you up."

"I had no way of reaching you." She hung her coat on the rack and headed for the bedroom. "I need a shower. My hair smells like cigars."

"Wait," Billy called after her. "Aren't you gonna show me?"

She gave him a coy smile. "You show me yours and I'll show you mine."

He tore his T-shirt over his head and began to unbuckle his belt.

"No." Reaching into her purse, she pulled out a small bag. "That."

She tossed it across the room.

When he opened it, he groaned.

"Exactly."

~

Kate took her time. She showered and washed her hair. Then she blew it dry so she'd look her best. Not that he deserved it, but she was enjoying making him wait. When she finally came out of the bathroom, he was sitting on the bed wearing his new thong and a goofy grin.

"Took you long enough," he said, trying—and failing—to sound annoyed.

She stood in the doorway, wrapped in a towel.

"Why are you smiling?" She tried to look stern. When she signaled for him to stand, he did, holding his hands over his crotch. "Uh-uh. Hands at your sides."

When she caught a glimpse of the state of his arousal, she had to press her lips together to keep from laughing. "I guess you really like your present."

"Funny. I showed you mine. Let's see yours."

She tightened her hold on the towel, suddenly feeling shy. If he laughed, she'd be mortified.

"C'mon."

"Don't laugh."

"I promise." He held up two fingers. "Scout's honor."

"You gonna act like a Boy Scout?"

"Hell no."

The towel fell, and he was on her like a rocket. He snatched her up and deposited her in the center of the bed, then covered her with kisses, working his way down for a closer look.

"I guess you like it." She giggled.

"Oh, yeah." His voice came from deep inside his throat. "Jeez, Katie, you didn't even get a landing strip."

She raised up onto her elbows so she could see his face. "The fact that you know what that means is pretty disturbing."

"Sorry," he said, swirling his tongue around her navel and not sounding sorry at all.

CHAPTER 21

"A day? You have sex several times a day?"

Kate focused on not throwing up all over the examining room floor.

"Usually," she croaked. "At least twice a day."

The doctor scribbled in her chart. Kate shivered and tried to keep from doubling over.

She had woken early that morning, burning up with fever and impaled by sharp pains in her stomach. Not wanting to wake Billy, she had curled up on the bathroom floor. As the pain grew worse, she pressed a towel against her mouth to keep from crying out. That was how he'd found her.

"What the hell?" He'd squatted beside her. "What's wrong?"

"I didn't want to wake you."

"That's the stupidest—" When she let out a small cry, he picked her up and carried her back to bed.

"What hurts?" he asked, setting her down gently.

"Here." She waved her hand below her abdomen. After making sure she was comfortable, he'd gone into the kitchen and began calling doctors until he found one who would see her that morning.

The relief she'd felt a few minutes earlier at seeing the doctor was a woman vanished. She stared at her strawberry pink toenail polish, now chipped and worn.

Dr. Landry set down the chart and folded her arms. "How many partners?"

Kate looked up, confused. "What?"

"How many men do you have sex with each day?"

Nerves made her feel like laughing, but what the doctor was implying wasn't at all funny. She felt frozen.

"Are you sexually promiscuous, Miss Daniels? It seems you have cystitis, or what we sometimes call honeymoon cystitis. It's often triggered by frequent intercourse and the introduction of bacteria into the urethra. It's also possible to contract it if anything unclean is inserted into the vagina. How many partners do you have sex with each day, and has anything other than a penis been inserted into your vagina?"

Kate winced. The pain was almost preferable to this interrogation.

Dr. Landry continued.

"Ironically, the use of condoms can also spread the infection. I assume, being as sexually active as you are, you're using condoms."

"Not exactly." Her face was on fire. "I was on the pill, but . . . um . . . If you can give me a new prescription, that would be great."

"The pill isn't going to protect you from sexually transmitted diseases, Miss Daniels, especially if you have multiple partners, or your partners have multiple partners." She flipped through Kate's chart. "You didn't complete the section on drug and alcohol use."

"My boyfriend filled it out. I'm really not feeling well." She rocked back and forth, trying to keep her mind off the pain.

"We won't be much longer. Do you drink alcohol?"

"Sometimes."

"How often?"

"Couple times a week, more or less."

"I don't suppose I need to point out that you're only eighteen, if that."

She squirmed under the doctor's gaze.

"Drugs?"

Kate stared at her feet and nodded.

"Which?"

"Which?"

"Yes. Which drugs are you using?"

Nervous fingers folded pleats into her paper gown. "Some pot. Some other stuff, pills sometimes. And something in a capsule."

Dr. Landry jotted notes into her chart. "What kind of capsule? Something you swallow?"

"No."

"Amyl nitrate?"

"I dunno."

"Do you break it open and hold it under your nose?"

She nodded.

"Miss Daniels, I need to write you a prescription for the infection and one for the pain. I can't do that because I don't know what kind of drugs you've been taking or if I can trust you not to drink alcohol while you're taking the medication I prescribe."

Kate squirmed under the doctor's harsh gaze.

"Would your boyfriend know what drugs you've been using?"

"I guess."

"What's his name?"

"Billy Donaldson."

Dr. Landry opened the door. "Naomi, could you please bring Mr. Donaldson in here?"

While they waited, she listened to Kate's chest, took her pulse, and then had her lie down on the table while she palpated her abdomen. She was helping Kate into a sitting position when Billy entered.

"Oh, you." Dr. Landry scowled. "Not one woman on my staff, save Naomi there, has gotten one bit of work done since you walked in the door.

Now I see why." She snatched up Kate's chart. "Well, I'm not enchanted, Mr. Donaldson, but I do have a few questions."

Billy stiffened and jutted out his chin.

"Do you and Miss Daniels live together?"

"Yeah."

"Are you her sole source of support?"

"Yeah."

"She doesn't work for you in any capacity?"

"Work for me? She's my girlfriend."

"How old is Miss Daniels?"

"Eighteen." He looked at Kate curiously.

"Miss Daniels tells me the two of you are extremely sexually active."

A sardonic smile played across his lips. "Yeah. So?"

"She's also admitted to drinking and drug use."

Billy's jaw tightened and his nostrils flared. His eyes narrowed as he looked at Kate.

"Don't intimidate my patient, Mr. Donaldson," Dr. Landry said. "I won't tolerate it."

"Wait a minute—"

"No," Kate gasped, wrapping her arms around her waist. "It isn't like that."

The doctor continued as if she hadn't spoken. "Mr. Donaldson, your girlfriend has cystitis. It can be caused by frequent, vigorous, and often rough sex. She has an infection and needs an antibiotic and something for pain. I can't prescribe those medications if I don't know what type of drugs she's been using. You can either tell me, or you can take her home as is."

Billy glared at her. "Since when?"

"I beg your pardon?"

"You want to know what drugs. I asked you since when. What do you want to know?" He seemed as irritated as the doctor.

"Why don't you just tell me—and Miss Daniels, since she seems to be clueless—what drugs you've given her? At least this way, she knows what she's dealing with."

The muscles pulsed along his jaw.

"Quaaludes, Seconal, amyl nitrate, coke." He hesitated for a second. "And pot."

The doctor wrote it all down in Kate's chart, then looked up at him.

"How old are you?"

"Almost twenty-four."

"So old enough to know better?"

Kate cringed.

"Look, I didn't come here for a lecture," he snarled. "We're here because she's sick, and if you're gonna write her a prescription, then write the fucking prescription. If not, just say so, and I'll take her where they'll care more about what's wrong with her and less about what I'm doing."

"You think I don't care about her?" Dr. Landry took a step toward him, looking like she was about to drive her finger into his chest. "Then you're sadly mistaken. If I didn't care, I'd have written those prescriptions already, and maybe they would've interacted with some drug that might still be in her system. But that's not happening on my watch."

When she turned to Kate, she regained a mantle of professionalism.

"When was the last time you took any type of drug, Miss Daniels, legal or illegal?"

"I took an aspirin this morning," she said, softly, "but it didn't help."

Dr. Landry looked at Billy.

"She smoked pot about two or three days ago." He looked at Kate for confirmation. "Other than that, we split a popper over the weekend."

"That's it?"

"For her." He glowered as the doctor pulled out her pad and scribbled two prescriptions.

"Get these filled. Take them as soon as you get home. This one is for the infection. Take it for seven days. This one's for pain. You should feel a little better by tonight. I'm only giving you enough for two days. If you still have pain after that, call me. In the meantime, no drugs or alcohol of any kind. I'd like to see you in two weeks to follow up and for a regular checkup. We can talk about birth control then." She pointed her finger at Billy. "No sex until this clears up."

Billy shot Kate a look of utter shock. "Birth control? You're not on birth control?"

"What?" The doctor stopped in the doorway. "How long have you two been together?"

"Three months," Kate said miserably.

"You're having sex like a couple of rabbits and you haven't discussed birth control?"

"I thought you were on the pill," Billy said, raising his voice.

Kate opened her mouth, but Dr. Landry interrupted.

"Mr. Donaldson, do you know what they call men who assume their girlfriends are on the pill?"

He shook his head, his eyes still fixed on Kate.

"Daddy. They call them daddy."

Kate wished she could disappear inside her paper dress.

Billy glared at the doctor. "Are we done here?"

"See Naomi on your way out and make an appointment for two weeks."

After the door closed, Billy grabbed Kate's clothes and thrust them at her.

"If she thinks we're coming back, she can kiss my ass. Get dressed. Let's get the hell out of here."

It was hard not to cry as he helped her into her clothes. He squeezed her arm a little too tightly as he led her down the hall. When the receptionist asked about scheduling a follow-up, Kate hesitated.

"Don't expect me to come with you," he snapped.

She promised to call in a couple days.

Billy didn't say a word as he helped her to the car, nor did he speak while they drove to the pharmacy to drop off her prescriptions or as he helped her into the apartment.

"Do you need help getting undressed?" he snapped.

She did, but she wasn't about to say so.

"Before I pick up your prescription, I'll go to the store and get ginger ale. That should help with the nausea. You want anything else? Soup?"

"I don't know."

"Yes or no, Kate? I don't read minds."

"Soup, please." She tried to keep from trembling. "I'm sorry," she said as

159

he grabbed his keys.

"What?"

"I said I'm sorry."

"For what? For getting sick? For letting me be humiliated by that rabid doctor? For not telling me you aren't using any fucking birth control?"

"I thought you knew," she cried.

"You're right." He threw his hands up, frustrated. "I should've asked. I just assumed you wouldn't wanna get pregnant. Jesus, Kate!" He stepped toward her, then stopped. "This is what I get for shacking up with a goddamn kid."

He stalked out of the apartment. The echo of the slamming door hurt as much as his words.

By the time Billy returned, Kate was buried under the covers, shivering uncontrollably. Her face was pale except for two bright, pink triangles on her cheeks. The deterioration in her appearance was startling. He touched his lips to her forehead like his grandmother would do. She was on fire.

In spite of his still pulsing anger, he tried to be gentle. "Katie, you need to take off these blankets until your fever goes down. You're too warm."

She made a low, mewling sound.

"C'mon. Just for a little while. The pills should kick in soon. Then you can have them back. That sweatshirt has to come off, too."

He helped her sit, then pulled the sweatshirt over her head, yanking her hair in the process. She didn't complain or cry out; she just looked at him, her big, sad eyes shining like glass. Then she lay down, shivering. He pulled the sheet over her, then lay beside her, curling himself around her when she continued to shake.

Eventually her body stilled and her breathing grew even. When he was certain she'd fallen asleep, he rolled away and stared at the ceiling. He'd used her like his own personal playground, and now she was paying the price. Guilt wedged itself in beside his anger.

Careful not to wake her, he slipped out of bed. He grabbed a beer, then picked up his unplugged guitar. Practicing was out of the question, as he was too agitated to focus. Watching TV didn't help either. He needed to get out of there, needed some distance. He'd never been angry with her before, and he didn't like it. He needed to leave before he said or did something he'd be sorry for.

Before leaving, he stood over the bed. She was in a deep sleep. Her forehead was still warm, but she was no longer burning up. He pulled the quilt over her shoulders, then left a note on the bathroom mirror in case she woke while he was gone.

It was almost midnight when he returned, his anger dulled courtesy of Jack Daniels, Molson, and a sympathetic bartender. Kate was asleep, wrapped cocoon-like in the quilt.

He rubbed his hand over her shoulder. "How're you feeling?"

"Little better," she mumbled.

"Here. Take these." He held out the pills and some water. She did as she was told, and within a few minutes, she fell back to sleep. He took a few aspirin himself to ward off a hangover, then shucked off his clothes and climbed into bed.

He stared into the muted gray light coming through the window. He was too drunk for much coherent thought, but that didn't stop him from mulling over this mess. It was not totally her fault. He had made the decision—or the lack of a decision, if he was being honest—to skip condoms. He wanted nothing between them. Fucking her had been amazing from the first time, and he didn't want it to feel any different. And she'd told him she'd gone to a clinic or something, had started on the pill. He'd just assumed she'd kept up the prescription. Or something.

Maybe he should have worried more about the "or something."

Angry, muffled voices penetrated the bedroom walls. Somewhere in the building, a couple argued. Kate's back was to him. He didn't like being angry with her. He used enough energy being angry with the rest of the world. She was the peace he hadn't even known was possible.

A horn blasted outside the window. The voices grew quiet. Still, he couldn't sleep. Frustrated, he rolled toward her, curling himself tight against her back. He kissed her hair.

"Damn you, Katie," he whispered into the darkness.

The next morning, he was sitting on the couch watching TV when Kate shuffled into the living room wearing nothing but one of his T-shirts, her hair still messy from sleep. It was a kick in the gut when she hesitated, looking as if she wasn't sure it was safe to go near him. He raised his arm, and she curled into a ball beside him.

"Any better?"

She nodded. "What're you watching?"

"*I Love Lucy*." He handed her his mug of coffee. She took a sip. When he offered to put on a fresh pot, she shook her head, then rested her cheek against his bare chest.

"You know," she said, running her hand over his stomach, "if you keep walking around naked, it's gonna be a lot harder not having sex for the next few days."

He looked down at her. "She said *you* couldn't have sex. She didn't say anything about me."

She grabbed his nipple and lightly twisted it.

"Ow!"

"Next time, it won't be a nipple."

He covered his exposed crotch. "Truce?"

Nodding, she nestled back into the crook of his arm. When the show ended, she sat up and faced him.

"Do you want me to leave?"

Emotions swirled, and for a moment, he thought he might actually be sick.

"No. Why would you think that?"

"You're pretty angry with me. I just figured—"

"I know, and I'm sorry. But just because I got pissed doesn't mean it's over. Jeez, Katie." Panic flowed through him like ice water. He'd never experienced anything like this. He stood and headed for the bedroom. He was zipping his jeans when she walked in.

"What are you doing?"

"Getting dressed," he said, more harshly than he'd intended. "I can't argue with you when I'm naked."

"I don't wanna argue."

"Then what do you want?" To hide his shaking hands, he balled his fists into the T-shirt he'd been about to slip over his head.

"I just want you to be happy." She bit her lip. He wanted to step across the room and bite it for her.

"What about you? Don't you want to be happy?"

She looked as if she didn't know how to answer.

"Katie? Are you happy?"

"At this moment? No. But the rest of the time, yeah. With you. I really am." She whispered, as if she wasn't sure it was the right thing to say.

"Katie," he said softly, "I'm happy, too, at least when it comes to you. I want you here. I know we jumped into this way too soon, but I don't care. And I'm sorry I can't keep my hands off you." He tossed his shirt on the bed and pulled her toward him. "Look what I've done to you. It's my fault you're sick."

He brushed her hair from her face and guided her to the edge of the bed. "Don't leave me. Things aren't perfect, but we'll figure it out." He kissed the tip of her nose. "Some days, I can't believe how lucky I am."

Her lips quivered, and he took her hands in his. "You call and make that appointment. Make sure you're all better, and then you get that psychopath to give you another prescription for birth control, okay?"

She nodded.

"In the meantime, I'll buy a case of condoms. That should last until the end of the week, right?"

She snorted and punched his arm.

"I hate them, but I'll use them until it's safe."

CHAPTER 22

Kate was still tired and queasy but felt well enough to participate in a promotional event for Bailey Swift and his introduction to record industry execs and the American press. The only problem was working out the logistics of her coming and going.

Joey jumped at the chance to tag along. After class, he met Kate a block from the soundstage, where she waited with Billy.

"I can't believe you agreed to this," Joey said as they walked down Flatbush Avenue, bundled up against the late February chill.

"You can't kick me any more than I've been kicking myself, so don't even try. I kinda get it. I used to have crushes on George Michael and David Lee Roth. A few months ago I was convinced I'd meet George Michael and move to England, where we'd live happily ever after in his castle." Her chattering teeth were making it difficult to speak. "But I'm crazy about Billy. He's better than George Michael and David Lee Roth combined. And you can throw in Tom Cruise as well."

As they waited for the light to change, she could feel Joey's eyes on her. "First of all, Tom Cruise is married and has had plenty of high-profile girlfriends. Second, David Lee Roth is a whore. And third, George Michael is gay."

She huffed. "No he isn't! Look at him! Where do you come up with this stuff?"

Joey stopped short. "What does that mean: *Look at him?* Because he's handsome, he's not gay? Because he's talented, he's not gay? Because he's macho, he's not gay?"

She shrugged. "I don't know. He doesn't look gay."

"That's the stupidest thing I've ever heard. Do I look gay?"

She surveyed the crown of curly hair, the neat but not-appearing-to-be-plucked eyebrows, his vintage wing tips, and the jaunty scarf tied around the neck of his navy pea coat.

"Um, yeah."

He waved his hand as if tossing her notion aside. "That's beside the point."

"I thought that was the point."

"Mark my words. He's gay."

"It doesn't matter." Kate linked her arm through his. "If he pulled up in his limo right now and offered to whisk me away, I'd turn him down."

"More likely he'd pull up and offer to whisk *me* away, but whatever."

On the other side of the parking lot, Billy was climbing out of his van. He glanced in their direction, then locked up and went inside.

"I'm so glad you invited me to come along," Joey said, practically giggling. He rubbed his hands together like some evil schemer. "Can I make believe I don't know him, too?"

"Just behave yourself."

"No way. This is gonna be too much fun."

⁓

While the girls had costumes, if you could call something the size of a dinner napkin a costume, the musicians wore black. Christa had lobbied for Billy to play shirtless, but to no avail. Bailey Swift had to stand out, and once

Kate saw him, she could see why. He looked more like a lounge singer than a rock star. His long, spiky black hair looked like a punk version of a bearskin hat. He wore a silky floral shirt unbuttoned to his navel, while several gold chains tangled in a thick carpet of black hair.

Across the room, men in dark suits conversed near a table set up as a bar. A tall, thin man with a dark beard, turtleneck sweater, and loud sport coat appeared to be the center of attention.

"That must be Davy Steinman," Kate whispered. "He's the producer. Billy said the money would be here tonight. I guess they must be backers or something. He's trying to sell this Swift guy." She motioned with her head to Bailey, who was circling the bar. "Billy said tonight is mostly about hearing the song, seeing the set, and getting some publicity shots with the window dressing, which includes yours truly." She curtsied.

Joey soaked up the goings-on of big business and money, while Kate tried to keep an eye on Billy without actually looking at him. She assumed the tiny blonde hanging all over him was Christa Dunphy. Noticing the proprietary hand on his arm, she wondered if Christa's insistence that Billy keep their relationship a secret had more to do with her wants than his needs. She was about to comment when Tiffany and Crystal arrived.

"Jeez," she whispered. "They're even taller standing up."

Joey gave her a quizzical look. "Most people are."

"You know what I mean. I'm gonna look like a shrimp next to them."

"Fried shrimp, if you fall off that trapeze."

"Don't remind me."

"You," the wardrobe mistress barked at Kate, "and you two. You need to get into costume."

Kate squeezed Joey's arm. "I wish I'd asked Billy for one of those little pills, but I'm afraid I'd be so mellow, I'd fall off my perch." She laughed nervously.

"You don't need a pill," he scolded. "You'll be great."

"Here's hoping. I'm also hoping someone turns up the heat, or swinging over a fire might be the best part."

⌒⌒

While Kate went off to get dressed, Joey began making the rounds, beginning with Billy and Christa.

"Hellooo," he said with a toothy smile, extending his hand. "I'm Joey Buccacino. My friend is one of the models."

Already sorry he'd agreed to let Joey come along, Billy accepted his hand, suppressing a mild look of annoyance.

"Billy McDonald," he muttered, shooting Joey a warning glance.

"I know a McDonald." Ignoring him, Joey furrowed his brow as if deep in thought. "Maybe I'm thinking of 'Old McDonald's Farm.'"

Billy scowled, but Christa cackled.

"I'm Christa Dunphy, Billy's agent."

"Oh, how fun!" Joey squealed. "I'll have to get me one of those."

"Why?" She seemed amused. "Are you a musician?"

"No, stylist—hair, makeup, clothing, you name it. Still in school, but already fabulous."

"I'll keep that in mind."

Joey gave her his best smile. "It was lovely to meet you, Christa." He nodded at Billy. "Barney."

Billy glared as he moved on to the other members of the band.

"Barney?" Christa said with a laugh. "How the hell did he get that from Billy?"

"He did that on purpose. He's Kate's friend."

"Oh." Her lips puckered as if she tasted something sour. "Where is she?"

"I dunno. Guess she's getting changed."

"I'm looking forward to meeting her." She sounded as if she'd be more excited about a root canal.

"You wanted to know who took Kate's photos." He pointed at Joey. "And he did her hair, makeup, all of it."

"Really?" She watched Joey work the room. "If he's that good, he just might need my services after all."

~

Without shoes, Kate was inches shorter than the two Amazons. Christa must have really wanted to please Billy to get her this gig.

She surveyed herself in the full-length mirror. Her breasts seemed much larger, and the top showed them off well. The other girls were overflowing theirs, which was probably exactly what the producer wanted. While they waited for the hair and makeup people, she slipped into her robe and wandered out onto the soundstage, looking for Joey. He was chatting with some suits, but when she caught his eye, he waved and excused himself.

"Oh my God, they're so boring," he whined. "Let's see." He pointed at the robe.

"Uh-uh."

"In a very short time, everyone here will see. Show me first." He tugged at her belt, but she slapped his hand away. Then she stepped back and flashed him.

"Too fast." He grabbed the edges of her robe and held it open. "Very nice." He nodded approvingly. "You almost gave *me* an erection!"

It seemed Joey wasn't the only one who appreciated Kate's figure. From across the room, Billy caught a glimpse of the exhibition and immediately began to berate himself—more so when he realized Bailey Swift had also noticed.

"Sorry, gentlemen," Bailey said, excusing himself. "I see something that needs my immediate attention." He headed for the bar amid the catcalls and whistles of the drummer and bass player, where he poured two glasses of Scotch. He strolled over and handed one to Kate, then he leaned in and said something to Joey, pointing to the other side of the room. Joey headed away, catching Billy's eye as he crossed the room. He flashed him a big smile and waved.

Sonofabitch.

Bailey rested his hand on the wall above Kate's head, while Billy clenched his jaw so hard it hurt.

"Well, well," Joey said, materializing alongside him. "Whaddaya plan to do about that?"

"I thought you were taking care of her."

"I was asked to walk her back and forth from the subway," Joey reminded him. "You didn't hire a babysitter. And frankly, she doesn't need one."

"You want her hanging out with that fucking jerk?"

"I don't know. What's one fucking jerk compared to another? Besides, they make a cute couple."

As he turned to walk away, Christa called out.

"Joey, right?"

He stopped and nodded.

"They've got a problem you might be able to solve."

"Me?"

"Somebody screwed up, and the makeup and hair people are scheduled for next Tuesday, not tonight. Can you do it?"

"Hell, yeah! I mean, I'll have to make do with what I have on me, but I can do it."

Christa looped her hand into the crook of his arm. "C'mon, I'll introduce you to Davy."

Joey shrugged. "We've met."

As Christa led him away, he grinned at Billy over his shoulder. "Look at me, saving the day!"

Scowling, Billy turned back toward Kate, but she was no longer visible. Bailey had been joined by one of the other guitar players and a sound tech. If he could figure out how to kick himself right now, he'd do it.

Joey set up shop in the small dressing room. He plugged in electric curlers, and set about putting the finishing touches on Kate's hair. She already knew how to blow it out and curl it, so all he needed was to make it bigger. He teased and sprayed until it was as big as it was going to get while she made faces at him in the mirror.

"I look like I could be in a Whitesnake video," she marveled, taking in the big hair and smoky eyes.

"You're a regular Tawny Kitaen."

"Could be, cuz I sure don't look like me."

Vacating the chair for Tiffany, she reached for her robe and headed toward the soundstage.

"Kate, wait." Joey motioned for her to come closer. "I think you should stay here with me. Somebody's about to blow an aneurysm."

A smile tugged at the corners of her mouth. "Oh really? Too bad, because I'm thirsty. Are you thirsty?"

"Well, I am a little dry." He grinned wickedly. "If you could just dart out and hurry back, I can't see what harm it would do."

She pursed her bright red lips, untied the robe and tossed it on a chair, and slipped into her black heels.

When she reached the soundstage, she hung back where she couldn't be seen and mentally prepared for what she was about to do. She'd have one chance, and since she'd be the first to be seen in costume, she had to make it good. The band was rehearsing. If she walked to the right side of the craft table, she'd be facing them. Of course, a view from behind could also be good. When had she had become so evil?

This is for you, Billy.

She hadn't gone but a few steps when the lead guitar screeched to a halt. The other instruments followed. It sounded like a musical car wreck, and it took all her resolve not to look in Billy's direction. She struggled to keep from smiling. She made her pass, her back to the now silent room, stretching across the table to grab a few olives. Then she walked to the bar, where she picked up two bottles of water. Moving deliberately, hips swinging naturally from the height of the heels, she made her way backstage.

As she cleared the partition, Joey yanked her into the back, causing her to almost stumble out of her shoes.

"Oh my God!" he squealed. "I had to come out when I heard the music stop. Holy shit, girl! If you'd been in Times Square, there wouldn't be enough hospitals to hold all the victims."

She giggled. "I can't believe that was because of me. I didn't expect that!"

"Are you kidding? You could stop traffic."

Behind her on the soundstage, they heard the director yell. "Back to work—show's over."

Joey squealed, then quickly lowered his voice. "I'd hate to be you tonight."

"You think he's mad?"

"Oh, I think he's a lot of things: hot, bothered, horny—and yeah, probably pissed. Your biggest problem is that just about every other man out there is also hot, bothered, and horny, including Bailey. Pretty sure he was drooling."

"Crap." She chewed on her finger. "If anyone says anything, I'll just say I have a boyfriend."

"Good idea. Just don't tell Billy that. Let him stew a bit."

"You're mean." She poked him in the gut.

"I know," he sang over his shoulder.

If Billy had been upset by Kate's little performance, she was equally upset by what followed as Joey put the finishing touches on Tiffany. Kate was reading in a chair behind him when she heard Billy's name.

"Oh, trust me," Tiffany was saying. "I'm nailing that before the week is out."

Kate's head shot up. Joey struggled to keep from smiling.

"Not if I get him first," Crystal said.

"Well, we could share. There's certainly enough of him to go around."

Crystal hummed in agreement.

Tiffany caught sight of Kate glaring at her in the mirror. "You got a problem?"

"Me? Nope." Kate smiled sweetly. When the girl looked back at her friend, Kate narrowed her eyes and clenched her teeth.

Joey coughed to keep from laughing.

"We have an early rehearsal Thursday." Tiffany continued as if she and Crystal were alone. "I'll invite him over afterward. Guys like that can't turn down a threesome."

Kate cursed under her breath. She flipped the page of her book so hard it tore.

Tiffany was about to respond to Kate's grumbling when Joey yanked her hair. "Sorry, love," he cooed. "Knot." She scowled, then went back to discussing how they planned to seduce the hot, blond guitarist.

Kate pretended to read, swinging her foot furiously. When she glanced up at Joey, he pressed his lips together and tried to hide his smile.

Billy didn't say a word when he picked them up at the subway station, and he did little more than grunt when he dropped Joey off at his station a few blocks later. He remained quiet as they drove through Brooklyn, over the Williamsburg Bridge, and into Lower Manhattan. Kate tried several times to engage him in conversation, but he just stared straight ahead, saying nothing.

After they pulled into the parking lot behind their apartment, he turned off the van and sat drumming his fingers on the steering wheel. She waited until he got out, then followed, expecting to help carry his bags.

"I got it," he snapped.

"Fine." It was her turn to get angry. She'd only agreed to do this video because of him. Plus it was his idea—or Christa's, the little blond weasel—that no one know they were a couple. It wasn't her fault she caused a stir. Not totally.

She bolted ahead, letting the door slam shut as he approached, and stomped up the stairs and down the hall to their apartment. Throwing her bag on the couch, she went into the bathroom to take off her makeup.

When she came out, Billy was sitting on the bed.

"You think you're pretty funny, don't you?"

"Me? I think I'm hilarious."

As she stormed past him, Billy grabbed her by the hand and pulled her into his lap, locking his arms around her. She sat stiffly, staring straight ahead, her jaw tight, not willing to look at him.

"I'm sorry," he said finally, pressing his forehead into her shoulder. "I'm not mad at you. I'm mad at me."

"That makes two of us."

"I'm an idiot. I shouldn't have talked you into this, and I shouldn't have agreed to keep you a secret."

"Are you saying that because you didn't like Bailey hitting on me or the other guys looking at me?"

"I didn't like any of it. I also didn't like you having to walk in without me and leave without me, even with Joey—who hates me, by the way."

"He doesn't hate you."

He snorted. "I'll call Christa tomorrow. Tell her we're not doing this."

"The video?"

"No. That we have to do. But I'm not making believe we're not a couple. I don't see the need for it. I'm not in this for the women. I'm a musician, not a gigolo."

"You don't want to be both?"

He shook his head.

"Aww," she purred. "Too bad."

He looked up, surprised. "What does that mean?"

"You'll see."

By the next morning, Kate had convinced Billy to go along with Christa, insisting she should know what's best for his career. He reluctantly agreed. So just like they'd done earlier, they arrived at rehearsal Thursday like two strangers. Billy dropped Kate off a block away and insisted on waiting until she turned into the soundstage parking lot. Then because his rehearsal didn't start for another two hours, he hung out at a bar around the corner.

Kate had just changed into a leotard and was slipping into the high heels she'd be wearing to rehearse when she heard the director shout something across the set.

"Yeah, you. Shorty," he called when she looked up. "C'mere." Tiffany was standing beside him, her arms folded, legs a mile long, glaring in Kate's direction.

She threw a quick glance over her shoulder, and seeing no one there, assumed that she must be "Shorty."

"Yes, sir?"

"Change of plans. You're the lead dancer now."

Nausea gave way to full-blown panic. "That can't be right. I . . . um . . ." *Um what, Kate? Excuse me, sir. I'm only here because my secret boyfriend is in the band.*

"Um nothing," the director finished for her. "Bailey's too freakin' short. Next to them, he looks like a mutant." He aimed a thumb at Legs 1 and 2. "You're up, Shorty."

"I'm five six," Kate said in a squeaky voice, as if it would make a difference.

"Perfect," he said as he led her over to the choreographer.

The dance moves amounted to little more than wiggling her hips, draping herself all over Bailey, and tossing her head an obscene number of times.

The worst part—worse than having to run her hands over Bailey's coarse, black chest hair—was the trapeze. Instead of just standing on one of the two swings like she'd originally been told, she would be in the spotlight with Bailey. Tiffany would now join Crystal in the back, which explained the evil stares aimed in her direction. She would've traded with either of them in a heartbeat, especially after seeing the look on Billy's face when he walked in the door, just as she leaned back in Bailey's arms and he buried his face in her neck.

On the plus side, if there was one, it turned out they would be swinging over a make-believe fire. The real fire would be filmed separately and spliced into the final footage. The most dangerous thing she had to do was hook her legs on the trapeze bar, lean back, and reach for Bailey while swinging.

As the night wore on, Bailey bounced between practicing with the band and practicing with Kate. It wasn't going well. She was having a hard time letting go of the ropes, and the director, whom she now thought of as Hitler, kept yelling at her.

"One more time," he called. Kate settled onto the swing. The band gathered around to watch.

Great. She wanted to throw up. Billy stood with his arms folded, looking nervous. From the corner of her eye, she spied Crystal and Tiffany making their way toward him. *Just great.* She hadn't told him of their plans. Maybe it was wrong, but she wanted to know she could trust him. She could still hear Tiffany's claim that "guys like that" couldn't resist a threesome, and she needed to know that he could.

"C'mon, love," Bailey said, pulling back her focus. "You can do it."

Fueled by anger and adrenaline, Kate gripped the thick ropes and pumped her legs, building up speed. On the director's command, she let go. Leaning back gracefully, she made the connection, grazing Bailey's hands with her own.

"Finally!" Hitler yelled. "Take five!"

Billy flashed her a wink and joined the rest of the crew in applauding. The only people not celebrating were Crystal and Tiffany, whose efforts at seducing Billy had been waylaid by Kate's brief brush with success.

If nothing else, they were determined. Kate remained on her perch and watched as Tiffany ran her fingers down Billy's arm. She could only imagine what the Amazonian slut might be saying.

Kate was torn between not letting Billy catch her watching and shooting daggers at him so he'd know she was on to them. But when she caught his eye a short time later, he winked. She responded by batting her eyes.

Rehearsal had run late, thanks to her. She was gathering her things and preparing to walk to the subway when Bailey came over and asked if she'd like to go for a drink, to "see where the night takes them."

She gave him a stiff smile. "I'm sorry, I'm not old enough to drink." He looked surprised. "Plus I'm in a pretty serious relationship."

"Oh." His obvious disappointment gave her ego the boost it needed. "No harm done."

"Absolutely not, but thank you. I'm flattered."

Billy observed their encounter from across the room as he rolled his guitar cord in a loop around his elbow and his thumb. What he really wanted, was to wrap the cord around the Limey's neck.

"Strike out?" he asked as Bailey approached.

Bailey looked at Kate wistfully. "Afraid so. Says she's in a serious relationship."

Billy smiled. "That so?"

"Apparently."

"Lucky guy," he said, his smile spreading into a grin.

Bailey nodded.

Billy hurried to pack the rest of his things, finishing as Kate slipped into her coat. She was heading toward the door, chatting with one of the director's assistants, when he called to her from across the soundstage.

"Katie!"

She looked up.

"Hang on."

He hoisted his bag and guitar case, then jogged toward her. He took her bag and slipped it over his shoulder, then cupped her stunned face with both hands and kissed her.

"C'mon, babe," he said, draping his arm around her neck and dropping another kiss on top of her head. "Let's go home."

CHAPTER 23

It didn't take long for the news to reach Christa.

"I hope you understand you blew it." Her voice screeched across the long-distance connection. "Bailey's pissed. Apparently he had a thing for your little girlfriend. He thinks the two of you made him look like a fool."

"That was your idea, not mine."

"It was my idea to keep it quiet, not to broadcast it two seconds after he hit on her. Jesus, Billy. He wanted you off the video, but Davy smoothed it over. He's not too happy either, by the way."

"Why? He have designs on Kate, too?" Billy gripped the phone in one hand while he squeezed the other into a fist.

"You pissed off his star, sweetheart. You're lucky I know how to write a contract, or you'd be back playing dive bars tout suite. When this video comes out, no one will know your name. If you're happy playing in the background, I can get you all the two-bit gigs you want. You know what? Strike that. I deal in the big time, babe. So if you want to be front and center, then you better start listening to me. Otherwise, you can handle your own career, and see how far you go."

He was still worked up a few hours later. Kate wasn't home yet, and he had to be out on Long Island by six thirty. If they hit traffic, it could take them well over an hour.

Although he was relieved when he heard her key in the lock, he still nearly erupted when he saw her.

"Do you know what time it is?"

Her face blank, she shook her head.

"It's almost five. I told you this morning I wanted to leave by four thirty. Where's your watch?"

She dropped her purse on the kitchen table, along with the paper sacks of groceries she'd been carrying. "I think it's on the dresser."

"Jesus, Kate." He stormed into the bedroom and returned with the watch. "Are you ready to go?"

"I just need to eat something." She began putting the perishables away.

"There's no time. You know what traffic's gonna be like on a Friday."

"I haven't eaten since this morning."

"We'll eat later. I can't eat before playing, anyway. Just go." He turned her in the direction of the bathroom. "Five minutes."

While Kate did whatever it was she needed to do, he carried his guitars to the van. She was still in the bathroom when he returned.

He rapped on the door. "What're you doing?" It was wrong for him to take his anger out on her, but he couldn't stop himself. Besides, she knew he hated to be late.

"I'll be right out." Her voice was strained. "Could you please make me a sandwich? I'll eat it in the car."

"Christ," he yelled. "Hurry up!"

He stalked into the kitchen, where he began slamming cabinets and drawers. Why shouldn't he take it out on her? If it wasn't for her, he wouldn't be in this position. If he hadn't fucking fallen in love, he wouldn't be jeopardizing everything he had worked for. He opened the packet of lunch meat she'd bought and nearly gagged. Liverwurst. He hated liver. He'd be damned if he was going to smell that all the way to Massapequa. He threw the packet in the fridge and grabbed a banana off the counter.

"Kate!" he yelled. "Now!"

Kate had come to believe that if anything could destroy their relationship, it would be Billy's obsession with being early.

If it were only that simple.

They made it to the club just before six thirty, even with stopping to pick up Joey in Brooklyn. They were still on time—but since they weren't the first to arrive, in his mind that made them late.

Billy had been silent the entire trip, which was usually the case when Joey was around. On the other hand, she had been quiet as well, but Joey had jabbered nonstop about the phone call from Davy Steinman asking him to do hair and makeup for the video. Steinman had been so impressed with what Joey had been able to pull off the night of the promotional event, he fired the other crew and gave Joey the job. He was already lining Joey up for some of his other projects as well.

They had barely claimed their seats at a table near the stage when Joey turned on her.

"What the hell is wrong with you?" he demanded, swiping at a curl that had dropped into his eye. "You didn't say two words the entire trip. I expect that from Mr. Personality, but not from you."

Billy was still hauling in amps and instruments, so now was as good a time as any. *Here goes nothing.* She slid her chair close enough that they were almost touching, then she leaned forward and whispered in his ear.

"*What?*"

"Lower your voice," she whispered urgently.

"How long?"

"Eight or nine weeks."

Joey looked toward Billy, who was joking around with Denny.

"He's taking it well."

She looked up cautiously. Afraid to speak, she could only nod.

Joey's eyes widened. "He doesn't know?"

"No. I just found out. Then when I got home, he was barking at me because we were gonna be late. And then I threw up."

He let out a long stream of air. "Guess that explains all the vomiting."

"Ya think?"

"Weren't you on some kind of birth control?"

She shook her head. When he opened his mouth, she cut him off. "Don't start. I was, and then . . ." She pressed her fist against her mouth as hot tears blurred her vision. "I screwed up. I don't know what to do. He's gonna kill me."

Joey gripped her shoulders, forcing her to look at him. It was rare to see him look so serious. "He lays one hand on you, I'll kill him with my bare hands."

"Thanks, but he'd swat you away like a fly."

"Still."

"He won't hurt me. Not physically. But he's not going to be okay with this."

Joey turned in his seat and watched Billy. She was actually afraid he might jump up and go after him. When he turned back to face her, he seemed calmer, more resigned.

"You gonna keep it?"

"Of course!" She placed a protective hand over her belly. Clearly, not everyone was cut out to be a mother—this she knew first-hand. But to not want a baby created with someone she loved? She couldn't even imagine.

"I'm glad, but you know there're options."

"Not for me."

Joey pulled her in for a hug. "You know Uncle Joey's here for you."

The tears fell harder.

"Stop. You're gonna look like a drag queen on prom night." He grabbed a paper napkin from the dispenser on the table and handed it to her. "When are you gonna tell him?"

"I don't know. He's been in a terrible mood. I'll probably wait until after the video."

He was about to respond but stopped and squeezed her arm. When she looked up, she saw Billy walking toward them.

"Hey," he said, spinning a chair around and straddling it. "The kitchen won't be open for another hour, but I asked, and they could make you a burger or something. That okay?" He gave Joey a less than friendly look. "You too."

"Aren't you a doll?" Joey exclaimed, his voice dripping with sarcasm.

Billy scowled, then turned back to Kate. "I'm sorry."

She tried to smile. "A burger would be great."

"You feeling okay?"

"I'm fine."

"I forgot to ask you. What did the doctor say?"

She dropped her eyes and focused on the serpent hanging from a thick silver chain around his neck. "The infection's gone."

"That's good. What about the nausea? Were you throwing up again?"

"That should stop soon."

"She say what's causing it?"

Her eyes widening, she shot a quick glance at Joey. "I, um, need to eat on a regular basis. Smaller meals. I've been skipping meals. That could make it worse."

"You should do that then."

"I know."

Billy nodded as he stood. "We okay?"

Kate smiled and blinked back tears, glad that the large room was so dimly lit. "Uh-huh."

"Good." He squeezed her shoulder, then bent to kiss her.

"Kate, don't," Joey begged after Billy had walked away, but it was no use. She covered her face with her hands and sobbed into the paper napkin.

CHAPTER 24

Kate nibbled on a saltine as she watched two fat squirrels chase each other across the sidewalk. She reached into her pocket for another cracker, broke it in half, and tossed the pieces on the ground. The squirrels scampered forward, each snatching a half.

She'd spent a good part of the afternoon huddled on a bench near the hotel where she and Billy were staying during the video shoot, rehearsing scenarios in her head of how to tell him she was pregnant. She would have preferred a grand gesture: having him unwrap a pair of booties or finding a rattle hiding in the pocket of his guitar case. She imagined those methods probably worked better when a couple had been together longer than three months and had at least had a conversation about becoming a family.

No, stashing a pacifier in with his guitar picks probably wouldn't go over well at this stage of the game. She'd just have to be honest and straightforward.

Billy was filming the music portion of the video on location in Manhattan. Tonight they'd be shooting in the studio and then wrapping up tomorrow. Depending what time they got home, she would make him a nice dinner—maybe meat loaf—and then she'd tell him.

And if not tomorrow, then definitely the next night.

She brushed bread crumbs from her lap and stood. At least she had a plan. It wasn't a great plan, but it was the best she could come up with.

~

Kate unlocked the door to their room to find Billy standing at the window, staring out over the street. He didn't turn when she opened the door, even though he must have seen her walking up the block.

"Where've you been?" he asked, his voice unusually flat.

Slipping off her coat, she tossed it onto the bed. "I took a walk, then I went to the park. I didn't expect you back so early."

He didn't answer; he just stood there, staring. Had something gone wrong during filming? If it had, it couldn't have been his fault. He'd been brilliant during rehearsal, like always. His reflection in the glass offered no clue to what he was thinking.

"I'll get ready now. I just want to brush my teeth and throw some things in my bag."

When she entered the bathroom, she was surprised to see the contents of her cosmetics case had been dumped into the sink. She anxiously swirled her hand through the mess, then snatched the bag from the floor. It was empty. She spun around to find Billy standing in the doorway.

"Looking for these?" He held up her bottle of prenatal vitamins.

Her heart hammering, she clutched the empty bag to her chest.

"I hope what you want to tell me is that you bought these by mistake." The muscles flickered along his jawline.

She couldn't answer; she couldn't even move.

He pounded his fist into the frame of the door. She flinched and pressed herself against the sink.

"How long?" he demanded.

"How long have I known or how far along am I?" Her throat was tight and the words so low, she was surprised he'd heard her.

"Both, actually." The look he gave her was hard and cold.

She hugged her arms around her waist. "About nine weeks," she stammered. "And I've known since I saw the doctor last week. I was going to tell you tomorrow, after we finished." She didn't think he would hit her, but he looked like he wanted to. "I had an ultrasound Monday. The baby's due October 2."

Turning away, he drifted toward the bed and sat. He dropped his head into his hands. It seemed a few times as if he would say something, but nothing came out.

"Billy, I'm sorry. I didn't mean—" She took a few steps toward him, but he raised his hand for her to stop. When he finally looked up, his eyes were two blue chips of ice.

"What are you going to do about it?"

"What?"

"What are you planning to do?"

Other than having the baby, she didn't have a clue what she was doing. She assumed they'd figure it out together. She was about to say so, when he stood.

"I have to go."

"Billy!"

He raised his hands in warning. "Back off, Kate."

"But the video—"

"Back. Off."

So she did.

CHAPTER 25

"Fuck!" Billy pounded his fist into the steering wheel. *This cannot be happening.* He pounded it again.

How could she do this to me?

He jammed the key into the ignition, shifted the van into gear, and squealed out of the parking lot onto Montague Street. At the first liquor store he came to, he bought a bottle of Jack, then drove to the pier to drink it. There were no answers at the bottom of the bottle, and whiskey sure as hell wasn't going to improve his temper, but at this moment, he really didn't give a shit.

Boats passed on the East River while the Statue of Liberty loomed in the distance, most likely giving him the finger. Why not? The whole fucking world was out to get him. He should've known better than to think things were finally going his way.

He watched the sun sinking into the horizon. His head dropped back, and he took one last swig before he capped the bottle and stowed it under his seat.

By the time he arrived at the soundstage, he was ugly drunk. Carrying his half-empty bottle, he pushed past Bailey and the director, waving them off when they complained about how late he was or asked about Kate.

He headed straight for the dressing room. Joey was working on the brunette. The other, the blonde, sat near the door, thumbing through a magazine. He swept everything off the makeup table and perched on the edge, glaring at Joey.

"Hey!" Joey yelled as the brunette jumped from the chair. "What the hell is wrong with you?"

"You knew."

Joey glared at him. "Of course I knew!" he shouted. "You'd have known, too, if you thought about someone other than yourself."

Billy made a fist and pulled back. He ought to punch the arrogant sonofabitch in his pretty little face. He surprised himself when he didn't, because he sure as hell wanted to hit somebody.

"Fuck you." He swayed as he stood. He started out of the dressing room, then grabbed the blonde and yanked her to her feet. He shot Joey an evil smile as he trundled her out the door.

"Fuck you, too, you loser!" Joey called after him.

He dragged the girl across the soundstage, drawing lewd comments from the band and crew.

"It's okay, baby," she said as she stumbled behind him. "You don't have to force me. I'm coming."

He pulled her inside the small office near the entrance and slammed the door. Slumping against the wall, he unscrewed the cap from the whiskey and drank deeply. He dragged the back of his hand across his mouth. His tongue felt thick and heavy.

"What's your name again?" he asked as she tugged at his belt buckle.

"Tiffany," she whispered into his neck. She caught the tip of his ear in her teeth.

"Take off your clothes, Tiffany." He took another long pull on the bottle.

The leather bikini wasn't coming off easily. She struggled with the top for so long he finally reached around and unhooked the clasp, exposing a pair of breasts that had clearly been enhanced. The bottom half wouldn't budge.

"There's plenty of time for that," she purred. "In the meantime, let me take your mind off whatever's got you so worked up."

In her heels, she stood just a few inches shorter than him. She tried to press her lips against his, but he turned his face.

"No. No kissing."

"Oh," she cooed, "I left lipstick on your chin." She rubbed at it with her thumb, smearing it along his jaw. She picked up his hand and placed it over her breast. When she let go, he let it fall, staring at the opposite wall. He took another drink.

His lack of participation didn't deter her. She slipped her hands under his shirt, raking her nails over his skin as she lowered herself to a squat, balancing on her heels like a pro. "You just relax and let me see if I can get little Billy to come out and play."

She unzipped his jeans and slid them over his hips. He leaned his head against the wall and closed his eyes. This was the way it was supposed to be. No emotion. No commitment. Take what he could and move the fuck on.

When her hand wrapped around his dick, his eyes flew open.

Fuck.

He grabbed her wrist, squeezing until she let go.

"What's the matter, baby?"

Baby? Fuck!

"Stop. Don't." He gave her a shove, and she landed on her leather-covered ass.

"What the fuck is your problem?" she said, as he tugged at his zipper.

He looked around the room as if he'd suddenly realized where he was. "Nothing. I changed my mind."

"You changed your mind? What the hell?"

What the hell was right. What was he thinking? He'd had hundreds of girls like this one. This wasn't what he wanted. Not anymore. He reached into his wallet, pulled out a twenty, and tossed it to her.

"What the—?" She threw it back. "Fuck you!"

"No thanks."

Kate had no idea how long she stared at the door. Voices floated down the corridor. Tiny footsteps ran past, a mother scolded. Slivers of light cast a patchwork onto the floor as the room grew dark. She turned on the lamp, then she sat down on the bed. Still she waited.

Nearly two hours had passed. The watch Billy insisted she wear weighed heavy on her wrist. She emptied the contents of her wallet onto the bed. Four dollars and change, a subway token, and a button from her winter coat that she kept forgetting to sew back on. There wasn't enough money to get back to Bayonne. And evens if she could, then what? Every minute that ticked by pushed them farther apart. She couldn't stay, and she couldn't get home. Joey would be at the soundstage by now, so she couldn't even reach him. He would be wondering where she was by now.

A different kind of nausea gripped her. She picked up the phone and dialed.

"Mom?" The tightness in her throat prevented her from speaking above a whisper.

"Yes?"

"It's Kate. How are you?"

"Fine."

"I haven't spoken to you and—"

"That was your choice. Are you in trouble?"

"Not really, but—"

"Then what is it?" She seemed annoyed, as if Kate was interrupting something important. Then again, wasn't that how she'd always spoke to Kate? She covered the receiver, and although her voice was muffled, Kate could still hear. "No one. Hand me my drink, please."

It was nearly seven. Cocktail time would be winding down. Her mother would be finishing her Rob Roy about now, and then it would be time for dinner. Did they still eat in the dining room, or had they settled for the informality of the kitchen now that she was gone?

"You were saying?" Her voice was as cold as the ice Kate could hear clinking in her glass.

"I wanted to let you know I'm okay and say I'm sorry I left like I did. That was wrong."

"Yes, it was. Is there anything else?"

"Not really. Um—"

"Good. Thank you for calling."

Kate waited until she heard the dial tone before hanging up.

It didn't take long to pack. She stuffed her money into the front pocket of her jeans, put her purse over her shoulder, and her coat on over that. Then she hoisted the duffle bag, lifted her suitcase, and left, closing the door behind her with a quiet thump.

It was dark now and colder. She reached into her pockets, but all she found was the empty cellophane sleeve from the crackers she'd fed to the squirrels and one glove. The other must have fallen when she pulled the room key from her pocket. She'd left the key upstairs on the dresser, next to the watch she'd also left behind. She slipped on the glove and picked up her suitcase, then shoved her bare hand into her pocket.

The street was nearly empty. Dead leaves skittered around her feet. A paper cup cartwheeled across the sidewalk. Two men stood in the doorway of a bodega on Joralemon Street. They called to her as she passed. Eyes straight ahead, she quickened her pace. As she rounded the corner onto Court Street, she nearly stumbled over a homeless man curled atop a subway grate. She hurried past, but before she reached the entrance to Borough Hall Station, she slowed, then turned back.

"Here," she said, holding out one of her precious dollars. Blue eyes stared up at her, one clear, one milky. "Take it." The man uncurled a filthy hand. She pressed the bill into his palm, then pulled off her glove and gave him that as well. "I only have the one," she said apologetically.

"Bless you." His voice rasped, as if it hadn't been used for a long time.

"Thank you," she said with a sniff. She grabbed her suitcase and headed for the station.

She didn't have much, but at least she'd have a roof over her head tonight.

CHAPTER 26

Billy leaned against the wall in the dingy hall. He was drunk. Drunk enough not to have been driving. Drunk enough not to have any conversations about being a father. And drunk enough to know if he didn't get back to Kate, he was likely to do something really stupid.

He was also too drunk to get the fucking key into the fucking lock. With an angry toss of his head, he brushed the hair from his eyes, aimed the key toward the hole, and pushed open the door.

Before his eyes could adjust to the darkness, he felt his way to the bathroom and flipped on the light. The bed was empty. He scanned the room, as if Kate might have been sitting in the dark, even though he knew damn well she was afraid of the dark. One of her sweaters was folded neatly at the foot of the bed. Two pairs of dangly earrings he'd just bought her and the book she'd been reading lay on top. He picked up the book and turned it over in his hands. *Flowers for Algernon*. It was one of his. Her place was marked with the ticket stub from *Cats*.

He hurled the book across the room. The ticket stub fluttered through the air and landed near a lone glove.

"Ah jeez, Katie." It was freezing outside.

He lifted her sweater and pressed it to his nose. The clean, sweet scent of oranges curled around him, soothing him for just a moment. There were the potholders she'd been making, as well as the spool of thread and the little pair of scissors he'd bought her. Maybe she hadn't left. Maybe she'd just gone out. That thought didn't calm him any.

He checked the bathroom. Her toothbrush and makeup kit were gone. He wheeled around and scanned the bedroom again, as if it might hold a clue to where she'd gone.

A glint of metal caught his eye. Her watch. Her fucking watch. It sat on the dresser next to the key. He picked it up, then dropped it to the floor, crushing it beneath the heel of his boot.

"Happy?" he yelled.

Nausea turned his stomach, and he gripped the edge of the dresser until it passed. Then he picked up a chair and threw it across the room. It slammed into the wall, the leg snapping off.

"Fuck you, Kate!" he yelled. An angry fist pounded on the wall from the room next door. "Fuck you, too!"

He yanked at the lamp, but it was bolted to the table. His heart was beating against his chest like he'd just run up twenty flights of stairs. He dropped heavily onto the edge of the bed and held his head in his hands. The room was spinning, and the images going through his mind weren't helping. Tiffany. The feel of her hand on his dick.

Tearing off his clothes, he headed for the shower where he caught a glimpse of himself in the mirror. Red lipstick stained his cheek, and he was filled with sadness and disgust.

He stepped into the shower, letting the scalding water punish him, ignoring the burning for as long as he could stand it. A chunk of Kate's soap sat on the edge of the tub. Picking it up, he held it to his nose. He scrubbed his face and his body until there was nothing left but a sliver. When he was done, he dragged himself into bed, the rough sheets small penance against his irritated skin.

Hours later, still awake and feeling only slightly less drunk, he grew more anxious. There was no reason to stay. Kate wasn't coming back. She probably wasn't home, either. He imagined she'd gone to Joey's. Too bad he didn't know where Joey lived or how to get in touch with him.

He needed coffee. And something to calm his stomach so he could think. After jamming his things into his bag, along with everything Kate had left behind, he checked out and drove to a nearby diner. The place was packed with the morning rush. The clatter of dishes and the cacophony of caffeinated patrons almost made him walk out, but the need for caffeine of his own trumped his aching head.

Bent over a cup of black coffee, he tried to determine what he could've done differently. There were a lot of things. Wearing a condom would have been a good start, or at making sure Kate had renewed her birth control prescription.

He racked his brain so hard, his head hurt even worse.

"Bullshit." This was as much his fault as it was hers. Or was it? Could he have been this lax on purpose?

"What the fuck, Donaldson?" he muttered into his cup, wishing it held something stronger. If that was what he'd done—gotten her pregnant on purpose—it had to be subconscious. He pressed his fingers into his eyes until spots danced behind the lids.

"More coffee?"

He looked up to find a waitress with a warm smile and a fresh pot. He pushed his cup forward.

"You need someone to talk to?" she asked as she poured. "Or you just gonna sit there mumblin' and scarin' my customers?"

"Sorry. Was I talking out loud?"

"Little bit. You okay?"

"Not really."

She set the pot down, then leaned on the counter. "What's wrong, honey?"

What the hell? "I just found out my girlfriend's having a baby." *Baby.* The word suddenly felt foreign on his tongue.

"Is it yours?"

He shot her a look. "Of course it's mine." A short silence. "Yeah. Of course."

She lifted her shoulders. "Ya never know."

The busboy dropped a tray of dirty dishes behind him. Silverware clattered to the floor. Dishes shattered. Billy cringed as the noise ricocheted inside his aching head.

He rubbed his fingers in circles over his temples. "I know."

"You love her?"

He nodded.

"She love you?"

"Yeah." His voice quavered and almost broke. He hoped she wouldn't notice.

"Then what's the problem? Kids are great. Got three of my own. The oldest starts college in the fall."

He forced a wan smile. "Seriously? You don't look old enough for a kid in college."

Her laugh was so loud, he winced.

"I'm not! Got knocked up in high school, but it turned out okay."

"You get married?"

"Nah. Bastard disappeared two seconds after he found out. Good riddance, right? But he did give me a terrific present. Wanna see a picture?"

Billy read the tag over her left pocket: Susie. "Sure."

She headed for the kitchen, topping off other customers on the way. When she returned, she handed him two wallet-sized photos.

"This is my oldest, Bethany." Looked like the girl's senior picture.

"Very pretty."

She pointed at the second picture. "This is Bethany, of course. This is Matt, my boy, and that's my youngest, Kathleen, but we call her Katie."

An elephant backed into his chest and sat down. "Katie, huh? She's a cutie."

"Yep. They're the best thing that ever happened to me. Even if every one of their fathers was a rat bastard."

He sat up straighter. "That sucks."

She shrugged. "It is what it is. Whaddabout you? You gonna be a rat bastard?"

"Huh?"

"You don't seem over the moon about this baby thing. You're not thinkin' about runnin', are ya?"

"No. She already did that."

She snorted. "That's a new one. You goin' after her?"

"You ask a lot of questions, you know that?"

She smiled and crossed her arms. "That's my job—part waitress, part conscience. So waddaya gonna to do about it?"

Why did his conscience suddenly sounded like it was in the mob?

"You're pretty pushy for someone who expects a tip."

"And you don't seem like the kinda guy who'd stiff a single workin' mother with three kids to raise."

He nodded.

"Well?"

He leaned back. "Yeah."

"Yeah, what?"

"Yeah, I'm going after her, okay?"

"Then what?"

"Beats the hell outta me. First I have to find her."

A customer signaled for Susie. She patted his hand. "You'll figure it out."

As he spooned sugar into his cup, trying to figure it out, it dawned on him that something hadn't been right with the hotel bill. He pulled it from his pocket and unfolded it. One night, plus tax. Under additional charges there was $25 for the stupid chair leg, and $11.85 for a phone call

He threw a ten on the counter, called his thanks to Susie, and bolted out the door. A few minutes later he was back at the hotel, pounding on the front desk bell.

"Look at this," he said when the clerk appeared, stabbing the paper repeatedly with his finger. "Right here. What's this?" She looked nervous. He pointed again. "Here."

"That's for a phone call."

"When? Do you know when it was made and to where?"

"That may take a few minutes."

"Look it up," he demanded. "I need to know."

Fifteen minutes later, he was on his way to New Jersey. The call had been made last night, 6:46 p.m., a 201 number.

Katie had called her parents.

CHAPTER 27

Billy rang the bell, then knocked impatiently. Peering through the front windows, he could see the parlor was empty. It was the same when he peeked through the lace curtains at the back door. He circled the house, then sat on the porch. He'd wait all day if he had to.

He'd been there about twenty minutes when a girl about Kate's age came out of the neighboring house, walking a small dog.

"You okay?" she asked when she saw him.

"No," he answered. "Do you know where Katie is?"

"Katie?" She seemed confused. "Oh, Kate! No. I haven't seen her since Christmas. Sorry. Apparently she ran off with some deadbeat. Quit school and everything. Broke her parents' hearts." She laughed, which seemed odd given what she was saying. "She's a cautionary tale around here."

He shook his head. "I think her parents brought her home last night."

"I don't think so. There was a school board meeting, and my dad went with Mr. Daniels. Mrs. Daniels' car was parked out front all night." She pointed toward her house. "That's my room. I was up pretty late. Unless she came home in the middle of the night, she's not here."

"I'm almost positive."

"Nope."

This was getting him nowhere. "Do you know where her parents are?"

"School, I guess. I have the Dragon Lady this year for English." She leaned closer and lowered her voice. "Honestly, if they were my parents, I'd have run away a long time ago."

"Why aren't you in school?"

She coughed. "I have a headache."

"Where's the school?"

"Just keep going that way." She pointed back in the direction he'd come. "You can't miss it. I'm Debby, by the way. Who're you?"

"I'm the deadbeat," he said as he headed for his van.

~

Classes were changing as Billy entered the high school. He pushed his way through the crowded lobby to the office and waited at the counter. An older woman, her back to him, was leafing through a filing cabinet. Stella Blazczykowski read the sign on her desk.

When she turned, he flashed his best smile. "Stella? Is it okay if I call you Stella?"

Her hand floated up to pat a hairdo that roughly resembled a football helmet. "Of course." She smiled as if they were old friends.

"Stella," he said, lowering his voice, forcing her to lean closer. "I need to see Mr. and Mrs. Daniels."

"They're probably in class, but let me check." She flipped through a log book on her desk. "Here we go. Mr. Daniels has a class, but Mrs. Daniels should be free."

"Where can I find them?"

She directed him toward an adjacent conference room. "You can wait in there while I page them. Who should I say is here?"

"It's a surprise." He winked. "You wouldn't want to spoil the surprise, would you?"

"I guess not." She flushed a warm pink. "Have a seat. I'll see what I can do."

He wasn't about to sit. Instead, he leaned against the table, arms folded and waited.

Mrs. Daniels arrived first. Judging by the sour expression on her face, she was not happy to see him.

"What do you want?"

Before he could answer, Mr. Daniels joined them. Billy got a sick feeling when he saw them exchange curious glances.

"What's going on here?" Kate's father asked. Unlike his wife, who didn't have a single wrinkle in her navy dress or a hair out of place, his suit was rumpled and he looked as if he'd combed his hair with his fingers.

"Where's Katie?" Billy asked.

"Kate," her mother corrected. "And what do you mean, where is she? Did you lose her?"

He could do without the sarcasm. He lowered his head and began to count. When he looked up, he met her icy glare with equal hostility.

"I know she called last night. I want to know where she is."

Mr. Daniels shook his head. "We haven't spoken to Kate since she left."

His wife touched his arm. "Yes, she called."

"What?" he stammered. "Evelyn, you never—"

She silenced him with a wave of her hand.

"I spoke with Kate. She said she was fine. I asked if she was in trouble, she said no, then she apologized for running off." She leveled a smug gaze at Billy. "I asked if there was anything else, she said there wasn't, and I thanked her for calling."

"Why didn't you tell me?" Mr. Daniels asked.

She gave him a cursory glance. "There was no need to concern you. Kate needs to suffer the consequences of her actions or she'll never learn. She said she was fine. I saw no reason to believe otherwise."

Returning her attention to Billy, she continued. "I don't know your reason for showing up here, but if you're looking for money, you're out of luck. Kate emptied her bank account, and if you've blown through that already, I suggest you both find jobs. I'm sure she would make a competent waitress."

He had never hit a woman, but this bitch was begging for it.

"Look, if Evelyn says she doesn't know where Kate is, then she doesn't know," Mr. Daniels insisted. "If anyone knows, it would be Joey. Other than that, I'm afraid we can't help you."

Disgusted by their lack of concern, Billy stared down at them. "Aren't you the least bit concerned about her?"

"No," her mother answered. "Kate has always been flighty and headstrong. She demonstrated that when she threw away a promising future to run off with you. The fact that she left you just proves I'm right."

One more word, and his head might explode. "Was she adopted or something? I mean, man—I had some shitty parents, but at least I had grandparents who loved me. You two? Unbelievable. Sad thing is, I don't think you even know her. She's sweet and funny. She's the kindest person I've ever known, and let me tell you, my grandma was a saint. Katie? Hell, she even puts *her* to shame."

"Kate," her mother corrected.

"You are fucking unbelievable, lady!" He took a step toward her and almost smiled when she stumbled backwards.

"I'm outta here, but let me say this. I'd rather our kid have no grandparents than to have either of you in his life."

"What?" Mr. Daniels stammered, but Billy just kept on walking. As far as he was concerned, they didn't deserve one more second of his time.

⁓

The apartment was empty. He hadn't expected Kate to be there, but knowing she hadn't come home made him feel worse. She had to be with Joey. Why didn't he know where that fucker lived?

Although he doubted he would take the call, especially after firing him, the only person he could think of who might know how to reach Joey was Davy Steinman. Or maybe Christa, since she'd been quick to glom onto him. He wasn't ready to wake that hornet yet.

"I'm sorry," the woman at Steinman's service said. "He's attending a benefit this evening, then heading for the airport. I don't expect he'll call for his messages until sometime tomorrow afternoon when he reaches LA."

Dammit. "Look, I know he's probably not gonna want to talk to me, but could you please ask him to call? It's an emergency."

All he could do now was wait. And think. He wasn't a fan of either.

⁓

Since the day Kate had moved in, Billy couldn't remember being in the apartment without her. And even though he'd lived there for almost three years, alone, it suddenly felt empty. His body quivered with exhaustion, but he couldn't bear the thought of climbing into his empty bed. He grabbed Kate's pillow and a blanket. Then he snatched the ratty-looking tiger she kept on her nightstand, the one he teased her about, and carried them into the living room.

He was a grown man about to curl up on the couch with a stuffed tiger.

At best, he'd slept no more than an hour or two. His brain wouldn't shut off. Different scenarios kept running through his mind. What if she wouldn't forgive him? What if she hated him? The worst one, the one that kept him awake the rest of the night, was what if she'd never made it to Joey's? If ever there was a time he needed to chill, it was now, but he wouldn't dare. Not even a little Jack or weed to take the edge off.

By the time Steinman called the following afternoon, he was damn near losing his mind.

"I'm sorry we had to let you go, Billy," Steinman began, "but you walked out on an expensive project, and that girl you recommended never showed either. You're a talented musician, but—"

"I don't blame you for firing me," Billy interrupted. "I'm sorry about what happened, but that's not why I'm calling. I need to get hold of Joey Buccacino. I need his address."

"I thought he was a friend of yours."

"He's a friend of Katie's. I don't know where he lives."

All Steinman had was a phone number. His office, however, had all of Joey's information. He promised to have his secretary call with the address.

Billy was out the door seconds after she called. There was just one quick stop he needed to make.

⌒

"What do you want?" Joey scowled when he opened the door.

Billy refrained from grabbing him around the throat. "Where is she?"

Joey glanced at the apricot-colored roses Billy held, then stepped out into the hall, pulling the door closed behind him. "She's sleeping. Just go."

"I'm not going anywhere, even if that means I have to shove you down that trash chute." He pointed to the metal box in the wall.

"You think behaving like a caveman is going to win her back? You don't deserve her."

He had him there. "You're right. But I'm not leaving until I see her, even if I have to sit here all night."

"Suit yourself." Joey opened the door, but before he could step inside and close it, Billy blocked him.

"Please," he said, nearly choking on the word. "I was wrong."

"I'll say." He stared Billy up and down, but made no move to head inside. He did nothing for so long, Billy assumed the next move was his.

"I over-reacted," he said after a long sigh.

Joey narrowed his eyes, then finally, he spoke. "What took you so long?"

"I didn't have your number or know where you lived," Billy said, unable to contain the sarcasm.

"Why didn't you just look in the little yellow address book Kate keeps next to the phone in your kitchen?"

Address book? *Shit.* "Why don't you just shut the fuck up?"

Joey reached back, grudgingly, and opened the door. "Kate really hit the jackpot the day she met you."

Two steps into the apartment, Billy found himself already halfway across the living room. "Holy crap, this is small." The ceiling was high, but if he stood with his arms outstretched, he could probably touch the walls on either side of him.

"It's New York. What did you expect?"

"Where is she?"

Joey pointed to a door on the opposite wall. "Like I said, she's sleeping. She's had a rough couple days."

"Can I wait in there?"

"You asking my permission?"

"I guess I am."

Joey sized him up before answering. "Look, I kinda have a date. I was gonna cancel, but since you're here, and if you promise not to upset her—"

"I won't upset her."

"The flowers are a nice start, but don't hold your breath." After what seemed like some internal debating, Joey grabbed his coat from a rack by the door. "I'll call in about an hour. If she's still sleeping, be by the phone. It's on the wall by the fridge. If she wants you gone, you better be gone before I get back."

"Or what?" Billy sneered.

"Or you may destroy whatever slim chance you might still have with her."

Billy stood in the doorway of the tiny bedroom. Kate lay on her side, knee up, her hand curled against her chest like a kitten. Wanting desperately to touch her, he crammed his hands into his pockets until he could finally trust himself. When he was sure, he sat on the floor across from the bed. It was uncomfortable, but it was the closest to heaven he'd been in days. He watched the rise and fall of her chest, and with each breath she took, he felt his fear slowly dissipate. For the first time in forty-eight hours he was able to take a full breath. If he could just close his eyes for one minute.

It couldn't have been more than a few minutes. His body jerked and his head snapped up. Kate was watching him, her eyes pink and rimmed with tears.

"Katie Baby." His voice thick, he scrambled to his knees. "I'm so sorry. Please forgive me." The sadness in her eyes was killing him. He handed her the roses. "Please."

She held the flowers to her nose, then cradled them beside her. Her lip quivered, but she didn't speak.

"I've been trying to find you for the past two days, which has given me a lot of time to think, and a lot of time to panic." When she looked like she would start to cry, he spoke faster. "Not about the baby. I mean I did at first, but the real panic, the real fear set in when I thought I might've lost you. That scared me more than I could've thought possible."

Emotion—and more than a little fear—was making it difficult for him to speak clearly. No girl had ever made him feel this way; made him trip over his words like this. He'd built walls. He was immune to this. Or so he'd thought. He held his hand to his mouth until he was confident he could say what he needed to say.

Might as well do this right. He shifted his body so that he balanced on one knee.

"There was always a place in me that was dark and empty. I don't know when it happened, maybe from the very beginning, you filled that space, made me whole. I can't imagine my life without you. I don't want a life without you."

He reached into his shirt pocket.

"Marry me. You're the best thing that's ever happened to me. I don't want to spend another day without you."

He helped her to sit up, then he placed the modest engagement ring on the tip of her finger.

"Like I said, I did a lot of thinking, and I know I would've asked you sooner or later. I love you, and I want to marry you. I want a big, noisy, crazy life with you."

"Are you sure?" Her voice was barely a whisper.

"Oh, Katie." He held her face in his hands. "Way more than sure."

CHAPTER 28

"What the fuck were you thinking?" Christa demanded as soon as Billy walked through the door of her borrowed office.

"Nice to see you, too." He dropped defiantly into the chair across from her, his don't-fuck-with-me attitude turned up as high as it would go.

Too bad she didn't notice. "I don't know what you expect from me. Bad enough I tell you to keep the girlfriend under wraps, and you listen for all of two minutes. Next thing I know, I'm fielding threatening phone calls from Davy Steinman and Bailey's manager!"

He twisted the guitar-string bracelet on his wrist and was getting close to telling this bitch where she could get off. Yeah, he'd fucked up, but he wasn't going to be screamed at like he was some stupid, snot-nosed kid.

"It's too late to fix it, but I'd still like to know what the hell happened."

He cleared his throat. "I had a situation with Kate."

"Are you fucking kidding me? You walked off the set of a music video because of some girl?"

"Not just some girl."

"Billy. Baby." Christa lowered her voice as she came around the front of the desk. "I keep telling you, you can have any girl you want. You can have a thousand girls. But didn't I warn you that a girlfriend right now is foolish? She's never going to understand what you need or what you have to do to succeed." She leaned forward and caressed his cheek. "You have to cut this off now or this kind of thing is going to happen over and over."

"That's not an option."

"Well, sweetheart you better make it an option." She reached for a cigarette.

His teeth were clenched so tightly his jaw began to ache. "Not an option."

"Billy. Listen to me, and you can really go places." She was practically purring. "With your looks and your talent, you'll be unstoppable. But you have to trust me. I know what I'm doing. You need to cut your losses and move on."

"I'm getting married."

She froze.

"Have you lost your fucking mind?" She yanked the unlit cigarette from her mouth. "You said yourself you've only known her a short time. Why the hell are you getting married?" Her eyes widened. "She's pregnant, right?"

"Yeah, but—"

"But nothing." She jabbed a finger in his direction. "Are you certain? Have you spoken to her doctor? This shit happens all the time. She's probably trying to trap you. Then what? Then you're stuck. Well, not really, but it could get messy."

He listened quietly. If she had known him better, she would've noticed his hands curled into fists and the muscle twitching in his jaw. But she didn't. Instead, she lit her cigarette and took a deep drag as she walked back to the other side of the desk.

"Here's what we're going to do. First, go to the doctor with her and make sure she's actually pregnant. If she is, then you suggest—strongly—that she terminate it because you are not in a position to play daddy right now. You have your entire career ahead of you, and you can't let some teenager and her brat—"

"That's enough." He spoke so low it might have been difficult to hear the words, but the look he was giving her carried plenty of warning.

"Excuse me?"

"I said that's enough."

"Billy."

"I didn't come here to discuss my personal life with you—just my professional life. Two different things. Got it?"

"You're making a huge mistake."

"Got it?" he repeated, louder this time.

She leaned back and flashed him a phony smile. "Absolutely." She snuffed out her cigarette. "Let's talk about your career then, shall we?"

He nodded.

"Two possibilities. The first could be quite lucrative, but we're going to have to change your appearance before you audition. One of the big three is casting a new show, kind of like *The Monkees* or *The Partridge Family*. They're trying to take advantage of the boy band craze. Think New Kids on the Block. We'll go back to the dirty blond hair. You'll need to cut it short and get it styled."

"A TV show?"

She nodded. "The network wants real musicians to play band members. You've got that going for you—and your looks, of course. What teenage girl won't want your poster hanging on her bedroom wall?" She snorted. "Clearly you're a hit with kids."

He bristled at her thinly veiled reference to Kate.

"I'm not an actor."

"No, but how hard would it be to act like a musician?"

"They want real musicians to act like real musicians, for a kids' TV show?"

"Teenagers, but yes. If they can't find musicians who fit their image, they'll just hire actors."

"Then what? Teach them to play instruments?"

She shook her head. "That's the magic of television, sweetheart. They'd make it look like they were playing while another musician played the actual music."

"What music would I play?"

"Pop. Things their writers create for the show. There would be tours and albums—of course, only if the show was a hit."

"So I wouldn't play my own music or even what I wanna play."

"They would have complete control. But again, because they're looking to attract preteens and teens, the pregnant teen girlfriend probably won't fly. But it's worth a shot. The money could be good, especially if it gets picked up. Then there's the marketing."

"Marketing?" She was giving him a headache.

"T-shirts, lunch boxes, posters. Teenage girls are an endless revenue stream. We could be looking at some serious coin here." He'd gone from potential disaster to cash cow in less than sixty seconds.

"I'm a serious musician, Christa. Bleaching my hair was one thing, but dyeing it again and cutting it to look like some teen idol faggot isn't happening. I don't want anyone telling me what I can and can't play, and I sure as hell don't want my picture on a lunch box."

"A 'serious' musician wouldn't have fucked up the most important job of his career because he and his teenage girlfriend had a 'situation.'" She used air quotes to make her point.

"No TV show," he said through gritted teeth.

"Fine." Christa folded her hands in her lap. "The only other option is a full-on push to book Viper. If we can get you out there over the next few months and demonstrate a strong following, I can work on getting you a record deal, but no guarantees."

"Booking me where?"

"Everywhere. All the way to LA and every stop in between. No record company is going to take a chance on you without knowing they're going to make money. If you can prove yourself on the road, put some distance between what happened here and yourself, in six months or so I might be able to get some A&R people out to look at you."

He leaned back in his chair. "I can't go on the road right now. At least not for long hauls."

"Jesus Christ. Why not?"

"I told you. I'm getting married and Kate is pregnant. I'm not leaving her and taking off for the next six months."

She slammed both palms against her desk. "Then take her with you! I don't give a shit! You're making this a lot harder than you're worth, you know that?"

"You work for me, right?"

Her eyes widened and the corner of her mouth curled up. "No, baby. It doesn't work that way. You do what I tell you. Then everybody's happy."

"Not me."

"You know what?" She pulled out her briefcase and flipped through a stack of papers. "Here's your contract. I'm done. I'm not even charging you a cancellation fee. I'm just not wasting my time."

She tore the contract in half and dropped it into the wastebasket next to her desk.

"You're on your own, babe. See how far you get without me."

CHAPTER 29

Kate watched Joey over the Sicilian pizza they were sharing at a midtown Sbarro's. "Yes, I want you to give me away."

His curls bounced as he shook his head. "Sorry. No can do." Not even the hint of a smile.

Her mouth fell open. "You have to. You're all I have."

"Can't I just be the best man? I mean, I'll actually *be* the best man anyway."

"The groom picks his own best man."

"Still."

"Besides, Billy's asking his cousin."

"Cousin? I didn't think he had any family."

"He has a cousin back in Kansas."

"Kansas? Like *Wizard of Oz* Kansas?" He shook his head, muttering. "I should've known he was a hillbilly."

Kate glared.

"How about man of honor?"

"You can be both. You can give me away and be the man of honor. I'm asking Toni to be maid of honor."

He clapped his hands and squealed. "I love her!"

"I know!" Kate imitated his enthusiasm. "You two are so much alike, I'm not surprised. All sass and sarcasm."

With that one burst of excitement over, Joey reeled himself in and returned to his pizza. He slipped a paper napkin from the holder and dabbed at some nonexistent oil, then he picked a piece of pepperoni off his slice and nibbled it slowly.

She was about ready to bean him. "Well?"

He looked up and blinked. "Well, what?"

"Joey!"

His shoulders sagged along with his face. "Fine. But I won't like it."

Squeezing his cheeks between her fingers, she made him look at her. "I love Billy. I'm happy. I may not have planned my life this way, but I'd still choose him." She squeezed harder. "I mean it."

"Fine!" He twisted from her grip. "If you're happy, I'm happy." He gave her a wild-eyed, toothy smile. "See?" He looked almost deranged.

He wiped his fingers on a paper napkin and pulled a small notepad from his backpack. "I guess if we're gonna do this, you better give me the details so I can start planning. We've got the who and the what. The why is becoming more obvious every day." His eyes raked over her belly. "When, where, and what are we wearing?"

"May 20 at the Methodist church in Bayonne."

"*Methodist?*" He slammed the notebook on the table.

Nearby diners turned and stared. He was acting as if she'd said they would be exchanging vows at the local House of Devil Worship.

"Yes, Methodist—and lower your voice. I haven't been to church lately and since I'm also pregnant and living in sin, I didn't think the nuns would be hanging a banner to welcome me back."

"But we're Catholic!"

"You and I are Catholic. Billy was raised Methodist—not that he practices, but at least it's his church. We're still being married in the eyes of God. Isn't that all that matters?"

"Who are you?" Joey demanded.

Exasperated, she lobbed a rolled-up napkin at him. "I'm the same girl I always was. Please don't be like this."

"Fine." He tossed his head. "I'm nothing if not flexible."

"Ha!"

"So what are we wearing?" He tapped his pen, suddenly impatient.

"Something simple. It's going to be a small wedding. Maybe just dinner afterward."

"Absolutely not. You're having a real wedding. It can be simple and elegant, and it can also be cheap, just like that piece of glass you call an engagement ring. I'll take care of the dress. In fact, let me take care of all of you." He became more animated, like someone had flipped a switch. "I'll do your hair and makeup, of course. Oh!" He nearly bounced from his seat. "Let me design your dress with my friend Leslie from F.I.T. I'll be the man of honor *and* your fairy godfather." Linking his fingers under his chin, he batted his eyes.

She laughed in spite of her frustration. "Okay, but one condition?"

He visibly deflated. "What?"

"No beads, poufs, or feathers. Nothing sprouting out the top of my head. And I don't want it to be bright white. White, but not white-white."

"That's five conditions."

"Promise."

"Fine. You'll look beautiful, I promise." He lowered his voice to a stage whisper. "You'd look beautiful in feathers and sequins, too, but what-everrr," he trilled.

"And no sequins."

He picked up his slice of pizza. "You can be such a party pooper."

CHAPTER 30

Everything had gone so smoothly in the weeks leading up to the wedding that Kate shouldn't have been surprised when Billy dropped his bombshell.

She gaped at his reflection above hers in the mirror.

"You wait until hours before I meet them and the day before we get married to tell me your cousin is married to your ex-girlfriend?"

"Former girlfriend. 'Ex' makes it sound more serious than it was."

She whirled around. "You're splitting hairs."

"Relax." He gave her the half-smile that usually turned her to mush, but she wasn't buying it this time. "You'll love them."

He was clueless.

"I'm more worried about what they'll think of me."

"They'll love you." He shrugged as if it was a foregone conclusion.

All he'd told her previously was that his cousin was an attorney and his wife was a teacher. That Luann was also the girl he'd dated for three years in high school and college had somehow slipped his mind.

"It's no big deal," he insisted. "If I didn't think it might come up, I wouldn't have mentioned it at all."

Her eyebrows creased into a deep V. "Is that supposed to make me feel better?"

"We went to different schools. We drifted apart. I dated someone else. I left school and moved east." He sat on the edge of the bed and pulled on his boots. "End of story."

All her little insecurities came flooding back. It would be bad enough to be judged by his cousin, who she knew almost nothing about, but by an ex-girlfriend? Someone he'd been with for years, instead of months? She felt sick. And fat.

"It just would've been nice to meet your ex-girlfriend when I wasn't all bloated."

"Former girlfriend." He stood and wrapped his arms around her. "And you're not bloated, you're pregnant. And you're the most beautiful girl I've ever known. I love you more than I'd ever imagined was possible. I swear on this little lump right here." He gave her belly a gentle squeeze. "Why are you freaking out? Luann and I are friends. I didn't get upset when she and Robbie hooked up. I was happy for them. Besides, if we're all okay with it, you certainly should be."

A horrible thought popped into her head. Feeling a little sweaty behind the knees suddenly, she leaned against the dresser. "Did you . . . you know . . . with her?"

It took him a few seconds to read her mind. "Seriously?"

She nodded.

"No. I never slept with her."

"Three years is a long time for someone who—"

"Someone who what?"

The worms were already peeking over the rim of their can—might as well open it up the rest of the way. "For someone who had trouble keeping his pants on."

Those familiar little muscles began to dance along his jawline.

"I wasn't a saint, Katie. You asked if I slept with Luann, and I said no." He shot her a level gaze. "I really don't want to have this conversation, okay?"

She should let it go; she really should, but she couldn't.

"So you cheated?"

For a moment, she thought he was going to walk out, but he didn't. He grabbed her hand, led her to the edge of the bed, and pulled her down beside him. Then he put his hands on either side of her face and leaned in until they were practically breathing the same air.

"I love you. Tomorrow it'll be official, but I've been committed to you since the day we met and I will stay committed to you until the day I die. Even before we had a clue where this was going, the thought of you pushed anyone else from my mind. I've never felt that way before. Not with Luann, not with anyone. Yeah, I was wrong, but I was also a horny seventeen-year-old."

"Now you're a horny twenty-four-year-old. What's changed?"

"Me," he said softly, drawing his nose across hers. "That's what's changed. You have nothing to worry about."

She wanted to believe him, but it was hard. He was so talented and so gorgeous. How could he ever be satisfied with just plain Kate? And if he couldn't?

"Just so you know, it's a deal breaker. If you ever cheat on me, it's over. Just the thought of you with . . ."

A tear slid down her cheek. Billy wiped it away with his thumb. "Never gonna happen. I'm in this for the long haul, Katie. Till death."

⁓

When the doorbell rang a few hours later, Kate took one last look in the mirror. Then she scooped up the half-dozen dresses lying on the bed, dumped them on the floor of her closet, and went to greet Billy's cousin and his wife, the former-slash-ex-girlfriend.

"Here she is." Billy beamed. "This is Katie."

There was no denying Robbie and Billy were related. Although not as tall as Billy, and with sandy brown hair, not blond, Robbie had the same blue-gray eyes and chiseled features. And if Robbie was attractive, then Luann was a knockout with black hair and pale green eyes.

Feeling self-conscious as they turned to greet her, Kate resisted the urge to fidget. She reached out to shake Robbie's hand, stiffening as he gathered her into a bear hug. When he let go, he held her at arm's length, smiling. "Well, buddy, you've done well for yourself." His twang was similar to Billy's, although more pronounced.

Luann, on the other hand, was one hundred percent southern belle.

"I hope you don't mind," Luann said, already pressing the palm of her hand against Kate's belly. "We just started trying for our own."

Robbie winked at Billy. "Who knows? That little stop by the hotel may have done the trick."

Luann smacked him on the wrist. "Don't listen to him!"

Kate didn't know if that meant they had or had not had sex at the hotel within the last hour, although if Robbie was anything like his cousin, that would be a big yes. Probably twice.

After encouraging everyone to sit, Billy offered to get drinks while Kate tried to make small talk. He returned with chardonnay for Luann and a glass of Hi-C for Kate.

When Luann stared at her glass and asked what she was drinking, Kate felt like a little kid in a roomful of grownups.

"Hi-C," Billy said, laughing, as he handed Robbie a Molson. "She's been craving it. That and watermelon, half-dill pickles, Jersey corn, and tomatoes. I'm glad summer's coming because it's been hell finding some of that stuff."

Luann laughed. "I'm a Hawaiian Punch gal myself."

Robbie slipped his hand around her shoulders. "She'll be in a twelve-step program one of these days."

She poked him good-naturedly. "It's my one big weakness."

Kate felt a knot inside her unwind. She liked Luann, even though she was so beautiful, it was intimidating.

The conversation soon veered to the old days, but Kate didn't mind. She loved seeing Billy looking happy and relaxed. Besides, she was busy focusing on drinking her Hi-C without getting a red mustache. When the doorbell rang, she was out of her seat before Billy could move.

"I'll get it," she waved him back. "It's probably Joey."

"Oh my God!" he squealed when she opened the door. "Could you just die?"

She stuck her finger in her ear to stop the ringing. "Could you reel it in a bit?"

"Not possible." He pushed his way past her, trying to peek over her shoulder down the long hallway. "Are they here? What does she look like?"

"Lower your voice."

"No." He dumped his bags in the kitchen and dragged Kate toward the living room.

"Hello!" he sang, his hand outstretched. "I'm Joey, father of the bride."

Robbie looked confused but accepted Joey's hand.

Joey gawked at him. "Wow, those apples didn't fall far from the tree." He looked at Billy, then Robbie. "You could be twins." He turned to Robbie. "Let me guess. You got all the personality." Without waiting for a response, he zeroed in on Luann. "Good lord, you're gorgeous!"

"Well, thank you! Aren't you sweet?"

Billy was shooting daggers, but Robbie grinned. "This is our own Miss Mississippi right here," he said proudly. "Runner-up in the Miss America pageant three years ago."

Kate blanched. Billy had forgotten to mention that, too. He conveniently also refused to catch her eye when she glared at him.

Joey was gushing. "I thought you looked familiar! What was your talent— and don't tell me just wearing your swimsuit, because honey, I'd believe you!"

"She sings," said Robbie.

"Is that how you two met?" Joey asked, looking from Billy to Luann.

Luann shook her head. "We met in high school, right after I moved to Kansas from Mississippi. I don't sing Billy's kind of music."

"Luann sings opera," Robbie explained. "She could've turned professional if she wanted."

"Katie loves opera," Billy said.

Luann beamed at her. "You do? That's wonderful."

"You do?" Joey gave her an incredulous look. "Since when?"

If Joey was closer, Kate would have pinched him. Instead, she blushed.

"I liked the part in *Cats* when they sing opera, and I love 'Nessun Dorma'—not that I have a clue what it's about. But I think I'd like to see a real opera someday."

"Billy," Luann scolded. "You have the Met right here. Why haven't you taken her? He could explain it to you, Kate."

Kate looked at Billy, surprised.

"He's not a fan," Luann continued, "but he understands it well enough."

"Time to go," Billy announced, making a valiant attempt to change the subject as he steered them toward the door. He snatched Kate's sweater off the end of the sofa and settled it over her shoulders.

"So Robbie, you think Derrick Thomas can pull the Chiefs out of the toilet this year?

Knuckling under to Joey's nagging, Kate agreed to spend the night in a hotel—the same hotel where everyone was staying but Billy, who insisted on driving her himself after the rehearsal dinner at their favorite pizza restaurant. She tried to convince him it was silly when she could've hitched a ride. But truthfully, she was glad he did.

Billy was kissing her good-bye, a kiss that suggested he might not be leaving so soon, when they were interrupted by a knock.

"C'mon, buddy," Robbie said when Billy opened the hotel room door. "Time for your bachelor party. Luann's going to help Kate unpack while you and I throw back a few. Then I'm sending you home for a good night's rest."

"I guess that's my cue."

Kate settled for a quick kiss before Robbie pulled Billy out the door.

Luann rested her hands on her hips. "You look exhausted. Go slip into your jammies and get comfortable. I promised I'd take good care of you."

Kate stifled a yawn. "I'd argue, but that sounds wonderful."

"How about something to drink?" Luann asked. "I could go for a Coca-Cola myself. There's a machine down the hall, or I can call room service. How about some herbal tea?"

Surrendering to another yawn, Kate nodded. "Chamomile, if they have it. You know, I was afraid I might not be able to sleep without Billy, but I'm beginning to think that won't be a problem after all."

Luann insisted on unpacking for her, so after she removed her makeup and slipped into one of Billy's old T-shirts, she climbed onto the king-sized bed to watch Luann bustle about the room.

"We're just so tickled," Luann said as she smoothed out the special slip Kate would wear under her gown. "Robbie worries about Billy. We both do. To see him happy is just wonderful. I don't know that I've ever seen him smile as much as I have tonight, and we dated for almost three years." Luann's face fell. "I hope you don't mind me sayin' that."

"No, although I didn't know that until this morning."

Luann's eyes grew round. "You're kidding!"

"Nope. It kind of stunned me, but it's okay. He'd told me he had two long-time girlfriends—one in high school and his first year of college—which I guess was you, and then another girl he dated for a while afterward."

"Samantha." Luann's nose crinkled. "Robbie said she was pretty but a little rough."

"Rough?"

"Let's just say she didn't bring out the best in him. He had enough problems. Lord knows he didn't need her encouraging him to do things that were bad for him."

"What kind of problems?"

"Oh, you know. With his mama and daddy."

Kate nodded, even though she knew nothing about Billy's parents.

"It's a shame, really." Luann busied herself as she spoke. "I never knew his daddy. He took off long before we met. From what I've been told, he was a real S.O.B., and that was when he wasn't drinking. When he was—which was most of the time he was a nasty drunk. That last time, he beat Billy so bad his grandfather ran him off with a shotgun. Ain't nobody seen or heard from him since." She turned toward Kate. "Rumor was their grandpa shot him and buried him in the cow pasture."

Kate's mouth went dry.

"Their grandfather thought the sun rose and set on Billy," Luann called from the bathroom as she unpacked Kate's makeup case. "Took care of him like he was his own, 'specially after his mama ran off."

A lump formed in the pit of her stomach. Billy had never spoken about his parents other than to say they were gone. She had assumed that meant they were dead.

"What's his mother like?" She asked when Luann rejoined her in the bedroom.

"Oh, she's a beauty. Tall, blond, blue eyes like Billy. Just picked the wrong man, I guess. She also likes to drink, among other things." Luann gave her a wink and a nod, as if she would know what that meant.

"When Grandpa ran his daddy off, she went with him. She'd come home every now and then, when she'd run out of money, but Grandpa put a stop to that. After he died, she started coming around again, playing on Gram's sweet nature, but she'd disappear soon enough. Last time I saw her, Billy and I were still dating. She stayed a few days, and then one morning, she was gone. So was Gram's jewelry, a few of Grandpa's guns that were supposed to go to Robbie and Billy, and the guitar Grandpa gave Billy."

"The Martin?"

Luann nodded dramatically. "Yep. Gram went to every pawn shop within fifty miles till she found it and bought it back."

No wonder the guitar meant so much to him.

"His mama would call now and then after that, try and talk Gram into letting her come home, but Gram would just hang up, then cry for days. When she died, there was no one to protect Billy anymore. He stayed with Robbie's parents before he went off to college, but he already had a pretty big chip on his shoulder by then. He didn't like anybody telling him what to do."

The more Luann talked, the broader her accent became. After a while, it was like they were sitting on a porch overlooking the delta, swatting mosquitoes.

A knock from room service interrupted Luann's story. While she poured the tea, Kate tried to nudge her back on track.

"So, Billy's mother?" She wrapped her hand around the warm mug, hoping the tea would settle her churning stomach.

"Awful. How she could live with herself, I have no idea."

"What happened?"

There was another knock. Luann scrambled from the corner of the bed to answer it.

"I thought you were going to help Kate unpack and then let her get to sleep," Robbie scolded after Luann let him in.

"We just got to talking." She smiled apologetically. Robbie planted a kiss on her forehead, then turned to Kate. "Billy's on his way home. He only had one beer."

Luann stashed Kate's empty suitcase in the closet. "Is there anything else I can do before I go?"

She shook her head and thanked her, still feeling a bit uneasy.

"We'll see you in the morning," Robbie called. As he ushered Luann toward the door she pulled free.

"I just wanna give you a li'l sugar." She kissed Kate on the cheek. "Sleep tight, honey."

Kate's tea had gone cold. She knew that because her hands were shaking and several drops sloshed from the cup onto her wrist. She tried to imagine Billy as a little boy, but couldn't. There were no pictures of him. She didn't even know if any existed. The more she thought about it, the more she wished he had told her himself. She not only felt horrible about his childhood, she felt guilty knowing something he clearly hadn't wanted her to know. He'd just let her believe his parents were dead.

When she was finally calm enough to stand, she slipped the chain lock into place, then she brushed her teeth, turned out the light, and slipped into bed. The sheets were cold, and she was lonely. She'd been exhausted earlier, but now she doubted she would sleep. When the phone rang a short time later, she was still wide awake.

"I miss you."

"I miss you, too." *Desperately.*

"Were you asleep? I wasn't sure if I should call."

"It's okay. I'm glad you got home safely."

He chuckled. "I'm safe."

"Good . . . Billy?"

"Yeah."

"I love you."

His voice grew lower. "I love you, too." They were silent again. "I guess I should let you get some sleep."

"I guess. This was a dumb idea. I don't think I'm gonna get much sleep."

"Me either."

She felt even lonelier after hanging up. The bed was harder than the one at home, and she couldn't get settled. She lay on her back, then rolled to the side and stuck a pillow between her knees. Even when she found a spot where she was somewhat comfortable, her mind replayed Luann's story.

She loved Billy. Deeply. She might be just a stupid kid who got herself knocked up, and maybe she didn't know much about anything, but she knew she loved him. She also knew there was something dark living inside him, although she didn't have a clue as to what it was. But it was there among the things he kept hidden; the things he couldn't—or wouldn't—share with her. Maybe that was what had connected them in the first place—those dark, secret places. The ones they both kept hidden.

She knew he loved her, too. And if she was going to have a child, she wanted it to be with him. He was the one who wanted her; who loved her right back. This she was certain of. Not just because he couldn't keep his hands off her, but because he literally could not keep his hands off her. If they were sitting in a restaurant, or surrounded by his bandmates, if she was close enough to him, his hand found hers, or it rested on her knee. Or his foot snaked beneath the table until the toe of his boot connected with hers. It was as if he didn't touch her, she might float away on him. Would she? Not on purpose, but without him to anchor her, make her feel wanted, maybe she would slip back into her old life. A balloon. Untethered. A shrug and she'd be gone. It was a scary thought.

She loved him, and not just because he was insanely attractive and talented. She loved him in spite of that, for all the things he wasn't. She loved the boy she'd come to know in that crummy motel room, the one who'd listened to her. The one who taught her what love is.

If she'd had a way to get home, she would have gone, just to hold him and tell him again how much she loved him.

Forcing her eyes closed, she tried to think of happy things. Like the first time he danced with her, and all the times since when he'd pull her to her feet and twirl her across the living room or up the canned goods aisle at the A&P. Watching him perform and knowing that someday, the world would know how talented he was.

And how he always made her feel cherished and safe—although tonight, that thought hurt. Thinking of Billy as a little boy with an abusive father made her stomach turn. Her parents hadn't been much better, but she couldn't remember them ever laying a hand on her.

She was debating getting up to see if she could find some ginger ale when she heard a soft tap on the door. Joey, she assumed, or maybe Toni. She climbed out of bed and peered through the peephole. She hurriedly dragged the chain from the lock, then turned the deadbolts.

"You never went home, did you?"

A sly smile worked its way across his lips.

Grabbing Billy by his loosened tie, Kate pulled him into the room. Before closing the door, she hung the Do Not Disturb sign on the doorknob. As she kissed him, her fingers tugged on the buttons of his shirt.

"I guess you're not upset I didn't go home," he whispered between kisses.

"Nope," she answered, relief and happiness washing over her. "Definitely not upset."

CHAPTER 31

Having started their honeymoon a night early, they slept late. Kate opened her eyes to sunlight streaming through the slatted blinds, and a loud, persistent knock.

"Uh-oh," she mumbled, pulling on her robe. "Who is it?"

"Me!" Joey's voice rang out, loud enough to wake anyone still asleep on the third floor. When she opened the door, he burst in like a dervish, then came to an abrupt halt.

"Are you kidding me? One night? You couldn't leave her alone for one lousy night?" Billy shrugged and stretched lazily. "Out! Don't you know it's bad luck to see the bride before the wedding? Let alone do what you two have been doing!"

"We didn't do that this morning," Billy pointed out. "We were interrupted."

"Besides," she assured Joey, "our bad luck is behind us. Relax."

"You two are unbelievable." Joey began bundling in his bags and cases.

"Why do you need all that stuff anyway?" Billy asked. "Look at her. There's no improving on that. She's more beautiful than any woman deserves to be."

Planting his hands on his hips, Joey turned to Kate. "Leslie will be here any minute. Do you want him to see the dress?"

She grimaced as she turned to Billy.

"Okay, okay, I'm going." Billy looked at his watch, the only thing he was wearing, then got up and walked into the bathroom.

Joey let out a long, low whistle once the bathroom door closed. "Sometimes I can almost see what attracts you. Straight men should not be that good-looking."

She flashed him a smug smile. "I'll bring him his clothes so you can keep your composure."

"Thank you," he said, fanning himself.

There was another knock and Joey answered it, stepping aside for Robbie and Luann. Fresh-faced with her hair pulled into a tight ponytail, she looked as beautiful as she had the night before.

"Mornin', sugar." She kissed Joey on the cheek. "Kate, honey, we brought you some breakfast." A waiter followed with a cart. When he left, Luann lifted the silver dome. "I ordered you an omelet for protein, with a slice of ham—I thought bacon might upset your tummy—two pieces of whole wheat toast, herbal tea, and orange juice. Folic acid is good for the baby." There was even a red rose in a vase.

At the third knock, Kate began to wonder if she'd woken up in Grand Central Station.

"Here you are!" Toni walked in and looked at Joey. "I went to your room and there was no answer. Then I went up to see you guys, and you were gone. I didn't want to wake Kate, but you're all here anyway." She looked at the tray. "Breakfast! I'm starving."

"We're heading to the dining room," Luann explained. "I just wanted to make sure Kate got off to a good start."

"She almost got off to a great start, right Kate?" Joey batted his eyes. "I wasn't planning on breakfast, but I guess Kate wouldn't mind a few minutes alone, would you dear?" He looked at her pointedly, his eyebrows inching toward his hairline.

She tried to look demure, but then the bathroom door opened.

"Oh jeez!" Billy said.

"Billy!" Luann cried. "What're you doing here?"

"What do you think?" Joey answered, dryly. "At least he finally put some clothes on."

Billy shrugged as he slipped his arms around Kate. "I'm in love."

Luann clucked her tongue. "Well, I hope you let her get some sleep."

"We slept very well," Kate assured her.

With the door still open from Toni's entrance, Leslie's arrival with the dress caused an even bigger stir.

"No!" cried five voices. Leslie spun on her heels and marched back into the hallway with Joey right behind her.

"What the hell?" she cried from the hallway.

"The groom is here!" Joey began regaling her with their supposed indiscretions of the previous evening.

"I'm going," Billy yelled from within. "But if you all don't mind, I'd like to kiss my fiancée good-bye."

"C'mon," Luann said, ushering the rest of them out of the room. "Billy, you're hopeless."

He looked down at Kate and spoke so low, only she could hear. "Hopelessly in love."

~

Kate's eyes filled with tears, threatening her carefully applied makeup, as she stared at her reflection in the full-length mirror in the pastor's office.

"Cry and I'll pinch you!" Joey threatened.

"I can't help it." She pressed a finger into the corner of her eye, hoping to stem the tide. Joey shoved a tissue into her hand. When the threat was over, he took it back, dabbed it on his tongue, and wiped the black eyeliner from the tip of her finger before she could yank it away.

"Ew!"

"Hush. Close your eyes." He angled her face toward him so he could repair the damage.

"You two are like little kids," said Leslie, offering a rare smile.

Although Joey's classmate cultivated a dark, Gothic look, the dress she had designed for Kate was perfect.

Kate smoothed her hand over the soft, ivory charmeuse, almost afraid to touch it. The gown featured cap sleeves of Battenberg lace and a lace-covered bodice. It flowed softly to the floor, concealing her growing belly. Joey had styled her hair into a loose bun at the nape of her neck and fastened two small gardenias above her ear. She carried a bouquet of gardenias, lilacs, and sprigs of lavender that matched Toni's tea-length dress to perfection.

Joey had outdone himself. The only thing he couldn't do, was fill the hole created by the absence of her parents, but he was sure as hell trying.

There was a knock at the door. Luann entered, all smiles in mint green with a big pageant hairstyle. For a moment, Kate was afraid Luann would outshine her, but Joey's expression as he looked at her a few seconds later assured her that wasn't the case.

"I hope Romeo realizes what a gift he's getting today." Joey's voice was uncharacteristically low, and his soft gray eyes were awash with tears. "It would break my heart to give you to anyone who won't love you at least as much as I do."

Tears stung her eyes as well, but before they could fall, he pinched her.

"Ow!" She rubbed at the bright red patch blooming on her forearm. "What's wrong with you?"

Joey's hand flew to his mouth. "I'm sorry! I didn't want you to ruin your makeup. I didn't know what else to do."

"Well, I don't think being black and blue is better."

"Sorry. If I pinch you again, I'll find a part that's covered." He scanned her body, searching for a likely spot.

She pictured herself covered with bruises for her honeymoon. "How about not pinching me at all?"

"I'll try." He didn't sound too convincing.

Outside, the clock tower chimed three times.

"You ready, sugar?" Luann asked.

Kate rolled her lips and nodded.

"Lipstick!" Joey called.

Leslie responded like a surgical nurse, slapping the tube into his hand. "Don't do that!" he scolded as he twirled a brush in the peachy shade he'd chosen, then swiped it over Kate's lips.

She glanced over at Luann. "How did you deal with this on a regular basis?"

"Are you kidding?" Luann said. "I'd have paid big money to have someone like him trailing me around, making sure I always looked my best." She turned to Joey. "You should think about that. There are good jobs for stylists on the circuit. You're a natural."

"Worth thinking about," Joey grumbled. "At least I'd be appreciated."

Kate wriggled under his artistic assault. "Can I smile if I feel the urge?"

"Yeah, but let me rub some Vaseline on your teeth." He snapped his fingers at Leslie.

Kate yanked her head back and waved her arms so hard several petals detached themselves from her bouquet and fluttered to the floor at her feet. "No! Enough!"

Luann hid a smile as she guided them into place. She opened the doors to the nave, which cued the music. First a cello, followed by violins. Then more strings filled the small church.

The music was Billy's gift to Kate. He had chosen all of it, as well as the musicians to perform. When she recognized Pachelbel's "Canon in D," she let it embrace her. The tiny hairs on her arm stood up as Toni took her first steps up the aisle.

"There's even a harpsichord," she exclaimed, dabbing carefully at her eyes with a tissue that had appeared out of nowhere.

Joey also seemed overcome. Unable able to speak, he mouthed the words, "I love you." Then he straightened his back, readying himself to do what he had warned her would be impossible.

~

The soles of Kate's feet vibrated with the first notes of the "Trumpet Voluntary," the swell of the organ and the timbre of the trumpet resonating through her body. As they stepped out onto the runner and she saw Billy waiting for her at the end of the aisle, the tears threatened again.

Joey shot her a sideways glance. "I just realized we never had the honeymoon talk. Are you good? If not, I'll try to explain quickly, but it might be a little different from what you're used to."

She couldn't help but laugh, and as she did, the nervousness faded away. "Thank you," she whispered, squeezing his arm.

He patted her hand. "Any time."

When they reached the altar, Billy looked down at her, his eyes shining. "Hello, beautiful," he whispered. Her heart was about to flutter right out of her chest.

"Friends," said the minister, "we are gathered here together in the sight of God to witness the joining together of William and Kate in Christian marriage."

Billy leaned forward. "Billy. And Katie."

"Sorry," the reverend whispered.

"Katie, will you have Billy to be your husband, to live together in holy marriage? Will you love him, comfort him, honor and keep him, in sickness and in health, and forsaking all others, be faithful to him for as long as you both shall live?"

Her throat dry, she croaked out a weak "I will."

The reverend posed the same questions to Billy, who answered in a clear, loud voice.

The minister turned to Joey. "Who presents this woman for marriage?"

When Joey didn't move, Kate nudged him gently. Reverend Ohlsen eyed him nervously. "Go ahead, son."

Silence. Billy glared at Joey over Kate's head. The minister spoke louder.

"Who presents this woman for marriage?"

Joey seemed almost catatonic. Kate handed her flowers to Billy, then reached over and pinched the soft skin on the back of Joey's hand.

"Ow!" he cried, snapping out of his trance. Muffled laughter filtered through the nave. Reverend Ohlsen rolled his eyes heavenward, sighed heavily, and posed the question a third time.

"I do," Joey whispered, rubbing his hand.

The minister turned and proceeded up the steps toward the altar. Kate passed her flowers to Toni and linked her arm in Billy's. They began to follow the reverend until she was jerked back sharply. Joey still had a tight grip on her arm. When the reverend turned and saw what was happening, he motioned with his eyes and a tilt of his head for Joey to step back.

"Joey, please," Kate whispered.

He didn't budge.

Billy leaned around her. "Dude! Step back!"

Kate looked helplessly at the minister, who came down the steps and whispered in Joey's ear. "Your part is over, son. Now you need to step over there."

The low murmur of voices rippled through the church.

"Joey, please let go." With her free hand, Kate reached over to peel his fingers away.

The look on his face was heartbreaking. At that moment, she saw the little boy she'd grown up with. The one who had woken up one morning and no longer had a mother. The one who'd been teased and bullied for the way he dressed and the way he spoke, yet was the first to battle for her when she'd been tormented in high school because her mother was the reviled Dragon Lady. She saw the twelve year old boy, all arms and legs, sitting on the floor of her bedroom, styling the hair on dolls she hadn't played with in years, and the teenager, tall and handsome, who gently rebuffed her clumsy first attempts at flirting.

Joey. Her first love.

She pressed her forehead against his shoulder. "No matter what, you know I'll always love you. Nothing is going to change that."

Slowly, she felt his grip relax. Then he leaned down, placed a gentle kiss in the center of her forehead and let go.

When it was time to recite the vows they had written, Kate was so nervous she was afraid no sound would come out. But when Billy took her hands and looked into her eyes, it felt as if they were the only two people in the church.

"Katie, not too long ago you thanked me for rescuing you, but in truth, it's you who rescued me. Until you came into my life, I was free falling. I had goals, but no direction. You threw me a lifeline, and now you're my anchor, my rock. It's for you I want to reach those goals, for you I want to succeed, and it's with you I want to share my life, whatever comes our way—both the good and the bad. In the words of Pedro Calderon de la Barca, 'When love is not madness, it is not love.' You are my madness and my love."

A tear slipped down her cheek. He wiped it away, then touched his fingers to his lips, sharing the intimacy of that tear.

"Billy," she began. "You are my Mr. Darcy, my Beowulf, my Prince Charming all rolled into one." He was grinning at her literary references, and she began to relax. "You make me feel safe and secure and loved. I trust you not only with my heart, but my life. I promise to follow you wherever you go and be by your side always. I promise to love you until my dying breath and if possible, until the end of time."

The rest of the service flew by without a hitch. When the minister pronounced them married, Billy took her face in his hands and kissed her. It wasn't an innocent, church-approved peck, but a passionate promise. She hadn't known it was possible to love someone so much that her heart actually hurt.

Instead of fireworks and rockets, electric guitars and cymbals burst forth from the choir loft with a heavy metal arrangement of the "Wedding March."

She clung to Billy's sleeves, stunned, gaping up at the choir loft. "I had to have a little something for myself, didn't I?" Billy grinned down at her.

Laughing, she took his hand and pressed it against her belly.

"Here's a little something else for you."

His eyes widened, and she could feel the baby moving against his palm. He dropped to his knees and kissed the spot.

"Fuck, yeah." He grinned up at her. "You're both my family now."

CHAPTER 32

The honeymoon was to last for three months, at least for Kate. Not wanting to go out on the road and leave her behind while she was pregnant, Billy booked Viper at a Pocono honeymoon resort for the entire summer. A small apartment was afforded them as part of the contract he negotiated, while Denny, Steve and the rest of the guys were given rooms in the staff quarters.

For their actual honeymoon—five days—Billy reserved one of the regular guest suites.

They stood in the doorway, Kate's eyes widening as she surveyed the large round bed with mirrored headboard, the heart-shaped tub, and the mini indoor pool. There was so much red—on the floor, on the walls, on the furniture—it made her eyes hurt.

"This has to be the tackiest thing I've ever seen," Billy said finally.

"There's a fireplace," she said, pointing to the brass box tucked into a faux marble wall and surrounded by Grecian columns. She pushed the door closed behind him. "This is great. I love it."

He gave her a look that indicated he didn't believe her for one second.

"Seriously," she said, slipping off her sweater and tossing it on a table near the door. "What are you supposed to do on your honeymoon?"

His mouth opened, but she didn't give him a chance to answer.

"Have sex. Right? If nothing else, this is a great place to have sex. Lots of it. We can have sex in the tub, in the pool, by the fireplace." She pointed to each area of the room.

"And if we don't fall off the edge," she added, wondering how one doesn't fall off a round bed, "maybe even on the bed."

To prove her point, she dropped her bag and purse on the red velvet sofa and jumped on the bed. Giving him a wicked smile, she shimmied into the center and patted the space beside her.

She gasped when she looked up at the ceiling. "Oh dear, God."

"What?" he asked, putting down the bags and joining her.

"How about that?" He grinned at his reflection in the large mirror positioned over the bed. "This place may not be so bad after all." He began humming a familiar refrain from "Hotel California."

Kate squinched her face up at the ceiling. "Too bad I can't have any of that pink champagne."

~

In spite of being holed up at a resort, the next three months turned out to be mind-numbingly boring. It rained almost every day and the novelty of unlimited ping pong and air hockey wore off pretty quick. The only bright spot of the summer for Kate was her birthday. Since it fell on a Thursday, Billy took the night off. And since she had scheduled an appointment with Dr. Landry, they would spend the evening in their own apartment.

Billy offered to take her wherever she wanted for dinner but she had insisted on Palermo's. Not the most romantic choice, but she was craving French fries with brown gravy and a meatball hoagie. That was all she wanted;

that, and to sleep in her own bed.

"Do you want your present now?" He looked like he was about to burst.

She stopped chewing and looked up in surprise. "I thought this was my present."

He shook his head. "Now don't be mad."

"The last time you said something like that I ended up half-naked, hanging from a trapeze."

"I think you'll like this."

"Do I get to keep my clothes on?"

"Only when we have company."

Kate wiped her hands on her napkin and waited.

He flashed a wide grin as he drum-rolled his index fingers on the table. "We're moving."

She felt a flutter of panic. "Moving? Where?"

"Up." He pointed toward the ceiling. Her eyes followed.

"Above the restaurant?"

"What?" Confusion flooded his face. "No. Our building, just a bigger apartment. Up. Three floors to be exact. Obviously we need more room. I spoke with the building manager last month, and asked him to let me know if anything bigger comes up. He left me a message a few days ago saying that a two-bedroom will be available at the end of the summer. I went to look at this afternoon while you were napping, and it's great. I went down to the realty office and signed the lease."

Don't look a gift horse in the mouth, Kate. Even when that horse signs a lease without discussing it with you.

"Well?" He was looking a bit nervous.

"Can you afford a bigger apartment?"

"Yeah, I think so. It's not that much more. Same layout, not much bigger, but the baby will have its own room. Right?"

"Right." She forced a nervous smile. "When?"

"October first."

Her hand slid over her belly. "The baby's due on the second."

"I know, but we have plenty of time to pack. And didn't Dr. Landry say first babies are usually late?"

He sat forward and threaded his fingers between hers. "So. Good present?"

After making him wait, she finally let him off the hook. "Yeah. Great present."

He pumped his fist.

"Don't get carried away." Grabbing a French fry, she waved it in the air. "I love the idea, but you're officially on notice: We should be making these decisions together."

He drew a cross over his heart with his index finger. "Promise."

That finger touched her heart as well. The last time she'd seen him do that, he'd promised Toni he'd get Kate home safely. And she loved the way that had turned out.

CHAPTER 33

"I hate country," Billy said. He folded his guitar strap into the pocket of his case, then lowered the Stratocaster into place. "I'd rather puncture my own eardrums."

"I know, man, but it's all I have right now for the hours you're willing to work. The only artists booking studio time during the day play country," said Steejan, holding up the studio schedule. "Slither wants you, and you'd be a perfect fit for them. You just have to be available to go on tour if they're happy with your lead work."

Billy shook his head. He'd told Steejan about a thousand times already.

"I've got my own band. That's why I'm not available in the evening, remember? Which also means no touring. At least not with someone else's band."

Steejan tossed the scheduling book on the table near the console.

"Well, then all I've got is country. The rest of the artists I got booked are repped by Bennett-Friedman, and you're a no-go as far as they're concerned."

"Fucking Christa," Billy muttered.

"That's exactly what you should've done—fucked Christa," Steejan said. "There are far worse things if you want to survive in this business, my friend."

There was a knock on the door to the control room. "C'mon in," he called, lowering his voice as the engineer entered. "Plus, I hear she's a pretty hot piece of ass."

Billy scowled as he hoisted his guitar case.

"I'm married now, remember? And I'm also one talented sonofabitch. I'm not fucking my way into or out of anything."

"Suit yourself. So I guess I'll be seeing you Tuesday with the Lonesome Rangers?"

"I guess I don't have a choice. Not if we wanna eat."

"Eating's good," Steejan called after him. "But fucking's better."

An hour and a half later, Billy was sitting in rush hour traffic on 278, still trying to get out of New York. His only night off all week, and he couldn't even get home. As he stared at the endless line of red taillights, there was a small part of him that wished he'd finished college and was just doing the nine-to-five gig, teaching or something. He cursed as he inched along the highway. Too much time to think. It was the last thing he needed.

He'd spent too much money on the wedding, and that had come back to bite him in the ass. Because of all the favors he'd traded, he would have to work for nothing a few days a month for who knows how long. Going on the road wasn't an option, and the money he made playing locally wasn't cutting it. On top of that, he'd had to put a security deposit on the new apartment, as well as first and last month's rent. He would get some of that back after they vacated the old apartment, but still. Money was tight, and he was supporting two people; in a few weeks, it would be three. At least Kate was planning to breastfeed. He wouldn't have to worry about feeding it right away.

He was being torn in two. Part of him was crazy in love, blown away by the knowledge that his baby was growing under Kate's heart. Then there was the part with all his dreams. If he'd listened to Christa, he'd be on the other side of the country by now, maybe even with a recording contract in his pocket.

The best he could hope for today was to get home, eat, stretch out on the couch, and drink himself numb.

~

Hearing Billy's key turn in the lock, Kate struggled to get up off the living room floor, where she'd been packing books. The door banged open, followed by the crash of his guitar case into the large box leaning up against the wall.

"What the fuck?" He slammed his palm against the light switch. Nothing happened.

"The bulb blew out, remember?" she said from the end of the hall. "And that's a crib. Robbie and Luann sent it. I couldn't exactly ask them to bring it back in a few weeks, could I?"

"You should've just told them to take it back altogether."

She pressed her hands against the ache in her back. "Why?"

He looked at her as if she'd grown a second head. "Because I don't need Robbie and Luann buying my kid a crib. I can buy my own damn crib."

Where was this fresh spate of anger coming from? Puzzled, she followed him into the kitchen. "I didn't think—"

"No. I guess you didn't think how I'd feel being made to look like I can't take care of my own family." He opened the cabinet over the kitchen sink, then slammed it hard enough to make her jump.

"No one thinks that."

"Forget it." Grabbing the keys he'd just tossed on the counter, he headed for the door. "How come there's never any goddamn aspirin in this house?"

"Wait," she called after him. "Dinner's ready."

"Not now. I gotta get outta here."

The door banged shut.

She leaned against the counter, wondering what she'd done to trigger his latest blowup. Everything was getting to him lately, but it had escalated after the Video Music Awards on TV the other night. As the camera panned the theater, they'd caught a glimpse of Asher Drake. She had nothing to do with Billy's not getting the gig with Asher's band, but it was her fault he was stuck doing session work during the day and playing two-bit clubs at night. He hadn't said it, but it didn't take much to imagine what he was thinking.

She pulled the baking dish from the oven. Not only wasn't his foul mood passing, he'd gone from sulking to just plain angry.

⁓

When Billy returned a couple hours later, Kate was asleep. Tired and hungry, he pulled a foil-covered plate from the refrigerator. He'd had plenty to drink at Kozakowski's, but he grabbed another beer anyway. He pulled off the foil and picked up the cold pork chop.

As he began to eat, he saw the note propped against the sugar bowl. There was just enough light coming through the curtained window to read Kate's handwriting.

Billy,
I called Luann and thanked her for the crib and told her we couldn't accept it, as we already bought one. She insists we return it and use the money to get whatever we need. I told her it was too generous and we couldn't accept, but she wouldn't take no for an answer.
I'm sorry,
Katie

She'd drawn a small heart next to her name.

If it was even possible, he felt worse. He was turning her into a liar on his behalf. She didn't get it. He crumpled the note and threw it at the trash can. It bounced off the wall and rolled onto the floor.

He pushed the plate away and sat in the dark with the walls closing in around him, a cold, fatty pork chop cramping his gut, a wife asleep in the other room, and another mouth to feed on the way. On top of that, his cousin and his former girlfriend were buying things for his baby he couldn't afford to buy himself.

He grabbed another beer and kicked the refrigerator door closed. Then he sprawled out on the couch, flipping channels until he came to MTV. He grabbed his unplugged Epiphone from its stand and silently fingered the lead break to "One," note for note, along with Kirk Hammett.

Maybe he should be writing. He hadn't written any new music for a while. He should take what he was feeling and write, put this angst to good use. Problem was, he had nowhere to work. He couldn't ask Kate to leave or go sit in the bedroom so he could be alone.

Of course, that might be preferable to blowing up at her over nothing. It was like a punch in the gut to see hurt in those big green eyes, knowing he'd put it there. But she never fought back. It was just so easy to blame her, and he was a big enough jerk to do it.

His mood shot from ugly to black with the next video. The song haunted his nightmares. He could play it in his sleep. He wanted to turn it off, but he couldn't move. Asher Drake was touring the country with a new hit single and smiling from his seat at the VMAs, and now Bailey Swift's fucking video was on MTV. And here he sat playing his unplugged guitar on his fucking couch, in fucking Bayonne, wondering how he was supposed to make ends meet.

When the video ended, he set his guitar down and headed for the kitchen. He pulled a bottle of Jack from the top shelf of the pantry. Not bothering with a glass, he settled onto the couch and drank until he didn't care about the music awards or Bailey Swift or his cousin, the fucking crib-buying lawyer.

~

It had been awhile since she had woken up alone. At first Kate panicked when she saw Billy's side of the bed empty. She was only slightly less worried when she found him passed out on the couch. Empty beer bottles on the coffee table and the empty bottle of Jack Daniels on the floor explained why. With MTV still playing in the background, she assumed he'd sat there half the night, drinking away his disappointment. She gathered up the empties, and as she disposed of them in the kitchen, she found her crumpled note on the floor next to the trash.

Billy was angry and frustrated, probably with himself, but he must be blaming her as well. Why wouldn't he? You couldn't turn on the radio without hearing Bailey's stupid song. If she was alone, she'd turn it off, but when they were together, neither moved, as if they didn't want the other to know how bad they each felt.

She scraped his dinner into the trash, then poured herself a bowl of cereal. He wouldn't go on the road now, not with the baby due soon, but afterward, she would insist he pick up where he left off. It was the only way, if they had any hope of staying together.

After breakfast Kate got dressed and went out to the courtyard with her copy of *What to Expect When You're Expecting*, but she couldn't concentrate. Not with the sky such a brilliant blue and the sunlight glinting on the Hudson. A walk might be just what she needed. She had packing to do, but given the way Billy had been snoring, he wouldn't be waking any time soon.

At the little park at the end of the block, she settled on a bench overlooking the water, the sun warming her face. She watched the boats. Some sailed under the Bayonne Bridge into Newark Bay. Heading north, they would pass the Statue of Liberty. If they went south, they would head out to sea. At this moment, she wished she could be on any one of them, sailing the smooth seas, not a care in the world.

A pigeon strutted nearby, poking in the grass and along the sidewalk. Another hopped onto the bench beside her and cocked its head, as if checking up on her.

"I'm sorry." She spoke low so not to frighten them. "If I'd known I was coming, I would've brought you some crackers." They took off in an angry rush of feathers.

"You always sit on park benches and talk to yourself?"

Hurt bubbled up at the sound of Billy's voice. He came around the bench and sat beside her, hands thrust in his pockets, close enough that his arm touched hers.

"Nice day," he said, tilting his face toward the sun and closing his eyes. He didn't speak again right away. When he did, he apologized. "I shouldn't take it out on you. I just feel overwhelmed sometimes."

She nodded. "What are you feeling that—"

"I said I was sorry." There was an edge to his voice. "Could we just drop it?"

She chewed her lip, and nodded.

They sat, neither of them speaking, watching the boats. After a while, she dipped her head enough to steal a glance. He was staring at the water, his eyes narrowed, his jaw clenched, and she wondered if he imagined himself heading home to a safe harbor, or out to sea in search of adventure.

CHAPTER 34

Her meat loaf had been a hit at dinner. Its return engagement around midnight, not so much.

It had taken some convincing, but Kate finally understood that meat loaf really was Billy's favorite. To make it special, she had seasoned and toasted bread for breadcrumbs and chopped onions until she cried. She mixed it gently by hand, adding one egg and just enough water to hold it together. Then she lovingly patted it into a loaf pan and topped it with a tomato sauce flavored with green peppers, yellow mustard, and brown sugar. She wanted it to be perfect, wanted to do something to make him happy, to make him see he hadn't made a mistake.

It was a lot to ask of a meat loaf, which might explain why it was now trying to kill her.

Her gut burning, Kate hoisted herself out of bed. Her antacid tablets were still on the coffee table in the living room, where she'd been eating them like candy since dinner. She popped two chalky tablets in her mouth, then headed to the kitchen for a glass of water.

As she padded back to bed, she felt a tightening in her groin. It spread until her belly was as hard and dense as a basketball.

The next contraction came while she sat on the edge of the bed, followed by another a few minutes later. She felt a flutter of excitement. The baby wasn't due for another week, but still. She pumped her fists into the air. *Yes!*

With all the packing she'd done for the move, she hadn't had time to pack for the hospital. Holding on to the edge of the mattress, she shimmied to her knees and dragged her suitcase out from under the bed. Getting up wasn't as easy. She carelessly threw a handful of panties into her bag, then tossed in her new nightgown, robe and nursing bras. When she was done, she snapped the suitcase shut and set it near the bedroom door.

The contractions were sporadic and pain-free. Unlike the indigestion, which was tormenting her. She chewed a couple more antacid tablets, then climbed back into bed. Too excited to sleep, she practiced her Lamaze breathing, drawing lazy circles over her belly while she waited for Billy to get home.

She awoke a few hours later to another contraction and an empty bed. The couch was empty as well.

Other than the staggered beams from street lamps, Avenue C was dark and deserted. Lights from Staten Island flickered on the small patch of river she could see from her living room window. Empty parking spots dotted the street, but there was no sign of Billy's van. Invisible bands tightened around her chest. When she felt the baby press against the palm of her hand, she stroked her belly.

Her eyes focused on her reflection mirrored in the glass as her belly grew hard, then relaxed beneath her fingers. Watching the street wouldn't do her any good. She forced herself back to bed, where her imagination offered up all kinds of frightening scenarios.

It was after five when she heard a loud thump outside the apartment. The door banged open. There were two sets of voices, neither familiar. From where she lay on the bed she could see three dark figures silhouetted in her doorway.

She wanted to scream, but nothing came out. Her shaking hands twisted the sheets up to her neck. The men made their way into her apartment, the hall light reflecting on the white-blond hair of the shorter man—Gordon, Billy's rhythm player. The taller man was unfamiliar, but she could see that they each had a shoulder under Billy's arms. His head flopped on his chest, and his legs appeared to be made of rubber.

She scrambled out of bed.

"What happened?" she cried, flipping on the light and moving as quickly as she could.

He appeared to be unconscious. His eyes fluttered and his jaw hung slack.

"Where can we drop him?" Gordon asked, gasping for air. "This sonofabitch is heavy."

She pointed toward the bedroom, but they only made it as far as the couch before dumping him roughly on the cushions. He rolled onto his stomach with a groan.

"What's wrong with him?"

The taller man laughed. He had a long beard caught up with several rubber bands. "He's drunk. What the fuck you think's wrong with him?"

Gordon shot him a look. "Kate, this is Snatch. He's new. Keyboard and background vocals."

"Snatch?"

He started to explain how he'd gotten his nickname.

"Not now," Gordon said.

Billy's shirt tails were out. His hair was damp and knotted. It spread across his face and into his open mouth. The stench of sweat, stale alcohol, and cigarettes coming off the three of them was nauseating.

"What happened?"

"He's drunk," Gordon said with a shrug, as if that was all she needed to know.

Snatch started to laugh, but stopped when he caught the dangerous look she gave him.

"I dunno why he was drinking so much," Gordon said. "I've never seen him this drunk."

Neither had she. She couldn't decide if she was angry, afraid, or just extremely disappointed. Scratch that. She was disgusted.

"Where are Denny and Steve?"

"They left soon after we were done."

"If you were playing at the college, where were you drinking?"

"There's a bar not too far from the student center. We went to have a couple beers."

The mess lying on her couch clearly had more than a couple beers. "Bars close at two."

"Yeah, but he wanted to keep playing, so the owner let him. When she locked up, we just jammed and drank."

"Holy shit! You're pregnant!" Snatch announced loudly.

She couldn't tell if he was completely wasted or just incredibly stupid.

"Do you want us to move him into the bedroom?" Gordon asked.

"No." He was hers to deal with. "Thanks for bringing him home. Is the van still in Montclair?"

"Almost forgot." Gordon pulled the keys from his pocket. "It's around back. I figured you weren't in any position to be without a vehicle."

"Thanks. At least someone's thinking."

"Sorry, Kate. Is there anything I can do for you? Anything you need?"

"No, thanks."

"Cool," said Snatch.

After locking up, she returned to the living room. She felt another, much milder twinge as she watched Billy snoring on the couch. The contractions had been intermittent, and none of them painful. False labor, most likely. She rubbed a hand over her belly. But what if she did go into labor? What if her water broke? Or the contractions that had started during the night came back, regular and painful? What would she do? Drive herself to the hospital?

Billy moaned and let out a long, loud burp. She couldn't remember ever being this disappointed in anyone.

She pulled a bucket and trash bag from under the kitchen sink and arranged them next to the couch, close to his head. She contemplated getting him out of his clothes, but at that moment, she didn't really care if he got sick all over himself. At least he was on his stomach. She yanked his wallet from his back pocket, plucked out three twenties, and tossed it on the coffee table. Then she got dressed. On her way out, she grabbed her suitcase and the keys to the van. She wanted to slam the door, but what was the point?

CHAPTER 35

Shrieks and shouting pierced Billy's eardrums. The sound was shrill enough to cause pain in his temporal lobes that seemed to shoot straight out his eyelids. A foul taste filled his mouth, and his tongue felt as if it were made of cotton. Keeping his eyes clamped shut, he reached for his pillow and fell hard onto the living room floor, hitting his face on the rim of a bucket and banging his shoulder into a corner of the coffee table.

Shit. He peered through one eye, trying to figure out where he was and why.

The afternoon sun was blinding, and the noise was getting worse. It was only children playing in the courtyard, but it might as well have been multiple air raid sirens. He dragged himself onto the couch, cursing as he pulled off his shirt to survey the damage, which included a large scrape across his upper arm. A huge red knot on his shoulder was already turning purple.

"Kate!" he cried, painfully regretting the volume of his own voice, which caromed off the inside of his skull like billiard balls after the break. The silence that answered was dull and flat. He stood, swayed, then made his way to the window, where in spite of the threat of another hot late September day, he slammed it shut, wincing at the bang as it crashed down.

If there had been a gun in the house, he might have shot himself to stop the pain in his head. He stumbled to the bathroom. After peeing for an impressively long time, he found a bottle of aspirin in the medicine cabinet. Praying for relief, he opened it. One lone tablet stared up at him.

"Fuck!"

He swallowed the pill without water, but with his mouth as dry as the Sahara, it stuck. Coughing to dislodge it from his throat only intensified the agony. Maybe one of the neighbors had a gun.

"Katie!" he yelled again, then shushed himself loudly. He held his throbbing head with both hands as he staggered toward the kitchen, feeling his way with one eye open just a sliver to avoid the bright, white light from the sun, which he was certain had moved closer to Earth just to sear his retinas. Squinting, he looked for a note, praying he'd find one telling him she'd gone to the store for more aspirin.

There was no note. And no additional bottle of aspirin, either.

"Where the fuck are you?" he yelled to the empty apartment.

The stink of the night before was strong on him, and though he longed to climb into bed, he was clearheaded enough to know he'd catch shit if he stunk up the sheets. Maybe the hot water of a shower on his head and neck might be some panacea for the pain. It wasn't. Wet, nauseous, and suffering from a Guinness record-breaking hangover, he climbed into bed and passed out.

When the phone rang a couple hours later, his head was still throbbing but not so badly that he was praying for a quick death. Why the fuck wasn't she picking up the phone? He pulled the pillow over his head to drown out the noise, determined to sleep until the pain was gone.

After a few minutes, the ringing started again.

"Kate! Pick up the goddamn phone!"

Either she was ignoring him, or she wasn't home. He glanced at the clock on the dresser. It was almost three. Given that the sun was still shining painfully, it must be afternoon. That, or God really did hate him.

He stalked into the kitchen. "What?" he yelled into the phone.

"Well, if it isn't Little Mary Sunshine."

"Whaddaya want?"

"Not you, that's for sure," Joey said. "Where's Kate?"

"I dunno."

"What do you mean, you don't know?"

"It means I don't know where she is. Maybe she went to the store."

There was a brief silence. "You don't know where your pregnant wife is?"

He rubbed his eyes. He needed coffee. And another fifteen hours sleep. "I don't know. I woke up and she was gone."

"You just woke up? Do you know what time it is?"

"Do you know how fuckin' loud you are?"

"Oh, honey, you have no idea."

After a moment of silence, Joey demanded he have Kate call when she returned.

"Yeah, whatever." He was talking to himself; Joey had already hung up.

He grabbed his sunglasses, then went to the kitchen window and pulled aside the handmade curtains. Mrs. Lombardi and Mrs. Calabrese were sitting on their bench as usual, but there was no sign of Kate.

She couldn't have gone far, either to the park or maybe the A&P—although now that he thought about it, the walk had become too much for her lately. The keys to the van weren't where he usually left them. After digging around in the junk drawer, he found the spare set and headed out to the parking lot. No van. He doubled back. How the hell had he gotten home alive if he couldn't even remember where he'd parked? As he passed through the courtyard, he was flagged down by the two old crows wilting in the late afternoon sun.

"Where's Caterina?" asked Mrs. Lombardi in her heavily accented English. "We havena seen her for two days." She held up two arthritic fingers. Mrs. Calabrese nodded in agreement, producing a couple misshapen fingers of her own.

"Busy," he answered. "Getting ready to move, you know?"

"And the bambini, eh?"

He nodded and forced a smile. The old ladies loved him, even though until Kate moved in, he'd had no idea who anyone in the building was, nor had he cared. Now she knew the whole damn building, and as a result, they all seemed to know him.

"Have you seen her?" he asked, squinting in spite of the dark glasses. "I was taking a nap. She must've gone out."

"Not for two days." Mrs. Lombardi shook her head. Mrs. Calabrese held up two fingers again, since he hadn't gotten the message the first time.

He nodded. "Right. If you see her, would you tell her I'm looking for her?"

Mrs. Lombardi nodded. Mrs. Calabrese continued to hold up her fingers.

When he got to the street, he searched the block. Still no sign of his van. Kate rarely drove it; she couldn't even park it. So if she had taken it, where the hell could she have gone?

A few hours later, Billy was knocking on Toni's door. One look at her face and he knew he'd fucked up again. Big time.

"Is she here?"

Toni folded her arms and glared. "Hello to you, too."

"Sorry. Hello. Is she here?"

Opening the door wider, she stepped aside to let him in.

"She's in the bathroom."

"Why didn't she call me?" he asked, his voice unusually tight. "I've been worried sick."

Toni shook her head and shrugged.

"She okay?"

"Beats me," she said dryly. "She hasn't really said much, and she's too good to speak badly of someone, no matter how much he deserves it."

He waited in the doorway, not sure if he should go in or go home. Toni wasn't making it any easier.

"How'd you get here?" she asked.

"Denny. Since she wasn't with Joey and she wasn't at the hospital, I figured she must be here. I saw the van out by the street." This time he'd remembered to look in Kate's phonebook. Otherwise, he'd never have known where Toni's new apartment was located.

She motioned to an empty basket on the kitchen table. "I was heading to the laundry room. I'll fold down there so you can have some privacy."

After she left, he stood near the door, his hands jammed in his pockets. He straightened up when he heard the bathroom door open.

"Seems all I want to do lately is sleep and pee." She stopped when she saw him.

"Where's Toni?"

"She went to the laundry room."

She remained in the hallway, one hand resting on her belly, the other on the small of her back. Her hair had been loosely braided, and she wore a lightweight sundress. Some of the weight she gained over the last few weeks showed in her face, and without makeup, she really did look like jailbait.

He took a few cautious steps. "If you keep running away, you're gonna destroy my ego."

She looked down, refusing to meet his gaze. Okay. Humor was out. He covered the rest of the distance between them.

"I'm sorry, Katie." He tilted her chin and lifted her face, forcing her to look at him. "It was stupid of me to drink so much."

She looked sad and tired, her face pale under what remained of her summer tan. "You could've missed it, you know? You could've missed the whole thing."

It didn't take long to figure out why she was so pissed.

"The contractions started around midnight. I was so excited. I couldn't wait for you to get home." She looked disgusted as she turned away.

Shit. "Are you okay?"

She folded her arms across her chest and nodded. "False labor."

"Katie." He reached for her, but the look she gave him stilled his hand.

"How would you have felt if you missed it, Billy? How would you have felt if you woke up this morning, and your child had been born while you were passed out on the couch?"

The lump in his throat felt about the same size as the baby she was still—thank God—carrying. If he tried to answer, no sound would emerge.

"Why?" Her voice broke on the single syllable.

Why? Because I'm scared to death. Because I don't know what I'm doing, or how I'm going to take care of you and a baby. Because you're the best thing that's ever happened to me and I know someday I'm just going to fuck it all up.

He couldn't say any of that. Instead, he just shrugged. "Dunno. Just got out of control, I guess." Knowing he'd disappointed her was the worst feeling he could imagine. If he'd had a tail, it would be between his legs. "I'm sorry. I really am. I won't ever drink like that again. I promise."

She seemed to be weighing his words.

"Come home, Katie. Please?"

"You mean it? You won't ever drink like that again?"

"I do." And he did—mean it. At that moment, he really did.

CHAPTER 36

The worst Billy had ever gotten from Kate was some occasional moodiness, but here in the final days of her pregnancy with her hormones on overdrive, he was having a hard time keeping ahead of her tears and snippy remarks. If he hadn't done so much reading about pregnancy and birth, he might've thought she hated him.

Although the way he'd been behaving, he wouldn't blame her if she did.

Trying to redeem himself, he took charge of the move and the unpacking. There was a lot to do, and not much time to do it. In order to get it all done, not to mention still earn a living, he snuck a little speed now and then. And really, he was doing it for her. If he needed a little help himself, what was the harm?

The only thing they were waiting on now was the baby.

"First babies are often late," Dr. Landry reminded them. "If we go two weeks past your due date, then we'll talk about inducing, but in the meantime, just sit tight."

"Maybe that's the problem," Billy said, straight-faced. "You're sitting too tight."

Kate shot him a dirty look.

"Okay, folks," Dr. Landry gave him a sympathetic smile, while Kate continued to glare. "I'll see you next Monday, if not sooner. And this probably isn't advice I need to give you two, but sex could help move things along." She winked as she slipped out the door.

"This baby is never coming out," Kate grumbled as he slipped her panties over her swollen ankles.

"Yes, it will."

"I can't remember the last time I saw my feet." She pointed her toes inward, then outward. "They're enormous."

"They're not enormous." He said this several times a day, either about her ankles, her belly, or her ass. He helped her off the table, and when she couldn't reach to pull her panties up, he did it for her. No wonder she was cranky. Being pregnant was a pain in the ass.

They were almost to the front desk when she stopped. "I have to pee."

He almost pointed out that she'd just gone, but caught himself in time. "Do you need help with your underwear?"

"No, I don't need help with my underwear." The bathroom door slammed shut. What happened to the sweet girl he married?

He was waiting to make an appointment for the following Monday when Kate waddled up and poked him with her elbow. When he looked down, she shoved something into his hands.

"Stick this in your pocket."

"What is it?"

"Just take it," she insisted.

In the elevator, he pulled the wadded ball of fabric from his pocket and burst out laughing. "Your underwear?"

"I couldn't pull them back up, so I just took them off."

He grinned as he backed her into the corner of the elevator and slipped his hand under her dress.

"No underwear, huh? You heard what the doctor said."

She pushed her hand against his chest, laughing. "Don't even think about it."

~

Back at home, Billy made her comfortable on the couch, then headed for the market. She was asleep with a magazine open in her lap when he got back. Her eyes popped open when he kissed the top of her head.

"I have to pee." She held her arms up so he could help her stand.

Instead of returning to the couch, she waddled into the kitchen. There was barely enough room for him, let alone her and her belly, but he'd been trying so hard lately, and she'd been so crabby. Helping with dinner was the least she could do.

She pulled two plump, red beefsteaks from a paper sack. "Fresh tomatoes!"

"We haven't had a frost yet, so you're in luck. I got them at the farmer's market on Avenue B. They also had sweet corn. I told him I had a pregnant wife who was a week overdue, and if the corn wasn't fresh, you'd be by tomorrow. I think I scared him."

"Yeah, well." She laughed.

She didn't hold out much hope for the weathered-looking ears, but this was the Billy she'd fallen in love with. The one who listened when she spoke; who paid attention to the things she loved, then did his best to give them to her, whether it be tickets to the theater or a jar of green olives. A couple ears of stale field corn couldn't mar what she was feeling right now.

She watched as he tucked a loose strand of hair behind his ear as he leaned over her cookbook and studied the recipe for béarnaise sauce.

This Billy? He made dealing with the other Billy worth it.

When everything was put away, the steaks seasoned and the potatoes baking in the oven, he insisted she go sit in the living room and put her feet up.

"I'm tired of sitting. I want this baby to come out. How about a bumpy ride after dinner?"

His gaze flickered over her face. "I have a better idea."

Taking her hand, he led her into the living room and flipped on the stereo. Dancing wasn't easy with her belly in the way, but they muddled through, and for a few minutes, with her fingers in his hair and his hands pressed against the small of her back, she felt almost normal.

When the song ended, he continued to sway with her until the buzzer sounded over the stove.

"Kitchen or couch?"

"Kitchen. The couch keeps trying to swallow me."

After a detour to the bathroom, she followed Billy into the kitchen. The table was set, including a small vase filled with pink carnations. She was about to thank him for the flowers, when he cursed.

"I left a bag of lemons in the van."

"I'll go." She dreaded having to sit again.

"Sorry, but I can run down three flights of stairs and back before you make it to the elevator."

She would've argued, but he was right. While he was gone, she rinsed the tomatoes and sliced them, then drizzled them with olive oil and sprinkled them with salt and pepper. She was licking her fingers when she heard him knock.

"You're lucky I didn't sit down." She pulled the door open and gasped. "Daddy!"

She wrapped her arms over her belly as if trying to hide her pregnancy.

"Hello, Kate."

Her father looked older, tired. His hair more salt than pepper, and badly in need of a trim.

"Aren't you going to invite me in?" He smiled nervously.

Where are your manners, Kate? She heard her mother so clearly, she peeked into the hall to see if she was there.

"Of course. Please." She stepped back, although part of her wanted to slam the door and go hide in her room.

He glanced at the kitchen table. "You're making dinner."

"It's okay," she said as she led him down the narrow hall to the living room. She took in the room as if seeing it for the first time. There was an unknown stain on the cushion and a tear in the arm of the sofa. Magazines, her *What to Expect* book, and empty guitar string packets were strewn across the coffee table, as well as a dirty glass. He took a seat on the sofa and turned to face her as she reached for the glass.

"Can I get you something to drink?" Her voice sounded strangely distant to her own ears.

"No, thanks. I don't want you to go to any trouble."

Kate looked at her secondhand wing chair. The floral fabric was faded and the piping frayed around the seat cushion. It clashed with the horrid orange sofa. She sat, still holding the glass, and faced her father.

"How are you feeling?" he asked.

"I'm fine." To be honest, it felt as if there was a foot wedged against her cervix, and her bladder was the size of a pea, but he probably didn't want to hear any of that.

"You look beautiful, Kate. You really are glowing."

Before she could thank him, the front door opened.

"Sorry I took so long," Billy yelled. "Mrs. Lombardi wants to come over later and look at your eyes and do some hocus-pocus so she can figure out when the baby's coming." His voice grew louder as he came down the hallway. When he saw her father sitting on the couch, he stopped.

"What're you doing here?" he asked, his tone flat. Not quite threatening, but close.

"Billy!" She swiveled toward him as best she could with no waist to swivel with.

His hand settled on her shoulder. "I asked you a question." That time, he sounded threatening.

"I wanted to see my daughter." Her father sat up straighter.

Like her furniture, she saw Billy through her father's eyes now, too. Although his hair was much blonder, the roots, like his mustache and goatee, were darker. In his left ear, he wore a hoop earring. A cross dangled from a second hole. On his left arm, he wore a watch with a thick black leather strap; on his right, a braided leather bracelet as well as the one made from guitar wires she'd given him at Christmas. Black tribal tattoos snaked up his forearms. His jeans were frayed and torn in the knees, and his feet were bare.

As intimidating as he appeared, none of that really mattered. Her father's eyes had landed on Billy's black Soundgarden T-shirt, declaring in bold white letters that Fuck Happens. Her parents hadn't approved of him when he was clean-shaven, nicely dressed, and on his best behavior. What difference did it make what he looked like now?

"Babe," she said as Billy stared at her father menacingly, the small muscle twitching along his jaw. "Why don't you bring a chair in from the kitchen and sit next to me?"

Turning to her father with the manners that had been drilled into her for eighteen years, she asked again if he would like something to drink.

"Maybe a glass of water." He cleared his throat.

Billy looked down at her. "You need anything?" When their eyes met, she saw something else: *Are you okay?*

She nodded. "I'm good."

He ran his hand along her shoulders, then rested it there, his thumb gently rubbing the back of her neck. The tight coil that had formed in her chest began to unwind.

"How's Mom?" she asked after Billy had left the room. The name tasted bitter on her tongue.

"Fine. Same as always."

Too bad.

"How's school?"

"I wouldn't know." He gave her a tremulous smile. "We retired in June."

"Good. I understand she's wanted to do that for a long time."

With his hands folded in his lap, his eyes flitted about the room nervously, as if he couldn't remember why he was there.

He cleared his throat. "Look, sweetheart. I know you've been hurt. We've been hurt, too. And frightened. We had no idea where you went or how you were. We wouldn't have known about the baby if Billy hadn't come looking for you."

"What?" She looked up at Billy, who had returned with water for her father. There was no ice in the glass, she noticed. He probably hadn't even let the faucet run until it was cold. "When?"

She looked from one to the other, but neither answered. Other than the little tic along his jaw, which said plenty, Billy gave nothing away. He sat beside her, folded his arms, and stared at her father.

"To be honest, Kate," her father continued, "we thought you'd eventually come home when—"

"When what? When I grew up? When I came to my senses? When I ran out of money?" Her voice grew higher with each question. "When what?"

"I didn't come here to upset you."

"Exactly why are you here?" Billy asked, his Midwestern twang more distinct.

As her father struggled for the right words, his eyes fell on the large, framed portrait leaning against the wall.

"You're married?"

Kate nodded. Billy slipped his arm around her shoulders.

"When?" He stood and went to take a better look.

"May 20."

He picked up the photograph and held it in his outstretched arms. Did he feel bad that he'd missed her wedding?

"You look lovely, Kate," he said, resting the frame against the wall. "I wish I could have seen you myself."

She tried to swallow the lump that had formed in her throat.

"I'm glad you did the honorable thing," he said to Billy as he returned to his perch on the edge of the sofa.

The twitch in Billy's jaw flickered angrily.

"I wouldn't call it that, Arthur." Kate cringed at the way Billy articulated the name. "I didn't ask Katie to marry me out of any sense of obligation, and although I can't speak for her, I don't think she accepted for that reason. I love this woman. I plan to spend the rest of my life with her."

"Woman?" Her father almost laughed. "She's a teenager. She should be in college, making new friends, trying to figure out what she wants to do with her life."

Billy stood, and Kate watched her father grow tense.

"Billy, please," she begged. He acted as if she weren't in the room.

"Trying to figure out what she wants to do or what you want her to do?"

"At least we had her best interests at heart."

Billy turned to her. "Are you gonna listen to this bullshit?"

She wanted to lie down. When she didn't answer, he turned back to her father.

"So, Arthur, you never did say why you were here. Katie's been gone over nine months. Why now?"

"It's not that I haven't looked for you." He answered as if Kate had asked the question. "You told us his name was Donaldson. I didn't realize he went by an alias."

Billy snorted. "It's not an alias, for fuck's sake. It's a stage name."

Her father ignored him. "I couldn't find any listings for a William Donaldson, so I assumed he had an unlisted number. I couldn't find Joey either—not that he would've told me anything. I called the number you had given us for your roommate's mother, but she said she didn't even know you."

She bunched up a handful of her dress, and wondered if she was in trouble for lying.

"A few weeks ago, I was talking with an old classmate who's on the alumni committee at Rutgers. He's involved with planning homecoming festivities, and he had a list of prospective bands. I thought I recognized the name of your band, so I called the booking agent. Her secretary was very helpful and with just a few phone calls, I was able to track you down."

"We just moved," she said.

"I thought I'd hit a dead end, but the woman who answered the door said you had just moved up three floors, so here I am."

"That still doesn't explain why," Billy said.

"Because I don't like the way things were left. That's the easy answer. I also wanted to make sure my daughter was all right and see if she needs anything."

"She doesn't. What's the hard answer?"

Her father looked directly at her. "We need to talk."

There was nothing he could say that would fix any of it. But she owed it to herself to listen. She drew her fingers along the inside of Billy's arm. "Babe," she said, her voice thin as paper. "Could you leave us alone for a minute? I'm fine. I promise."

Billy nodded reluctantly. He warned Arthur that their dinner was ready and reminded him Kate needed to eat. When the banging of pots and slamming of cabinet doors indicated he was finishing their dinner, she turned to her father.

"Go ahead," she said evenly, her voice belying the sick feeling that had hold of her stomach.

He cleared his throat. "Your mother tells me you took one of her journals." When she didn't respond, he continued. "We were concerned that you might get the wrong impression."

She rolled her eyes. That kind of response usually elicited a reprimand, and she was hard-wired to issue an apology, but not this time. There were no words that could justify or explain what she'd read. But that didn't stop him from struggling to find them.

"Kate. Sweetheart." He picked at an invisible piece of lint on his slacks.

He could call her whatever he wanted. It wouldn't change anything, at least as far as her mother was concerned. The only reason her father was still sitting in her living room was that he had refused to allow her mother to have an abortion. For that, she must owe him something.

"Why didn't she come with you? If you were so certain I had the wrong impression."

"She didn't think you'd want to see her."

"She was right."

"I understand that, but it was a long time ago. You were a surprise for both of us. We believed we couldn't have children, so we never expected it. For you to come along, especially so late in life, was a mixed blessing." He quickly added, "But still a blessing."

"C'mon, Dad. You and I both know she never considered me a blessing. As for you? I honestly don't know. Maybe you did after a while. Maybe not. But after reading her journal, my life and how unwanted I was finally made sense."

He seemed to be struggling for a way to defend her mother. She almost felt sorry for him.

A pot clattered to the kitchen floor.

"Never mind. You don't need to make excuses. I'm happy. Really happy, for the first time ever. If that's what you wanted to see, then you've seen it."

She struggled to hoist herself out of the chair.

As if on cue, Billy returned. Had he been listening, and if so, what had he heard?

"Thank you for coming," she said politely.

Billy's hand rested on her hip, grounding her. It was exactly what she needed.

Her father stood. "I hope we can put this behind us."

Nodding, she fought back tears.

As he made his way across the room, he pulled out his wallet.

"Do you need anything? Can I give you some money? You can buy something for the baby."

Billy began to speak, but stopped when Kate touched his forearm. "Thank you, no. We don't need a thing."

"All right," he said, although he didn't seem quite convinced. When he reached the door, he turned to Billy.

"Will you call us when the baby comes?"

"Yes," she answered. "He'll call."

CHAPTER 37

They ate in silence. Playing with her food, Kate dragged a slice of tomato around her plate like a kid pulling a wagon.

"You okay?" Billy asked. Her change in mood since her father's visit was weighing him down.

She speared a piece of steak, then dipped it in a puddle of béarnaise sauce and popped it into her mouth.

"This is so good."

"I have watermelon for dessert."

She set down her fork and smiled up at him. "Thank you for being so good to me."

"I love you. You're having our baby. Why wouldn't I be good to you?"

"I haven't been the easiest person to live with lately."

He chuckled. "Yeah, and I'm a day at the beach."

"Oh hell no, but at least I'll eventually have this baby and get back to normal." She gave him a stern look. "On second thought, I haven't given you enough trouble."

He threw a string bean at her.

"So, you ready to tell me what that was all about?" He rose to get the watermelon and looked back at her over the door of the refrigerator. She shrugged, focused on the remnants of the dinner he had hoped she'd enjoy.

"How much did you hear?"

"I don't think it matters what I heard or didn't hear. What I care about is you. I can't make you tell me anything, but I know you're hurting, and that makes me want to hurt someone. So I can get in the car and drive to Belleville and demand some answers, or I can stay here and hold your hand while you tell me the truth."

She cocked her head. "If we're telling the truth, it sounds like you've been there more recently than I have."

He jutted out his chin. "I have."

"Well?"

"Well," he began, "that one time I was acting like a giant ass?"

"Which one time would that be?" The sparkle had returned to her eyes.

"Funny." He tried to frown but couldn't. "When you told me you were pregnant? And I had that bout of temporary insanity?"

Kate's eyebrows rocketed up. "Is that what we're calling that?"

"Yes," he continued with little more than a sidelong glance. "I came back, you know."

"Yes, I know. We got married, remember?"

"I mean that night. I came back to the hotel, but you were gone. I was stupid, ugly drunk, but I came back because I wanted to—because I love you, and I was afraid if I didn't . . ."

He hadn't meant to go that far. This was dangerous territory. He stared at the leftover steak bleeding onto her plate.

"I came back because I knew I couldn't live without you." He raised her fingers to his lips and kissed them. He explained how he'd discovered she had called her parents and assumed that they had come for her.

"You drove all the way to Belleville to bring me back?"

He looked into her eyes. "Yeah. I did."

When the tea kettle whistled, he made her a cup of herbal tea and opened a beer for himself, then he pulled out the chair beside her and sat. He couldn't bear seeing her looking so sad and distracted. If he could take away whatever it was she was feeling right now, he'd do it in a heartbeat.

"On the outside, my childhood probably looked pretty good," she began after a few minutes. "I grew up in a nice house. I had almost everything I needed and plenty that I didn't. On the inside? It was empty. I just never really understood it until recently."

While she spoke, he pressed his leg against hers and drew circles on her hand with his thumb. If her childhood was anything like his, she needed to feel safe, grounded in the present.

"For as long as I can remember, I've had nightmares. When I was little, I used to hear noises up on the third floor, right over my bedroom. Thumps and scraping sounds, like something was being dragged across the floor. Once, when I was playing hide-and-go-seek, I saw a bat hanging on one of the light fixtures in the hallway between the nursery and the servants' quarters."

He nearly choked on his beer. "Your house has servants' quarters?"

Kate nodded. "We didn't have servants, of course, but my great-grandfather did, and my father said his parents had a live-in maid when he was growing up."

"Jeez. So a bat, huh?"

"Yeah." She shuddered.

"Sure it wasn't your mother?"

"Doubtful. Hanging upside down would mess up her hair."

At least she was smiling—but it didn't last long. He nudged her with his knee to go on.

"This is kinda embarrassing, but I'm afraid of the dark."

"I know."

She looked up, surprised. "You know?"

He nodded. "When we were in that motel in New Brunswick, I had almost fallen asleep when I heard you get up. I saw you turn the light on. You did it again when we were in New York."

"But you always leave the bathroom light on."

"Yeah. For you."

Her mouth formed a little O, and it looked for a moment as if she were about to cry. She pinched the bridge of her nose and then continued.

"Like I said, I'd hear noises upstairs. The old nursery was over my bedroom." She twisted her napkin into a rope around her finger. "One night, it was really bad. The wind was howling, which made it worse, and it probably was mostly my imagination, but I was frightened. I was only around six or seven, and I tried to get in bed with my dad. My mother was furious that I'd woken her."

As she spoke, she started to rock. Her voice was so low he could hardly hear her.

"She dragged me upstairs and locked me in the attic. She wanted to teach me a lesson, to prove that I was wrong, that there was nothing there. My dad argued with her, but he didn't stop her. He left me there, too. It was cold, and I was so scared I wet myself. She didn't come back for me until morning."

If Evelyn Daniels had been anywhere nearby, he didn't think he would've been able to control himself.

"You're hurting me."

"What?"

"My hand. You're hurting my hand."

He had been grasping her hand so tightly, her fingers were turning red.

"Sorry." He loosened his grip but didn't let go.

"I was still afraid of the dark and the noises after that, and even though the nightmares got worse, I didn't dare set foot in their room, no matter what."

A startling image of Kate flashed through his mind. "Is that why I found you curled up on the bathroom floor with a towel in your mouth that time you were sick? To keep from waking me?"

"I guess." She looked uncertain.

He gripped her gently by the shoulders. "Don't ever do that again. Don't you ever worry about needing me." He pushed a stray lock of hair behind her ear. "How do you manage when I'm away? When you're alone?"

"I miss you of course, but I'm not as frightened. A little bit, but it's not so bad. Maybe because there are so many people around me. The neighbors and all. If I really needed someone, there are people here I could call."

He'd hated her involvement with the neighbors, the steady stream of people in and out of his apartment. Now, he wanted to go door to door and thank them.

"Come with me." She led him into the living room and asked him to wait on the couch. She disappeared into the bedroom, returning a few minutes later with a small notebook. Holding it close, she settled down beside him.

"Growing up, I always felt like I was a huge disappointment. No matter how hard I tried to be good and do what they wanted, I couldn't make my parents happy. Mostly my mother. My father just seemed indifferent. I became more insecure. I was afraid to try new things, believing I'd just do it wrong and disappoint them. As I got older, my friends all but disappeared, except Joey."

She seemed to drift off for a moment. "I think he was a buffer. With him around, they didn't have to deal with me. After his mother died, he was always at my house. He went on vacations with us, and sometimes he'd even spend holidays with us. When he was around, my life seemed normal—at least to me, not having anything to compare it to. I don't know how I would've survived without him."

The pain in her eyes was like a knife in his belly.

"When I left home, it wasn't only because my parents said I couldn't see you. Remember my mother had taken Joey's pictures and hid them?"

He nodded.

"When I was looking for them, I found a box of journals in her closet. She must've been writing them for years. I was curious, so I leafed through a few."

He glanced at the notebook on her lap.

"You took one of your mother's journals?"

Running her hand over the faux leather finish, she nodded. "I did, but I'm sure this one was meant for me."

He studied her face. "Did she write something in there for you?"

"Sort of."

When she tried to hand it to him, he pulled away.

"I'm not comfortable reading your mother's personal thoughts, Katie."

"I understand, but I want you to read the last part. It's easier for me if you read it, rather than for me to say it."

"I don't know."

"Please." Her lip quivered.

He took the journal. As he read, his stomach turned. He read it again, then snapped the book shut.

"What the fuck is this?" he said finally, holding up the journal. "Your mother wrote this?"

When she nodded, he grit his teeth so hard his jaw hurt. White-hot anger clouded his brain. Evelyn Daniels was more than just a bitch. She may have been an amateur compared to his parents, but the pain she inflicted was no less real.

"Why didn't you tell me you found this?"

She stared at her hands, tightly clenched in her lap. "I didn't want you to know I was unwanted and unloved." The tears she'd been holding back spilled down her cheeks.

"Oh, baby! You are not unwanted or unloved." He tossed the book aside and held her tight against him. "No fucking way. I want you every second of every day, and it's not just about sex. I want to share everything with you. I love you more than I even thought it was possible to love someone. Remember telling me you wanted to be adored? Well, I adore you. I freakin' worship you."

He held her for a while, until it all clicked into place. He snatched the book off the table. "Why do you still have this?"

She shrugged.

"How often have you read it?"

"I don't know. A few times. It's who I am."

"Bullshit." He stood and headed for the door.

"What're you doing?" She struggled to get off the couch.

"What you should've done when you found this." He pulled open the door and stormed into the corridor. When he reached the trash chute, he opened it and dropped the book into the incinerator. Kate stood in the doorway, her mouth hanging open.

"That's where it belongs. It's garbage—and as far as I'm concerned, so are your fucking parents." He pulled her back inside their apartment.

"Katie, look . . ."

She tilted her face up toward his. Open. Vulnerable. Trusting. He wanted to tell her she wasn't alone; that she wasn't the only child to grow up with horrible parents, but he couldn't. What was the point? It wouldn't make things better for either of them. They were their own family now. Wasn't that all that mattered?

Besides, he had a better idea.

"Go put on some underwear. We're going out."

~

A few hours later, lying side by side, Kate reread the shiny black letters inked in script along Billy's ribcage.

"Does it hurt?" She gently prodded the angry red welts beneath the new tattoo.

"It's fine. But it hurt like a sonofabitch while he was doing it."

"I thought you were gonna cry," she teased, laughing at the look he gave her. "I can't believe you did this for me."

"I've been thinking about it for a while. I just wasn't sure exactly what I wanted it to say. Tonight, you helped me figure it out. Now if you ever get it in your head that you aren't loved or wanted, all you have to do is look here, alongside my heart, right where I keep you."

Her smile widened as she read the words again.

My precious Katie. Always wanted. Always loved. Always adored.

CHAPTER 38

The aroma of fresh-baked bread greeted Billy as he walked through the door. Italian wedding soup simmered on the stove. A third scent, one not so pleasing, accosted him as he continued down the hall and stepped into the living room.

"Katie?"

A muffled response came from the baby's room.

"What the hell are you doing?" he yelled as he turned the corner.

Kate looked down at him from her perch atop the secondhand dresser where she stood to stencil a border on the wall near the ceiling.

"What do you think?" She waved her arm like Vanna White. "I thought it still looked kinda blah, so I took a walk up to the five and dime. They had this in stock. Isn't it great?"

A row of pastel bunnies hopped two-thirds of the way around the room. The towel shifted beneath her feet as she displayed her work.

"Freeze!"

"Why?"

He put an arm out to steady her, then dragged the chair she was using as a step stool closer to the dresser.

"Get down. Now!"

"But I'm almost done."

"Now!" He held out both arms. "Step down."

Grumbling, she leaned forward to hand him the paintbrush. Afraid she would fall, he grabbed her around the legs and lifted her from the dresser to the floor.

"Christ," he exclaimed. "How much does that baby weigh?"

Her mouth dropped open.

"I've picked you up plenty of times. You weigh a hell of a lot more now."

"Thanks a lot." She threw her paint rag onto the newspaper covering the floor and planted her hands on her hips. "I have to check on dinner. After that crack, you may not get any."

"Have you been climbing up and down on that dresser all day?"

"No. I told you I went to the store."

"How?" He threw his hands up. "You can barely get off the couch."

She had the nerve to look affronted. "You really don't want dinner, do you?"

"Not at the risk of something happening to you or the baby, no."

"I need to finish this," she insisted.

"I'll finish it."

When she realized she wasn't going to win, she explained the process of stenciling in great detail. His eyes began to glaze over before long, so she handed him the brush and went to check on dinner.

It took less than a half-hour to finish. He tried to be as neat as possible, afraid if she wasn't satisfied, she'd be back up there the minute he wasn't looking. After he put the paint away and finished cleaning up, he found her asleep on the sofa, her feet on the coffee table. He smiled at the little trickle of saliva in the corner of her open mouth.

"Babe?" He trailed a hand across her belly. "You hungry?"

Kate opened her eyes and yawned. "I have to pee."

He laughed as he reached down to help her up. "Those are four words I won't be sorry not to hear much longer."

"You?" She grunted. "I'll be happier not having to say them."

She swayed a little, pressing her hand into her back.

"You okay?"

"Yeah." Her nose wrinkled. "Just a twinge in my back."

He gave her a stern look. "Why do you think that is?"

Ignoring his comment, she tugged his over-sized T-shirt over her belly and headed for the bathroom.

"Want to tell me where you found all this energy?" he asked a few minutes later. He filled their soup bowls and carried them to the table.

Her eyes lit up. "I think I'm nesting. The books say women start nesting—making everything ready for the baby—right before they go into labor."

"Jeez, I hope so."

"Why? This getting to be too much for you?"

"Not at all." He smiled sweetly. "You've been a regular little gift from heaven."

"I'd be mad, only I agree."

When she was done, she groaned as she pushed herself out of her chair, then put her bowl in the sink.

"I'll do the dishes. I just want to see the baby's room first."

"I'll do the dishes. You've done enough nesting for one day. Go look at the room, then put your feet up."

"I'm fine."

"Go!"

He was putting the leftovers away when she called his name. He mumbled a curse. So the last bunny's ear was a little too big. It's not like the kid would even notice. Now he'd probably have to repaint the whole damn room.

"What?" he asked, coming around the corner, ready to defend his painting skills. Kate stood in the middle of the room, her eyes wide. "What?"

She pointed to a small puddle on the floor.

271

"Oh shit. Did you pee yourself?"

"No!"

The look of horror that had crossed his face when he'd thought she could no longer control her bladder shifted into a huge grin. "Seriously?"

She nodded.

"Yahoo! I'm calling the doctor." He galloped down the hall, then rushed back. "Any contractions?"

"No. Just a backache."

When he returned, Kate was on her hands and knees cleaning the floor.

"Oh, for crying out loud. I'll do that. Go take a shower." He helped her to her feet.

"You ready to be a daddy?" A wide grin split her face.

He smiled back as he pulled her in for a hug. "Nope."

~

Kate's contractions didn't start for several hours. Even then, they were inconsistent. Since her water had broken, Dr. Landry gave her a twenty-four-hour window to deliver and instructed Billy to bring her to the hospital around two in the morning.

They were given one of the newer rooms designed for both labor and delivery and decorated to look more like a bedroom than a hospital room. It even had a stereo system. Kate brought along a cassette of Glenn Miller's big band music, somehow convinced the up-tempo beat would "move things along." It hadn't, and she was already sick of it.

"I warned you," Billy said.

"I'm not pushing a baby out into the world listening to 'Highway to Hell' or 'Eruption.'"

He shrugged. "Just saying, the baby probably would've come out faster."

After the nurse examined her, Kate was even more frustrated.

"You have a ways to go, honey." She smiled as she snapped off the latex gloves.

Kate threw her head back on the pillow.

"Anything we can do to move it along?" he asked. They had done things repeatedly during the week "to move it along," but nothing had worked. She looked as if she was about to tell him that she wasn't in the mood, when the nurse suggested she take a walk.

Grabbing the side rails, Kate struggled to sit up. "Anything," she grunted. "I'll do anything. I feel like I've been pregnant for a year."

The nurse took her elbow. "I'm sure it feels that way, but trust me, once you hold that little baby, you'll forget all about this part."

Billy slid a pair of flip-flops on her feet and helped her stand.

"Are you okay?" she asked, reaching for his arm.

"Me? I'm fine. Why?"

"It's late. You must be exhausted."

"You think I should take a nap while you do a few laps? Maybe I'll sleep through the whole thing, and you can wake me in the morning when breakfast is ready."

Kate poked him in the ribs. "No, but I feel bad about keeping you awake."

"I'm a musician." He kissed the inside of her wrist. "This is my time of day."

They made several laps around the nurses' station with only one contraction to show for it.

"This baby is never coming out," she grumbled.

It was plain to see she needed to relax. Sex was out of the question, but Billy knew another way. He led her toward the darker end of a corridor.

"What're you doing?"

"Be quiet." He put his arms around her and began to sing as he rocked her back and forth. She rested her check against his chest and closed her eyes. After a while, he could feel her sinking into him. Dancing might not make her labor progress any faster, but it was a nice way to pass the time.

"I think you're causing a stir." Kate planted her chin in his chest and pointed at the nurses' station. The nurses snapped back to their papers and monitors as if they hadn't been ogling him.

"Wouldn't be the first time." Ignoring the clucks and sighs coming from across the way, he bent down and kissed her.

Kate stopped swaying and took a deep breath. "Keep it up, because whatever you're doing, it's working."

Oh God. He needed a deep breath of his own. "You okay?"

She nodded, then exhaled slowly. "The contractions are coming more regularly now. Keep dancing. Dance me all the way to the delivery room, if you have to."

CHAPTER 39

It had been almost two weeks, yet Billy was as much in awe of the miracle of his daughter's birth as he had been when the nurse first placed her in his arms. He stood over the bassinet watching her sleep. She was so tiny. Once he got over the fear that he might break her, he realized he could cradle her in just the palms of his hands.

On the bed beside the bassinet, Kate was also asleep. Rhiannon had been fussy, and Kate had been up with her most of the night. So had he, even though Kate had taken her into the other room.

He'd spent twelve hours holed up in the studio yesterday, waiting for Jake Woodson to show. When he finally did, he was so fucked up his manager ended up canceling the session. This morning, he dragged himself back to

Manhattan, fueled on coffee and Ritalin, only to wait another three hours and then get sent home after Woodson's manager checked him into rehab. At least he'd get paid for the fifteen hours. The rest of the week was a bust.

He pulled the bedroom door closed. He needed sleep, but was too wired on caffeine and speed to lie down. He needed food, too. Maybe a beer. Something to mellow him out. A couple hits would help, but if he toked up, he'd wake Kate. He wasn't in the mood for another lecture about smoking weed with a baby in the house.

Other than a large pot of meatballs and sauce, the refrigerator was almost empty. Someone would have to go grocery shopping, and since he didn't have functional breasts, it would have to be him. There was a box of spaghetti on the kitchen counter. One of the neighbors must have dropped off the sauce. At least there would be dinner. Maybe later he'd feel like going shopping. Right now, he just needed to chill.

He set the pot of sauce on the stove to heat, and before long, his mouth was watering from the scent wafting in from the kitchen. Just as he was about to sneak a meatball, there was a loud rap on the front door. Cursing, he hurried to the door. Two burly deliverymen in overalls, with thick, oversized mustaches, stood next to a large item swathed in layers of bubble wrap and moving blankets. The whiff of cheap cigars and sweat was overpowering.

"Yeah?" His tone suggested they should have thought twice before knocking on his door.

"We have a delivery for Kate Donaldson," said one.

"From who?" He eyed them suspiciously.

"Is this the right address?"

"Yeah. I asked who it's from."

The second one looked at his clipboard. "Mrs. Daniels, Belleville."

"Swell. What is it?"

"Some kinda chair."

"We have our own chairs."

"Look, buddy. I'm the deliveryman, not the interior decorator. I get paid to drop off the chair, not discuss it wit-choo."

He spoke as if he was auditioning for a part in *West Side Story*.

"What if I refuse it?"

"Then I leave it in the hallway unless you wanna pay me to take it back."

He was considering that option when Kate came up behind him.

"What's this?"

The second man looked at his clipboard. "Delivery for Kate Donaldson. Goldilocks here don't wanna sign for it."

Billy's hands closed into fists as she forced her way between him and the deliveryman. "I'm Kate."

He wasn't sure if he was angrier with Evelyn Daniels for presuming to send something, the deliveryman for his piss-poor attitude, or Kate for stopping him from decking the sonofabitch.

"You don't even know what it is," he said.

"I'm sure it's nothing dangerous. Then again, it's from my mother. But, I'd rather not stand here and discuss it with these gentlemen, nor do I want to bail you out of jail, so I'll sign for it."

Looking smug, the wise-ass shifted his cigar from one side of his mouth to the other. Kate returned the clipboard, then asked if they could bring it inside.

"Sorry. We just deliver door to door."

"Fine with me." Billy turned away. "Leave it out there for all I care."

"Please?" Kate asked. "I just had a baby. I can't lift it right now."

The man softened. "For you? Yeah. And cuz he don't want it."

As the men carried the chair into the living room, Kate rooted through her purse, looking for a tip. She turned to Billy.

"I didn't even want them to bring it in."

"I'm sorry." She looked sheepish, and he felt bad about that, but he wasn't about to tip the sonsofbitches.

"Don't sweat it," the man assured her. "The look on his face was worth it."

"What the hell was that about?" Kate demanded after she closed the door.

"What?"

"That! Why were you so rude?"

"I told you. I don't want anything from your parents, especially after what they've done to you. Your father shows up out of the blue, and for some reason they think all is forgiven? Then they send you a flower arrangement when

Rhiannon was born, appropriate for the winner of the Kentucky Derby."

"Billy—"

"No!" He couldn't help raising his voice. "What about the package last week with that baby gown and the hints that we should have her christened there instead of here? You know they're only trying to look good for their friends. They haven't even come to see her."

"No—but my dad called. They want to come Saturday."

He was dumbfounded. "You weren't gonna tell me?"

"It was just this morning." She seemed flustered. "I didn't say yes or no. I said I needed to talk to you. What are you doing home, anyway?"

"Fucking Woodson's in rehab. The whole album's on hold." He yanked the elastic from his hair and tossed it on the counter. "What do you wanna do, Katie?"

"I dunno. I grew up without grandparents. I don't want that for Rhiannon. She should have the unconditional love of her grandparents. You did."

He wanted to scream. These people were nothing like his grandparents. Instead, he threw his hands up in frustration. "You're right. Of course you're right. But I guarantee you, I can go down to that courtyard and pick ten strangers off any of those benches who'd be better grandparents than either of your parents." He stood in front of the window. "You want grandparents? How about Mrs. Lombardi? The lady who probably made what we're having for dinner. Or Mrs. Calabrese? She made the afghan the kid's sleeping under and, if I remember correctly, a pot roast when you came home from the hospital." Once started, he couldn't seem to stop. "How about a grandfather, Kate? Every kid needs a grandfather. I loved my grandfather. You don't think I want that for my kid?"

Too wired and agitated to calm down, he paced back and forth, then returned to the window.

"Let's see." He searched the courtyard. "I know! Mr. Esposito. Isn't he the old guy who gives the kids butterscotch and yells if they get too close to the street? Sounds like a good grandpa to me. What about Mrs. O'Brien's husband? The one who takes his teeth out and chases the kids? Kinda creepy, but okay for a grandfather. Pick one, Kate. Hell—pick four! Rhiannon is entitled to at least four grandparents."

Kate was looking at him, stunned.

"I'm sorry." He folded his arms in front of his chest and tried to calm down. "I don't trust them, and I don't want them to hurt you again."

"I see you're upset. It's just that—"

He signaled for her to stop. "Do what you want. It's your decision. But I swear, they hurt my daughter, then I call the shots, understand?"

A low mewling came from the bedroom. Kate turned to go, but he stopped her. He pulled out the kitchen shears instead. "I'll get her. Go open your present."

By the time he had calmed Rhiannon and changed her diaper, Kate had stripped several layers of bubble wrap from an ornate Victorian wicker rocker. It had serpentine arms and a highly detailed back with carved rosettes and fancy wooden beadwork.

She was gushing. "It was my great-grandmother's. She rocked my grandmother in it, and my grandmother rocked my father, and my mother rocked me."

He felt a flush of embarrassment at his earlier tirade, but it didn't change his feelings about Kate's parents, in spite of the gift, which was probably an expensive antique. Although, honestly, it was hideous.

"It's beautiful," he said.

Kate sat, then held out her arms. He handed her the swaddled bundle, then watched her face as she rocked Rhiannon back and forth.

"Doesn't look very comfortable." There—something he could be honest about.

"No, but I can make a cushion for the seat and the back."

"That'll be nice. You should call your parents after dinner and thank them." He tried to keep his tone even. "And if you want them to come Saturday, that's up to you. I have a gig, so you're on your own."

She nodded. "I understand."

CHAPTER 40

Saturday morning, Billy woke to find Kate sitting in the rocker in Rhiannon's room. Both of them were crying.

"What's wrong?" He assumed the answer was a combination of hormones, a lack of sleep, and her mother's impending visit.

She rambled for a few minutes, but he had a hard time hearing her over the crying baby and the pounding in his head.

"Go take a shower." He reached for Rhiannon. "I'll give her a bottle. Then I'll put her down for a nap and run to the A&P and pick up a couple hoagies."

"Hoagies?" Kate sputtered, as if he'd suggested she serve bologna skins and eggshells.

"They can eat a hoagie. They're not coming for the meal—they're coming to brainwash you, remember?" He raised Rhiannon to his shoulder and rubbed her back.

She started to explain something about some kind of salad and dessert. He shushed her, pointing out she could either take a shower or argue. Thankfully, she chose the shower.

After he got Rhiannon settled, he went to the market, where he grabbed a bottle of Excedrin, opened it, and swallowed three pills dry, then snagged a large coffee and ordered the hoagies. While he waited, he sipped the coffee impatiently, hoping the combination of caffeine and aspirin would take the edge off his aching head.

He picked up a quart of potato salad, a bag of chips, and a couple bottles of soda, grudgingly forked over thirty-five dollars, and rushed home. He wanted to be long gone before Kate's parents arrived.

Laughter greeted him as he entered the apartment. *Shit.* His eyes leapt to his watch. Kate had said they were expected at one, and it was just a few minutes past noon. He slipped into the kitchen to stow the hoagies and the salad in the refrigerator and found several Zabar's bags on the counter.

Joey. Of course.

In the bedroom, Rhiannon was asleep in her bassinet while Kate sat on a chair, her back to him, as Joey set her hair in hot rollers. She was calm, dressed, and wearing makeup. There was no sign of the hysterical girl he'd left an hour earlier.

She caught his reflection in the mirror.

"Joey came early to give me a hand. Isn't that great?"

Joey looked over his shoulder and batted his eyes.

Billy gave them both a bland smile. "Yep. Great. What about the hoagies?"

"Oh." She looked sheepish.

"Yeah."

"Just put them in the fridge. We'll have them for dinner."

"You'll have them for dinner. I'm leaving."

"So where is this gig you're playing tonight that you have to leave before one o'clock in the afternoon?" Joey asked pointedly. "Maine?"

Kate shot Joey a warning look, but Billy just ignored him. Besides, what could he say? He was right.

When he stepped out of the shower a short time later, Billy heard voices—one loud one and the occasional murmurings of three others. He pressed his ear against the door.

"Beautiful," Joey said. "The most beautiful baby I've ever seen."

He couldn't hear what Evelyn was saying.

"She should wake soon." Kate's voice was high and tight.

Another low murmur. Probably her father.

"No," Kate answered, "not really. A schedule might be more convenient, but we believe she should eat when she's hungry and sleep when she's tired, and we hold her when she cries."

Kate's mother was speaking. He couldn't make out what she was saying, but she was probably giving Kate shit for not being an uptight bitch.

From what he could hear, Kate seemed to be holding her own. "This is what we decided is best. We did a lot of reading. She's a baby for such a short time, and this is how we want to raise her. I don't believe loving her will spoil her." A chair scraped. "Can I get you more iced tea, Mother?" Her voice was strained. He felt guilty about skulking behind the bathroom door.

He slipped quietly into the bedroom and began to get dressed.

He didn't need to be at the club until eight. There was no reason to leave now. Kate knew that. She needed him, and he was being a jerk. He was rolling up the sleeves on his buttoned-down shirt, exposing his tattoos and wishing he had a reason to walk through the living room bare-chested, when Rhiannon began to whimper.

He picked her up, then cradled her gently. She stretched, raising her arms with a great yawn, and pushed her feet against his chest. Pulling up her chin, she squeezed her eyes together and blinked as she focused on his face.

"I swear we'll never do to you what your grandparents did to your mother or what my parents did to me," he whispered. "I promise. I don't ever want to sit across from you and have you wishing you were somewhere else."

Kate's hand gripped the back of his shirt. "You don't have to worry. That won't happen." She cooed a greeting at their daughter, then uncovered one of Rhiannon's feet and kissed her tiny toes.

"I'm sorry for not being supportive. I'll stay if you want."

"Really?" She looked so hopeful, and he nodded. "Thank you." She stood on her toes to kiss him.

"I'm sorry." Evelyn stood in the doorway of their bedroom. "I didn't realize you'd be starting on a second child so soon."

Kate pulled away, wiping her mouth as if she'd done something wrong. Evelyn was smiling, but it didn't reach her eyes. The woman was cold and fake. He'd thought so the first time he met her. He was certain of it now.

"Hello, Evelyn. I'm sorry I didn't get to greet you when you arrived." His voice matched her tone. Judging by the arch of her brow, it was obvious she didn't like being addressed by her first name.

"Nice to see you again, Billy."

Evelyn had eyes like a cat, tilted slightly over high, pronounced cheekbones. It was easy to see she had once been a beautiful woman. Now, she looked as if she had spotted her prey and was about to pounce.

"Are you going to let us see the reason we're all here?" she asked, attempting to sound lighthearted.

"Is she awake?" Kate's father came up behind her.

"Yes, but they're hiding her for some reason."

Billy handed Rhiannon to Kate, who took the baby straight to her parents.

"Mother, Daddy, this is Rhiannon."

Arthur reached for the baby, but Evelyn was quicker. She whisked Rhiannon into her arms and scrutinized every inch of her face. Finding no flaws, she settled on the matter of her name.

"Rhiannon. Such an odd name. How will she be baptized without a Christian name?"

He couldn't help but wonder if this woman even knew how to say something nice. "It's Welsh," he explained. "Actually, it's the name of a Welsh witch."

Kate shot him a look. "We just like the name, Mother."

Billy wondered how she could speak with her throat that constricted.

"Her middle name is Grace," she continued, "after Billy's grandmother. She'll be baptized. I'm sure there won't be any issue with her name."

Evelyn seemed about to disagree, but Arthur stepped in. "Let me see that baby," he cooed, taking her easily from his wife.

"Look, Evelyn she has Kate's nose and chin." He smiled up at Billy. "Kate was a beautiful baby."

"She's still beautiful," Billy said, noting that Arthur seemed to be trying. He also seemed taken with his new granddaughter. Evelyn looked like she'd been sucking on a lemon.

"Come see her room," Kate said, ushering everyone out the door. She was wound like a top, probably more than a little embarrassed to be standing in the bedroom, especially with an unmade bed, which from what he understood had been a cardinal sin when she was growing up. Not to mention what the bed symbolized. He wanted to give his own tour of the apartment:

And this, Evelyn, this is where I fuck your daughter's brains out. And she loves it.

The baby's room was too small for everyone to crowd into, so Billy remained in the hallway. Arthur held Rhiannon while Kate pointed out all of the things she had made.

"Good heavens," Evelyn exclaimed. "How did you get that hideous chair?"

For a moment, there was nothing but silence. Kate stared at her mother.

"You sent it to me," she said finally.

"I did not!"

"I did, sweetheart," Arthur chimed in. "I thought you might like it for the baby's room. It was my grandmother's."

Kate looked from her father to her mother. "I know, but the delivery man said it came from Mrs. Daniels."

"It certainly did not," Evelyn said. "I hate that thing. Although it is quite valuable."

"I thought you rocked me in it." Kate sounded deflated.

"Heavens, no. Rocking children is another way of spoiling them. Once you were old enough, I propped your bottle. Coddling a baby does them no good. You'll learn soon enough."

"Oh, brother," Joey muttered from behind Billy. He clapped his hands brightly. "Okay, everybody, lunch is served!"

Evelyn swept past them into the hall. "We weren't planning to stay for lunch, but since you've gone to so much trouble Joey, I guess we can impose a little longer. Plus, Kate and I still need to discuss the christening."

Kate looked as if she'd been punched in the stomach. Arthur handed the baby to Billy.

"I rocked you," he said to Kate, his voice nearly a whisper. "Until I had to move the chair back into the attic."

She gave him a thin smile.

Joey chattered away as he hustled Evelyn and Arthur back to the living room, where he had set up his little feast. Kate seemed unable to move, but she nodded when Billy asked if she was okay. Rhiannon was fussing, so he led Kate to the rocker and guided her into it.

"Here." He placed Rhiannon in her arms. "Feed your daughter and rock her."

Kate seemed almost catatonic. She began unbuttoning her shirt as he squatted beside her. "You're gonna be a wonderful mother in spite of her, you hear me?"

He gave her shoulder a light shake. "Katie. Don't let her get to you."

Kate began to rock. "She's something else, isn't she?"

He nodded.

"My dad seems like he's trying."

"Yeah, until she eats him."

At that, she laughed. "Tell them I'll be out as soon as I'm done nursing." He turned for the door. "No, wait."

She slipped a finger into Rhiannon's mouth, breaking the suction from her nipple, which was met with a cry of distress from the hungry baby.

"What're you doing?"

"I'm going to feed our daughter and eat my lunch." She yanked a receiving blanket from the dresser and nestled Rhiannon against her breast, where she resumed nursing, then draped the blanket over her shoulder. "My mother thinks breastfeeding is barbaric, by the way."

She turned down the hall.

"That's my girl."

Evelyn looked up when Kate entered the room. She was about to say something, but Billy leveled a cold, hard stare, daring her to open her mouth. She snapped it shut. But he had no such luck a short time later when she learned Joey would be Rhiannon's godfather.

"Joey?" She turned to Joey as if she expected him to agree that it was ridiculous. "Surely, you can't mean that." She looked from Kate to Joey, her lips curled into a half-smile, waiting for the punch line.

"Why wouldn't I mean that?" Kate asked.

"But . . . well . . . I don't think I should have to draw you a picture."

"I'm sorry, Evelyn," Joey said. All pretense of formality had vanished. "Would you like me to find you a crayon?"

Evelyn shifted uncomfortably. "I don't wish to be blunt."

"Please," he sneered. "Be blunt."

Her jaw dropped. "You're so confrontational, Joey. You've never spoken to me like this before." She threw a fiery glance at Billy. *Oh no you don't.* She couldn't pin this on him.

"Fine. You're a homosexual." She waved her hand as if it was settled.

"No shit," Joey said dully.

Kate looked startled. Billy stifled a laugh.

Evelyn sucked in her cheeks, furious, as Arthur pushed tuna salad around his plate. He suggested Evelyn try the coleslaw.

"I've lost my appetite." She leaned forward and set her plate on the coffee table. "Joseph, how do you expect to be my granddaughter's godfather when you are a practicing homosexual?"

"I'm not practicing. I'm quite good at it. I don't need to practice."

Kate rocked back and forth, her eyes wide. Billy was glad he'd stayed. He wouldn't have missed this for the world.

"And while you're worried about what I'm practicing or not practicing, *Evelyn*," Joey dragged out her name, knowing how it grated on her, "I am a practicing Catholic. I go to church every Sunday. To the best of my recollection, I haven't missed a single one. Ever. So put that in your pipe and smoke it!"

Kate giggled. Billy didn't know if it was nerves or if she really thought it was funny. He thought it was fucking hilarious. In fact, he needed to get out of there before he completely lost control.

"Anybody want a beer? Anybody? Nobody? Well, I could use one." He rocketed from his seat.

Evelyn forged onward, all but squirming under Joey's gaze. "Who's the godmother?"

"Toni," Kate answered.

"Who's that?" She snarled at Joey. "Your boyfriend?"

Joey stared back, expressionless.

"Mother, Toni was my college roommate. She was also my maid of honor." Kate pointed to the photos hanging on the wall. "She's standing next to me in the one outside the church."

Billy returned to his seat beside Kate as Evelyn stood to look at the photographs. In the center hung the large portrait taken in the park, the one Kate's father had admired when he'd visited previously. Smaller photos surrounded it, some from their wedding, others taken by Joey.

"Very nice." Evelyn didn't really seem interested.

"The wedding was spectacular," Joey said. He seemed to be enjoying reminding Evelyn that she had missed her only child's wedding. "The music itself was worth the price of admission."

"Thank you," Billy said with a companionable nod.

"You're welcome." Joey not only sounded sincere, he smiled at Billy.

"Best day of my life," Kate added. She glanced down at Rhiannon. "Well, one of the two best days, although much less painful."

Billy leaned down and kissed her full on the lips. He even slipped his hand into Kate's hair—a little extra "fuck you" for Evelyn.

Evelyn gave the picture a closer look. "This doesn't look like a Catholic church."

"It wasn't," Kate said. "It was a Methodist church. Billy is Methodist. It was my decision not to get married in the Catholic Church."

"I guess if you ever want an annulment, it will be easier this way." Evelyn studied the other pictures on the wall.

Seriously. If he ever started hitting women—

"Which I guess," she continued, brightening, "brings us back to the question of Rhiannon's baptism."

Kate maintained her serenity. "There is no question. Rhiannon will be christened at St. Vincent de Paul here in town."

Evelyn stiffened. "When?"

"November or December. The second Sunday of the month. I have to find out which date is best for Toni. We have to take a parenting class, but once it's settled, I'll let you know."

"I guess that's that." Evelyn snatched her purse from the end of the sofa. "Arthur, let's go."

"There's dessert," Joey said, although it sounded more like a warning than an invitation.

"No, thank you." She shot him an evil look. "As I said, we hadn't planned to stay."

She kissed the air about Kate's head, touched Rhiannon's forehead, and then headed down the hall, expecting Arthur to fall in step behind her. He set his plate on the coffee table. Kate stood and he kissed her cheek, then planted a delicate kiss on the baby's forehead.

"She's beautiful, Kate."

"Thank you, Daddy."

"Arthur," Evelyn called.

"Yes, dear." He hurried down the hall after her.

"Kate?" Evelyn said from the doorway. "We'll hear from you shortly?"

"Yes, ma'am."

Billy followed them to the door. Evelyn had already made a beeline for the elevator, but Arthur paused and held out his hand. "Thank you," he said before rushing to catch up with his wife. Billy had the distinct impression that he wasn't talking about lunch.

⌒⌒

Joey stood at the window, his back stiff, his arms folded across his chest.

"Well," Billy said. "That was fun."

Kate sat on the couch, still stunned. "Un-freaking-believable."

"You okay?" Billy asked.

"I'm fine." She turned to Joey. "What about you?"

"What about me?" he snapped.

She and Billy exchanged glances.

"Here," he said quietly, reaching for Rhiannon. "I'll change her and put her down." When he'd left the room, Kate stood beside Joey, who was watching her mother march across the courtyard, her father trying to keep up. Slipping her arms around his waist, she rested her head against Joey's shoulder.

"You know," he said after a while, "if you'd asked me this morning how your mother felt about me, I would've said she treated me like a son. I had a hard time visualizing some of what you told me. I believed you, don't get me wrong, but it was hard to imagine her being that cruel." He sighed heavily. "I certainly underestimated her."

"I'm sorry," she said into the soft folds of his sweater. "You didn't deserve that."

He turned to face her. "No, I didn't. Neither did you." He glanced out the window. "Bitch."

She chuckled.

"I wonder if you were adopted," he added, the hard glint fading from his eyes.

"I've wondered the same thing myself," Billy said, returning to clear the dishes.

Joey picked up Evelyn's half-empty plate. "I'll get that."

Billy continued clearing. "I got it. You two sit and lick your wounds. I'm pretty much unscathed this time around. I might not be so lucky next time."

CHAPTER 41

Kate had just kissed him goodbye and left to go to Mass with Joey, who had spent the night, when Rhiannon began to fuss. He held his breath, hoping she'd fall back to sleep so he could do the same, but she had something else in mind—not to mention in her diaper.

"Do you save these little treats for me?" he asked, after he'd dragged himself out of bed and into last night's jeans. "Because I'm pretty sure Mommy likes doing this more than I do." He wiped her bottom efficiently, and although he was getting better at changing diapers, it didn't mean he enjoyed it. When his daughter was clean and dry, and was cradled in his arms, it dawned on him that this was the first time they'd ever really been alone together. Rhiannon blinked at him; her eyes a deep navy that Kate insisted would change before too long. If they did, they should be green, like Kate's. Although he was sure she already had him wrapped around her little finger. If she had her mother's eyes, he would be putty in her hands.

"Are you gonna be trouble, little one, like your old man?" he cooed. "Or are you gonna be good like your mother?" Her little brow furrowed, and he couldn't help but laugh. "God help us. I think that means trouble."

Since it was clear Rhiannon was no longer sleepy, he settled himself into Kate's rocker—barely. People must have been a hell of a lot smaller back in the day. It creaked mournfully as he rocked, so he stopped, envisioning a scene from Goldilocks and the three bears, which triggered a memory of the obnoxious deliverymen. There was a flash of anger, but looking down at his daughter, nestled safely in his arms, it passed.

He had a handle on his anger now, didn't he? He knew when he needed to walk away, at least with Kate. It had gotten him into trouble a couple times, but still. It was better than the alternative. A shiver ran through him, strong enough to startle Rhiannon. Her arms flew up in the air and she settled her gaze on his face, studying him carefully. He watched her just as intently.

He'd always wondered how a parent could look at a child—their own flesh and blood—and feel that dark anger. It made even less sense now. Yeah, he'd probably be pissed if someday Rhiannon drew on the wall with permanent markers or dented the car—or worse.

But real anger? The kind that dissolves reason; that fills your ears with a roar so loud the only thing you can hear is the sound of your own blood pulsing through your veins; the kind that makes your vision turn black around the edges. That anger? That was the kind he kept on a very tight leash.

He drew his finger the length of Rhiannon's left leg. Spindly and soft as velvet. Not even as long as the length of his hand. He kissed her shin, close to the spot that his leg sometimes ached. Then he kissed the top of her foot, knowing first-hand how thin and fragile those bones were. He kissed her belly, and her ribs. By the time he pressed his lips to the soft, pulsing top of her head, his cheeks were wet. One fat drop landed near her nose, and she startled once again.

He swore silently as he brushed the tear away. He hadn't cried in years. Not since . . .

He lurched from the chair, sending it crashing into the wall. He stalked into the kitchen where he pulled down the bottle of Jack Daniels he hadn't touched in weeks. He settled the baby over his shoulder, then opened the bottle and poured three fingers into a glass. It wasn't even ten o'clock, yet he raised it to his lips. The scent of the whiskey was so strong, his father could have been standing right beside him.

The memories caught him unaware, raining down on him hard and fast. And just like that, he was a wise-ass ten-year-old.

~

Katydids chirped in the tall, dry grass. A warm breeze brushed his face.

"I do, too," he insisted.

"You're fulla shit," the kid with the buzz cut and freckles said. "I think he's lying."

"It's true! It's a genuine autographed baseball."

"Liar, liar," two of the boys chanted.

Billy closed his fists. He would punch the next kid who called him a liar. They hadn't lived there long, and he didn't know how long they'd be staying. It was hard enough to make friends, let alone if you went around passing out bloody noses.

"You don't believe me? I'll prove it!" He was sorry as soon as the words left his mouth. His father had warned him not to touch that ball. On one of the rare occasions Big Bill was home and sober, he'd told Billy that his great-grandfather had seen the Kansas City Monarchs play Babe Ruth and his All Stars in 1922. His pappy had fielded a fly ball during batting practice, and after the game, the Babe had signed it.

The ball was old and stained. His father kept it in a plastic box to protect it. Billy wasn't allowed to touch it, but his old man was at the base, and Fort Riley was nearly an hour away.

"You better not, Billy," warned Robbie, who at twelve was two years older and wiser. But he was tired of getting pushed around. He'd commanded respect on the baseball diamond with a wicked change-up and an even meaner four-seamer, but off the field, he was just the new kid. He was trying not to let his fists do his talking, but it was hard.

"Wait here." Billy dashed into the house.

"Dammit." Robbie ran after him. "Your father will pitch a fit if he knows you touched that ball."

"Well, unless you tell him, he's not gonna find out." Billy took the steps two at a time. He brought the ball, box and all, down to the yard.

"Take it out," said Wheezer. "I wanna see for myself."

"You can see it in the box," Robbie said. "It's real."

"Says you," said Wheezer.

"Yeah, says you!" the kid with the freckles echoed.

Billy took the box from Wheezer and opened it. "See?"

Wheezer snatched the ball and turned so Billy couldn't grab it.

He watched with his heart in his throat, praying they wouldn't drop it. He didn't feel like a tough guy anymore. In fact, he was afraid he might start crying.

"Here, Andy," Wheezer said. "Catch!" He tossed the ball to Andy, who scrambled into the field along the driveway.

"Shit!" Robbie yelled. "Don't throw the fucking ball!"

He felt sick to his stomach as he watched Andy and Wheezer toss his father's prized baseball.

"Hey, look at me," Wheezer cried. "I'm Babe Ruth!" He threw a high fast ball. Andy snagged it just before it sailed over his head.

"All right, that's enough. Give it back. You wanted to see it, and you saw it. I've gotta put it back before my old man gets home."

As if on cue, they heard the rumble of a truck. Clouds of dust appeared at the end of the driveway. The sound distracted the boys, but not before Andy threw the ball to Wheezer, who was turning to look down the driveway. The ball hit him in the shoulder, bounced, and rolled into a puddle.

Robbie dove for it. He snatched it up, wiping it on his shirt, smearing it with mud and erasing part of the signature. "Oh, man!" He looked up, panic-stricken, as he held out the ball.

Billy couldn't move. Wheezer and Andy took off through the field. He wanted to go with them and never come back.

"Billy!" Robbie yelled, snapping him out of his fear.

"Gimme!" Billy held out his hand, then crammed the ball back into the box. "Keep him outside until I can put this away."

"No. If you disappear, he'll be more suspicious. Give it here. Where was it?"

"On top of his dresser."

Billy stood at the end of the driveway, his heart pounding, praying Robbie would get it in exactly the right spot. The back door slammed shut behind Robbie just as his dad climbed out of his pickup.

"What're you boys up to?" Big Bill was wearing his MP uniform. He threw his cigarette in the driveway. It rolled until it hit a rock, then continued to smolder.

"Nothin'."

"You have practice today?"

"No, sir."

"Why not?" He narrowed his gaze at Billy, then Robbie. Billy hoped he wouldn't notice how hard Robbie was breathing.

"Because the season's over," Robbie answered, a note of sarcasm in his voice.

Big Bill glared at him.

"You got a problem, boy?"

"No, sir."

Please don't piss him off, please don't piss him off.

"You best be running on home then. Your mama's probably lookin' for you."

Robbie glanced at Billy.

"Mama said Billy can sleep over. She said to ask if it's okay."

"Where's your mama?" he asked Billy.

"Workin'." His voice was dry and thick.

His father squinted at him suspiciously. "You okay?"

"Yes, sir."

"You finish your chores?"

"Yes, sir."

"Fetch me a beer. Then you can go."

"Yes, sir." He ran into the house and grabbed his father a beer. He opened it, sipped the foam off the top, and brought it to him, then ran upstairs to pack his things. Robbie was already on his bike when he came back outside.

He threw his backpack over his shoulder and climbed onto his bike.

"Wait a minute, boy. Ain't you gonna give your old man a kiss good-bye?"

He climbed off his bike, casting an embarrassed glance at Robbie, then gently lowered the bike to the ground. His father was sitting in a rocker on the porch. He was leaning over to kiss him on the cheek when a strong hand clamped onto a handful of his T-shirt and pulled him closer.

"You better not have been getting' yourself in trouble." From this close, Billy knew the beer wasn't his father's first drink of the day. Combined with the stale smell of cigarettes and the shabby state of his uniform, he guessed he'd spent the better part of the day in a bar.

"We weren't." He tried to wriggle free.

"I'm warnin' you. Better not let me find out you were gettin' into any mischief."

"No, sir."

His father let go but grabbed a handful of Billy's hair, which had grown well past his ears. "You need a haircut, boy." He shook his hand and Billy's head along with it. "You're startin' to look like a girl—or are you gonna grow up to be one of them little faggots?" He let Billy go, and gave him a shove.

"No, sir." Billy rubbed his scalp.

"Go. Get outta here."

They were about a half-mile from the house when Billy skidded to a stop. He dropped his bike and walked off into the woods.

"What're you doin'?" Robbie called after him.

Billy could hear him crunching through the brush toward him.

"Do you think he'll notice?" He peered up at Robbie from where he'd been crouched to let loose his lunch. The smear on the baseball was obvious and they both knew it, but Robbie shook his head.

"Nah. It's fine. He can't tell. I turned it so it doesn't even show. Once it dries, it won't be noticeable at all."

Billy dragged the back of his hand across his mouth. "Yeah, you're probably right."

"Come on. Let's get goin' before someone calls my mother and finds out we lied."

They headed back to the road.

"Robbie," Billy said as he picked up his bike.

"Yeah?"

"You're the best friend I've ever had."

"I'm not your friend, knucklehead. I'm your cousin."

"Yeah, well, you're my best friend, too."

Robbie hid a smile. "Let's go, squirt. I'll race you home."

The following week, Billy had forgotten about the baseball. His mother was working at the hospital, and Gram was with her church group. From the steady hum drifting through the air, he guessed his grandfather was out on the tractor harvesting alfalfa.

He poured himself a bowl of cereal and filled it with milk, then carried it into the living room, where he set it on the coffee table. He was so engrossed in *Scooby Doo* a short while later that he jumped when the refrigerator door slammed.

"What're you doing there, sport?" His father stood in the doorway, popping the top on a can of beer. The clock on the mantel said it was ten to ten.

"Watchin' cartoons." He didn't like being around his father when he drank, which was most of the time.

Keeping his eyes on Billy, his father pulled a cigarette from a pack in his shirt pocket. He pulled out a lighter, lit it, then took a long drag.

"Gram said you can't smoke in the house."

"I don't see her right now, do you?"

"No, sir." Billy picked up his bowl and carried it to the kitchen. His father was spoiling for a fight.

"Where you goin'?"

"I promised Robbie I'd go fishin'."

"I didn't hear you ask permission."

"Can I go fishin'?"

"How you gonna get there?"

"My bike."

"Really? I don't think you got a bike no more, cuz if I'm not mistaken, when I come home last night I saw a bike lyin' in the driveway where it wasn't supposed to be."

Billy raced to the back door, where he could see his crumpled bike lying in a stand of tall weeds. He turned around and slammed immediately into his father. Bill was a big man, tall and solid. He grabbed a handful of Billy's shirt and lifted him off his feet as if he weighed nothing.

"How's it feel, boy? How's it feel to see somethin' you love destroyed?"

"Why'd you run over my bike?" Billy yelled, struggling to get down.

"How 'bout you tell me what happened to my baseball."

His father's face was inches from his, and he stank of booze and cigarettes. Billy started kicking, and his father let go, dropping him to the floor. He ran for the front door, but his father caught him by his hair, yanking him back. He slapped Billy hard, causing him to slam his forehead against the corner of the table. Blood gushed warm and sticky into his eye and down his cheek, making it difficult to see. He pulled himself onto the couch, then bolted for the door, but his father was too fast. He threw Billy against the cushions, then came down hard, holding him in place with his knee.

"Don't you dare run from me, cuz if I have to chase you, this is gonna hurt a hell of a lot more than it needs to." He grasped at his belt, unbuckling the heavy brass buckle and sliding it out through the loops of his pants. He doubled it up and demanded Billy roll over.

"No," he cried, kicking at his father and trying to get away. Blood ran down his face. It was smeared over his hands and onto the couch.

His father flipped him over with a grunt and began hitting him. When he was distracted by a fit of coughing, Billy pushed back and slid off the couch, crying out when he landed. He rolled over and tried to catch his breath. Scrambling to his feet, he made it partway out the front door before his father caught him by the shirt.

Billy went flying through the air like a rag doll, slamming into the side of the doorjamb. His ear was ringing. It was difficult to see. His father pushed him back onto the couch and threw the belt aside, determined to teach his son a permanent lesson. With his fists.

There was little more he could do other than cover his face. The sound of grunts and fists mutated into a loud buzzing. Everything turned white. Then there was nothing.

Billy's eyes flew open. He was home, in his kitchen in Bayonne. He was an adult. Able to protect himself and his family. But that didn't stop his hands from shaking.

If his grandfather hadn't come back to the house when he had, his father might have killed him. Over a fucking baseball. He had woken up in the hospital days later with his eyes blackened, his skull fractured, his lung punctured, and more broken bones than he could count. When he was finally released, his parents were gone. There was a warrant out for his father's arrest, and no one—other than his mother, he assumed—had seen him since.

He settled Rhiannon into the crook of his arm and threw back the whiskey. Then he poured himself another.

CHAPTER 42

"When did you become such a bagel snob?" Kate asked, carrying a bag of bagels that she was certain were fresh, while Joey groused behind her.

"I'm not a snob. I'm just saying, if you told me you wanted bagels, I would have brought fresh ones from New York." He let out an exasperated sigh for her benefit.

"New York is right there," she said, pointing out the kitchen window. "If you had brought them yesterday, they would have been day-old bagels, when I have fresh right here." She held up the bag.

"For as long as it takes to get here from New York, those bagels are probably a week old."

It was pointless to argue. Instead, she pulled three plates down from the cupboard.

"Would you get me a platter from the top of the pantry please? I'll put on a fresh pot of coffee."

"Don't think I don't know you're changing the subject," Joey responded, slipping off the leather bomber jacket he'd worn to church. "What's that?"

She stopped to listen. Music drifted in from the back of the apartment. Billy was playing his guitar, probably for Rhiannon. She stepped out into the hall. "Stairway to Heaven." She smiled at Joey and motioned for him to follow her. They tiptoed down the hall and peeked into the nursery. Billy was sitting on a stool, bent over his guitar as Rhiannon listened intently, her tiny brow furrowed.

"Get your camera," she whispered.

When he heard the click of Joey's Olympus, Billy glanced up and winked before continuing to serenade his rapt little audience.

"He plays for her all the time," Kate explained back in the kitchen as she set the bagels on the platter. "It's sweet. She just watches and listens. He'll get up with her in the middle of the night and play if she's fussy. Sometimes it's the only thing that calms her down. She's definitely Daddy's little girl."

"It's good," Joey said. "It's almost like a lullaby like that. What else does he play for her?"

"Some of his own stuff. Some Metallica, Guns N' Roses. He just slows the tempo way down. Depends if we want her to go to sleep or not. Sometimes just silly little songs he makes up."

Joey stood outside the kitchen and listened. "He should record them."

She laughed.

"Seriously. He should record them—as lullabies."

"He can't." She dumped stale coffee into the sink and filled the pot with fresh water. "They're not his."

"He can get permission. He'd have to pay royalties, but that would come out of what he makes. It's genius, if I must say so myself."

"Well, you must, because it's crazy. Billy's music is loud. It's distorted riffs and angry, angst-filled lyrics. What part of that says lullaby to you?"

"The other stuff. Like what he's playing in there. I bet he could convince a record company to put out an album of baby rock."

"Who'd buy it? Baby stoners?"

He huffed. "No, their parents. Let me talk to Christa."

He was serious. "No way. Billy doesn't have anything to do with her, you know that. Besides, I don't trust her."

"I can at least put it out there, see what she thinks."

"And if she thinks it's a good idea, she'll take it and run with it."

"She wouldn't do that. And if she can help his career, why are you standing in the way?"

"Since when do you care about his career?"

"I care for your sake. I'm just saying what he's doing is good. I bet other parents would pay for something like that. Parents who can't pick up a guitar and play their little ones to sleep."

Billy was good, and maybe it was a good idea. And he sure as hell deserved a break.

"Let me talk with Christa. If she can help him, wouldn't you be okay with it?"

"I'm more worried about what Christa would want in return."

"Oh, she's not so bad. I like her. She's funny, and she's got a great sense of style. She gets a bad rap because she's so aggressive, but isn't that what you want in that business? Think about it. If she were a guy, no one would bat an eye at what she's done to promote her clients. She's a woman succeeding in a man's world, and that's what makes her scary."

It wasn't Christa's success that scared Kate, but she wasn't about to tell Joey that.

"She's a shrewd businesswoman. I guarantee, all she'd want is her cut." He folded his arms and gave Kate a look that made her feel like she was being selfish.

"Just let me see what she thinks. Then we'll suggest it to him. There's no harm in that, right?"

She nodded, trying to ignore the giant red flag waving in the back of her mind.

"Right."

CHAPTER 43

It was one of the stupidest things he'd ever heard. Rock lullabies. Yet here he was, sitting on an uncomfortable leather sofa while Christa Dunphy made him wait.

Billy glanced at his watch. It was three minutes later than the last time he'd looked, thirty-three minutes since he'd arrived. He'd been on time, although he'd expected her to keep him waiting. And she did.

Not that it wasn't interesting.

Christa was now the lead agent at Bennett-Friedman's New York office, which encompassed an entire floor of an ultramodern building across from the park. A study in chrome and glass, the reception area appeared to have been lifted from the set of a futuristic movie. Even the receptionist, who looked as if she'd just stepped off the cover of Swedish *Playboy*, had an otherworldly look about her.

Not that he would've expected anything less, but he was surprised to see the apparent fringe benefits of signing with the agency so prominently displayed.

After he'd given his name to the legs at the front desk, she'd alerted Christa that he had arrived and offered him a single barrel bourbon, which surprisingly, he'd refused.

He glanced around the large waiting room. Other than the long, low sofa on which he sat, there were two zebra-print side chairs. Both had been occupied when he entered, or he would have chosen one of those. They didn't look much more comfortable, but at least they weren't as low to the ground. He felt like a praying mantis. The slope of the sofa was so steep that his knees jutted out and his legs splayed open. When he looked up, the receptionist smiled. It seemed he wasn't the only one having a problem keeping his knees together.

"Are you sure there isn't something I can interest you in?" She uncrossed her long, bare legs, giving him a direct shot of her pantyless crotch before crossing them again.

Damn if his jeans didn't get a little tighter. He dragged his eyes up to her face.

"Positive, but thank you."

He shifted uncomfortably. It had been six weeks. The last thing he needed was a beaver shot burned into his brain. Wait. *Six weeks?*

"What's today's date? The twenty-first, right?"

The way she nodded and smiled, you would've thought he'd asked for her phone number.

He grinned. Six weeks. Tomorrow Rhiannon would be six weeks old. Hot damn. He'd pick up a bottle of wine, and tonight, as soon as Kate put the baby to bed—

"Ms. Dunphy will see you now."

Another knockout, a brunette this time, waited in front of the glass door that led to the inner sanctum. He glanced at his watch. Forty minutes. Definitely payback. The way the blonde smiled as he stood, her eyes climbing the length of him from his boots to the double black hoops in his ears, he knew he could walk out of here with her when he'd finished with Christa. He wouldn't, but it was still a powerful feeling.

Christa rose to greet him. "I'm sorry to keep you waiting. You know how it is."

She gestured for him to sit while she floated over to a bar built into the wall. Ice clinked as she poured. She didn't bother to ask what he wanted.

She handed him the glass, then clicked the rim with her's.

"I understand congratulations are in order. Seems like you've fathered yourself a little muse."

It had been awhile since he'd had whiskey this good. He let it sit on his tongue, enjoying the burn, savoring it before swallowing. "Thanks. Although I think the muse in this case would be Joey."

She laughed. "Well, he certainly is excited. I have to say I am, too. Not that it's something I'd normally be interested in, but Joey can be a little relentless, and," she flashed him a wide grin, "I'm already familiar with your abilities." She settled back into the buttery soft leather chair next to his, slowly drawing one leg over the other. Was she wearing panties?

"It's good, Billy. I think there's a market. I've put out a few feelers, and I have some record companies who might be willing to bite. Of course, I need to know where we stand before I go any further." The lift of her eyebrows as she raised her glass to her lips filled in the blanks.

He should have expected this. He'd known she wouldn't stick her neck out without some kind of commitment from him. And was that so bad? He'd been busting his ass and getting nowhere fast since they'd parted ways. The least he could do was hear her out. "You mean represent me again?"

She threw her head back and laughed. "Did you think I was going to invest my time and energy as a favor to you or to Joey? The fact that I'm willing to work with you after what you pulled the last time is a testament to my belief in your talent."

She reached for a cigarette. "Since you're pitching this to me, I assume you're not working with another agent or producer, which leads me to believe the dissolution of our partnership wasn't in your best interest. As for me," she waved her hand to encompass the corner office and its expansive view of Central Park, "I'm doing just fine. To be honest, if I do take you on, I'll probably hand you off to a junior agent." She gave his arm a little squeeze. "But don't worry, everything goes through me. If you live up to my expectations, who knows?" Smoke swirled around her head. "So, tell me. How's it going?"

"I'm busy, but it could be better."

"Busy with . . .?"

"I have a lot of studio work."

"I see." She took a deep drag on her cigarette. "You certainly don't need me if you're just looking to be a hired gun. But I guess that's good. Keeps you close to home and your little family?"

"Yeah, it's good. Not exactly where I'm planning to take my career, though."

"No. I didn't think so." Her eyes flickered over him. "Why don't I call Patrick in to join us? I had him do some legwork in case you'd want to come back into the fold. Let's see what he's come up with. Perhaps he can give you an idea of where we see you going if you come on board."

Dozens of faces looked down at him from the wall over the bar. Famous faces. Faces of musicians he revered, emulated—in one or two cases, maybe even idolized. Christa's clients.

He nodded.

"Excellent." She picked up his glass and refilled it at the bar while they waited for Patrick.

Christa knew what he wanted, and she knew how to make it happen.

Over the protests of her throbbing arms and aching back, Kate stood at the window and bounced a wailing Rhiannon on one shoulder. The streetlights cast a milky blue light over the courtyard. Circles of dried leaves swirled across the pavement, starting and stopping with the wind as it blew off the river.

She'd been at it for hours. *Hours.* Since early afternoon, she'd put the baby down just three times: twice so she could go to the bathroom and a third time when she needed to walk away before she lost her mind. Rhiannon's gasping howls had reached all the way to the kitchen, so after a few minutes, she'd gone back to get her. The crying had to be her fault. In trying to eat healthier, she'd probably given Rhiannon gas or something.

She paced the living room, singing and rubbing her daughter's back until she heard Billy's key turn in the lock.

"Finally." She flew down the hallway. "Here. Take her."

"Gimme a second." He slipped off his jacket, then hung it on the rack. "What's the matter?" he cooed to the beet-red, tear-streaked face.

If Rhiannon stopped crying for him, she swore she'd go right off the deep end. A tiny part of her was almost relieved when Rhiannon took one look at him and screamed even harder.

"What happened?" He was looking at her as if she'd been pinching his daughter all afternoon. "You're not even dressed." He wrinkled his nose at her stained T-shirt and flannel pajama bottoms. He, on the other hand, looked as if he'd just stepped off the cover of *Rolling Stone*.

She slumped against the wall, as if her body could no longer hold her upright. "She's been screaming since you left, which was about seven hours ago. I haven't eaten or showered. And I hope you're not hungry, because I haven't even thought about dinner yet."

"What're you yelling at me for?" he asked calmly, which made her even angrier. Not because any of it was his fault, but because he was capable of being calm—not to mention showered and dressed. "And don't worry about dinner. I've already eaten."

There was a small explosion inside her head. "Great. Not because I'd want to eat or anything." She stormed down the hall. "You're on for the rest of the night." She tossed the words over her shoulder. "I'm done!"

To emphasize her point, she slammed the bathroom door, flipped on the noisy overhead exhaust fan, and burst into tears.

⁓

It was quiet when she stepped out of the bathroom an hour later. Soft jazz played on the stereo. Whatever was cooking in the kitchen smelled wonderful. When she peeked into the bassinet next to the bed, it was empty. Rhiannon's door was closed.

She wasn't sure whether to cry again or laugh like a hyena. Neither seemed a particularly appropriate response.

It was after nine, and since there was no reason to get dressed, she slipped a fresh nightgown over her head, braided her hair, and headed for the kitchen to eat a little crow. And if her nose was correct, it would be sautéed in onions and garlic.

A pot of water was simmering on the stove next to a skillet of sautéed vegetables. An open box of fettucine sat on the counter. The table was set. Next to each place was a wine glass. Billy stood at the kitchen window holding a tumbler of what she assumed was whiskey.

"Feeling better?" he asked when he noticed her standing in the doorway.

She nodded and mumbled an apology.

He turned up the heat on the stove. "Fettucine primavera okay?"

It sounded delicious, actually. "Yes. Thank you." She pointed to the wine glass. "You know I'm not supposed to drink."

"One glass won't hurt. Besides, I'll get up during the night if you want. We have formula—I checked. "

"It's pretty quiet. I assumed you'd given her to the gypsies."

He chuckled softly. "Not likely. I'm already in too deep. I think she was just exhausted. Finally wore herself out." He pulled a bottle of white zinfandel from the refrigerator and filled Kate's glass, drained his whiskey, and filled his wine glass as well.

"To better days," he said, raising his glass.

"Amen." She took a sip of her wine. "Speaking of which, how'd it go?"

Billy turned his back to her as he emptied the box of fettucine into the boiling water. "Um, okay. Good. Different." He picked up a wooden spoon and began stirring the stiff strips.

"And? Does she think it's a good project?"

"She does." He unwrapped a stick of butter for the Alfredo sauce.

She waited. When he didn't elaborate, she pushed again.

"What happens now? Do you have to find a producer? Do you record it on your own? I guess that's possible. Can we afford that?"

"Um, no."

"No, we can't afford it?"

He shook his head.

"Billy!"

He gave the pasta another stir, then sat down across from her.

"Christa's gonna find a producer—or more likely, her assistant will. I met with the both of them, actually." He tossed back more than half of his wine. "They think it's a great project. Very marketable. If that's the case, and I can make some money, I can get back out there with the band. More concerts, you know? Doing what I really want."

She twirled the stem of her wineglass. "Yeah, but the studio work—that's good, too. You're home more and it pays pretty well, right?"

"Yeah, sure." He smiled nervously. "Of course."

She gave him space as he finished his wine in one long swallow.

"But it's not what you want, is it?"

His eyes met hers. "Not really."

Needing a moment to process, she raised her glass and took a sip. *You can do this, Kate. This is what he wants.*

"What's next then?"

Billy stared at the plate in front of him. He grabbed the bottle and refilled his glass and took another sip before he spoke. "I know we should've talked about this, but I also know I would've done it anyway. I'm sorry. And I hope you're not disappointed or mad, but I've had to put my career on hold for a while now. I can't keep doing that. I signed another contract with Christa today. She's already got a record producer interested in the album. On top of that, Patrick, her assistant, has been putting out feelers to get Viper out on the road as an opener. They're talking concerts, Katie, like Bon Jovi, Van Halen, Metallica. Maybe not right away, and nothing's definite, but it's possible. I can't do it on my own."

He pushed away from the table so suddenly, the chair nearly tipped over. With his back to her, he stood at the stove, the spoon clenched in his fist.

"I'm losing ground here. I can't do the nine-to-five thing. I'm not Mike Fucking Brady!"

She heard what he was saying. But what she also heard, the part he'd be the first to deny, was the tone in which he'd said it. He was defensive, almost daring her to argue. If she did, she knew he'd use it as an excuse to storm out. To prove he was right, that she didn't know him or understand him.

Christa scared her. She didn't trust her. And in spite of this new talk of an assistant, she still didn't feel comfortable—but this wasn't her decision to make.

She swallowed the wine, along with the lump in her throat. "I think it's wonderful. Christa's the best in the business, right? And you deserve the best. I'm on your side, Billy. I'm your biggest fan."

He visibly relaxed, as if he'd been holding his breath since they'd begun talking.

"Really?" He turned. "You're okay with this, with me going back on the road? What about days like today? What will you do when you need a break?"

"We'll be okay. I've got a whole building full of substitute grandmas here to help if I need them."

"Oh, babe. You don't know how glad I am to hear you say this." He pulled her to her feet and buried his face against her neck. "God, I love you."

She squeezed him tightly. She knew what he wanted and what he needed. And she knew she loved him enough to risk everything so he could have it.

CHAPTER 44

"I can't believe of all the places I could've taken you for your birthday, this is where you wanted to come—again."

Billy buckled Rhiannon into the highchair at Palermo's as Kate slid across the red leatherette bench and picked up the menu.

"You like it, too. Besides, I like to think of it as our place."

"Yeah, but we could come here any time. We could've gotten a babysitter, gone into the city, seen a show. Your parents offered to watch her."

"I'm not sure I'm ready for that yet. And with you gone so much lately, I didn't think you'd want her away overnight."

He ran his fingers through Rhiannon's yellow curls before he slipped into the booth. "Just as long as I get some alone time with the birthday girl, I'm good." He handed Rhiannon a spoon, which she began banging on the tray of the highchair.

It felt good to have Billy home. He'd finished recording the lullaby album in late February, and Christa had kept her promise. Viper had so many bookings he was away more than he was home. Some of the trips, especially the ones to the West Coast, had lasted several weeks.

They weren't opening for any big names yet, but Billy seemed content. In fact, although he swore he didn't like being gone so long, he was about as happy as she had ever seen him, especially whenever they were booked in the Pacific Northwest. The music emerging from that area, especially the alternative rock coming out of Seattle, struck a chord with him. It was all he could talk about some days.

"So, the usual?" he asked, scanning the menu.

"I don't know. I might have eggplant parmigiana."

"Really?" He looked up surprised. "You always order the same thing—meatball sub, French fries, brown gravy. I thought that was the main reason we come here."

"I'm just craving something different." She glanced at him over her menu, watching as he read the specials.

He flopped his menu onto the table. "I'm gonna have the mussels in garlic and butter over linguine."

Her stomach pitched, and bile rose to the back of her throat. "Please don't. All that garlic, you know, and the smell?"

He smirked as he reached for the menu he'd just set down. "Oh, but you can eat liverwurst?"

She clapped her hand over her mouth and scrambled to her feet. "Excuse me," she gasped, rushing toward the hallway leading to the restrooms. The ladies' room door was locked. *Dammit!* Thank God no one was in the men's room. She yanked open the door and made it to the toilet just in time. After she'd emptied her stomach and was sure the nausea had passed, she ran cold water into the palm of her hand and tried to rinse out her mouth.

"Subtle," she muttered to her reflection as she dabbed a wet paper towel over her runny mascara.

When she opened the door, she was startled to find Billy leaning against the wall opposite the men's room, his arms folded. From where she stood she could see the waitress playing with Rhiannon. Pressing her lips together, she raised her eyes slowly until they met Billy's.

"I'm guessing there's something you'd like to tell me."

She tried to gauge his mood—not that it mattered. Not only was the cat out of the bag, it had just caused her to hurl in the men's room.

"Surprise!" she said in a shaky voice.

His lips curled into the smile that still made her knees weak.

"It certainly is."

Billy set his Martin in the corner of Rhiannon's room, careful not to wake her. He leaned over the crib, soothed by the rhythm of her breathing. It was one of the things he missed when he was away: sitting in the dark, listening to the sounds his child makes, knowing she was safe.

He twirled a soft curl between his fingers. Although he'd been away a lot, he hadn't missed most of the important firsts—yet. He'd been there when she rolled over, when she sat up, and when she crawled. He'd even been there the first time she stood. She'd crawled toward him while he was changing strings, then pulled herself up using his foot and then his amp.

What he would miss was her first birthday, and that was killing him. He was booked on a tour through Europe. Given the timing, chances were pretty good he'd miss her first steps, too. That was one of the reasons he'd given Katie the video camera for her birthday. It had all the latest technology and was small enough to drop into the diaper bag. It had cost him almost $1,800, but it would be worth it. Of course, that was before he knew they were having another baby. He planted a kiss on his daughter's soft cheek and pulled the bedroom door shut.

Kate was sitting up in bed, thumbing through the instruction manual. The video camera lay on the bed in a jumble of cords and blank cassettes. It was hard to look at her without feeling as if his heart would bust wide open, not to mention the other part of him that responded just as enthusiastically.

"She asleep?"

"Yep." He pulled his T-shirt over his head and tossed it into the corner. "Although she was fighting it, especially while I was singing." He unbuckled his belt and the button on his jeans. They dropped to the floor. He kicked them into the corner, then fell onto the bed beside her.

"I'm not surprised. She misses you."

He picked up the camera and peered at her through the viewfinder. "What about you? You miss me, too?"

Sad eyes met his. She never complained, never said she didn't want him to leave, but he knew she wasn't happy he was gone so much. Even if she didn't say it, he could feel it. Somehow, that made it worse. She gave him a tremulous smile. "Of course I do."

He tugged the manual from her hands and scooted forward to nibble at her lower lip. "How about I show you how much I've missed you?"

Later, as Kate lay curled around him like a vine, she pointed out that he was taking the news of her pregnancy well.

He was. He was also being careful not to make another misstep like the last time he found out she was pregnant. He smiled indulgently and rubbed his thumb against the base of her neck. "I'm kind of surprised, since I thought you couldn't get pregnant while you were nursing. But I knew we'd eventually have more kids. If I remember correctly, you want five."

"I do. Just not all before my twenty-first birthday." She shimmied on top of him, her hair raining down on either side of his face. "So you're really okay? You're not angry? I didn't plan this, you know. I was as surprised as you."

Her eyes were a deep jade in the low light. He tucked her hair behind her ear.

"You want an honest answer?"

Her face fell.

He pressed two fingers against her lips. "Just listen. Before I met you, I didn't want any kids. I didn't want to be responsible for fucking up somebody else's life. I didn't even want a relationship. I wanted to worry about me and nobody else. And then there you were. All you did was look at me, and I was a goner. Falling in love with you was the best thing I've ever done. I have no idea how to be a parent, but as long as I get to do it with you, then whatever you want, Katie. You want another kid? Two more? Three? I'm okay with that. In fact, I think it's great."

CHAPTER 45

FEBRUARY 20, 1991

"Slimming?" Kate held the green velvet gown over her swollen belly. "I look like a whale."

"It's perfect," Joey yelled over his mobile phone. "Would I make you wear something that didn't make you look beautiful? You're my best advertisement."

"You're full of shit and you know it. I thought Christa was your best advertisement."

"She pays me to make her look good. You, I do for free. The dress is perfect. I just feel bad I can't do your hair and makeup."

"Like you said, she pays you. I'm not paying you, because whether you work your magic or not, I'm gonna look like a whale in an evening gown."

"You're breaking up!" His words were bracketed by static. "I'm almost to Christa's. I'll see you later. You're going to look fabulous!"

With Joey's voice ringing in her ears, Kate fingered the buttery velvet as she slipped the gown onto its padded hanger. It was a beautiful dress, and she was lucky he'd found it. If only she didn't look like—

A sharp pain shot through her abdomen. She gripped the doorknob until it passed.

Nature was telling her to slow down. And she would. Tomorrow. In the meantime, she had to make lunch and get Rhiannon down for a nap, or she'd be miserable by the time the babysitter arrived.

On her way to the kitchen, Kate peeked in on her daughter. Billy sat cross-legged on the floor while Rhiannon brushed his hair. Judging by the tiny jewel-studded tiara and strands of multicolored beads he wore, she guessed their daughter was getting him ready for his big night.

"I think that's exactly how you should go."

He looked up, his face splitting into a wide grin.

"Tempting, but I'm sure Joey didn't go through all that trouble to find a tux in my size so I could go in a T-shirt and tiara. I'd hate to disappoint him."

"You'd rather disappoint your daughter?" she asked in mock horror. "Besides, if you go looking like that, no one will notice I look like Shamu."

Rockin' My Baby had not only been an enormous hit, it had landed Billy a Grammy nomination for Best Instrumental Arrangement. While the album didn't lend itself to a concert tour—nobody wanted to sit through a concert with an audience of wailing infants—Billy's success meant Viper was booked solid for the next few months. That, combined with the record sales, had finally provided them with a measure of financial security.

They were even looking to buy a house. The timing was perfect, since they were outgrowing their tiny apartment at warp speed. The only thing standing in their way was that they couldn't agree on where to live.

Having come to a tense but civil understanding with her parents, the idea of moving back to Belleville had begun to sound more and more attractive. The promise of trustworthy babysitters and the possibility of spending a night or two on the road with Billy had been dangled in front of her like a carrot. But Billy adamantly refused; he wouldn't even discuss it. He wanted to remain closer to Manhattan and the airports. And lately he'd begun dropping hints about moving to Seattle. The thought of moving across the country was terrifying.

They had looked at houses in Bayonne, but they were small, with little more to offer than a third bedroom, maybe a garage or a basement, and a huge price tag. The last time she'd gone back home for a visit, she'd fallen in love with a two-hundred-year-old farmhouse that, while also small, was bigger than anything they'd seen in the city. It needed work, but it had potential: two relatively private acres, a garage, and was more than $50,000 cheaper than anything else they'd seen. Billy agreed it was a better deal, but he wouldn't budge. At this rate, they'd be living in their cramped apartment forever.

"How about some lunch?" she asked. "Then a nap."

"Good, cuz I need one." He faked a yawn, then grabbed Rhiannon and tickled her. "But I think Mommy means you!" Rhiannon dissolved into giggles as Kate headed for the kitchen. She was thinking there was no sweeter sound than her daughter's laughter, when another stabbing pain shot through her. Placing her hand on the swell of her belly, she felt the abdominal wall grow hard beneath her fingers.

"Oh dear God." She inhaled sharply. "This can't be happening."

A third contraction gripped her as she was making lunch. Sinking into a seat at the kitchen table, she took long, slow breaths until it was over.

When it had passed, she set the grilled cheese sandwiches on the plates and called Billy and Rhiannon in for lunch.

Afraid of another contraction while they were eating, she quickly downed half her sandwich, then told Billy she was going to lie down for a bit.

He was trying to coax Rhiannon into finishing her lunch. "That's a great idea," he said distractedly. "That way you won't be tired later." He looked up hopefully. "I know it's asking a lot, but I'd really like to hit that afterparty."

"Sure." She hurried from the kitchen as another contraction formed low in her belly. They were starting out so strong, she held out slim hope that it was false labor. Once it passed, she dialed Joey and left a message with his service. Then she lay down, hoping that whatever seemed determined to start would stop.

Twenty minutes and two contractions later, the bedroom door opened.

Billy quietly stripped down for his shower. When he'd gone into the bathroom, she opened her eyes and looked mournfully at the beautiful gown hanging next to his borrowed tux. She'd spent hours agonizing over a dress, and now she might not get to wear it after all.

Once the shower had been running awhile and she was sure the bathroom would be filled with steam, making her face difficult to see, she opened the door.

"Babe? I'm not feeling well."

He pulled the curtain aside, then swiped at the lather dripping into his eyes.

"What do you mean?"

"I kinda have a headache, and I feel sick to my stomach." She was such a terrible liar.

"You're kidding." His face fell. "Do you think you're in labor?"

Shit. A direct question. "It isn't like last time," she stammered. This was true. Last time, her water had broken first, and she hadn't had any pain or contractions for hours. This time, though, her water was intact but she was in a hell of a lot of pain.

"Oh, Katie. I don't want to go without you."

She wasn't going to let anything short of crowning keep him from going.

"I know, but you have to go. Maybe I'm just tired. Maybe I ate something that didn't agree with me. Maybe it's a bug." *Maybe I'm about to pop out a baby.*

"Lie down. We'll see how you feel later. Then we'll decide."

She nodded, although she was pretty sure things were only going to progress from here.

The phone was ringing when she stepped into the hall.

"What?" Joey yelled over the street noise.

"Where are you?"

"I just finished up at Christa's. I'm heading home to change."

"How does she look?" She hoped he'd describe a huge zit or say he was unable to do anything with the hairy wart on her chin, or maybe that her giant boobs had deflated.

"Fabulous," he gloated.

"Fuck you," she mumbled.

"What?"

"So true."

"Yeah, that's what I thought you said. What's up?"

If she told him the truth, he'd make her tell Billy. Lie number two coming up.

"I'm sick. I'm not going."

"You have to go!"

"Trust me, it's not a good idea. I was hoping you'd keep me company."

Silence.

"Are you contagious?"

"Pretty sure I'm not contagious."

"Then what's wrong with you?"

"Headache and upset stomach."

"Sounds contagious."

Joey wasn't going to the awards, but Christa had wrangled him invitations to some of the afterparties, including the one hosted by Sirenic Records.

"I promise." Kate gritted her teeth against another contraction. "I'm not contagious. Maybe a little food poisoning." All this lying was giving her a real headache.

"Food poisoning?"

"Please. I'd just feel better having you here while Billy's gone. You can still make the party after he gets back."

"He's going without you?"

She hadn't gotten that far, but what was one more lie? "Yes. Please?"

"Jeez, Kate. This is my first awards season, and I'm gonna miss the first party of the year."

"Oh honey, you have so many parties in your future, you'll be turning down invitations left and right."

"Yeah, right." She could hear the disappointment in his voice, but she knew he wouldn't let her down. "I need to make a quick stop at my apartment, then I'll head out. Need me to bring anything?"

"Just your sense of humor."

She hung up before he could ask what she'd meant by that.

"Any better?" Billy stood in the doorway, his hair dripping and a towel wrapped around his waist.

She shook her head.

"This sucks." He rubbed a second towel over his head. "Can't you take an aspirin or something? This is a big night for me—for us."

He was trying to hide his irritation. The last thing she wanted was for him to be upset with her, but it would be better for him to be annoyed than to sit home and wait for something that could take hours. To distract him, she gave his towel a quick tug, and it fell to the floor. She ran her hands over his chest and the tight ridges of his stomach, then wrapped her arms around his waist, or at least tried to.

"I miss you," she whispered against his chest, still damp from the shower. "I miss this."

"If you're worried about how big you are, don't be," he said, trying to be helpful. "It's obvious you're not fat."

She rolled her eyes, glad that he couldn't see it.

He held her for a moment, then gave her a quick pat on the ass. "I guess if I'm going, I better get ready."

Kate ducked into the bathroom ahead of another contraction. Her knuckles turned white as she gripped the edge of the sink. It hurt like hell, but so far the contractions remained irregular and widely spaced. When she could move, she slunk out to the couch, trying to stay out of his way while he got ready.

When he finally emerged, he looked so incredibly handsome that the disappointment almost did her in. Maybe she would just take her chances. There were plenty of hospitals in New York if her labor progressed. But then common sense prevailed. It would be much worse to go and then have to make him leave.

"You'll be the best-looking one there." She tried to ignore the lump in her throat and straightened the black bow tie above his black wing collar shirt. "I wish I could see Asher Drake's face when he gets a load of you."

"I'm sure he's forgotten me by now," he said as she pulled a couple long blond strands from his jacket. "Are you sure you aren't up to going? It doesn't feel right to go without you."

"I'm sorry. If you really wanna take someone who deserves to be there, it would be Joey."

"I'm not taking Joey, but if by some miracle I win, I'll make sure to thank him."

"Did you write your speech?"

"No. Because I'm not gonna win. Besides, that would jinx me."

"You're gonna win."

"Did you listen to the other albums?"

"No. I just think you should win."

"From your lips to God's ears."

When he went to kiss Rhiannon good-bye, Kate ducked into the bathroom. She was breathing through another contraction when she heard a loud knock on the front door.

"Coming," Billy called. He tapped on the bathroom door. "You okay?"

She grit her teeth. "Be right there." If he didn't leave soon, she might give birth on the bathroom floor.

"You haven't left yet?" Joey's voice could be heard over jet engines. There was a second knock as she shuffled from the bathroom.

"That must be the car." Billy rushed toward her while Joey went to tell the driver Billy would be down shortly.

Lifting her chin in his hand, he searched her eyes. "Is there something you're not telling me?"

She felt a spurt of panic, but before she could tell another lie, Joey appeared behind him.

"Yes. I realized I'm not gay after all. I was able to convince Kate to run away with me. This whole Grammy nomination was just our way of getting you out of the house so she could pack. Oh yeah, and the baby's mine." He let out an exasperated sigh. "Good grief! Your limo's waiting. In this neighborhood, you'll be lucky if it's not up on blocks already."

Billy glared at him. "That's not even funny."

"It wasn't meant to be." Joey took Rhiannon from him.

"Promise me as soon as you win, you'll call." Kate tugged on his lapels.

"Promise!"

"I promise. I'll call you as soon as it's over."

"No. Right after you win."

"What if I don't win?"

"Not possible. But call me no matter what. As soon as your category's over. I'll feel better if you call. Please?" She was starting to sound desperate.

"I promise. I'll call you as—"

She pulled his mouth to hers and kissed him, hard, then softly, then hard again. When she stood back, he looked at her with a funny smile. "What was that about?"

"Everything. Everything and nothing. I want you to know how much I love you, and I want you to know how disappointed I am that I'm not going."

"That wasn't the kind of kiss someone with a headache gives."

"I do. I love you, and I believe in you."

He kissed her forehead. "I love you, too."

"Oh my God!" Joey cried. "Go already!"

As he slipped into his overcoat, Billy turned to Joey. "I feel better knowing you're here."

"That's too bad, then," Joey answered.

"Enough!" She glared at Joey as she walked Billy to the door. "Don't forget: Call me as soon as your category's over, win or lose."

When she returned to the living room, she gave Joey a weak smile.

"Pick Rhiannon up and let her wave until he drives away, okay? I'll be right back. I have a surprise for you."

"Oh, goody. Uncle Joey loves surprises!" He twirled his godchild across the room and over to the window. "Oh my God," he called out. "She's so cute. She's throwing kisses."

"Is he gone yet?" Kate called from the bedroom.

"They just pulled away." He set Rhiannon down and looked up to see Kate standing at the other end of the living room with her coat and her suitcase.

"Surprise!" she cried through clenched teeth.

His jaw dropped. "Oh shit—you *are* running away with me!"

"Even better: I'm in labor. Tag! You're it!"

~

Joey alternated between talking to himself and snapping at Kate as he loaded her bag into the back of his BMW the moment the babysitter arrived.

"I can't believe you think you can pull this off, missy." He grumbled through clenched teeth as he made a U-turn on Avenue C.

"Look," she explained as patiently as she could under the circumstances. "If I'd told him, he wouldn't have gone. I'd feel guilty he missed it. I couldn't do that to him."

"Don't you think he's gonna be pissed that you didn't tell him?" He took his eyes off the road long enough to glare at her. "Although not as pissed as I am."

"Hopefully he'll be back before the baby comes. I was in labor with Rhiannon for—" She gripped the armrest.

"Oh God," Joey cried, picking up speed.

"It's okay," she said through gritted teeth.

"The hell it is!"

CHAPTER 46

Billy slipped into his seat. Radio City Music Hall. At least he was on the aisle. Six four for two and a half hours in a cramped seat with no leg room was a recipe for an uncomfortable evening. He stuck a finger under his collar. He wasn't sure what he was feeling. Excitement? Nerves? It was unreal. Like he'd been transported from his couch through the TV screen and dropped into the audience. This was one weird fucking acid trip.

Bonnie Raitt strolled past in a jacket that shimmered like Christmas lights. The whole damn theater sparkled as if someone had peeled the roof back far enough to let thousands of stars sift over their human counterparts.

Then again, not everyone was decked out. Kirk Hammett and Lars Ulrich stood a few rows in front of him, neither even wearing a tie. He tugged at his collar again. Fucking Joey, convincing Katie he needed to wear a tuxedo.

Katie. He checked his watch. If he hurried, he should be able to find a payphone and check on her before the show started.

"This seat taken?" A bare leg pressed against his thigh.

"Oh, hey. Not really." He stood to step into the aisle, but Christa didn't wait, stepping past him and pushing her body against his in a tight squeeze, pinning him in place. His eyes dropped to her breasts, which threatened to spill from the top of her strapless black gown.

"Sorry," she said with a wry smile as she claimed Kate's empty seat. "I forgot how much space you take up."

"Where's Barry?"

"He's not coming." She dropped her head. "I'm not sure it's going to work out." She dabbed at the corner of her eye, although he noticed she was still wearing the golf ball she called an engagement ring. "We're from two different worlds. He's Wall Street and I'm Madison Square Garden. I'm getting home when he's getting up." She rested a hand on his arm. "I'm sure you of all people know what I'm talking about."

He was about to say he didn't when she asked about Kate.

"She's not feeling well. Thinks she might have a touch of food poisoning."

"Oh, that's too bad. It must have come on suddenly."

"More or less."

"Joey will be so disappointed. He was looking forward to their 'girl time.'" She crooked two fingers on each hand, forming quotes.

"What?"

"You know. Joey and Kate." She laughed. "Girl time. Trust me. I love girl time with Joey just as much." Christa had not only become one of Joey's clients, the two of them shared a love of all things bitchy.

He shook his head. "No, she's sick. Joey went over to stay with her."

She looked surprised. "Oh. I must've misunderstood. When I spoke to him I got the impression Kate just didn't feel like coming. I'm sure he said something about hanging out, watching TV, and eating popcorn. Although I imagine they'll also be trashing what everyone's wearing." She lowered her voice. "Speaking of which, did you get a look at—"

He glanced at his watch, his jaw tightening. "I'll be right back."

She grabbed his wrist as he stood.

"Where are you going?"

"I need to make phone call."

"You can't. They're about to start."

He hadn't noticed the house lights blinking. Pissed, he dropped back into his seat. Kate had been bitching for two weeks about how fat she looked in that dress, even though the damn thing had been made for her. It was perfect, and frankly, he'd been getting sick of telling her how good she looked. And now she pulls this bullshit and lies about not feeling well just so she can stay home? How could she do this to him? She knew how much he wanted her here, how much he needed her tonight.

The house lights went out. The orchestra started to play. Billy grit his teeth.

Christa leaned over, her head practically on his shoulder.

"I hope you're going to let me show you off later," she whispered. "There'll be a lot of people at that party I'd like you to meet, people who are dying to meet you."

He looked down at her, still scowling.

"Absolutely. Wouldn't think of missing it."

She ran her hand along his arm and gave him a squeeze.

"Perfect."

~

Joey waltzed in like a runway model in a pair of green scrubs.

"They're a little blah," he declared, "but they match my eyes."

"Your eyes are gray," Kate said, leaning into another contraction.

"Not tonight. I'm wearing green contacts. See?" He leaned closer.

The best she could do was shake her head and pant. Not getting the response he was hoping for, he pulled up a chair and gave Kate his hand.

"This sucks. We should be sitting on your ugly couch eating crap and drinking cheap wine." The harder she gripped, the louder he spoke. "Better yet! We should be dressed to the nines and sitting in the audience at Radio City Music Hall!"

A nurse rushed in. "Who's yelling?"

"He is," Kate gasped, collapsing against her pillow. "I thought it was supposed to be easier the second time."

"You want something for pain?"

"No," Joey replied stoically. "I'll be okay. Although I think she broke my hand."

Kate looked at the nurse and tried to smile. "I just need to get my bearings."

"When you get them, send some my way," Joey said, flexing his fingers.

The nurse gave her a wink. "I'll be back soon." She closed the door as she left, likely in deference to the volume of Joey's voice.

The next contraction coincided with the start of the Grammys broadcast.

"Are you squeezing from pain or excitement?" Joey asked as her fingers tightened around his.

"Both. I can't believe I'm missing this."

"You're not. You've got the best seat in the house. If you were there, you'd be sitting so far back you wouldn't be able to see a thing."

When the contraction ended, she closed her eyes. She was already exhausted. She made Joey promise to wake her if he heard Billy's name, although she was fooling herself if she thought she'd actually fall asleep anytime soon. Before he could answer, she grabbed his hand.

"I promise!" he cried as she squeezed.

She shook her head and grunted.

"Already? Honey, if you don't slow down you're gonna miss it, and he's never gonna get here in time. I love you, but I don't think I can do this."

She concentrated on her breathing, gluing her eyes to a print on the wall across from her of an idyllic beach. As the contraction wound down, another nurse appeared. She checked the printout from the last few contractions, then introduced herself.

"I'm Delia," she said with a warm smile. "I'll be your nurse tonight. How's Daddy doing?" She beamed at Joey.

He was staring at the TV screen. "Clueless. As usual."

Kate was grunting into another contraction, so he broke his focus to explain. He pointed at the television. "Daddy is there. At the Grammys."

Delia listened as Joey explained who Billy was and why he was there, detailing the role he'd played in Billy's success. When she asked if they knew when his category would be presented, he shook his head.

"No, but it better be soon. At the rate she's going, he may not get here in time. More importantly, I faint at the sight of blood. My people didn't sign up for this."

"I'm surprised you were able to get him to go," Delia said. "Although it is a pretty big deal."

Kate tried to roll to her side. Her back was killing her. "He doesn't know."

"What do you mean?"

Joey gave her a helpful heave. "She didn't tell him. She started having contractions but didn't want him to miss it, so she didn't tell him."

"I'm not due for two weeks," she said with a groan.

"How will he know you're here?"

"Oh, it's a brilliant plan. He's supposed to call home when he's done, and the babysitter will tell him." Joey's voice was loaded with sarcasm.

Delia looked at the monitor again. "Your contractions are very close. I'm going to give you some oxygen, which should help you and the baby." She slipped a nasal cannula into Kate's nostrils. "I'll be back in a bit," she promised.

Two more contractions came rolling in, one after the other. Delia returned with a doctor, who followed the printout from the monitor until the last contraction was over. As he introduced himself, Delia began pulling the curtain closed around them.

"Hi Kate, I'm Dr. Walters. I'm the resident on duty. How are we doing?"

She tried to resettle herself against the pillows. "Not good. I don't remember it being so hard last time."

"Your contractions are lasting a long time, and we're not getting a good enough read on the baby from the external monitor. I'm going to insert an internal fetal scalp electrode. It'll let us know exactly how the baby's doing. Okay?"

She nodded and closed her eyes, desperate to rest between contractions. It seemed no sooner had one finished than another began.

After Dr. Walters inserted the electrode, she heard him tell the nurse that she was still only dilated two centimeters. *Oh God!* That wasn't possible.

She'd been at this for hours already. That meant the baby wasn't coming soon. Given the amount of pain and her level of exhaustion, she didn't know how she would manage.

"Dr. Landry's on her way," Dr. Walters told her before he left.

At this moment, she couldn't care less. It was Billy she wanted. This had been a huge mistake. Another contraction gripped her. When she lost the ability to focus, Delia coached her through it, but it wasn't the same.

"Is something wrong?" she asked as she sank into the pillows.

Delia patted her leg. "Don't worry. Dr. Landry will be here soon."

And that's when she heard the presenter announce the category for Best Instrumental Arrangement. In spite of the fear and exhaustion, she tried to rally. "Turn it up," she begged.

Joey began punching buttons. The bed started to move. The hum drowning out the television.

"Turn it up!" she repeated.

"Stop yelling at me!"

He punched another button. The TV audio muted.

"Joey!"

Another nurse rushed into the room. "What's wrong?"

Kate pointed at the set. The presenter was reading Billy's name. The camera flashed to him in the audience. Through sheer willpower she sat bolt upright, grabbed Joey's arm, and squeezed harder than she had during any of her contractions.

"Was that Christa sitting with him?"

"Maybe." He tried to pull away.

"Why?"

He spoke so fast it sounded like one long word. "She was going anyway. When she heard you couldn't go, she said she'd sit with him so he wouldn't be alone." He tugged at his arm, to no avail. "You wouldn't want him sitting there with an empty seat, would you?"

"Yes, I would. Especially if she's the alternative."

"Calm down, Mrs. Donaldson," the nurse said.

"Yeah, calm down, Mrs. Donaldson," Joey repeated. With another yank, he was free.

" . . . Billy McDonald for *Rockin' My Baby!*"

She tried to speak, but it felt as if her insides were being ripped to shreds.

"Oh my God! He won!" Joey clawed for her hand.

Kate panted through the contraction and tried to focus on Billy as he made his way to the podium.

"Oh my goodness," exclaimed the new nurse. "That is one fine-looking man you have there."

Kate tried to smile but was pretty sure all she'd done was bare her teeth.

"Kate?" Dr. Walters appeared beside the bed. "Things aren't progressing."

"Not . . . now! Joey . . . turn it . . .up," she said between pants.

Joey didn't move. He was watching the doctor.

"One more contraction," Dr. Walters told Delia, "but tell them to get the OR ready."

"What's wrong?" Joey asked.

Dr. Walters raised his voice to address Kate. "Your contractions are coming too fast, and they're lasting too long. The baby isn't handling it well. You're not dilating either, so for all the work your body's doing, those contractions aren't proving effective. We're going to see how it goes with the next contraction, and if things don't improve, we're going to have to do a C-section."

She was too exhausted to be frightened. She looked up at the doctor, but what she saw was Billy just over his shoulder. He was with her, but he wasn't. He didn't know. If something happened, he'd never forgive her.

"Wait one minute," she begged. She angled her head toward Joey. "I can't hear."

The doctor stood back, but it was too late. Billy raised the little gold gramophone in the air. As the music came up, the camera cut to host Garry Shandling.

A nurse entered and whispered to Dr. Walters.

"Dr. Landry's here," he said. "She's going to meet us in the OR. What we need to do now is get that baby out, okay?" He gave her a reassuring pat and turned to Joey. "Mr. Donaldson? The nurse will show you where you can get ready."

Joey backed away, lifting his hands. "I'm not Mr. Donaldson. That was

Mr. Donaldson." He pointed to the television. The doctor looked up at Garry Shandling.

Kate couldn't speak. She was being sliced in two from the inside out. She grabbed the rail and let out a strangled cry.

Joey snapped to attention. "Kate. Listen to me. I won't leave you, I promise. Billy will be here soon. Everything will be fine."

His voice faded as the edges of her vision dimmed. Pain, sharp and jagged, tore through her. Lights flashed. She was moving. Fast. Faces swam over her. She tried to focus on just one. When she found it, she gripped his arm.

"Please," she gasped. "Save my baby."

~

Joey was on a slow burn, growing hotter by the minute.

Kate had returned from recovery shortly after midnight. Her eyes fluttered several times. She tried to wake, only to drift off again. He sat beside her, refusing to leave. There was no sign of Billy, and he couldn't bear the thought of her waking up alone.

An hour passed before she showed any real sign of life. She squeezed his hand, but it was nothing like the bone-crushing grip from earlier. Her voice was low and raspy. He had to lean closer to hear her.

"Please don't be hard on him," she whispered. "He's going to do a good job of that on his own. Promise you won't make it worse."

Her lids were heavy with anesthesia. She struggled to keep them open, intent on extracting a promise before she surrendered.

"You're an ass, you know that?" The words were harsh, but his voice was soft.

"I know." The ghost of a smile touched her lips as she drifted off.

The later it got, the harder it would be to keep his promise.

CHAPTER 47

Billy opened the front door, trying to be as quiet as he could. Joey's car was no longer parked out front, and since it was long past three, he was counting on slipping in undetected. The apartment was dark except for the flicker of blue light, and he was afraid Kate had fallen asleep in front of the TV. Instead, he found a strange teenager.

"Hey," he called softly, trying not to scare her. "Hey, you!"

The girl squinted at him, looking confused. When she appeared about to scream, he stepped back and lifted his hands, one of which held his Grammy. "Where's my wife?"

"Billy?" she asked hesitantly.

"Yeah. Where's Katie?"

"At the hospital." She yawned. "What time is it?"

"Almost three thirty. When did she go to the hospital?"

"Right after I got here, around six."

"What?" he demanded. "Why didn't she tell me?"

"Beats me." She yawned again. "Oh, yeah. Congratulations."

He stared at the little gold trophy as if seeing it for the first time and squelched the desire to hurl it against the wall. The only thing that mattered right now was getting to Katie.

There'd be plenty of time to beat himself up later.

Getting into the hospital in the middle of the night was a bitch. All the entrances were locked except for the emergency room, and he ended up running halfway around the block. Once he finally made it inside, he argued with four different people on his way upstairs. If he hadn't been holding Rhiannon, he would've busted someone's head open.

He expected things to be no different when the elevator opened onto the maternity ward. Instead, it seemed empty. The halls were dimly lit, and all was quiet except for the distant, frantic wail of a newborn. The nurses' station was unmanned.

He was pacing anxiously when Dr. Landry came around the corner.

"Oh, good. You're here." She reached up and stroked one of Rhiannon's golden curls.

"Where's Katie?"

"Follow me." She gave him a tired smile as she led him along the corridor. "Congratulations."

"Thanks. It was a big surprise."

"Two weeks early isn't that unusual. Of course, we didn't expect this."

His chest grew tight. "Excuse me?"

"You said you were surprised."

"The baby's here?"

"Yes." She looked confused. "You didn't know?"

He shook his head. "When?"

"Around eight thirty. Listen . . ."

His pulse quickened. "Is Katie okay? The baby?"

Dr. Landry directed him to a nearby bench.

"There were some complications."

His heart beat harder with every word until it was pounding so loudly, he had difficulty hearing.

"Kate suffered a placenta abruption. The placenta began to tear away from the uterine wall. She was in a great deal of pain and although she was in labor, she wasn't dilating. When the baby began to show signs of distress, we did an emergency C-section."

He felt dizzy; like he'd somehow ended up in a bad dream.

"We had some tense moments, but I got him out as fast as I could. His initial Apgar was a little low, but he improved on follow-ups. He's perfect."

"A boy?"

She nodded. "A beautiful, healthy boy. Kate will have a bit of a recovery, but she's going to be fine."

He began to shake. His voice was barely above a whisper. "How did it happen? I mean . . . her pregnancy. It was okay, right?"

"It was. She showed no signs anything was wrong at her last visit. I don't know why it happened. Once she got here, we monitored her and the baby closely, but when we saw he was having difficulty, we decided not to wait. We lost his heartbeat just before we got into the OR, but I had him out in less than sixty seconds." She stood. "We'll talk more tomorrow. What you need to know now is that in order to get Kate under as quickly as we did, we had to use a general anesthesia, so she's pretty groggy. She hasn't seen the baby yet. She may not even remember she had him. But she's fine, and so is your son." She smiled. "I'm sure Mr. Buccacino will heal nicely as well."

Nothing was making sense. "What happened to him?"

"Fainted." She chuckled. "He only needed a couple stitches. He wasn't too happy they had to shave the back of his head, though."

He held Rhiannon closer. The scent of baby shampoo and a hint of sweet citrus helped slow his heartbeat to its normal rhythm.

"Kate's probably asleep. Do you want me to take you to the nursery?"

"No. I need to see Katie."

"Of course." She escorted him to Kate's room, then promised she'd see them later that morning.

The room was nearly dark. He stood at the foot of the bed, his stomach in cramps. Kate lay motionless. A machine beeped steadily, attached to her by tubes and wires. Joey slept in a chair beside her, his head resting on the edge of the bed, his hand over hers. It was a touching scene, except the leading man was all wrong. Angry sobs welled in his chest, but he fought to hold them back.

Rhiannon whimpered. She rolled her face toward him. The feel of his daughter's warm, moist breath against his neck was calming. Joey lifted his head. He looked at Kate, and then his eyes narrowed into slits as he noticed Billy. He glanced at his watch, then stood and motioned for Billy to step into the corridor.

The door closed behind Billy with a soft click. He was about to offer his thanks when Joey turned on him.

"Where the fuck have you been?"

Billy's immediate defense was offense.

"Who the fuck do you think you're talking to? You know exactly where I was, and you know damn well she didn't tell me she was in labor."

Joey moved away from the door, speaking through gritted teeth. "You were supposed to call, remember? The babysitter said you never called."

"I did call. The line was busy. I figured Kate took the phone off the hook because she was mad at me for . . ." He stuck his chin out defiantly. "I called."

"You thought she'd be mad why?" Joey said.

"Nothing."

But he wouldn't let up. "Why? Because you forgot to mention her? Because you thanked fucking Christa and even me, and you forgot to mention your own wife?"

It was true. He hadn't thought he'd win, so he hadn't thought about what to say. It all happened so fast. He could say whatever he wanted now, but Joey was right. There was no excuse.

"I fucked up, okay? Happy?"

"Of course I'm not happy. While you were up there on the stage forgetting Kate, all hell was breaking loose here."

"Look, are you done yet?" He wanted Joey to stop talking. He already felt like shit; this wasn't helping.

"No. You wanna tell me why you were done over six hours ago and you're just showing up now?"

"Not really." Billy set his jaw stubbornly. What was he going to say, that he'd been pissed at Kate, so he'd used that as an excuse to go out and party? There was no excuse for the rest of his behavior. Joey needed to back the fuck down. He didn't need another conscience. He had one, and it was kicking his ass.

"Whatever," Joey said, clearly disgusted. "You don't owe me any explanation. She's the one you have to answer to. Although she'll just let you slide like usual. But before she does, let me tell you what her night was like."

Billy shifted Rhiannon into his other arm. "Make it fast. I wanna be with Katie."

"I'll take as long as I want."

"You're lucky I'm holding my daughter."

"Don't threaten me. I'm so pissed right now, you should be afraid of me!"

Part of him wished Joey *would* beat the shit out of him. What he had to say, however, was worse than any physical beating.

"Kate's contractions were bad, and the pain was excruciating. She squeezed my hand so hard I thought she'd broken the bones in my fingers."

Billy snorted. "Is that when you passed out?"

"Go ahead, make jokes. At least I was here."

Another kick in the gut.

"Did Dr. Landry tell you what happened? Did she tell you that they lost the baby's heartbeat, and because they only had seconds to spare, she had to start cutting before Kate was fully under anesthesia?"

His limbs had gone rubbery; his arms shook. Joey reached for Rhiannon. He let him take her, afraid he might drop her.

"Do you have any idea how close—," Joey's voice broke. He waited a second before he continued. "Do you have any idea how close we came to losing both her and the baby?"

It was becoming difficult to breathe.

"Where were you?" Joey's voice was plaintive and full of questions, questions he could never answer.

"I called." He tried to swallow. Whatever was stuck in his throat wouldn't budge. "Not right away. There were pictures, interviews, but within a half-hour or so, I called. The line was busy. It was after ten, and I knew you were with her. She never talks to anyone that late, so I figured she was mad." He ran his hands through his hair. "I thought she'd taken the phone of the hook, so I got even more pissed, especially after . . ." His mouth snapped shut. It all began to make sense. Christa. That fucking bitch. She'd played him, all night, with every move. Closing his eyes, he pinched the bridge of his nose and tried to calm the rage that was rising up within him. When he could speak again, he continued.

"Everyone went to the party at Sirenic, and part of me was feeling great because I'd won and the other part was pissed because I thought she'd blown off going with me and had taken the phone off the hook. It was stupid. I get it."

"She doesn't know."

"Doesn't know what?"

"She doesn't know you didn't mention her. She couldn't hear you."

All he wanted was to be with Katie, but he remained standing in the hallway, paralyzed with guilt.

"Here." Joey handed him the keys to his BMW. "Give me your keys. I'll take Rhiannon home and put her to bed. Go be with Kate."

Billy handed Joey his keys, then kissed his daughter.

"Hey," he called quietly as Joey made his way down the hall. "Thank you."

"Yeah," Joey answered, his voice flat. "Whatever. Congratulations."

CHAPTER 48

Several minutes passed before Billy could bring himself to go back inside. He was afraid to face her. Afraid she'd take one look at him and know. But once inside, once he got a better look at her, the hot shame of guilt crystallized into cold, jagged fear.

He watched, motionless, until he was certain he saw her chest rise and fall. She was breathing with the help of oxygen. Her arms were arranged stiffly at her sides. Her long, dark braid and the life-giving blood snaking its way through an IV into her hand were the only spots of color on her pale, still form. Her skin was waxy, and she seemed small and insignificant against the whiteness of her surroundings. A blanket covered her swollen belly. No longer ripe with promise, it resembled a lopsided pumpkin.

It was all wrong. Kate didn't sleep like that. Lying on her back made her feel vulnerable. If she wasn't on her stomach, she was curled into the curve of his arm. That was where he wanted her now. He wanted to feel her breath on his chest, to know he could protect her.

The feel of someone else in his arms made him shudder. It was as if his body were trying to erase the memory from earlier that evening. Beads of sweat bloomed at his temples. He tore off his overcoat, yanked off his tie, and tugged at the top buttons of his shirt. Swallowing the urge to vomit, he gripped the bed rail and sucked the air like it was pure Colombian Gold.

Kate looked so fragile, like she might shatter. He ran a finger down her arm. It was cold. She hated being cold. When he couldn't find another blanket, he placed his jacket across her chest, careful not to disturb the thin tube attached to her arm or the zigzag of wires snaking out from under her hospital gown.

"Is she awake yet?" A nurse moved silently to the opposite side of the bed. He shook his head.

"You must be Mr. Donaldson. I'm Delia. Congratulations."

"I should've been here." His voice was thin and reedy.

"She didn't want you to miss your big night, poor thing." She finished checking the monitors and IV, and then went to get another blanket.

When she returned, Billy tucked the blanket around Kate, then waited while Delia slipped a band on his wrist identifying him as the baby's father. His finger traced the words on the bright blue bracelet. This meant more than that statue mocking him at home—and he'd missed it.

He reached beneath the blankets and found Kate's hand. Then he leaned against the bed rail, closing his eyes. The nausea that choked him could have come from any number of things—a lack of food, too much coke and champagne—but he was betting it was guilt. He'd been thinking with his dick and his ego. He was terrified what it might cost him.

Christa had paraded him around like he was Slash, Eddie Van Halen, and Yngwie Malmsteen rolled into one. The next great rock guitar god—no one had been fooled but him. She introduced him to the biggest names in the record industry and convinced him they were as enthusiastic about his career as she was. She not only fed his ego, she made sure the Cristal kept flowing along with the high-grade cocaine.

What he really was, he realized too late, was her trained pet monkey.

While he had been hidden away in a back room with his pants open and the most powerful agent in the business on her knees, the girl he loved more than anything in the world was being sliced open like a ripe mango. A chill ran through him as he tried to shut out the image of Kate, terrified and alone on the operating table, while he— *Oh holy fuck.*

He rubbed the heels of his hands hard against his eyes. A kaleidoscope of sparks swirled beneath the lids. He staggered into the bathroom and puked until he thought his stomach would come up next.

When it stopped, he leaned against the sink until he could breathe. He rinsed his mouth, careful to avoid his image in the mirror. Night was fading. From the window in Kate's room, he could see thin pink threads of daylight along the horizon. He couldn't ever remember being so afraid of the dawn.

Unable to stomach his reflection in the glass, he returned to Kate's bedside just as she began to stir. She coughed, then groaned. Her eyes fluttered. It took a while before she was awake enough to recognize him.

"Congratulations," she rasped, her voice low and gritty.

"You, too." He lowered the railing. Leaning over, he kissed her and caressed her face. "I'm sorry," he said, his voice catching.

"For what? For having the best night of your life?" She tried to swallow, but it seemed painful. "I'm so proud of you."

He shook his head. "It wasn't. Not without you. You shouldn't have let me go, Kate."

"Uh-oh."

"What?"

"You're angry. You never call me Kate unless you're mad."

"I'm not mad. Not at you."

She struggled to keep her eyes open. "Is the baby here?"

"Yep." He sniffed. "It's a boy."

"Who does he look like?"

"I haven't seen him. I wanted to be with you."

"Can we go see him?"

"I don't think so. Maybe they'll bring him here."

"Please?"

He kissed her again. "Okay. I'll go find him. I love you, Katie." His voice was going to give out on him. "You know that, right?"

"I do."

"Always." He slipped his fingers between hers. "I'll always love you. As long as I live."

"Stop." She ran her tongue over her dry, cracked lips. "You're scaring me."

"I just wanna make sure you know."

"I know," she whispered.

~

The halls of the maternity ward were coming to life. Gone were the hushed tones that had greeted him earlier. Rather than one lone baby's cry, he heard a dissonant chorus. Outside the nursery, he searched the rows of see-through bassinets until he found the one he was looking for.

The guilt that had a choke hold on him earlier grew even stronger when he saw his son. It felt as if his heart were about to break in two.

By the time he returned with a nurse and his baby in tow, Delia had Kate sitting up. She even had a hint of color in her face, which was still pinched from pain and exhaustion.

"Close the door and pull the curtain," she said when the nurses left the room. "Then help me get this gown off."

"C'mon, Katie," he teased, trying to sound like himself. "Even you know it's too soon."

A weak smile won out. "We need to bond. Skin-to-skin contact is important. The doctor said I could try to nurse if I was up to it."

"Are you?"

She nodded. He didn't think so, but he wasn't about to argue. He slipped the hospital gown as low as it would go and helped her get into a comfortable position that would allow her to hold the baby against her. Then he unswaddled his son, who protested loudly until Billy nestled him against his mother's bare skin.

"Devin Joseph Donaldson." He drew on every ounce of strength he had to control his voice. "I'd like you to meet your angel here on earth. This is Katie, but you'll call her Mommy. She's the best person you will ever know."

He couldn't speak another word. The reality of what was before him and the knowledge that this day could have been very different almost brought him to his knees.

As he watched Kate fall in love with their son, there was another reality he needed to face.

He had all but made up his mind they were moving to Seattle. It had been all he could think about. He'd been trying to find a way to break it to Kate, and had decided it would be better to wait until after the baby came, when she wasn't so emotional and when he could convince her that moving close to her parents would be the worst thing they could do.

Now? That was over. He had no right to pressure her into doing anything she might not want to do. Not anymore. Whatever she wanted, he'd do it.

"I was thinking . . ." He hesitated, giving himself one last chance to change his mind, knowing what he was about to do was all about guilt and not at all about what was best for any of them. "I need to call Robbie and Luann."

Kate nodded, intent on studying the tiny foot she held in her hand.

"I need to give them a heads up," he continued, wondering if his smile looked as fake as it felt. "I have to let Robbie know to get Gram's piano ready."

"What?" She looked up, lost.

"I think we're moving to Belleville."

She couldn't speak. Neither could he. His emotions were gridlocked as he wondered how one huge, stupid mistake could have caused him to deliberately make another.

If he'd thought giving in on the house would lessen his guilt, he was wrong. It didn't change one damn thing. He was still a lying, cheating sonofabitch.

CHAPTER 49

After three months of negotiating, the Belleville house was theirs—or it would be the following month. Kate was thrilled, but Billy had begun to resemble a deer caught in the headlights. She assumed it was the impending responsibility of a thirty-year mortgage.

It didn't help that he'd had some kind of falling out with Christa and fired her right after the Grammys. There had been some angry phone calls and messages, but all he would say was that they'd had creative differences. Beyond that, he'd warned her to let it go. She knew when it was safe to poke the bear. This was not one of those times.

Trying to coexist with an infant and a toddler in a tiny apartment was also causing strain, which was why they were heading to the park earlier than usual. Rhiannon was being overly rambunctious, and since Billy hadn't gotten home until almost four, it was just easier to disappear for a couple hours instead of trying to keep her quiet.

Moving into a seven-room house with a big backyard couldn't happen soon enough.

It was warm for mid-May, one of those crystal-clear days when the sky was so blue and the sun so bright it hurt your eyes. There were far worse things than having to spend a morning in the park. Kate buckled Rhiannon and Devin into the double stroller, stopped to say hello to Mrs. Lombardi and Mrs. Calabrese, then headed down Avenue C.

The park was nearly empty. The scent of freshly mown grass hung in the air, and she felt a twinge of excitement that soon she'd have her own yard to sniff. Dappled sunlight filtered through the leaves of her favorite tree, where she spread her blanket on the damp grass. It was the perfect spot. Far enough from the busy street and close enough to watch the ships sail past. While Devin napped, Rhiannon sat surrounded by picture books, bubble solution, and goldfish crackers, which she swam across the blanket. When she grew bored, Rhiannon climbed into Kate's lap with her favorite book, wrapped her cheese-kissed fingers around Kate's ponytail, and rested her head against her chest. She kissed the top of her daughter's head, breathing in the scent of baby shampoo, maple syrup, and a hint of dehydrated cheddar cheese.

"Judy can pat the bunny," Kate read. "Now you pat the bunny."

Rhiannon left an orange trail as she ran her finger over the soft fur shape in her book. "If you're very good, maybe Daddy will let you get a bunny of your own when we move to the new house. Would you like that?"

With a nod, Rhiannon turned the page. Kate continued to read until Devin began to fuss.

"Uh-oh, Mommy." Rhiannon scrambled to her feet and peeked into the stroller. "Hiya, buddy," she cooed, imitating her father.

Devin broke into a wet, toothless grin, not sure of who to smile at first. In spite of the way he'd come into the world, he was a happy baby.

Kate lifted him from the stroller and set him on the blanket. While she changed his diaper, Rhiannon sang him a wordless, tuneless song that made him laugh and pump his legs, making the diaper change a bit of a challenge. When she finished, Kate held him up on his feet, and he wobbled on his chubby, bowed legs.

"Excuse me."

A woman stood a few feet away.

"I'm sorry to interrupt, but you've got the cutest li'l babies there. I was just taking a walk on my lunch hour, and I saw this itty-bitty angel and I just had to stop."

"Thank you." Kate smiled as she tried to place the stranger. She didn't look like any of the businesspeople who frequented the park at lunchtime. Large sunglasses rimmed in rhinestones covered her eyes. She wore tight-fitting jeans, a low-cut tank top, and a cropped denim jacket. Her high heels, which were currently sinking into the grass, matched the bright red that lined her mouth. Her blond spiral curls hung well past her shoulders, and an armful of bangles tinkled when she moved.

"These angels can't possibly be yours," she said in a deep Southern accent, peeking over the top of her sunglasses. "You must be the babysitter. You don't look old enough to have one child, let alone two." She gestured at Rhiannon. "Not to mention this li'l cutie looks nothing like you."

It was true. Rhiannon was Billy's child, right down to her temper.

"Oh, they're mine," Kate said proudly. "Rhiannon looks like her daddy."

"Rhiannon! That's beautiful. Like the Stevie Nicks song?"

Kate nodded. "And this is Devin."

"Hello, Rhiannon. My name is Jane." She reached for Rhiannon's hand and shook it. The toddler eyed her jewelry. At any moment, Kate knew her daughter, whose arms were covered with multicolored plastic bracelets, would expect the newcomer to share.

Jane leaned over Devin and made the sounds most people do when face to face with a baby. Then she looked at Kate. "And you are?"

"Sorry." She held out her hand. "I'm Kate."

"Katie!" Rhiannon giggled.

Kate pretended she was going to tickle her, and Rhiannon doubled over with laughter. "You know only Daddy calls me that!" She scooped her up with her free arm and kissed her cheek.

"They're beautiful," Jane said, settling onto a nearby bench. "You're very lucky."

"We've been blessed." She swallowed the lump that formed in her throat whenever she thought of how lucky she and Devin were to be alive.

"So, where do you work?" she asked, curiosity getting the better of her.

"Around the corner." Jane flicked her hand. "Seeing these li'l angels here certainly makes me miss my grandchildren." The corners of her bright red mouth turned down.

"You certainly don't look like a grandmother."

"I'll take that as a compliment. I haven't seen my grandchildren in a while." She ran a finger under her glasses as if wiping away a tear. "I hope it's not an imposition, but would you mind terribly if I held this little guy? Just for a moment. It's been so long since I held a baby."

It was an odd request, but she looked so dejected Kate found it hard to say no.

"I guess that's OK." She stood and settled Devin in Jane's lap.

Fine brows drawing together, he studied the stranger's face. He looked suspicious at first but then broke into a lopsided, drippy grin. Jane stood, cooing and bouncing him until he latched onto one of her large hoop earrings.

"No!" Kate cried. She reached out to unwind his chubby fingers from the gold circle. "Stay still," she warned. "I'm so sorry. He's at that grabby stage. I have to keep my hair in a ponytail or a braid—"

"Katie!"

Billy's voice came booming over the traffic on West First Street. She turned, surprised to see him standing at the crosswalk. He held up his hand and darted in front of a passing car, nearly getting hit, then jogged straight toward Jane and yanked the baby from her arms.

Startled, Devin began to howl.

"Pack up," Billy demanded, his voice hard and cold. "Now."

What on earth had gotten into him now? "Billy! What're you doing?"

He lowered his voice, but his eyes were blazing. "Now."

"And this must be Daddy," Jane said.

Mortified, Kate turned to apologize.

Billy kept his eyes fixed on Kate. "I said let's go."

"I'm going as fast as I can," she said, convinced he'd lost his mind.

He strapped Devin into the stroller, then Rhiannon, who was crying now as well. Then he snatched the blanket off the ground and waited for Kate to shove the rest of the things into her backpack.

"I'm so sorry," she said to Jane. "I don't—"

Billy grabbed her elbow and pulled. "Let's go, Kate. I mean it."

She glanced over her shoulder as Billy led her across the street.

"Don't worry, honey," Jane called after her, an odd smirk on her face. "He thinks he's protecting those precious babies."

As soon as they reached the courtyard, she yanked free of his grasp and stormed ahead to the building. She waited while he unbuckled Devin, then she scooped him up, and headed for the elevator, leaving Billy behind to fight with the stroller and a screaming toddler.

Upstairs, she settled into her father's rocker, trying to calm herself while she nursed Devin. He studied her face as if trying to figure out what she was all worked up about. After he drifted off and she settled him into his crib, she waited until she was certain she was calm enough to go find out what the hell had just happened.

Rhiannon was sitting on the floor in the living room, eating a peanut butter and jelly sandwich and watching Sesame Street. She found Billy in the kitchen, staring out the window.

"What in God's name is wrong with you?"

The frantic look he gave her took her by surprise. "Do you always let strangers hold our children?"

"No! Of course not. Jeez, Billy. It was no big deal. She seemed nice enough. I don't know what you're freaking out about. Give me a little credit, will you?" She yanked open the refrigerator door. There was nothing she wanted inside, but it gave her something to do that didn't involve looking at him or putting her hands around his neck.

"What if she'd run off with him?"

She slammed the door. "Did you see the ridiculous shoes she had on?"

Closing his eyes, he pinched the bridge of his nose, as if she were the one suddenly behaving irrationally.

She threw up her hands. "Why did you even come to the park? I left so you could sleep, and you got up anyway. Then you tracked me down like some kind of bloodhound."

"Sit down," he said, looking out the window again.

"No! You're getting pretty bossy. I don't like it."

"Kate." He stared at her for a few beats. "Just do as I ask, and sit down." His chest rose and fell as if he'd just run up three flights of stairs. "Please."

He was acting like an ass, and she didn't like it. She yanked a chair away from the table and sat.

He seemed as if he didn't have a clue as to what he wanted to say. Then he took two glasses from the drain board, reached into the pantry, and pulled down a bottle of whiskey.

"Are you serious?" She looked pointedly at the clock over the stove. It was quarter after eleven.

He didn't answer. Although she never drank whiskey, and wasn't drinking at all, since she was nursing, he poured a shot into each glass, pushed one in front of her, and threw his back. His hands shook as he poured a second glass.

What the hell. "Now you're scaring me."

He didn't answer. He just drained the contents of the glass, then poured another.

"Billy, talk to me."

When their eyes met, she saw something unfamiliar, unsettling.

"That woman in the park?" He watched her face. "That was my mother."

It took a few moments to process what he'd said.

"I don't understand. She said she worked around the corner—"

"She's lying," he shouted. "It just proves she's up to no good. If she wanted to see me, she'd have come to the apartment." He gestured wildly. "She obviously knows where to find us. She's probably been watching you, knows your routine."

He reached for the bottle, but Kate was quicker.

"That's enough. I get that you're upset, but please stop."

A tiny muscle pulsed through the scruff lining his jaw.

"She's probably looking for money."

"Money? We don't have any money. I don't understand."

Rhiannon called from the living room.

Before Kate could rise from the table, he stopped her. "I'll go. We'll talk later, okay? Tonight. After they're in bed."

Waiting for her to agree, he lifted his eyebrows, making the fine white scar above his eye stand out. She wasn't sure if the tightness in her chest was due to the sudden, bizarre appearance of his mother or because he might finally be ready to share some of his secrets.

CHAPTER 50

Kate sat across from him on the living room floor. She took one last bite of her pizza, then pushed the plate away.

"Not hungry?"

"Not really."

On any given day, Billy could easily put away three-quarters of a pie by himself, but not tonight. He couldn't eat. Drinking was another story. He filled his glass, then held out the bottle of wine.

"Yeah." She raised her glass. "I have formula for Devin."

"I'll get up with him during the night, give you a break."

The edges of her mouth curled. "In that case, fill 'er up."

The sound of children playing in the courtyard below had faded as evening settled in, and other than the occasional sound of traffic on Avenue C, it had grown quiet. Billy set the bottle on the floor beside him. There was a part of him that still didn't want to tell Kate anything about his past. A part that was afraid if she knew the kind of parents he'd had, she'd pack up the kids and leave. Especially when she figured out he wasn't much better than what he'd come from.

When he looked up, wide gray-green eyes were watching him. Her hair tumbled over her shoulders in long, loose waves. A small frown tugged at her mouth. God, she was beautiful.

"Would it help if I told you I already know a little?" she asked in a small voice. She pulled her knees up to her chin and wrapped her arms around her legs.

He leaned against the couch. A worm of apprehension gnawed at his belly, turning what little he had eaten into a doughy, indigestible lump. Maybe this wasn't such a good idea.

"What are you talking about?"

"Luann told me some things the night before we got married."

Fucking Luann. "Like what?"

"That your dad used to beat you and your grandfather ran him off." She began to rock. "I'm sorry. I should've told you I knew, but I just figured you'd tell me when you were ready."

He ran his hand through his hair. "What else did she say?"

"Isn't that enough?"

He shook his head. "I wish it were. There's a lot you don't know about me, about my past. And I'm sorry about that. Some of it I'm still not ready to talk about. But there are some things you need to know. Maybe it will help you understand why I'm so fucked up." He pulled her into his lap and kissed her hair as she rested against his shoulder.

He'd had all day to think about what to say, yet he still found himself stumbling over the words. "I guess I should start with an apology. I let you believe my parents were dead. Obviously, my mother isn't. I'm not sure about my father, although I hope he's rotting in hell."

Kate picked up his hand and wove her fingers between his. When she gave them a squeeze, he continued.

"My mother left when my father did. She'd come back from time to time.

Last time I saw her before today was right after I started my junior year at KU. She showed up, totally unexpected. I was happy to see her. I always thought this time would be different, ya know?" He snorted. "She took me out to dinner. I showed her around campus. It seemed almost normal, like anybody else's mom coming for a visit. The next day, she came to my apartment, acting all nervous and jerky. She wanted money. Told me she needed to get into rehab, said she couldn't afford it. I knew she drank, but she'd started using, too. Said she needed to get sober and I was the only one she could count on."

Kate's fingers were tracing circles over the muscles in his back. Her touch against his skin was soothing, helped keep the past from getting too close.

"She said if she could get clean, she could take care of herself, maybe even help me out. Not that I needed it. It was just nice knowing she wanted to. I had a free ride to KU, plus I played in a band. The money I made helped pay for extras. And I still had the money my grandmother left me. Of course she knew that."

He reached for his wine.

"You don't have to tell me any of this." He felt her words against his neck, soft as a kiss.

"Yes, I do." He emptied the glass, then refilled it.

"I gave her everything. Every last dime. She promised she'd pay it all back as soon as she could, and I believed her. My mom had been a nurse. I didn't know it at the time, but she'd lost her license for stealing drugs from patients."

"That's awful."

He nodded. "When I went to pick her up at the motel that afternoon, she was gone. Checked out that morning, before I even gave her the money. She took every cent I had and disappeared. I quit school that day, pawned what I could, and headed east. I slept in the van behind a bar in Jersey City. I washed dishes during the day and played at night until I had enough money for an apartment."

He closed his eyes and concentrated on the warm breath against his neck as the scent of sweet orange curled around him.

"What about your father?"

He paused, weighing his words. "I can't, babe. I'm sorry. Let's just say he was an evil bastard. Unfortunately, I inherited his temper. Other than that, I don't want to talk about him."

351

Gray dusk filtered in through the window, casting shadows on the half-packed boxes. Kate moved so he could see her face. In spite of the fading light, he saw the pain in her eyes. He'd never wanted her pity.

"I come from a great gene pool, Katie. I'm sorry it's too late to reconsider having kids with me. Like I said, I inherited my father's temper. At least I'm aware of it. I know when I need to walk away." There was a rock lodged in his throat, one he couldn't swallow. "I don't ever want you to be afraid. I'd never hurt you or my kids. I'd hurt myself first."

Kate slid to her knees between his legs. Cradling his face in both hands, she kissed him. Then she ran her thumbs over his tears, wiping them away. She trailed a finger over the scar above his eye and kissed that, too. Some of the barriers he'd used to protect himself began to crumble.

"Look at me."

He raised his eyes reluctantly.

"You don't scare me, Billy Donaldson. I'm not afraid of you. I know you love me, and I know you'd never do anything to hurt me."

With those words, the dam broke. He buried his face into her neck and cried. Kate's heart might be big enough to overlook his past, but if she ever found out what he'd done in the present, he knew she would never forgive him.

CHAPTER 51

It took less than a week for Billy to find out what his mother wanted.

Viper was back on the road, still playing gigs Christa's agency had booked. Breaks and rest stops were spent on the phone, acting as his own manager and agent, trying to book the band wherever he could. When he was home, he let every studio in the tristate area know he was available for session work. It was depressing, but if he had any hope of making mortgage payments, he didn't have a choice. His career was moving backward instead of forward—again.

He was backstage after opening for Loose Meat when Denny stuck his head into the dressing room.

"Hey, man. There's a woman out front says she needs to see you."

Billy pulled his T-shirt over his head and wiped the sweat from his neck. All he wanted was a quick shower and bed.

"You know I don't see anyone backstage. Especially women."

"She insists you'll see her."

He didn't know anyone in Atlanta, and he sure as hell wasn't interested in meeting anyone, either.

"Said to tell you her name is Janet."

His chest tightened. "What does she look like?"

Denny shrugged. "Flashy blonde, late forties, maybe. I'll tell them to send her away."

Shit. His throat went dry. "No. Send her back."

"Seriously?"

"You heard me." He dragged his hand through his hair. "I'm sorry. Just send her back."

He caught a glimpse of himself in the mirror. Fear lined his face. He paced the room, waiting for the knock. When Denny opened the door, his mother pushed her way inside.

"There he is!" She lifted her arms as if to hug him, but he stepped back. She turned to Denny apologetically. "You'd think he wasn't happy to see me."

He signaled for Denny to go and waited for the door to close. "I figured you'd show up sooner or later, *Jane*. What do you want?" He hoped he sounded as cold as he felt.

"Is that any way to greet your mother?" The exaggerated appearance of innocence was nauseating.

"I mean it. What do you want?"

"I wanted to see you. You rushed off so fast last time. Before that, I hadn't seen you since . . ." She tapped a finger against her lips. "How long has it been?"

"Seven years." The memory was as clear as ever.

"Oh, it can't be."

"Seven years. When you conned me into giving you all my money so you could go to rehab."

She looked shocked. "I did go to rehab! I'm one hundred percent now, thanks to my baby." She reached up to touch his cheek, but he yanked his head away.

"What do you want? I have a plane to catch." He was lying. They had driven this leg of the tour, and were heading home in the morning, but she didn't need to know that.

"I wanted to see you. It's been a long time. I wanted you to know how proud I am."

It all clicked into place. "You saw me on TV, didn't you? You're looking for money." He shook his head. "You're something else. How stupid do you think I am?"

"Stupid? Why on God's green earth would I think you were stupid? Not my baby. I know better." She wandered around the room, pausing in front of the tiny sofa where he'd set his guitar. She ran a finger over the strings. He snatched it away and set it in its case.

"Let's cut to the chase. Tell me what you want so I can tell you no. Then we can get on with our lives."

Her lip quivered. "You hurt me, you know that? And that is certainly no way to talk to your mother. I didn't raise you—"

"You're right. You didn't raise me. Your mother did." He stared down at her, daring her to contradict him.

"Look." The barest hint of a smile crossed her face. "I wanted to say congratulations."

"Thank you. Is that all?"

"Oh, I don't think we're talking about the same thing. I'm disappointed you never bothered to tell me I'm a grandmother."

Hearing her say it made his stomach clench.

"You're not. You would have to be a mother before you could be a grandmother. We both know how that turned out."

Ignoring him, she walked toward the dressing table. Two pictures were tucked into the mirror. One was his favorite of Kate. In the second, she held Devin while Rhiannon leaned forward to kiss him. Before he could stop her, she snatched the second picture.

"They're adorable. They look just like you." She pointed to the picture of Kate. "Now that surprises me. She's not at all the type I expected you to go for. She's pretty enough, but you could've done much better."

His jaw grew tight. He didn't need to justify himself or sing Kate's virtues to a woman who wouldn't know a virtue if she tripped over one.

"You wanna tell me why you're here? Like I said, I have a plane to catch."

She looked up at him. "I wanted to let you know we'll be coming for a visit. I want to officially meet my grandchildren."

"No, you're not. You're not coming within fifty miles of my family."

"Oh?" Her eyebrows arched as she dropped the photo into her purse. "I don't think there's a damn thing you can do to stop us." Her smile grew, but her eyes were two blue chips of ice.

His heart stilled. "What do you mean, 'us'?"

She looked up at him, wide-eyed at his naïveté.

"Your father is determined to meet his grandchildren. And if you won't introduce us yourself, he says we'll just wait until the next time you're on the road. By the way, he said to tell you that's a cute little house you bought. Small, but very private. Hardly any neighbors around."

A chill ran through him, causing him to shiver so violently it felt as if the floor had moved. When he met her eyes, she was watching him with a smile so evil, he shivered again. All the oxygen had been sucked from the room.

"How much to keep you both away?" He spoke through a jaw so tightly clenched, he thought his teeth might crack.

"Now see?" She snapped her purse shut. "I knew I didn't raise a stupid boy."

It was after four in the morning when Billy unlocked the door to the apartment. Not long after his mother had gone, he'd headed straight to the airport, leaving Denny to check out of the hotel and deal with the instruments and the long drive home. There had been a flight about to leave for Newark. He'd had to pay top dollar, but he needed to get home.

Kate was asleep. Devin nestled in the crook of her arm, a possessive hand resting on her breast. Rhiannon was curled against Kate's leg, a thumb in her mouth, her elbow on her mother's knee. A tiny pink toe poked through a hole in her footed pajamas.

Everything he loved was right here in a tangle of arms and legs. He slumped against the doorjamb and took what felt like his first full breath since seeing his mother backstage.

He needed a drink.

He made his way to the kitchen, and aided by the dim bulb over the stove, pulled down the Jameson Black Barrel Arthur had given him for his birthday. He took a glass from the cupboard, then reached into a drawer and dug out the checkbook.

In his place at the head of the small table, he opened the bottle and poured three fingers into the glass. Throwing his head back, he drained it, not even bothering to savor the high-end whiskey. He reached into his wallet and pulled out the scrap of paper his mother had stuffed into his hand before she left. He wrote out a check and slipped it into an envelope and affixed a stamp. Then he left the apartment.

It was blackmail, plain and simple. If he gave in, she'd never back off. But if he didn't, then what? Would he have to worry every time he was away that his father might resurface? Was he out there waiting for the chance to hurt him again—or worse?

All he knew for sure was that if he saw his father anywhere near Katie or the kids, he'd kill him. Without a second thought.

He yanked open the metal door on the mailbox and dropped the envelope inside. It was better this way. Safer. A day wouldn't go by that he wouldn't worry, but he had to believe that greed would make his mother keep her promise.

It was the best he could hope for.

CHAPTER 52

The closing on the new house was only a couple days away. Kate had taken Rhiannon with her to run some errands, and Devin was napping. Since he hadn't been sleeping well since seeing his mother in Atlanta, Billy thought he'd join him.

He had just stretched out on the couch when the phone rang.

"Hey, it's me," said Denny. "How's it going?"

Fan-fucking-tastic. "Okay. What's up?"

"Listen, I don't want to get into the middle or anything, but Christa called me."

His hand tightened around the phone. "Yeah?"

"She said she's called you several times. You won't return her calls."

"That's right, and it's none of your business."

Denny was quiet for a moment. "I get it, okay? I'm just the messenger."

"Is that all?"

"She says you better return her call or you're gonna be sorry."

"Are you threatening me?" He'd have put his fist through the wall if he wouldn't have to turn around and fix it.

"No, man! Like I said, I'm just the messenger. I don't like being in this position, and to be honest, I don't trust her. Maybe you should call her."

"Maybe you should mind your own fucking business."

"Listen to me. You think long and hard about whatever happened to cause this little rift between you two. Then you decide if her threats are empty or not and who's gonna be hurt if she follows through."

He could feel his blood pressure rising.

"I'm not trying to start a fight with you. Jesus, Billy, you're the last person I want on my case. I just think you oughta take a deep breath, then call her and straighten it out. Just detonate this bomb before it goes off in your face and hurts everyone around you."

Neither of them spoke for a few moments.

"You still there?" Denny asked.

"Yeah. I got it."

After hanging up, Billy stared at the phone before he picked it up and dialed.

"This is Billy McDonald for Christa Dunphy."

"Of course, Billy. Please hold," cooed the receptionist.

She was back a moment later.

"I'm sorry. Ms. Dunphy isn't available to talk at this moment. She said she will be available tomorrow at one at Smith & Wollensky. She'll be expecting you then." She cleared her throat. "She also said it would be in your best interest to make sure you don't disappoint her."

"Oh, she did, did she? Just put her on the fucking phone."

"I'm sorry. That's not possible. She's in a meeting." She hesitated a second, then added, "The restaurant is on the corner of Third and—"

He slammed the phone into the cradle so hard it loosened the base from the wall.

Between his mother and Christa, he wasn't sure how much more he could take.

Between his mother and Christa, he wasn't sure how much more he could take.

It was a few minutes after one when Billy walked through the door at Smith & Wollensky. He was deliberately late. He'd be damned if he'd be sitting there waiting when Christa walked in.

He waved off the hostess. "Don't bother. I see the bitch."

He pushed his way through the bar to Christa's table in the back. He'd almost reached her when she saw him. It pleased him to watch her recoil as she must have recognized the anger on his face.

"Billy." She smiled up at him, recovering quickly. "Nice of you to join me."

The chair scraped roughly across the wooden floor. He sat and folded his arms across his chest.

"What the fuck do you want? I've made it clear I want nothing to do with you."

She folded her perfectly manicured hands on the table in front of her. "Why? Because we had a little fun? I didn't rape you, Billy, and I sure as hell didn't force myself on you. We were two consenting adults who were drawn to each other. No one got hurt. Yet."

"I was drunk and dusted, and you know it. That's no excuse, but I was fucked up. It won't happen again—with you or anyone else."

She laughed. "We'll see about that. You're playing the doting husband—I get it. You feel guilty. But guilt fades, honey. Trust me."

He scooted back from the table. "Is there any point to this little meeting? Because if not, I'm outta here."

A waiter set a glass of whiskey on the rocks in front of him. God, he needed it, but he didn't dare pick it up.

Christa's voice was as smooth and solicitous as the drink before him. "See, I know what you need, what you want. You don't even have to ask. I told you a long time ago, I can lay the world at your feet."

She pulled two envelopes from her purse and slid them across the table.

He eyed them warily.

"Go on."

He picked up the first envelope, opened it, and scanned the text. It was an artist recording agreement, although the name of the record company was blacked out. On the second page was a list of terms, including the amount of money the band would be paid and the number of promotional appearances they would be expected to make.

The second envelope held another contract, and while the name of the record company was also inked out, the town wasn't. Seattle.

The advance for each contract was close to $750,000. He folded the documents slowly and slipped them back into their respective envelopes, trying to control his emotions. He looked up at Christa, hoping she couldn't tell his heart was drumming a thousand beats per minute.

"Like I said, Billy. I know what you need and what you want, and I can give it to you."

His gaze dropped to her lips. He hadn't kissed her. That meant something, right? *He never kissed her.* He cleared his throat. "And what do you want?"

She tossed her head. "My cut, of course. Fifteen percent of everything. That's fair, isn't it?"

A bead of condensation ran down the side of his untouched glass. He followed it with his thumb, then picked up the glass and took a long swallow. When he looked across the table, she was smiling.

"That's it?" he asked.

Her blue eyes had grown dark. "Of course that's not it. You know what else I want. No one has to know. It'll be our little secret."

He clenched his teeth.

"If not, that's your choice," she said with a casual wave of her hand. "If you decide to walk away from me and what I'm offering, that's up to you. Just understand I'll make it my business to see that not only do these offers disappear, no record company worth its salt will touch you." She lowered her voice enough that only he could hear. "Not only that, I'll make sure to let Katie know how much I like that little serpent tattooed above your dick."

He slammed his fist onto the table, sloshing her drink onto her sleeve. "You stay the hell away from my wife."

She dabbed at her sleeve with her heavy linen napkin and tossed it onto the table, where a corner of it slowly unfurled into what was left of her drink.

She stood, her face impassive. "Don't threaten me, Billy. You may be bigger, but I have better weapons. I've given you a lot to think about. I'll give you a week. After that, the deal's off the table."

She snatched up her purse and left.

Voices filled the crowded restaurant, flatware tinkled against the plates, waiters moved between the tables, but all he heard was the click of Christa's heels on the hardwood floor. He rubbed his hand over his face, then lifted his glass and drained it, relishing the burn. He signaled for a refill.

His life was turning into a fucking nightmare.

CHAPTER 53

Billy stood in the lobby of a building in lower Manhattan. He'd been loitering so long, he was surprised none of the residents had called the cops. He paced back and forth, trying to figure out what to say and how to say it. He'd been at it for hours. Pulled up every scenario. Turned every possibility over in his head. There was only one answer, and no matter how much it was going to suck, he couldn't think of any other way out.

Steeling himself, he rang the bell. The door buzzed, allowing him to enter without having to announce who he was. Skipping the elevator to give him more time to change his mind, he took the stairs to the fifth floor. When he reached the apartment, he convinced himself to stop thinking and just knock.

Turned out he didn't have to.

"What are you doing here?" Joey leaned into the hall, probably looking for Kate. He looked at Billy suspiciously. "Are you alone?"

"Yeah." His voice quavered.

"What's wrong with you?"

He shook his head. "Can I come in?"

"Where's Kate?"

"Home. Can I just come in?" He was already losing his temper. Bad idea. "May I please come in?"

Joey's eyebrows shot into his hairline.

"'Please,' huh? Learn a new word?"

"Something like that."

Stepping back, Joey waved him in with a dramatic sweep of his arm.

Although not as big as their apartment in New Jersey, Joey's new place was much bigger than the one he'd had in the Bronx.

"Have a seat," Joey said, already bustling away. "Do you want something to drink? I have a bottle of Malbec open, and some chardonnay in the fridge. I might even have some beer."

"Water will be fine."

Joey's head popped around the corner. "Water? Seriously?"

This was going to be a lot harder than he thought. Even an everyday encounter with Joey usually left Billy wanting to choke him.

"Yeah. Water."

"Perrier or tap?" Joey called from the kitchen.

"Just water, for fuck's sake." He wiped his palms on his thighs. "Tap."

Joey returned a minute later with a glass filled with ice and tap water and set a coaster down on the glass-topped coffee table. He sat across from Billy, crossed his legs, and rested his hands in his lap. "So, to what do I owe this pleasure?"

Billy took a sip of the water, hopefully enough to clear the dust from his throat, then set the glass onto the coaster. He looked around the room. A large black and white picture of Kate—naked, it seemed—holding Rhiannon as a baby was propped on a bookshelf on the opposite wall. Tears burned the backs of his eyes and he had to look away, but not before Joey saw what he was looking at.

"What makes her even more beautiful is that she doesn't have a clue how beautiful she really is," Joey said, angling his head toward the photograph.

Billy nodded. This was going to be even more difficult with Kate looking down at him from that shelf.

"You know, most men would have a problem with their wives or girlfriends posing au naturel."

Billy studied the calluses on his fingertips. "Well, I'm not most men."

Joey burst out laughing. "You and I both know you'd lose your shit all over the place if it had been anyone but me who had taken that picture."

"Yeah, I guess." He hesitated. He raised his eyes to meet Joey's. "But I know I can trust you. I know you'd never do anything to hurt her. Ever. Right?"

Tilting his head, Joey remained silent.

"Right?" he repeated.

"Of course I'd never hurt her."

Billy nodded. His throat was closing up again. He reached for the water. When he set the glass down, he stared at it as if the next move would come from the glass and not from him.

After a while, Joey cleared his throat. "Is there any specific reason you came to see me?"

Just as Billy opened his mouth to speak, the front door buzzer went off. Joey stood.

"That's probably Shanghai Dumpling, but the way my luck's going, it might be my father."

Billy frowned at the implied insult.

"I wasn't expecting company," he said as he buzzed in the delivery man. "But if you're hungry, there's usually enough for two."

"No, thanks. Not hungry."

While Joey dealt with his dinner, Billy checked out the rest of the room. He assumed most of the pictures on the walls had been taken by Joey. Some were iconic New York architecture: the Brooklyn Bridge, the Empire State Building, the World Trade Center. But most were people—his people, Kate and his children. A composition of details from photos he'd taken of Kate filled one wall: the slope of her neck, the swell of her breast, the sharp angle of her hip bone. He was intimately familiar with every part of her, and he could lose it all now so quickly.

A sob escaped before he could stop himself. He turned it into a cough, but it was too late.

"Billy?" Joey stuck his chopsticks into his container of beef chow fun. He dropped onto the sofa. "What's wrong? Is it Kate?"

Billy looked up though a veil of tears. The look on Joey's face was heartrending. This man loved his wife as much as he did. Maybe even more, since unlike him, Joey would never do anything to hurt her.

He shook his head. "Kate's fine. The kids are fine. They're all fine." He dragged his hand through his hair, then ran it over his face.

"Then what the hell is going on? Something's wrong. I've lived here for over a year, and no matter how many times you've been in the city, you've been here once, and I'm pretty sure you were kicking and screaming all the way. Start talking."

Billy nodded. "Yeah." *Here goes everything.* He looked up to meet Joey's gaze. "I love Katie more than anything. Since the day we met. She means more to me than anything."

Joey's features softened. "I know. I give you a hard time about all this, but I know. And I know she loves you, so if for some reason you think you needed to come here to convince me, you didn't have to. I know, okay?" He gave Billy a wicked smile. "It's just that it's so much fun watching you turn red when I get you going."

When Billy didn't respond, the smile slipped from Joey's face.

Billy's eyes swept the photos of Kate again. "I know, and I'm sorry about any misunderstandings in the past. I need your help."

Joey nodded. "Okay."

"This is hard. Really hard. And please believe me it was just once, and it won't ever happen again. I was drunk and I'd been doing coke and there was a lot of champagne, you know?"

Joey's eyes hardened. "What did you do?"

Billy stared at his hands, twisted together in his lap.

"The night of the Grammys . . ." The words were so painful, he struggled to swallow. When he looked up, the expression on Joey's face told him he'd already figured it out.

"It was Christa. It just happened. Before I knew it, we were in the back somewhere. I don't even remember it all. She was kind of all over me. I didn't even kiss her, honestly."

Neither of them seemed to be breathing. All he could hear was the sound of a clock ticking from somewhere deeper within the apartment.

"So that was it? She came on to you. You didn't touch her, and then you went home. Six fucking hours later, but you went home, right?" Joey's eyes were locked on Billy.

Billy shook his head so slightly that it would have been hard to see if Joey hadn't been staring at him.

"Oh my God."

"I didn't touch her. It was all her."

Joey's hands were flying about his head in a frenzy. "Do you really think that excuses anything? That if you just lie back and close your eyes, you're not accountable? What are you, some fucking stereotype?"

Billy buried his head in his hands. "I love my wife."

"Oh, well then. I guess whatever happened with Christa doesn't matter, right? You love Kate. What's the problem?"

Joey's hatred for him was palpable.

"The problem," he said, trying to remain calm, "is that Christa is threatening to go to Kate if I don't give her what she wants."

Joey snorted. "So you're some amazing stud and now no one else can satisfy her?"

"I don't know what her deal is, although I know I didn't satisfy her. I didn't fuck her. I wouldn't, and I won't. It was just a blow job." As soon as he said it, he regretted it.

"Why didn't you say so? Just a blow job. Well, damn, even Kate can't get upset about that. I mean, that doesn't even count, right?"

"Can we cut the sarcasm?"

"I don't think so."

This wasn't coming out right. "Listen to me. I need you to keep Christa from going to Kate. That's all. Beg her. Plead with her. Whatever you have to do."

"Why would I want to help you?"

It was what he'd been wondering all afternoon. Why? Why would Joey want to help him? There was only one reason, and he hoped he would see it his way.

"Because you don't want Kate to be hurt any more than I do. I love her, and I know I don't deserve her. But she loves me, too. We have a family. We have two kids, and you and I both know if she finds out, she'll leave me and she'll take my kids away." His voice broke. "And then everybody is hurt, and for what? One stupid, drunken moment? Don't you think she's been hurt enough in her life? Please don't let this happen. I don't care what Christa does to me. I don't care if she destroys my career. I don't care. I'll do anything to keep Katie from being hurt."

Neither of them spoke for several minutes. Billy stared at his feet. If Joey refused to help, chances were he'd go directly to Kate and tell her himself. It could all be over tonight.

"What if she won't listen to me?" Joey asked, his voice low.

Billy looked up, hopeful. "Make her listen."

They sat in silence. The clock ticking. Finally, Joey rose from the sofa.

"I think you should go."

Billy stood slowly. "Can I count on you?"

Joey looked away, and his eyes hung at the photograph of Kate with Rhiannon. He turned back to Billy, his expression flat and cold. "I'll see what I can do."

"You're the only hope I have." He took a few steps toward the door, then turned and held out his hand.

Joey stared at it, then shook his head. "No. We don't get to shake on this. We're not friends. You fucked up. What you've done could destroy the best person we both know. I won't shake your hand over that."

"Understood." Billy nodded.

As he turned to leave, Joey spoke.

"You know I hate you, don't you? I really hate you."

The words stung, but it was easier hearing them from Joey than from Kate. He nodded as he reached for the doorknob.

"If it's any consolation, you can't possibly hate me as much as I hate myself."

CHAPTER 54

"It's today!" Kate cried, popping up like an overexcited jack-in-the-box.

"Every day is today," Billy grumbled into his pillow. His head ached. A dense fog filtered through his brain.

"Today's *the* day. C'mon, grumpy. Get up." She traced her nails over his bare back. "I need to strip the sheets off the bed."

One bloodshot eye cracked open. "How 'bout I just strip you and we stay in bed all day?"

"Yeah," she snickered, "because people with two kids under the age of two get to do that all the time. Not to mention, we have to be out of here by five." She brushed her lips across his temple, then climbed out of bed. "We're buying a house today, remember?"

In his head, he was groaning. How could he forget? He didn't want to move. Didn't want to move closer to Kate's parents. Didn't want to move to some lame-ass little Jersey town so far from New York City it was almost in fucking Pennsylvania. He groaned again, this time not just in his head.

"You OK?"

"Yeah." He opened both eyes and rolled onto his back. Kate stood at the foot of the bed, wearing a lacy little bra. The angry red scar starting just below her naval and disappearing into the matching panties was a sharp reminder of what today was about. She stepped into her jeans, zipped them up, then climbed onto the bed and crawled up between his legs, planting kisses on his belly and chest along the way.

"We're buying a house today," she sang, a wide grin splitting her face.

He forced a smile. "Yep."

With one last kiss, she snatched the pillow out from under his head.

"Hey!"

"C'mon," she said. "Up! Besides, you're the one who never likes to be late for anything." She pulled a too-large Viper T-shirt over her head. "I'll nurse Devin, you can give Rhiannon breakfast. There are Cheerios and a plastic bowl and spoon on the kitchen table, and just enough milk in the fridge."

"What about coffee?"

"No coffee. I packed the coffeemaker. We can get coffee on the way. Think of it as incentive to get out of bed."

"Are you fucking kidding me? I can't get motivated to do all this shit without coffee. Besides, I have a headache."

Her smile faded, but she said nothing about the hangover they both knew was causing his headache.

"There's a full bottle of aspirin in my purse. We'll get coffee at the deli on the corner." With that, she yanked the sheet off him with a flourish. "I'll make it up to you. Soon. I promise." She batted her eyes before sailing out of the bedroom, calling to Devin that she was on her way.

Billy sat up and ran his hand over the scruff on his face, trying to remember the last time he'd shaved. Not that it made any difference. He'd be signing his life away today no matter what he looked like.

He pulled on the worn, ripped jeans he'd worn yesterday, then turned on the TV for Rhiannon and shuffled into the kitchen to get her breakfast.

Kate's purse sat on the counter, a bottle of Excedrin peeking out of the top. He tapped three into his palm.

After rinsing the dregs from a plastic sippy cup sitting on the counter, he filled it halfway with orange juice and the rest of the way with vodka he'd lifted from a box near the door. When he raised the cup to wash down the aspirin, his eyes settled on the new tattoo inked across the outside of his thumb and down his wrist:

When love is not madness, it is not love.—May 20, 1989

He had recited the quote from Pedro Calderón de la Barca as part of his wedding vows. After what happened the night Devin was born, he'd had it tattooed on his hand. He would never unzip his pants again without remembering all that he stood to lose.

He closed his eyes and prayed that the vodka and aspirin would kick in soon.

⁓

Kate's exuberance was deflating like a day-old birthday balloon. Billy had barely said two words since they'd left Bayonne, even after finishing his extra-large coffee. She studied his profile as he drove: hair pulled back, shades on, eyes focused straight ahead, jaw tight. Her anxiety grew with each passing mile.

"It's not too late to change your mind," she said as they pulled up in front of her parents' house to drop off Rhiannon and Devin.

He gave her a thin smile. "Yes, it is. Like you reminded me earlier, we have to be out of the apartment today. I don't wanna live in the van—or worse, with your parents." He ruffled the top of her head like she was one of the kids.

"I mean it. If you don't want to do this—"

"It's fine," he said as he climbed into the back of the van to unbuckle Rhiannon from her car seat.

It's fine? He was acting as if she'd just told him they were having leftovers for the third night in a row. She'd gotten carried away in the excitement of buying a house, while it was all too clear, if she'd bothered to pay closer attention, he was miserable.

Later at the lawyer's office, Billy stopped several times as he worked through the mountain of papers to drag his hand through his hair, a sure sign he was tense. By the time Mr. Reilly congratulated them and handed Billy the keys, he stared at them as if he wasn't sure what they were for. This was wrong—very, very wrong. Her stomach churned. How could she have woken up so excited and just a few hours later be filled with such doubt?

It took less than four minutes to drive from the attorney's office to their new home, but the uncomfortable silence made it seem much longer.

"I love you," she said after Billy pulled up in front of the two-car garage. Her voice lifted at the end, making it sound more like a question than a declaration.

He gave her hand a quick squeeze before climbing out of the van. "I know."

I know? This was some deep shit. She scanned the back yard where she had pictured her kids playing. Where she'd imagined barbecues and picnics on the patio, maybe a treehouse someday, and a pool. Now it just looked forlorn and shabby. Lost in thought, she climbed from the van and headed toward the front of the house while Billy tugged boxes from the back of the trailer.

"You're not gonna help?" Irritation crept into his voice.

She had assumed he would carry her over the threshold. She almost said as much, but thought better of it. "Sorry," she said instead, reaching for a box marked Kitchen.

"Not that one." He frowned. "That's too heavy. Grab the guitars from the van and take them into the room off the kitchen."

As she waited for him to unlock the back door, she set the two cases down. It would be okay if he carried her over that threshold. They'd probably be using that door most of the time anyway.

"What're you doing, Kate?" He was almost yelling. "If I'm gonna get back to Bayonne in time to meet Denny and Steve, I don't have time for this nonsense."

She mumbled another apology, then picked up the instruments and hurried toward the back room.

After everything was unloaded and Billy had left, she surveyed the disorganized mess. She had carefully labeled each box so that it would go into its designated room. That hadn't happened. Boxes were scattered among the kitchen, dining room, and living room.

"Begin at the beginning," she muttered, stooping to tear the tape off the nearest box. It was filled with boots, scarves, and hats. Probably the last box that needed to be opened. She carried it upstairs to the master bedroom and set it near the closet. The room wasn't much bigger than what they'd had, but it was theirs. Or at least it would be in thirty years.

After a couple hours of trying to organize and unpack, her growling stomach and aching breasts got the best of her. She needed to nurse Devin, and she wanted to get back before Billy returned. She cut through the alley and walked the few blocks to her parents' house, where she found Rhiannon in tears at the kitchen table. A ham sandwich sat on a plate in front of her.

She scooped up her weepy daughter and kissed her damp, gold curls as Rhiannon wrapped her arms around her neck and sobbed harder.

"I thought Mom was making macaroni and cheese."

"She is," her father said, sounding exasperated. "For dinner. We thought she'd eat a sandwich for lunch."

"Only peanut butter and jelly." She'd told her mother this numerous times. She made Rhiannon a new sandwich, then went upstairs to feed Devin. Once both children were down for a nap, she promised to return around dinnertime and headed back to the house, downing Rhiannon's discarded sandwich on the way.

After pausing to admire the Japanese quince in full bloom outside her new living room window, she made her way across the patio. She grabbed the doorknob, turned it, and slammed into the door. She twisted the knob again. Nothing. It was locked, and they only had one key—the one she'd watched Billy slip onto his keychain at the lawyer's office.

"Are you kidding me?" She kicked the door in frustration. There was no way she was walking back to her parents' house on the off chance that her father, who'd probably never picked up a screwdriver in his life, might be able to figure out how to get the door open. She didn't know any of the neighbors, and besides, she didn't want them to think she was a scatterbrain who locked herself out the first time she left the house.

As she slumped against the locked door, her eyes fell on a row of bricks edging an overgrown flowerbed. Desperate times and all that, she thought as she dropped to her knees. She tugged at each until she found a brick with some give, then wrested it from the ground. She slipped off her T-shirt, wrapped it around the brick, and took a swing at the pane of glass nearest the door knob. It did little more than shudder. She swung harder the second and third times. On the fourth try, it shattered. Using the sheathed brick, she knocked out the rest of the glass, then reached inside and unlocked the door, careful to avoid the jagged edges.

One of the boxes she'd unloaded earlier held a small broom and dustpan, but it wasn't among those in the kitchen or the dining room. She was in the living room, prying the tape off the one she thought she needed, when she heard the crunch of gravel in the driveway. A few moments later, the back door banged open.

"Katie!"

Before she could answer, Billy yelled again. She heard his heavy boots going up the stairs.

"I'm down here," she called.

"Kate!" He bellowed, pounding down the steps. She'd expected him to be pissed about the broken window, but he sounded frantic.

She appeared in the doorway to the living room just as he came rushing down the hall.

"What the hell happened?" he demanded, grabbing her by the arms.

She pulled away gently, confused by his urgency. "I couldn't get back in the house. The door locked on me and you have the only key."

He stared at her for an uncomfortable few seconds. "Did you try the front door?"

Oh, shit. "What?"

"Did you try the front door?" he repeated, dragging his hand through his hair. "It was unlocked."

She rolled her lips together and stared up at him.

"Good job." He yanked off his T-shirt and tossed it at her. "We have company. You should probably get dressed."

CHAPTER 55

Billy grabbed a beer from the cooler and downed it in two long gulps. The sight of the broken window and open door had sent him over the edge. His first thought was that someone had broken into the house—and the first person he'd thought of was his father. Why his old man might do something like that, he had no idea, but he'd been a vindictive bastard sixteen years ago, and he'd probably only gotten meaner and more spiteful since. And even though he'd agreed to his mother's blackmail, he couldn't help worrying that he'd show up anyway.

He raised a second beer to his lips and caught Denny staring at him. "What?"

Denny shrugged. "Guess you're thirsty."

He grabbed another from the cooler and tossed it to Denny, a little harder than necessary. "Yeah, I am. I'm sure you are, too." His tone contradicted his hospitality.

Once they'd emptied Billy's van, Kate left to go to the market and then to her parents' to put the kids to bed. By the time she returned toting a couple pizzas, they had finished unloading Steve's truck and were putting a hurting on a second case of beer.

In the face of her frown, he defiantly grabbed another.

"Denny's going to come back tomorrow afternoon to help get the furniture upstairs," he said after a long swig. "And he's offered to fix the window, so you're off the hook."

"I didn't realize I was on the hook, but thank you anyway."

She planted a kiss on Denny's cheek before heading upstairs to continue unpacking.

After they'd devoured the pizza, Billy walked Denny and Steve outside. While they talked about some of his ideas for converting the garage into a studio, Billy reached into the glove box in the van and pulled out the last of his stash. He filled the pipe and lit it. After taking a long hit, he passed it to Denny.

The tension he'd been feeling all day began to dissipate. He tilted his head back, looking up at the velvet night. He hadn't seen this many stars or heard this kind of quiet since he'd left Kansas. He exhaled slowly, visualizing the tightness around his chest leaving him. When he looked down, Denny was watching.

"What?"

Denny shook his head. "Nothing."

This was really starting to piss him off. "What?"

"What the fuck is wrong with you?" Denny asked.

"Excuse me?"

Denny snorted and turned away.

"Shut up, Denny," Steve said.

So much for feeling relaxed.

"You have something you wanna say to me?" Billy's hands curled at his sides.

"Yeah." Denny took a step closer. "If I was married to a girl like Kate, I wouldn't be barking at her all the time. You've got the world by the balls, brother. Yet you are angriest motherfucker I've ever known. You have a beautiful wife, two healthy kids, and a freaking Grammy." Denny stabbed one finger toward the house behind Billy. "You just bought a house, and you're only twenty-six fucking years old. If I hadn't moved in with Allison, I'd still be living in my parents' basement."

Billy pulled up to his full height. He ran his hand across his jaw as he stared down at Denny. "I think you better shut the fuck up."

"C'mon, guys," Steve said, trying to step between them.

"Look, man." Raising his hands, Denny took a step back. "I mean no disrespect. I love you like a brother, but I just think you're a damn fool. I've known Kate almost as long as you have, and that is one sweet little angel you have there. So you fucked up. Get over it and start treating her better, or I guarantee you, if she gets hipped, she won't think twice about kicking your sorry ass to the curb."

He wanted to pound Denny into the pavement, beat him senseless so he would never repeat what he'd just said. But he couldn't move. He was rooted to the ground. When he tried to speak, his voice was barely a whisper.

"What're you talking about?"

Denny threw his hands up. "You and Christa. Unless there're more."

The words hung in the air. "Where did you hear that?"

"More places than I care to remember. At first I didn't believe it. Steve will tell you. Neither of us did. Hell, I still can't believe it." Denny folded his arms and glared at him. "All I'm saying is that you've got it all. Be happy. And if you can't be happy, then pretend you're happy. Because if you don't? Then man, someday you are gonna be sorry."

CHAPTER 56

Hot water rained over his body, but still he shivered. Denny's words were ringing in his head. He felt sick.

If Denny and Steve knew, who else knew, and how long before it got back to Kate? He punched the wall. Cracks shot through two tiles. Dammit. Did he really think no would find out? It had to be Christa, because he sure as hell hadn't told anyone other than Joey. And he may have convinced her not to go to Kate, but if she told everyone else, what difference would it make? If she was within twenty miles right now, he'd find her and make sure she'd never open her mouth again.

Fuck. He slammed his head against the wall.

He couldn't allow Kate to find out. Never. She'd never forgive him, had made him promise if he ever wanted someone else to tell her and let her go. But he didn't want anyone else. Had never wanted anyone else. He was just a selfish, stupid prick. If only she had told him that night she was in labor.

He squeezed his eyes shut. Yeah, right. Because this was her fault.

"Fuck me," he muttered, then repeated the sentiment much louder as cold water needled his body. They hadn't owned the house twelve hours and he would already have to replace a window, broken tiles, and apparently they needed a new water heater. Stepping out of the shower, he swiped at the mirror with his hand and stared at his distorted reflection.

Denny was wrong. He didn't have the world by the balls. It was the other way around.

Exhausted, stressed, and wanting nothing but to collapse somewhere and go to sleep, Billy found Kate in the living room wearing a black lace nightgown he'd never seen before. Candles lined the mantle. A fire crackled on the hearth.

When she saw him in the doorway, she smiled and threw open her arms. "Ta-da—oh, wait." She rushed to the mattress they'd dragged into the living room earlier and pulled a bottle of champagne from a baggie filled with ice. "Ta-da!" She still didn't give him time to respond. "Shoot," she muttered as she scooted back toward the fireplace and pushed the button on a boom box. The sultry voice of Etta James filled the room. Kate rolled her eyes, struck another pose. "Ta-da!" she sang, with slightly less enthusiasm.

His heart tore just a little. Denny was right; she was an angel. She was a lot of things. All of them good. He didn't deserve her.

"Katie."

She raised her hand before he could make any excuses. "I know you're tired and kinda freaked out, but I want you to know how much I appreciate all this." She pressed a fist against her chest.

"Katie . . ."

A puff of smoke rose behind her.

"I love you," she continued, "and I want to show you just how much."

More smoke. The homey smell of a wood fire was stronger than he remembered—especially, he realized, since she hadn't opened the flue.

"Shit!" he cried, rushing forward and pushing her out of the way. "Dammit, Kate! Open the windows!"

Thick smoke rolled out above the flames, billowing to the ceiling, then swirling down around them. Kate dropped the bottle on the mattress and rushed to push up the window. The smoke, finding an escape, followed.

Trying to keep his hand above the flames, Billy reached into the firebox and grabbed the lever for the flue.

"Fuck!" he yelped. Yanking his hand back, he pressed it into the damp towel around his waist.

Kate grabbed the bag of ice and held it open for him to plunge his hand inside.

As the pain faded, he gave her a stern look. "Kinda foolish to burn the place down before we spend one night here, dontcha think?"

She sat beside him on the mattress, wide-eyed, looking almost afraid to breathe. "I'm sorry."

All things considered, it was almost comical. He tried to sound tough. "Yeah? You don't look sorry."

She rubbed her lips together, but the edges of her mouth were definitely curling up.

He didn't bother to hide his smile. "I could be wrong, but I think I was about to get lucky."

"Maybe."

He raised his eyebrows. "Maybe?"

"Does it hurt?"

He pulled his hand from the bag, wiggled his fingers, then dabbed them with the towel. A bright red streak marked his palm. "I think I'll live. I may even be able to play guitar again someday."

"Oh God." Her voice was barely a whisper.

"I'm kidding." He bumped her with his shoulder. "It's no worse than grabbing a hot pan." He rested his other hand on her knee. After a second, he slid it up her thigh and lifted the edge of her nightgown.

"Like I said." He grinned. "It appears I was about to get lucky."

"I kinda ruined our evening."

Slipping his arm around her waist, he kissed her behind her ear. "No, you didn't. You go ahead with whatever it was you were planning, and I'll try to forget you smell like bacon."

She jabbed a finger into his ribs. "Nice."

"I'm kidding. I'm all yours."

Kate took his hand in hers. She plucked an ice cube from the bag, and ran it over the burn. "I wanted to make this night all about you to let you know how much I appreciate what you've done for us, even though I know how hard it was and how much you didn't want to do this."

"Were you planning to do nasty things to me?"

"Pretty much."

He tossed the towel onto the floor and laid back on the mattress, his hands behind his head. "Go ahead. Show me how grateful you are." He closed his eyes, then popped one open. "And don't forget, you just made me burn my hand. I expect you to show me how sorry you are, too." He closed his eyes again. "Oh yeah, and the door." He leaned up on his elbows. "Don't forget the broken glass. I bet you're sorry about that."

"Oh, shut up." She pushed him down and climbed on top of him. Pressing her mouth against his, she kissed him until he finally stopped talking.

Later, as he held her body tight against his, he sighed deeply.

"What's wrong?" She leaned back to look up at him.

"How can you love me so much when I can be such a jerk?"

"Seriously?"

He nodded.

She shrugged. "I just do. So you get a little cranky now and then. I think that's to be expected of creative people."

He laughed. "Where'd you hear that?"

"I don't know. Seems like some of the most prolific musicians and painters were a bit . . . out there. What about Mozart?"

"You're comparing me to Mozart?"

"Not really, but he was a little strange. Didn't you see *Amadeus*?"

"That was a movie and highly fictionalized."

"Still, creative people can get kinda testy."

"If you say so."

"I know so."

"It's still no excuse for me to treat you badly."

"Where is this coming from?" She lifted up onto her elbows. "You don't treat me badly. If I do something to irritate you, I expect you to get irritated. I get irritated with you. It's normal. I know it doesn't change how I feel about you, and I assume it doesn't change how you feel about me."

He gently tucked a strand of hair behind her ear. "No. Nothing could change how I feel about you."

"Good. Let's celebrate that."

She reached for the champagne.

"I hope you know how much I love you, Katie. You are the best thing in my life. I still don't understand how I got this lucky."

He clicked his glass against hers. "So, no regrets?"

"None. Well . . . maybe one."

"Really?" Although she should have a laundry list of regrets where he was concerned, it still bothered him that there would be one.

"I was kinda hoping you would carry me across the threshold."

He could be so dense sometimes. "Is that what all that was about this afternoon?"

She looked at him sheepishly and shrugged.

"C'mon. I can do that." He set his glass on the floor.

"Nah. It's too late."

He looked at his watch. "It's only nine thirty."

"I mean, it's too late, we're already in the house."

"Nonsense." Standing, he helped her to her feet. "Let's go."

She pushed weakly against him. "It's silly. Besides, you're naked."

"I don't care. We're in the country. Clothing should be optional."

"Well, it's not!"

Undeterred, he scooped her up and tossed her over his shoulder.

"Stop!" she cried, hanging upside down. "What'll the neighbors think?"

"Like I give a shit. They'll just blame rock and roll."

She pommeled the backs of his thighs, laughing. "Billy, stop!"

"Nope, this is one mistake I can fix."

He carried her out the front door and set her down on the porch, then picked her up in the traditional way.

"You're gonna have to help." He squatted until she could reach the doorknob. After he'd stepped inside, he asked what was next.

"I don't know." When she looked up, her face was serious. "Just promise you'll always love me the way you do right now—at this moment. That's all I'll ever really need." Her hand floated up to his cheek. "Promise."

Looking down at her, he remembered the first time their eyes met. At Kildare's, when somehow, some part of him had known he was looking at his future.

"I can't do that." His voice finally broke.

Her eyes grew wide and her mouth dropped open.

"I can't do that because I know that every day I will love you more than I did the day before, for as long as I live." His voice deepened with conviction.

"And that, Katie, I promise, will be the easiest thing I ever do."

The End

NOTE TO READERS

Reviews are important to independent authors. If you decide to leave a review after you've read this book, please email me a link to your review at klcmaterialgirl@gmail.com and I'll send you an *At This Moment* bookmark as a thank you.

ABOUT THE AUTHOR

Karen Cimms is a writer, editor, and music lover. She was born and raised in New Jersey and still thinks of the Garden State as home. She began her career at an early age rewriting the endings to her favorite books. It was a mostly unsuccessful endeavor, but she likes to think she invented fanfiction.

Karen is a lifelong Jersey corn enthusiast, and is obsessed with (in no particular order) books, shoes, dishes, and Brad Pitt. In her spare time she likes to quilt, decorate, and entertain. Just kidding—she has no spare time.

Although she loves pigeons, she is terrified of pet birds, scary movies, and Mr. Peanut.

Karen is married to her favorite lead guitar player. Her children enjoy tormenting her with countless mean-spirited pranks because they love her. She currently lives in Northeast Pennsylvania, although her heart is usually in Maine.

ACKNOWLEDGEMENTS

While my name stands alone on the cover of this book, it was in no way a singular effort. In fact, without these people it might never have seen the light of day.

First I want to thank Liz Vigue. After reading several early chapters, she wanted to know more about Kate. Who was she and how did she become the woman in the story? And Billy? Why was he such a mess? I wasn't sure myself, so I began to write Kate's backstory. I sent her to college and gave her a cold, distant mother and a self-involved father. Then I dissected Billy and discovered his abusive parents and a weakness for drugs and alcohol. Kate, Billy, and Joey came to life. Each morning they piled into the backseat of my car, where they would speak over each other, trying to make sure I heard them as they told me their stories. Not until I was deep into what has become *At This Moment*, did they quiet down and begin to trust me. Those early chapters became the foundation for *We All Fall Down*, the second book in the series. So, thank you, Liz. Thank you for making me dig deeper, for your critiques and encouragement, and even for boggling my poor brain with Freytag's Pyramid.

Thank you to my earliest readers: Patty Morgan, Diane Stone, Ione Connelly, Kerry Palumbo, Marge Ayers, Karen McMillon, Beth Yaroszeufski, and Ace Leccese.

I'm eternally grateful to my beta readers for their feedback: Sarah Streby, Amber McKenney, Allison Hart, Dena Williams, Judi Rae Kessner, Desiree LaDuke, Soraya Gimenez, Sarah Elmore, Amy Levasseur, Sally McGarry, Shasta Anderson, Rhonda Donaldson, Deirdre Popp, and Valarie Savage Kinney. Extra special thanks to Marcia Evans, Ann Travis, and Lydia Fasteland for really digging in. You guys totally rock.

Lori Ryser, thank you for all of the above and then some.

Amanda Cimms, you are a far better writer than I can ever hope to be. Thank you for your early editing skills, not to mention the champagne, flowers, and cupcakes you and Ace brought when I finished the rough draft. Garrett Cimms, thank you for an awesome cover design and for expressing my vision. (You're also a great cover model.)

To my editor, Lisa Poisso, thank you for your professionalism and expertise. You not only guided me to become a better writer, you helped me make Billy and Kate much more vivid.

To my critique partner, Dr. Bella Ellwood-Clayton, thank you for everything. I hope I can be as big a help to you as you have been to me.

Thank you to my experts: Denise Cataudella for the "tour" of Brooklyn, Jennifer Sterner for the anatomy lesson, Blythe Holynski for seeing Kate through two births, and real-life rock star Glen Burtnik for answering all my silly questions. And thanks to all the musicians I've known over the years. For a girl who loves music, it's been a pretty sweet ride. And to Nancy Blaha, thank you for helping me see through the fog, among other things.

Karen, Margaux, Garrett, and Amanda, thanks for enabling and encouraging me to be more than just "Mom," although that will always be the best thing I've ever done. I love you all.

Most important, thank you to my husband, Jim. I couldn't have written one word without your support. Thank you for taking on all that you have so that I could write every day. Thank you for your patience and your feedback, even when I hated it. Thanks for sharing stories that were hard to hear, but that I needed to know. You not only made me a musician's wife, you helped bring Billy to life. You will always be my favorite lead guitar player. I love you.

TURN THE PAGE FOR AN EXCLUSIVE SNEAK PEEK OF

WE ALL FALL DOWN

BOOK TWO IN KAREN CIMMS'
OF LOVE AND MADNESS TRILOGY

DUE FOR RELEASE THIS FALL

CHAPTER 1
JULY 19, 2012

The short-term parking lot shimmered like an urban mirage.

Miami had been hot, but at least there was the occasional ocean breeze to punctuate the wet, heavy air. No such luck in Newark.

Fishing an elastic band from his pocket, Billy gathered his hair into a double loop, then leaned against the full-length windows of the terminal. The cool glass felt good against his sweat-soaked back.

Mirrored aviator shades covered his bloodshot eyes, but nothing could disguise the pounding in his head. The dizzying waves in the pavement and the familiar rocking motion of his latest hangover made him want to find a dark corner and sleep until this roller coaster came to a complete stop. And when it did, he'd like to get his hands around the neck of Stonestreet's tour manager and personally thank him for booking such a goddamn early flight.

Unfortunately, since he'd been fired hours earlier, the opportunity was unlikely to present itself.

A long line of cars and shuttles cozied up to the curb, spewing fumes into the dense, still air. If Eddie didn't show soon, Billy swore he'd leave the little shit's crap all over the sidewalk and hail a cab. Five more minutes. Folding his arms, he closed his eyes and tried to sort out the last twelve hours, figure out where he'd gone wrong.

Mistake number one had been dropping acid. He hadn't done it in years, but when Eddie showed up with a couple hits, he figured what the hell. He was no choir boy, and this tour was kicking his ass. One more night, then he would've been home free, at least for a couple weeks.

But what a night. He could still hear the roar of the crowd jammed into American Airlines Arena. When the band started playing "Escaping to Perdition," he did what he always did, what he was paid to do: hang back and provide the rhythm and accents, but somewhere after the first verse, something snapped. Maybe it was the acid. Or maybe he was just sick of playing second fiddle to a hack who couldn't even win at Guitar Hero without backup. Whatever the case, he lost himself in the music and before he knew it, he'd commandeered Mick's big solo.

And he was wailing on that motherfucker.

Even now, baking on the hot sidewalk a thousand miles from Miami, he could still feel those notes pulsing through his fingertips. It was like being in a trance. Before he knew it, he'd crossed Mick's invisible line.

His fingers had flown up and down the neck of his Les Paul custom. The frets had all but disappeared and his fingers moved as if on glass. He'd become the music. Each note reverberated through him, shooting out like sparks.

Mick let him have his moment. And it was the way he'd always dreamed it would be. He was front and center—Billy McDonald—and the crowd went crazy. When he'd opened his eyes and realized twenty thousand fans were screaming for him, he'd fallen to his knees. And he hadn't missed a single, fucking note.

The rest of the show was a blur, but the feeling stayed with him. It was the best night of his career—or at least it had been, until later.

The band was partying harder than usual back at the hotel, which was saying something. The booze flowed, the weed was plentiful, and there was more than enough high-grade cocaine and half-naked women to go around. It was tough sometimes, but he knew where to draw the line. The guilt he still felt from cheating on Katie twenty years ago would eat him alive if he let it. The risk of a few moments of pleasure wasn't worth losing the only thing in the world that had ever really mattered other than his music.

He'd tried to stay away from the hard stuff too, and he'd sworn to Katie he'd quit, but he was only human. If he needed a little something to help him get by now and then, he wasn't hurting anybody.

But last night? The shit had hit the fan. Fueled by whiskey and coke and twice as much resentment, Mick launched into a tirade about Billy stealing his solo. He'd tried to shine him on at first, but he wasn't about to apologize to that horse's ass. Everyone knew Billy was ten times better than Mick McAvoy on his worst day.

When things started getting ugly, he'd gotten up to leave. Mick threw the first punch. He missed, but it didn't matter. Not since Billy was ten had anyone taken a swing at him and been able to walk away unassisted. One punch, and Mick's feet had flown out from under him. He rolled ass-backward over a bench and onto the floor.

And after a couple roadies had helped him up, Mick fired him.

The rest of the night had been spent nursing his ego and a bottle of Jack. Things had been going so well. Last night's show had been amazing. And now it was over.

A horn blasted, and Billy opened his eyes. Still no Eddie. He looked at his watch. It was a little past eleven. Plenty of time to get home, although the thought of facing Katie made his head throb.

Happy birthday, babe. I got fired! That was gonna go over real well.

The rumbling of his stomach brought him back to the present. He couldn't remember when he'd last eaten, although the thought of food nauseated him—or maybe it was the heat. If he hadn't lost his license, he'd be on the road by now. In the meantime, he longed for a little hair of the dog and a shower. He'd been so out of it last night, he'd lost track of time. Not only hadn't he had time for a shower, he'd almost missed his plane.

He dug a toothpick from his pocket and clamped it between his teeth. Maybe that would get his mind off wanting a drink and a handful of aspirin. Another horn beeped. He looked up as Eddie pulled to up to the curb.

After throwing his duffle bag and guitar cases in the back, Billy slipped into the front seat while Eddie loaded his bags into the cargo area.

"Sorry about last night, man," Eddie said, navigating the rented SUV onto 78 heading west. "But you were amazing. Holy shit! You should've seen Mick's face. Acting like the big man, giving you the spotlight, but I could see that little vein pulsing on the side of his head."

Billy nodded. "It felt pretty good. I hope I get to feel that way again someday."

"It'll happen, brother. God doesn't give you that kinda talent to hide it under a bushel. Know what I'm sayin'?"

Hide it under a bushel? Hardly. He'd been fighting for twenty years to make his mark, only to have just about every opportunity snatched right out from under his nose, thanks to one vindictive little bitch with a long memory and too much influence.

"Yeah, we'll see," Billy muttered as he lowered his seat and closed his eyes. The cool breeze from the air conditioner was soothing on his aching head.

"Thanks for the lift. I was hoping my kid would pick me up, but I forgot he's working at some camp in Colorado."

"No problem. I enjoy the company. Hey, I'm a bit parched. You mind if we stop along the way for a little libation?"

Billy cocked an eye open. He needed a drink a hell of a lot more than he needed a nap. He turned to Eddie and grinned.

"I think I could be persuaded."

32275942R00251

Made in the USA
Middletown, DE
30 May 2016